Adriana Kraft

When It's Time to Heat Things Up

PUBLISHED BOOKS

SERIES

RIDERS UP Romantic Suspense novels
Book One *Cassie's Hope*
Book Two *Heat Wave*
Book Three *Detour Ahead*
Book Four *Willow Smoke*

SWINGING GAMES Erotic Romance novellas
Book One *Anticipation*
Book Two *Hook-Ups*
Book Three *A Tempting Taste*
Book Four *Complexities*
Book Five *The Adventure Continue*
Book Six *Who's the Coach?*
Book Seven *Dare to Adventure*
Book Eight *Pushing the Limits*
Book Nine *Too Close for Comfort*
Book Ten *Triple Play*
Book Eleven *Summer's End*
Book Twelve *Foursomes and More…*
Book Thirteen *Epicurean Delites*

COLORS OF THE NIGHT Erotic Romance novels
Book One *Colors of the Night*
Book Two *Aria Returns*

PURGATORY POINT Erotic Romance novels
Book One *The Mistress of Purgatory Point*
Book Two *Return to Purgatory Point*

THE DIARY Erotic Romance novels
Book One *The Diary*
Book Two *Writing Skin*

STAND ALONE NOVELS AND NOVELLAS
A Gift for Adam Erotic Romance novella
The Lady Wants More Erotic Romance novella
The Heist Romantic Suspense novel
The Unmasking Romantic Suspense novel
Cherry Tune-Up Erotic Romance novella
The Reunion Erotic Romance novel
Atlantis Woman Found Erotic Romance novella
The Best Man Erotic Romance novel
Santa's Boss Erotic Romance novella
Through the Mirror Erotic Romance novella
Sheila's Prenups Erotic Romance novella
Full Circle Erotic Romance novella

SHORT STORIES IN ANTHOLOGIES
Accidental Contact, in *Sapphic Planet*
A Taste of Ginger in *The Cougar Book*

WHAT THEY'RE SAYING
ABOUT ADRIANA KRAFT

Romantic Suspense

Heat Wave (Riders Up, Book 2) Five stars at Goodreads *Heartfelt with mystery and hope...made me cry. Spot on interplay between the main characters...well written and extremely enjoyable to read.* Donna H.

Cassie's Hope (Riders Up, Book 1) Five Stars at Goodreads *An emotional roller-coaster, with twists and turns you never see coming! ...I feel I know them, I took their journey with them. I felt their pain, their sadness, their struggles, and most of all their love. And that is the mark of a truly good book.* Faith

Erotic Romance

The Reunion, Winner of the 2014 Bisexual Book Award for Erotic Fiction. *This book sizzled as two incredibly sexy women and one gorgeous guy form a super hot triad, eventually. These three are by far and away the best smoldering trio I have read about. Oh, bring on more of this, but read this one first!* JJ, Rainbow Reviews

The Best Man, Top Pick at The Romance Reviews, Five Stars at Amazon *Kitty and Jared are my new favorite characters. I love this book. It kept me on edge because Kitty was so unpredictable, which gave this story its twist and turns.* Cheryl B.

Riders Up
Book Three

Willow Smoke

by

Adriana Kraft

Riders Up: Book Three

Willow Smoke
By
Adriana Kraft

ISBN: 978-0-9907476-6-6
Copyright © 2014 by Adriana Kraft

B&B Publishing
1970 N. Leslie St. #560
Pahrump, NV 89060

Cover by
Rebecca Poole
Dreams2Media.com

Riders Up

Book One: Cassie's Hope
Chicago, 1996

Book Two: Heat Wave
Iowa, 2000

Book Three: Willow Smoke
Chicago, 2002

Book Four: Detour Ahead
California, 2004

Chicago,

2002

Chapter One

"I won't let anything hurt you." Daisy Matthews finished wrapping the ankles of the chestnut mare and sat back on her haunches to evaluate her work. The mare's ankles were cooler than they had been two hours earlier.

It wasn't easy to convince a horse to stand in buckets of ice, but after three years of being a groom and an exercise rider, she could do it about as well as anybody at Arlington Park. At least that was what her boss said when he promoted her to assistant trainer.

Daisy grinned. There wasn't much prestige associated with being an assistant trainer for a fellow with a string of only twenty-some claimers and allowance horses, but it was something, particularly for a girl from the wrong side of the tracks.

RainbowBlaze took a step forward. "I know." Daisy groaned. "Step one: pay attention. Sorry, I got lost daydreaming. You're right. Taking care of you is an important job." She chuckled. "I can't think of anything I'd rather be doing."

"Hey kid, do you always talk to horses?"

The horse reared and pawed. "It's okay, girl." Daisy kept her voice soft and ran her hand slowly along the mare's neck.

When the mare had stopped trembling, Daisy stepped out of the stall, shaded her eyes from the sun and faced the interloper. She scowled at the man's new sneakers, monogrammed shirt and neatly pressed slacks. He looked liked he'd be more at home on a sailboat than in a barn.

The man peered over wire-rimmed glasses like he knew something she didn't. Or was he appraising her? Why? His dark hair set off a chiseled face; it was difficult to guess his age, but she could see a few gray hairs at his temples. He was money. Understated, but money. Probably the stock market. What was he doing in her barn?

She thrust her jaw at him. "So who the hell are you? Don't you know better than to sneak up on someone who's working with a horse?"

The man frowned and sputtered before speaking. "Sorry, kid, I didn't mean to put you in danger. Don't know a damn thing about horses. I'll be the first to admit that."

Daisy exhaled slowly. "Okay, so why are you here?" She shifted her weight from foot to foot. An odd sensation swept over her — one she didn't like. This man, although ignorant as hell about horses and barn etiquette, had an air of confidence that suggested he knew he belonged — whether in the board room, on a sailboat, or even in her barn. His staring made her uncomfortable, and she didn't like being uncomfortable.

She knew how to protect herself from males; she'd been doing that for years. That wasn't the problem. The guy was probably old enough to be her father. But he was dangerous; she just didn't know how, yet. "And do you have a name? Who let you in here? You know you got to have a pass to be back here."

"Good God kid, do you always welcome people by putting your dukes up first?" The man dug a visitor's badge out of his pocket. "Will this help?" he asked, handing it to her. "The name's Nicholas Underwood. My friends call me Nick."

Daisy examined the badge as if it contained the stranger's DNA. She handed it back. "You should wear it so it shows."

- o -

Underwood grunted an expletive under his breath. He studied the combative young woman. If only his employees were as protective of his plant as this woman was of her horse.

How old was she? Maybe twenty-four, twenty-five. Too young. He scanned her tight, willowy frame. Damn, was she blushing?

Who would have guessed that a slight overbite could be so attractive? It set off an angular face and a slightly oversized nose; yet all was in balance as if sculpted by a skilled craftsman. Strawberry blond hair fell to her shoulders and swept across her forehead. She stood tall and lanky with medium breasts.

Not the kind of woman that usually appealed to him. He'd never been attracted to younger women, preferring women with experience.

So why was this willowy kid with straw sticking in her hair leaving him tongue-tied like some damn adolescent? Maybe the overly pungent horse odors clogged his good sense.

Nick breathed deeply and clipped the identification badge to his shirt pocket. "If that satisfies you, maybe you can help me. I don't think I'm lost. The guy at the gate said Barn D. By the way, what's your name?"

She pursed her lips as if he'd just asked for her most closely guarded secret.

"You know my name and have me at an advantage, kid. So who are you and what were you doing with that horse? I didn't know horses wore socks."

The young woman giggled. It was a low pitched sound that did nothing to soothe Nick's nerves. He'd obviously said something funny.

Willow, he decided he'd call her Willow.

She brushed hair away from her eyes before responding. "I'm Daisy. Daisy Matthews. I'm assistant trainer for Sam Gallagher." She crossed her arms across her mid-section. "They're not socks. I just finished wrapping her ankles to help bring some heat down."

Nick nodded. There was a lot to learn if he wanted to take horseracing seriously, which he wasn't convinced was desirable. He wouldn't be here at all, if it wasn't for Michael Barnes going belly up on him. Daisy Matthews. He shook his head. All he had to do was locate the damn horse, arrange for its sale and get the hell out of here. No more horses. No more Willow.

This niggling indecisiveness was bad and so out of character for him. Cool. Collected. Poised. Skilled. Powerful. That was how he saw himself, and it'd better be the way others saw him.

He plopped down on a bale of hay in the shadow of the stable. The woman frowned at him. Wasn't that why the bales were there? He'd seen people sitting on them once at the state fair.

"I think I should have worn a hat," he said in way of explanation. "It must be ten degrees cooler here in the shade."

"It gets hot and muggy in July in Chicago. A hat would've been a good idea. And if you ever come back, shoes or boots are better than sneakers. On shedrow you never know when you'll be in a position for a horse to step on you."

"Shedrow?"

"All these barns on the backside, that's what they're called, shedrow."

"Oh. I'll try to remember—if there is a next time. So tell me, where can I find a horse named RainbowBlaze?"

"RainbowBlaze!" Daisy gasped and glared at him again. "Why? What do you want with her?"

"Damn, you've got to be the most protective woman I've ever encountered. If you must know, she's my horse."

Daisy opened her mouth as if to speak. She glanced quickly at the chestnut mare. "There must be a mistake," she stammered. "RainbowBlaze belongs to Michael Barnes."

7

Nick crossed his legs and leaned against the stable wall, giving Daisy Matthews a slow satisfied smile. He'd found his horse. And he had a new employee. This could be more interesting than he'd imagined.

Furthermore, being his employee made Matthews safe to be around. He had a firm rule against personal involvements with employees. He flashed a look at the slender woman's nipples that showed faintly through an orange tank top. Didn't she know what she looked like?

Too young. He closed his eyes. He might be old enough to be her father. His eyes sprang open and he appraised her again. Maybe, maybe not.

"The horse did belong to Michael Barnes." Fright flickered across the blonde's face and quickly disappeared behind a steely gaze. "Mike's fallen on bad economic times. Turned out he couldn't pay his debts. Showed up at my office with a bill of sale for some damn race horse and begged me to take it to clear what he owed me. Against my better judgment, I agreed." Nick raised his open palms upward. "So, here I am."

Daisy's hands, resting at her sides, curled into fists.

"You look like you'd like to slaughter me for your supper." Nick stood. Ignoring the woman, he pointed at the horse with the oversized socks. "So I take it this is RainbowBlaze." He glanced back over his shoulder at the woman. She gulped and nodded. "Is the horse any good? How much can I get for her?"

Daisy sputtered and Nick suppressed a laugh.

"She's a damn good mare. She'll run her heart out for you, if you treat her right. But she won't work just for anyone."

"Sounds like you've got a thing for my horse, kid."

"Suppose so." Daisy studied the dirt at her feet. "I've known her since she was foaled. Was there to help her mother give birth. I've been there every step of the way when Rainbow was with Cassie Travers, and then when Michael Barnes bought her it was with the understanding that she'd come to Sam's barn and be with me."

When the woman stopped to catch her breath, Nick said, "You didn't answer my question. How much is she worth?"

Daisy shrugged. "Maybe," her voice quaked, "fifty thousand. Maybe more."

"Hmm. Michael said a hundred grand." He watched the spirit flow out of the young woman. Her glistening eyes grabbed at something inside him that he hadn't experienced for a long time. Not thinking, he reached for her chin.

"That horse," he said softly, "means a lot more to you than a hundred grand, doesn't it?"

Daisy nodded, pulling away from his fingers and rubbing her eyes with her knuckles. "She's family," she mumbled. Then her watery eyes hardened. "But she's your horse, your property to sell or do with whatever you want."

"Exactly." So why did he feel like some kind of lowlife because he wanted to sell his own horse?

He glanced up and down the barn area where men and women were brushing, bathing or walking horses. The place was alive; he liked that. He kept his eyes on the strawberry blonde fighting desperately to maintain her composure. He wondered what it would feel like to be loved as much as she loved that four legged beast.

Hell, he'd always prided himself on being a risk-taker. He didn't have that much to lose, really. And maybe he could have some fun and learn a few things at the same time. He already liked teasing his newest employee—that was worth something. She tried so hard to be tough, yet he bet she had a heart the size of Texas. He smiled. Wasn't that a horsey thought?

Meeting Daisy eye to eye, he said, "Okay kid, I've got a deal for you."

"I couldn't come close to buying Rainbow if I lived to be a hundred."

Nick let his chin fall against his chest. "That's not the kind of deal I had in mind."

Daisy rolled her eyes and reached for a pitchfork sticking out of a nearby hay bale. "I'm not that kind of woman, old man. You're old enough to be my father."

"What?" Nick wrenched the fork away. "That's not what I had in mind either." He let out a ragged breath. "I might be old, but I wasn't *that* precocious."

He scowled at her. He half expected her to stick her tongue out at him. "What I had in mind was this kind of deal. If you can convince me why I should get involved in horseracing as a serious venture, then I won't sell Blaze and you can keep her in your care."

Daisy bristled. "Her name is Rainbow."

"Her name is RainbowBlaze. You call her what you want. I'm calling her Blaze. If she takes after her trainer at all, then I think that name is quite appropriate."

Daisy shrugged. "So what do I have to do?"

"Don't sound so excited. I don't know. How would you sell me on horseracing? Show me the place."

"Haven't you ever been to a race track?" He shook his head.

Daisy rolled her eyes skyward. "Then you haven't lived."

Nick laughed. "Apparently I've lived many more years than you, according to your own assessment."

Blushing, Daisy asked, "How long do I have? If I accept your deal."

"By the end of the day."

"What? That's not possible."

"I'm a busy fellow."

"Right. The races will start in another two hours. A quick barn tour will have to do." She gave him a quirky smile. "Soon we have to get you a hat or you'll be fried."

Nick smiled and reached for her hand. "Good idea. Come on, I'll buy you lunch. They must have a gift shop over there somewhere. We can do the barn tour later."

Jerking her hand out of his, Daisy cried, "Wait! I've got responsibilities here. I can't just run off. I've got to tell Sam what's up. If he's not around, then I'll leave a message with a groom. Besides, you should meet Sam."

"Not yet. Nope, the deal is with you, not with Sam. You do what you have to do and I'll wait for you here in the shade."

The lanky woman scurried down the length of the barn and around a corner. Even flustered, she moved with an unpretentious grace. She had to stand nearly six feet; he was six foot two and he didn't have to look down at her at all. She was a lot of woman. He didn't consider himself a betting man, but he'd bet a ton of money that Daisy Matthews could be quite convincing. So what kind of future did he have in horseracing?

- o -

Leaning against the barn for much needed support, Daisy pressed her throbbing temples. What in the hell had she gotten into now? Deal. Bullshit. The man already planned to sell Rainbow; he just enjoyed torturing women.

What choice did she have? She'd do most anything to stay with Rainbow. They'd been together since she moved out of the group home to live with Cassie and Clint Travers. Taking a kid from the inner city of Chicago to a quiet horse farm in McHenry County had been quite a reach. But it had worked. From that moment on, horses

12

had become her lifeblood. And RainbowBlaze stood above all others.

Rainbow was the first foal she'd helped birth.

Now she had to deal with Nicholas Underwood. What a pretentious name! She'd wanted to rip his glasses off and stomp on them. But she hadn't. Cassie would say that she was learning to live within herself, within her emotions. Sounded like just so much social work bullshit. But Cassie had been a good social worker when she worked at the group home, and she was now one of the best horse trainers in the Chicago area. And Daisy owed her a lot—even her life.

No, she could handle the Nicholas Underwoods of the world. She'd seen a lot worse. She'd survived a lot worse.

- o -

Daisy couldn't stop grinning at Underwood, who was stuffing half a hotdog overflowing with mustard and relish into his mouth. Mustard oozed out across his lips. His tongue flicked out to retrieve the yellow goo. He might be wealthy, but he certainly didn't act like how she thought rich folks behaved. At this moment he seemed more like a kid than she did.

"Haven't you ever seen a man eat a hotdog before?" he growled at her.

Daisy glanced down at her food and laughed. "I never paid that much attention, but you do put on quite a show."

"One of my mottos is that life ought to be enjoyed. I don't eat just to survive; I eat to have pleasure."

"The Buddhists claim that you ought to take time and enjoy each bite of food." Reaching for a second hotdog, Nick muttered, "To each his own."

Daisy picked up a potato chip. "Maybe it's the hat. It makes you look younger."

Nick pulled on the brim of the long billed Arlington Park cap. "Well, in that case, it was the best purchase of the day." His eyes sparkled. "I wouldn't want you to start calling me Gramps.

Daisy ignored his humor and began explaining how to read the racing program. Later, on their way to the stands, she'd stop at the windows and show him how to place bets.

Underwood was a good listener. He seemed quite interested in horseracing. That was good; that increased the chances of holding on to RainbowBlaze.

"So how do you know so much about Buddhists?"

"What?" Hadn't he been listening at all?

"You said the Buddhists think you should take time to enjoy each bite. Are you Buddhist?"

"No. I read a lot."

"On religion?"

She heard the incredulity in his voice. "Among other things. Shakespeare. Chaucer. Wolfe. Twain. Contemporary romance. Westerns. And, of course, anything to do with horses and horseracing. I like to read."

14

"Sounds like an English major."

Daisy blinked. "I'm majoring in English, at U.I.C."

She smiled at Underwood's raised eyebrows. Why did she enjoy surprising him so much?

"You go to college and work here full-time?"

Daisy sipped her Coke. Did he think she was just a kid off the street? "The track is full-time. I try to take a course a semester. In the winter, I can squeeze in a little more, since things are slower at the track."

"So what do you plan to do with your degree?"

"Do I have to *do* something with it?" She handed him a napkin. "You missed some."

"Where?"

"There." She pointed to the right corner of his mouth. He wiped the left corner. "No," she said, grimacing. She picked up a second napkin and leaned across the table to wipe off the remaining mustard. He gave her a wicked grin and a laugh bubbled from his lips.

"You! You knew what I meant all along. Why do you enjoy teasing me so?"

"Because you react so spontaneously."

She gave him her best pout.

"Seriously, what do you expect to do with your degree?"

"Train horses. What else? I like to read. Cassie told me college wouldn't hurt if I never did anything particular with the degree, or even if I never finished."

"That's twice you mentioned this Cassie

person. Sounds pretty important to you."

"You bet." Daisy dropped her gaze momentarily. "I lived with her and her family for a few years. And she taught me just about everything I know about horses."

"Sounds like she taught you a few things about life, too."

Daisy nodded. "Yeah, you could say that."

"Maybe I'll meet her, if I hang around the track or around you long enough."

What would Cassie Travers make of the man under the long billed cap? *Be careful, Daisy, girl* she'd say.

"My mother would agree with you and Cassie, by the way."

"Huh?"

"You don't listen too great, Matthews," Nick responded, draining his second cup of coffee. "I said my mother would agree with you. She's an English professor at the University of Minnesota."

"Really?"

Nick nodded. "She thinks people ought to read the classics and contemporary stuff and just about anything written in order to be well rounded."

Daisy glanced at her watch and then started clearing the table. "We better go. It's a half hour till post time. I hope you'll like the races."

"What I've seen of the track so far is impressive. Very clean. Staff seems welcoming and professional. And there's a pulse about the place that's appealing. Lead on, fair lady, and your eager protégé shall follow."

"So in this first race, which horse do you like best? I rather like the sound of MoonofGold." Nicholas sat next to Daisy in the Arlington Park grandstands.

She gave him a shocked look. He looked completely serious. She giggled. The man knew absolutely nothing about horses or horseracing. She hadn't been able to show him the barn area — that would have to wait for another day. She hoped there'd be another day. He couldn't sell RainbowBlaze — she wouldn't let him.

"I don't think he has much of a chance. He hasn't won a race in three years," she said, pointing to the Daily Racing Form spread across her lap. "He's only cheap speed. He'll run flat out for about four furlongs and then start going backward."

"How do you know all of that?"

"By going over this information on the horses' past performances. There's not enough time to teach you now, but trust me, if you want to be successful at the track over the long haul, you'll have to arm yourself with a lot of data, wade through it, and then make your best judgment."

He leaned over to get a closer look. Goosebumps. Daisy cocked her head at the man. She didn't get goosebumps — unless it was in the winner's circle, or maybe very early when the sun was rising over the track. She did not get goosebumps because of a man, and particularly an

17

older man. Although he did look younger as the afternoon wore on. *Must be the hat.*

Nick shook his head. "You're right, there's not enough time. But I definitely want to learn, if I decide to stay in this game." He stared blankly at Daisy. "Who has the best chance in your judgment?"

"MisterJames is the six to five favorite and on paper looks like the horse to beat."

"But you don't think he'll win."

"Nope. He's a speed horse, and there are three other speed horses who'll be battling for the lead. I think the winner will be a patient horse who can come from behind — like the ten horse, BreezySurprise. I also saw the favorite during his last workout. He ran too fast. The exercise rider couldn't control him. I don't think he saved enough for the race."

"You're talking in a language I don't fully understand, but I'm getting the gist of it. So what would you bet?"

"If I give you the winner, it's only right to split the winnings," she kidded, wrinkling up her nose. "I'd put two on the ten to win. He's eight to one, so he'll give you a nice return, if he wins."

"You're not certain?"

"Of course not. This is horseracing."

"Okay. Sounds like the stock market, but what the hell. I'll go make the wager."

Daisy tried not to stare at Underwood. The man must have an iron stomach; he had returned with a salty pretzel and a box of popcorn. "You must really like junk food."

"Not my typical fare," he responded, offering her some popcorn. "But I like to pig out now and then, particularly when I'm nervous. I'll work it off tomorrow."

She didn't doubt that. She hadn't seen any spare fat on the guy. "They're entering the gate," she said, pointing across the infield.

The starting bell clanged and the race was off. Daisy kept one eye on the horses and the other on her enthralled student. The muscles in his neck tightened and his eyes narrowed. He stood when everyone else stood to get a better view of the horses coming down the homestretch. Unlike most fans, he said nothing. His mouth fell open when the number ten horse swept past the favorite in the final sixteenth to win easily. At least he wasn't going to be one of those gushy fans who screamed at their favorite horse when he got stuck in the middle of the pack. Daisy liked that.

He turned and caught her up in a bear hug; his lips brushed her cheek. Before she had a chance to pound his shoulder she was back on her feet. His grin split his face in two.

"That was spectacular," he hollered, leaving his arm around her shoulders. "I've never seen anything like it. Such power. Determination. Guts.

My God, why didn't somebody tell me about this before?"

She watched Underwood nod at the horse standing in the winners circle as if he were acknowledging a champion. What did the man really see in the horse?

Certainly, more than the casual fan. Whatever, she was thrilled, and it didn't even bother her that he hadn't let her go.

"And you," he said, staring at her with bright shining eyes, "you're a guru. You had that race pegged."

Flushed by his admiration, Daisy countered, "Just don't count on that happening. We lose more often than we win."

"Yeah, but what a thrill it is to win. I couldn't believe how that horse was straining to get ahead. So do I collect our winnings now?"

"Sure. I don't see another worthwhile bet until the fifth race. I'll handicap that one while you're gone."

- o -

Daisy glanced up from the Form when Nick returned. He sat down looking quite pleased with himself. Once she'd finished her handicapping, she set the papers down and sipped her drink. She leaned back and swept her eyes across the tote board, the pond, and the horses coming onto the track.

She took a deep breath and let it out slowly.

20

This was about as good as it got. She didn't spend enough time sitting in the stands and appreciating the races. Usually, there wasn't enough opportunity.

Clearly, Underwood was enjoying his first day at the races. The odds of keeping RainbowBlaze had rocketed. Daisy's skin warmed.

"Oh," Underwood said, reaching into his pocket. "I forgot. Your share of the winnings."

Daisy held out her palm and he placed in it a stack of bills. Her mouth went dry. Her eyebrows narrowed. "What's this?" she managed to say.

"There you go, kid. Not listening again. I said it's your share of the winnings. You said two hundred on the ten to win. I thought that was a little light. So I put four hundred on him to win. There should be a little less than two thousand there. Not bad, I'd say."

"I can't take this," Daisy stammered, shrinking into the chair. "I meant two dollars, not two hundred. Good grief! I'd never bet two hundred dollars on a horse."

She shoved the money toward him. He closed her fingers over the bills and pushed her hand back on her lap. "It's yours, fair and square. You said yourself that if the horse wins we split the winnings."

"But I meant a two dollar bet," she squeaked.

"So, I misunderstood." He squinted and thinned his lips. "Of course, you wouldn't want to make me feel too stupid and utterly terrible about this whole horseracing thing."

Daisy shook her head. "I think I'm going to be sick," she mumbled.

She didn't resist when Nick grabbed her by the hand and helped her up the stairs to an inner lobby. Leaning against a cool marble wall, she slid to the floor. She held her head between her knees while he rubbed her taut neck muscles.

Two thousand dollars. She'd never held that much money in her hand. At least her stomach was settling some. It must have been a bad hotdog. She was about ready to float. She tried to open her eyes, but couldn't. It was his fingers. What were they doing to her neck? To her body? Good grief, what was happening to her?

"Why don't we get you outside," he said. His words were soothing, like a cool cloth on a hot forehead. "Maybe back to the barn. Do you think you can stand?"

She nodded, not trusting herself to form a single word. He held her firmly as they made their way back toward shedrow. By the time they got halfway there, she could breathe again.

"Sorry about that back there," she said, gruffly. "I'm not the swooning type."

Nick leaned back and laughed. "I never thought you were, kid. Anything but. You probably had some bad food."

She looked quickly at him and knew he was teasing her again. Without forethought, she punched his bicep. Her fist met rock-hard muscle.

"So how do you make all of this money?" she asked, not attempting to hide the accusation.

Again, Nick laughed. "It's all legitimate, kid; you haven't fallen into the hands of the crime syndicate." He sobered. "Most of it was made investing in the stock market—my money and other folks' money. Lately, I've gotten out of that line of work." He glanced at Daisy. "I own a canoe factory."

"Really?"

"Yep, handcrafted, very expensive canoes. You ever canoed?"

"Nope. I've hardly been out of the Chicago area. I don't imagine there's a big demand for canoes here."

"Actually, there is. A lot of our buyers vacation in Northern Minnesota, or maybe Wisconsin or Michigan. You really should try canoeing."

"Why? I'm too clumsy for that."

"Nonsense. You carry yourself with the grace of a tall woman who is comfortable with her body. You must drive the young studs up the wall. I suspect anyone who can be so at ease with horses can manage a canoe. And I think you'd love the serenity of it. Hang around me long enough and you'll find yourself in a canoe. You can count on that."

Daisy smiled to herself. She knew about as much about young studs as she did about canoeing, but she wasn't going to tell Nicholas Underwood that. Did he find her appealing?

They walked without saying anything more until they came to a halt in front of RainbowBlaze's stall. The horse stepped forward, obviously expecting a treat. Nick was pleased to see Daisy didn't disappoint her.

"So," she said, not meeting Nick's eyes, "what's your plan? Are you going to keep RainbowBlaze?"

A slow grin crossed Nick's lips. "I'm not sure I got a whole day's tour."

The blood seeped from the lanky woman's face. "Okay," he said, "I won't leave you hanging. Yeah, you've done a very convincing job. Two things stood out, really. First, listening to you talk to that horse earlier today before you knew I was standing here. I'm envious of that kind of relationship. Second, watching that number ten horse strive to win was something I'll never forget. I appreciate that desire."

"So you'll keep Rainbow?"

"I'll make a deal with you. I'll keep Blaze on two conditions."

Now why was she frowning? Would the woman ever learn to trust him? But then maybe she shouldn't. "First, you will continue to educate me regarding horses. How to be a heads-up owner. I'll likely want to expand. Don't look so shocked. You'll learn, kid, I never do anything halfway. When I decide I want something, I go after it."

So why was she blushing again? "Second, you

will teach me how to read that newspaper you were reading today — that form that looked like a jumble of numbers and letters to me. Do you agree?"

"Of course. I can do all of that, if you have the time. And it will take much of my time, too."

"Good. To cement the deal, when I draw up the papers on RainbowBlaze, you will appear as twenty percent owner."

"What?" Daisy gasped. "You can't..."

"Listen, kid, I'm beginning to think you're a slow learner. Don't tell me what I can't do." Nick took a handkerchief from his pocket and wiped the dust from his glasses; he studied the woman to see if she was again in danger of fainting.

"It's only good business. You know the horse business. I don't. But I do know that if someone owns a piece of the action, they'll likely make the wisest possible decisions about their investments."

"Do the people who build your canoes own part of the business?" Her brow furrowed.

"You don't miss much — but in fact, they do. I'm a firm believer in that principle. So is it a deal?"

Daisy stared into the stall at RainbowBlaze for the longest time. Was she afraid of him, or of something else? A full two minutes passed before she responded.

"Okay," she said, quietly. "What choice do I have? I still don't understand any of this. I don't know what you're really after."

"There is one stipulation I make with all my employees."

"What's that?"

"If they sell out, they have to sell to me. I don't want strangers owning any part of my businesses."

Nick glanced at his watch and shook his head. "I've got to get going. I'll catch up with you later, kid. Since we have a deal, you just go ahead and do what you were doing with Blaze. I'll have the papers ready for you to sign before the end of the week. Then we can work out a schedule for my equine education."

Uneasy with his own bravado and sudden awkwardness, he stared at Daisy. "This was one of the most enjoyable days I've had in a long time, kid. Keep up the good work."

- o -

Daisy waved in response, slumped down on a bale of hay and watched the strange man — no, her new partner — disappear down the alleyway and into the parking lot.

Had she been dreaming? She touched the wad of money in her pocket. It was there. She didn't have to count it. That would cover a good amount of tuition and books. She scratched her head with both hands. Did she believe in fairy godmothers or godfathers? Not hardly.

Holy Moses, she owned part of RainbowBlaze. She gawked at the sleek animal. Rainbow's large brown eyes had a special gleam in them, as if she knew what had transpired. Daisy began to giggle.

This had been an incredible day.

She sobered, remembering his fingers massaging her strained neck muscles and her breasts crushing into his chest after their horse won. The man might be a businessman, but he was powerfully built. And he walked like he knew where he was going but was in no particular hurry to get there. Had he been as aware of her body as she had been of his?

She recalled his gentle touch. Heat raced through her veins. Her nipples tightened. Daisy closed her eyes and shook her head. It couldn't be. She couldn't be attracted to Nicholas Underwood. He was too...

She didn't know what it'd feel like being attracted to a man. A slow grin worked its way across her lips. If this tingling was part of the attraction, then it wasn't all bad.

Chapter Two

"Why can't I think straight?" Daisy sprang off her living room loveseat and headed for the tiny kitchen in her first floor Cicero apartment. It was an eat-in kitchen only because she ate on a card table. She pried open a can of pop and swallowed deeply.

How many times had she rerun the events of the day? They still seemed beyond her wildest dreams. She owned part of Rainbow. And she'd tucked two thousand dollars away in the bank.

She wandered back through the small dining room. The room served as an office with a desk, computer, low-tech sound system, and several bookcases. No space remained for dining, but then she seldom had visitors. She plopped back down on the off-white loveseat only to immediately jump up and move to the matching wing chair.

Then there was the man. Nicholas Underwood. Brash. Gentle. Demanding. Laid back. Old, yet maybe not too old. He was a paradox.

She chewed her lower lip. Could he be the one?

Not in a romantic mushy sort of way. But in a practical way. Somehow, sometime she wanted to learn about those things that could happen between a man and a woman. She'd batted away every male, young or old, who had noticed her since she was ten. She intimidated males. For the most part, that was good. Her grandmother would be proud.

The fact that their worlds were so different made a man like Nicholas Underwood safe. They couldn't share any long term future. She could help him out — maybe he'd be able to help *her* out.

Her birthday wasn't far off. She'd probably be the only twenty-one year old virgin in Cicero if not all of Chicago. She wanted to experience being a woman before her birthday.

She'd studied several educational sex videos again and again. They'd been helpful, but only to a point. She'd have to decide fairly soon what to do with Nicholas Underwood. For now, he made an intriguing horseracing partner. She hugged herself. Would he make an equally intriguing partner in bed?

Yes or no, at least he'd be experienced. She wasn't about to give what her grandmother had called her most *prized treasure* to some bumbling kid or some horny macho man. She'd learned enough from those videos to know she was looking for a gentle, skilled lover. Maybe she'd finally found him.

What would Nick think of her small abode? It would probably look like a cell compared to his palatial surroundings. He never had said where he lived, but then neither had she.

The apartment buzzer rang. Daisy walked to the entry and peeked through the peephole. She groaned. Maxine and Reggie. Her brother-in-law had a nose for money; thank goodness she'd stopped at the bank and deposited her cash before coming home.

Daisy opened the door and Maxine led the way in. Reggie Lassiter followed her sister like a dog on a fresh scent.

"How are you, baby?" Maxine said, her voice only slightly slurred. It was still early in the evening. "We were nearby and thought we'd check in on my little sister."

"Right."

"Get me one of my beers." Reggie looked like a dark-haired, overweight nose tackle for the Chicago Bears. *In his dreams.* Daisy chuckled to herself on her way to the kitchen for his beer. She kept her fridge stocked for just such occasions. It didn't pay to get Reggie angry at her – or at her sister.

She retraced her steps and handed each of her guests a beer.

Maxine took three swallows from the bottle before asking, "So have you been keeping busy?"

"There's plenty of work at the track, and there's always homework."

Her petite sister twisted the loops of her purse nervously. Perspiration shone under the dark ringlets on her forehead. This wasn't just a social visit. Daisy knew the signs by now. They wanted something.

Maxine was her half sister; even then it was difficult to think of her as kin. She was older. She'd hit the streets right after their grandmother's funeral, when Daisy was twelve. Social services had taken Daisy to a group home.

Maxine and Reggie had never wanted anything to do with her even after they married. Not until she'd gotten a steady job working for Sam Gallagher. Reggie Lassiter seldom inspired confidence. After meeting Reggie, Cassie Travers refused to let the man on her property.

Daisy scowled. Why couldn't Maxine get her life together? Why couldn't she dump Reggie and move on? She was hooked, that was why. On booze, on drugs, on Reggie Lassiter.

"You're giving me that condescending look again," Maxine complained. "Why do you always have to look like you think you're better than me?"

Daisy blinked. "I'm sorry. I don't mean to do that. So what have you guys been up to?"

"Hanging." Reggie snickered.

"My Reggie lost his job again. Thought maybe you could help us out," Maxine purred. "Winchel's won't give me an advance. Said I already owe them. Don't remember getting the advance before. They treat their waitresses like shit anyway. So will you help?"

"How much do you need?"

"How much you got?" Reggie ran his eyes up and down her body like he was undressing her.

Daisy flinched. She was sure Reggie ogled her to make Maxine jealous.

"Not enough, I'm sure. I can loan you twenty-five until you get paid," Daisy said to Maxine.

"That's chicken shit," Reggie growled, lurching to his feet. "Look at this place. You make more money in a week than we see in a month. Thought you took family responsibilities seriously. You're always talking about family. So do something about it."

Daisy didn't stir. "I've got twenty-five dollars. You're welcome to borrow it or not. Maxine, will that help?"

"Yes darling, that will help a lot. Reggie," she said, pulling him back down beside her, "we've got to be grateful that Daisy wants to help at all. Your family certainly doesn't."

"What family?" He spat the words out. "All right, it's better than nothing, but not by much. How about some tips?" His voice turned sugary. "You're an insider now, Daisy Matthews. You gotta see some hot horses."

Daisy shook her head. How many times had they been around this one? She knew Reggie. If she gave him betting tips, he'd hold her responsible for how the horses ran and expect even more.

Reggie glared at Maxine for support.

"Daisy, he's not asking for money. Just for some help, some advice. He can make his own bets. Can't you honey?" She rested her head on Reggie's shoulder.

Daisy tried not to gag.

"I'll get the bets down. Just tell me who to bet on."

"Like I've said before, horseracing isn't that

predictable."

"He knows that," Maxine replied, squeezing Reggie's hand. "My man knows how things go down. Don't you dear?"

"That I do." He glared at Daisy. "This time I expect results, or someone may get hurt."

"Ouch," Maxine yelped, "don't squeeze my hand that hard."

"Sorry," he said, looking directly at Daisy. "Sometimes a guy just doesn't know his own strength."

Daisy closed her eyes. The man didn't have a subtle bone in his body. Either give Reggie some possible winners, or her sister would be hurt. Not that it would be a new experience for Maxine. Against her better judgment, she caved in.

"Okay, I'll give you three to five runners a week that appear ready to win. You know that doesn't mean they'll win."

Both Reggie and Maxine nodded. "You make your own bets, however you manage that, but not through me. I could get in trouble with my boss for that. I don't have time to run to the betting windows on race day."

"No problem. I can handle that." Reggie stood. "I'll drop by and get the picks Wednesdays."

"No!" Daisy jumped to her feet, towering over her beefy brother-in-law. "I'll leave messages on your answering machine. My work is so erratic I'm never certain when I'll be home."

"That'll be just fine, Daisy." Maxine rose and hugged Daisy loosely. She stood back and looked up at Daisy. "I never will understand how you got so tall and me so short. Mama was average height, but daddy was short."

Daisy snorted. "At least you know who your daddy was."

"Yours must have been a pro basketball player." Reggie laughed. "I hear your mother was a professional, too."

"Reggie!" Maxine pulled her husband toward the door. Daisy clenched her teeth and kept her hands to herself.

"Don't mind him," Maxine said. "Mama loved both of us. You know that. She did the best she could."

The door shut quietly. Daisy laid her forehead against the door jamb and let out a breath she hadn't known she was holding. She ran her fingers through her hair and walked back into the living room. Giving up on studying, she picked up the trash, turned off the lights and headed for her bedroom. A good novel might help remove the foul taste her sister and brother-in-law so often left in her mouth.

She changed into a sleeping shirt and pulled back the futon covers. Daisy smiled and drank in the warmth of her bedroom. She'd had a choice of a rental with two small bedrooms or one large. She'd opted for the latter.

It was her favorite room in the apartment. From her bed she could see her reflection in the mirrored closet doors at the end of the futon. In a corner near it stood a stuffed chair and a reading lamp. A small TV and VCR sat on a dresser in the opposite corner. Someday she'd break down and buy a proper bed, but she liked her simple futon floor mattress. It didn't require much upkeep. Another reading lamp stood between the bed and a four shelf bookcase.

The bedroom was light and breezy. She'd wallpapered the room with a simple floral design of daisies—her favorite flower. They made her feel special, like someone loved her.

She crawled under the covers and hugged Bear to her chest. Maxine was right. She knew their mother had loved them. There were good memories from when she was quite young. Times when her mother would read a children's story at bedtime.

And then everything had gone wrong. Her mother began working nights. Too many men came to visit. Most ignored the gangly string-bean of a girl, yet they still managed to scare her.

She'd only been seven when she found her mother lying naked on the kitchen floor. The woman who had read bedtime stories to her was no longer breathing.

Grandmother Matthews loved her. She knew that to be true. Daisy hugged Bear tighter. Her grandmother had been a solid rock and had taught her basic values. While Maxine had given their grandmother a difficult time, Daisy had listened and wanted to please. Grandmother Matthews was family.

Tears stung her eyes as she remembered her

grandmother's death—another death that turned her life upside down.

Raul and Cassie loved her. Raul Hernandez would love any stranded dog. He was the nicest man, and she was lucky it was his group home where she'd been sent. That was where she met Cassie Travers, her social worker, foster mother and mentor.

Yes, she'd grown up hard and had to defend herself from an early age, but she did know something about love. And then there were the horses. They knew how to love. And there was Bear, a gift from her mother so many years before. Things could have been much worse.

She drifted off to sleep. The image of a tall dark-haired man with glasses offered his hand. She reached for it, but sleep overcame her before she could feel his skin touching hers.

- o -

By Saturday night, Daisy was beginning to wonder if she'd imagined Nicholas Underwood. She sat at her desk, the words on the book she'd been studying starting to blur. Underwood intruded into her thoughts far too often.

The phone rang; she let the answering machine take it. "Hey kid, you still alive?"

Daisy laughed at the voice. Should she pick up the phone? She didn't want to appear too eager, but then she didn't want to seem irresponsible either.

She lifted the receiver. "I'm here." Her voice felt more husky than normal. "How did you get my number?"

"Ah, you are there. Hoped you hadn't gone to bed yet. Figured mornings wouldn't be a good time to catch you at home. Hell, you're my employee. I know all your numbers."

"Do I get yours?"

"Didn't know you could be coy, kid. Of course. I'll give you a list. There may be occasions when one of us will have to cancel. I don't have a lot of time to waste with missed appointments, and I don't imagine you do, either."

Daisy listened to his breathing; her own lungs strained.

"Are you phone shy? You were more talkative the other day."

"No, I don't think so."

"Am I interrupting something? It is Saturday night. You don't have a passionate date going on there, do you?"

"No. Not hardly. I thought you'd call at the barn."

"I'll call you when I can wherever you are. I've got Blaze's papers drawn up waiting for your signature. You'll have to fill out owner forms for the track before she can race again. I sent mine in yesterday. They already have a security check done on you, so it shouldn't take but a day or two. I've got to run over to the Twin Cities for business Monday so will leave tomorrow to say hi to the folks. Should be back Wednesday. I'd like to get with you sooner, but can't. God, I feel like I'm rattling on like a teenager."

Daisy chuckled. "You are." She looped the phone cord around her elbow, carried the phone into the living room, plopped down on the loveseat and draped her long legs over its arm. "Do you still want me to teach you stuff about horses and handicapping?"

"Sure do, teach. I'm sure you have your hands full in the mornings. Maybe Thursday..."

She heard him rummaging, probably through his appointment book.

"How about two o'clock? I've got the rest of the day open. How's that for you?"

Daisy didn't have to check her book. "It looks good for me. Why don't you come to Barn D? We can start from there."

"Great. I'm going to have a messenger bring by Blaze's papers for you to sign. The sooner we get the paperwork completed, the quicker she can race again."

"You know where I live?"

"It doesn't take a private investigator to determine that. Most of your personal information has to go on the ownership papers. As well as your Assistant Trainers License. Right?"

"Right. I didn't think about that."

"Besides, I make a point of knowing everything I can about my employees and partners."

"I'm not your employee, Mr. Underwood." She knew she must sound harsh, but she couldn't help it. Sometimes the man really galled her. Like right now. "We may be partners by some strange circumstance, but I *work* for Sam Gallagher."

"Whoa there, kid. The lady has a temper. I like that. Shows fire and will." He paused. "I'll have to think on that. You may be right. You may complicate my life yet."

Daisy frowned. "Well, you sure as hell have complicated mine."

"Yeah, but aren't they nice complications? A week ago you didn't even know I existed. You didn't own a race horse. And you were probably planning to waste time you could spend educating me playing around with some college guy."

Brushing hair off her brow, Daisy chewed on her lip. She wasn't experienced at this kind of repartee. She only knew how to tell guys *no*, not how to give them a let's-wait-and-see signal.

"Cat got your tongue, kid? Am I really going to complicate your life that much?"

He sounded far too pleased with himself. "I don't know. Depends on how much time you require, I suppose. I not only have my job—I do have to study, too."

"Will I be imposing on your social life? Do you have a steady man in your life?"

"Not hardly. Well, I mean," she stammered, "not one."

"Still playing the field, huh? Well, I shouldn't get in the way too much, then. If you're a good teacher, this may not require a lot of time."

"You mean if you're a good student, don't you?"

"Now, that's more like the woman I remember with straw in her hair. Do you realize that you are drop dead gorgeous with a half dozen pieces of straw sticking out of your hair? The guys must be lined up around your block with their tongues hanging out. I'm sure they won't like my intruding on their time, but I won't let that deter me. Are you still there?"

"I'm here." Daisy tried to keep her voice steady while her heart raced wildly.

"Maybe you'll just have to put some of the guys on ice for a while. I can be quite demanding, and I make no apologies for that. There never is enough time to do everything I want to do. But this horse thing is now at the top of my to-do list. And that includes you. Remember, you've been paid in advance."

"I remember. Owning a part of Rainbow far exceeds any of my dreams."

"Listen kid, if you hang around me much you'll have to get used to expanding your dreams. I don't dream small. It doesn't take any more time to dream big than small."

"Maybe, maybe not."

"What do you mean maybe? Weren't you listening to what I just said?"

"I heard you. It's just that some folks can dream all they want to, work as hard as they can, and still nothing happens."

She heard Underwood swallow. "Guess you're right," he said, "sometimes I get so wrapped up in what I'm doing that I forget where I've come from and what I've seen."

"What?"

"Some other time. Good to hear your voice, kid. There's a quality about it that I can't quite name. Maybe its youthful exuberance. Anyway, I'll see you next Thursday at two o'clock. Don't be late."

"I'll be there."

- o -

Nicholas Underwood sat staring at the cell phone long after he'd set it on the massive oak desk at the center of his study in his fourteen room Kenwood house. The woman stuck to his hide like a sandbur. *Sultry* described her voice. She probably didn't have a clue how sexy she sounded or looked.

He leaned back in his swivel chair and propped his feet on the desk. She had to be his employee. It was safer that way. But she might be right. He hired Sam Gallagher, and Sam hired Daisy Matthews. So what did that make Willow to him? One could probably cut it either way.

Who was he kidding? He didn't want to regard the tall, slender woman with the deep smoky voice as an employee. He closed his eyes. *Twenty-five from forty-two equals seventeen. Shit.* He slammed his feet back to the carpet and strolled over to one of the floor-to-ceiling bookcases that nearly ringed his study. He reached for a slim volume and turned the pages until words leapt out at him. *Let the world slip: we shall ne'er be younger.* It was from *Taming of the Shrew.*

Would that he could. What he really wished was that he could forget how Daisy Matthews' soft breasts crushed against his chest or how her gray eyes rounded in pools of pain and then turned iridescent in the delight of banter and the unexpectedness of surprise. She possessed a vitality that he found intoxicating and difficult to shake.

If he was a smart man, he'd go to the Twin Cities, conduct his business and arrange for the sale of RainbowBlaze while out of town. But that would be too much like the coward's way out. No, he'd stay the course. He wasn't about to cheat destiny. Certainly a man of his experience and talent could best a woman who'd probably lived no more than a quarter century.

But why even bother to enter the contest? He could simply flee. No one was watching.

He could no more flee than sprout wings. There was something about Daisy Matthews that drew him like the sorrowful call of the loon. He wanted to know more about her. He wanted to listen to her story. He wanted to have some excuse to hug her again. Given her youthfulness, she might not be good for his pride, but she seemed good for his soul.

A rap on his office door jolted Nick from his reverie. "Yes, come in." Mary Brown entered and Nick tried not to smile.

Other than his bedroom, his office was the only room in the house where she knocked before entering. How often had he felt like an intruder in his own home before the inquisitive eyes of Mrs. B.?

Maybe it was because he'd inherited her; well, sort of. She came with the house. The eighty-something bent African American woman had been taking care of residents in this house since she was a teenager. And she had an uncanny sense of showing up when he least wanted to talk. He often threatened to fire her, but they both knew that he cared for her like a favorite aunt. And if he didn't watch out, she could easily smother him with love. She'd outlived her family and her friends. She hardly had anyone else to irritate or to love.

"So, Mister Nick, I was worried when you didn't come home for supper. You usually call." Mrs. Brown stood in front of his desk peering at him with large dark questioning eyes.

He waved his hand dismissing her concern. "Sorry, I must have gotten overly involved at work."

"Harumph. That usually don't make you forget your manners." Mary Brown bent over and straightened two stacks of papers on Nick's desk.

Nick scowled. She backed away abruptly. "Oh, I forgot. Don't touch a thing in the master's office," she chided.

"I'm not your master," Nick responded quickly. "But you're right about not touching things in here."

"Sounds to me like you're the one who's

touchy."

Nick always found it hard to ignore Mrs. Brown, but he tried his best.

"My, my," she said, "how many years has it been since you've had a woman throw you off stride?"

"What?" Nick nearly shouted.

"A woman. You know. You remember what they are."

"I know what a woman is."

"Good." Mrs. Brown gave him a toothless grin. "I was hoping you wouldn't forget. She must be something."

Nick closed his eyes, took a deep breath and reopened them. The housekeeper was still there. "What do you mean by that?"

"For the last several days you've been moping around here like a tomcat returning from the street who had no luck. There's no bounce in your step. Indecision about a woman will do that, you know."

"I didn't know that," Nick responded sharply. "And don't you have something better to do than worry about my love life?"

"No need to get huffy." Mrs. Brown took another step back from the desk. "If you ask me, you could use some good loving. This old house could use a good woman. It's getting to be more than I can manage alone. And I'd like to hear the sounds of children again in these walls before I die."

"Go to the park and rent a kid or two. Bring

them here and let them scream their heads off. Just as long as I'm gone." He glanced at the papers on his desk. "Now, Mrs. B., if you have nothing further, I do need to get back to work."

"Didn't look like you were working before. Looked like you were staring off into space."

Nick raised an eyebrow and cleared his throat.

"Okay, Mr. Nick, I can take a hint. I just want you to know that you can bring a woman here anytime. It won't bother me none. I may be old, but I know how things are with you young people these days. Even my old Andrew thought we should test out the equipment before we got married."

"Mrs. B.!"

"I'll leave you now, Mr. Nick. Maybe you'll get a skip in your walk soon enough." Nick shook his head and watched Mrs. B. leave the room. A skip, indeed.

He turned more pages of the Taming of the Shrew. The words blurred. Gray sultry eyes stared back at him. A long elegant nose and narrow chin emerged. Then there were full lips and a slight overbite. The mouth turned upward in a shy grin.

Nick frowned. The only thing that skipped was his heartbeat.

- o -

Ten miles away, Daisy hugged Bear and drifted off to sleep. Words from *Twelfth Night* teased her mind: *Then come kiss me, sweet and twenty, youth's a stuff will not endure.* She wet her lips. The image of his face sharpened. His lips parted, inviting. She leaned forward. His image swirled, fading into the night.

"Underwood checks out. Clean as a whistle, according to the guys in the Racing Office." Sam Gallagher sat at the desk in his tiny track office and chewed on the stem of a crusty pipe. He hadn't lit it in years. "Not to worry. He's legit."

Daisy nodded and grinned at him. "Thanks for checking him out for me." Gallagher had taken off his University of Maryland ball cap, exposing his gleaming white bald crown. She respected Sam's skill with horses and his judgments regarding people. "So what do you think of him?"

"Hard to know. Only talked with him twice by phone. He's a businessman. That's clear. And he's honest. At least he admits to knowing nothing about horses." Gallagher idly scraped caked mud from his boots with a ball point pen. "You sure got him hooked. He's ready to get involved with racing, and apparently he has a checkbook that can back him up."

"That's not surprising." Daisy took a seat on the straight-backed wooden chair. "So do we work with him?"

Gallagher smiled. "Do *you* work with him? I think that's the question. Oh, Underwood was respectful enough toward me. But he clearly sees himself as somehow sponsoring you in this training business. Every trainer needs to find an owner who will provide enough financial backing to carry him through the bad times as well as the good."

"But I'm not ready to go out on my own." Daisy shuddered. "I like working for you. And there's so much more to learn."

"Underwood has good business sense. He seems to know that. Talked to me about being your coach, and that I'd continue getting my training fees with any horses he might purchase." Gallagher eyed Daisy. "Frankly, you'll get a raise for bringing in a fair amount of business. Sounds like I'll be picking up a small piece of the next horse he buys.

"A lot of owners want to do business that way. Makes them feel like the trainer will be more committed to their horses. Maybe it's true. I've done it both ways. And either works all right. There's more potential profit when you own a share of the horse — and there's more potential for loss." He shrugged. "Like horses, each owner is different, and you have to kind of read their cues and shape the game for them without losing your own integrity."

Daisy sighed. "There's so much to learn."

"You'll do fine." Gallagher glanced away. "I know I'm old enough to be your grandfather, and you're a young woman on your own." He stopped talking and then looked back at her. "I just want you to be careful with Underwood. He's a legitimate businessman, but he's still a man. He's smitten by racing. And he may be smitten by you.

That's neither good nor bad. Depends on what you want. My only suggestion is be careful, and sort out what you really want. Being business partners is one thing, being something else — well, that's something else."

Daisy blushed. "Thanks, Sam. I'll try. You've been like the grandfather I've never known. Right now my head is spinning in ways I never knew possible. But I've got street smarts. I won't get easily hurt."

"I know. I should be giving the same advice to Underwood. He may be at more risk than you. Doubt if he has any real grasp of the tenaciousness of the woman he's selected for a partner." Gallagher chuckled. "But it's the right of grandfather types to worry some. Sort of like on the day before a big race."

Nicholas Underwood was proving an able student. Daisy watched him pour over the past performances for the next day's races at Arlington, his broad shoulders slumping forward. They'd spent two hours a day together for the past four days. It was always two to four, like clockwork.

She vaguely wondered what he did after he left the track. He talked very little about himself. He was brooding about something. Hopefully, there weren't any problems with his business. Or with his women. Good grief, she didn't even know if the man was married.

Daisy cleared her throat, setting down Chaucer's *Canterbury Tales* on which she had a paper due the following week. He hadn't heard her. They sat in a corner of the track kitchen; half chilled coffee and crumbs remained from their study break.

"Mr. Underwood."

Across the small table, Nicholas Underwood glanced up sharply. "How often do I have to ask you to call me Nick? We're partners. Strangers call me Mr. Underwood. Partners and friends call me Nick."

Daisy frowned.

"So what did you want?"

She had to know. "Are you married?"

That ridiculous, lazy smiled worked across Spec's lips. She was going to die. Her toes curled.

"Shouldn't the question be are you married..."

Her head pounded. "Okay, damn it. Are you married, Nick?"

"Ah, I've heard my name roll off a woman's lips more smoothly and with more passion than that. But that will have to do for now." He folded the paper and laid it down beside his empty plate. "To answer your question and unasked questions. First, I am not married. Second, I was married to a beautiful woman with a lot of class and money. She wanted more class and money than I did. We parted amicably and still greet each other now and then. The marriage has been over for fifteen years, probably when you were still in training bras.

"With all her makeup and designer clothes, Ashley couldn't hold a candle to your natural beauty. Third, there have been many women, but

50

none currently. I'm finding that you cramp my style in that way. You keep me studying these forms and the horse books so much, there's no time for women. Even if I were so inclined. Does that about answer your questions?"

Daisy nodded. She chewed her lower lip. How could he read her mind? She felt like such a neophyte.

"So how about you, Matthews? Ever been married?"

Her eyes rounded. Underwood was dead serious. His crack about the training bra sank into her awareness. Good grief, he thought she was considerably older than she was. "No," she stammered. "Never."

"No live-in boyfriend?"

She shook her head. "Current men?"

"None," she mumbled. "There's no time."

"Good." Nicholas leaned back and graced her with a satisfied grin. "Maybe I'm cramping your style, too." He unfolded the newspaper and redirected his attention to the Saturday races.

Daisy picked up her book and blew air through pursed lips. She'd learned what she had to know. How fast would he run when he discovered she wasn't even of legal drinking age?

Chapter Three

The sputtering sounds of the apartment buzzer penetrated Daisy's sleep. She rolled over and pulled a pillow over her head. The buzzer continued ringing sporadically. "Go away," she grumbled. "It's Monday. It's my day off."

Scrambling off the futon, she grabbed her robe and poked her arms through the armholes as she strode angrily toward the entry. She'd have to remember to get the landlord to fix that damn buzzer. Maybe she should just snip its wires.

Daisy peered through the peephole and grew deathly still. Why had he come? She didn't want him to know this part of her world. With fingers trembling slightly, she turned the knob and opened the door.

"Morning, kid. Damn, you look quite fetching with sleep still in those lovely smoky eyes of yours." Nicholas Underwood strolled into her living room like he'd been there many times before, like he belonged. "Come on, girl. Get your butt in gear—hell, it's mid-morning. It's your day off. We're going to do Wrigley today. Enough of the books and pedigrees. I need a break. *We* need a break."

Daisy stood in the entryway as if her feet were poured in cement and she was still waiting for it to dry.

"You got any coffee here? I'll make it while you get into some clothes." Nick licked his lips. "Don't know why you bothered to put that robe on; it doesn't hide a damn thing unless you tie it."

Daisy's hands flew to her ears. "Stop. Stop talking, please. How did you get here? Why are you here? My robe!" She pulled the robe tight around her body and knotted the sash. Her cheeks must be scarlet.

"Damn, I hope you don't go answering the door like that for just any guy who happens by."

"Guys don't *happen by* without calling first. Now that you're here, you might as well make yourself useful. The coffee is on the counter in the kitchen. Two scoops for eight cups. I'm going to get dressed."

Daisy padded toward her bedroom with as much grace as she could muster and then slammed the door behind her so hard the hinges rattled.

The nerve of the man getting her out of bed. Was he checking up on her? A boyfriend could have slept over. Right! Well, it was possible. *Yeah, and sewer rats can sprout wings.*

Had he said something about the Cubs? Wrigley. The Cubs. What did you wear to a baseball game? Probably no different than the track. She tugged on a pair of white shorts and wiggled into a yellow spaghetti-string tank top. Under the tank top was a sheer bra that held things in place, but didn't cover much up. She

54

touched each nipple playfully until they were on full alert. Looking in the mirror, she chuckled softly. Underwood had come to her uninvited; she wasn't about to run away and hide. He might think of her as a kid, but someday he'd realize she was more than enough woman for him to handle.

She entered the kitchen running a brush through her tangled hair. Underwood sat at the card table sipping coffee. He took one brief look at her and spewed coffee from his lips. Quickly, he grabbed a paper towel to clean up the mess. Daisy continued brushing her hair, ignoring his discomfort.

"Geez, kid, if you're going to put on a show, save it for a guy your own age. Can't you find anything that'd cover up your belly button? I'm not sure I'll be able to keep all the guys from pawing you, if you go out like that."

"I'm used to taking care of myself." Daisy set the hairbrush down and poured herself a cup of coffee. She hid her smile. She had his attention. Was Nicholas Underwood as aware of his arousal as she was? "I didn't ask you here. If I'm too ugly for your taste, you can leave now."

"Holy shit. I never meant to imply that you're ugly. You're too damn gorgeous for my heart."

She sat down, crossed her legs and followed his eyes as they took in the view. Nonchalantly, she wiggled her toes.

He gasped.

Thank God for those tapes on seduction. Nicholas Underwood was going to be easier than she'd thought. If he got any hotter, his glasses would steam over. But not yet. No, there were still things to be done. She wasn't ready for the momentous event. Soon, but not now.

"So, I take it you're a Cubs fan."

He nodded, shook his head and seemed to regain his equilibrium. "My neighbors think I'm a traitor. If you live on the South Side, you're traditionally a White Sox fan; if you live on the North Side then you root for the Cubs."

"But you're not a traditionalist."

"Hardly."

"So where do you live?"

"Kenwood."

"Ah."

Nick frowned. "I believe I detected a little reverse classism. Yes, I have a lot of money. Yes, I live in a big house. Yes, I give to a lot of good causes. Yes, I'm hooked on...race horses, for the moment. I want to talk to you about how I go about buying some more, but not today. That sounds too much like work. This is your day off. It's the Cubs."

"How do you know I didn't have other plans?"

"I guessed. Maybe it was a hope more than a guess." He scowled. "But maybe it was a mistake. You look different here in your own space. More domestic. More at home. More..."

"More woman, maybe?"

Nick blew out air and coughed. "Oh, I've not missed that fact." He righted his glasses on his nose. "I've got to use the head, and then we better

56

think about driving to the ballpark. It'll be good to be in a crowd. You've got a nice pad here, kid. Nice library. You could use a better computer, though. The one in your office area is ancient."

"It's what I can afford." She stood and placed their cups in the sink.

"Didn't mean to make you defensive."

Daisy rinsed the dishes while Underwood used her bathroom. Did Underwood have a maid? He probably did, as well as a gardener. Well, her space was adequate for her needs. She hadn't invited him here. That would never have occurred to her.

"Only one toothbrush," he said, coming up behind her.

She spun around to face him. "What did you expect?"

"There you go getting your back up again. I wasn't expecting anything. I was just commenting. One toothbrush looked lonely, but I liked it that way."

"I guess I'm pleased I didn't disappoint you." He was standing too close. She could hardly breathe.

He brushed a lock of hair back off her forehead and ran an index finger down the length of her nose before pressing it against her lips. His eyes flared with passion and then immediately cooled. He backed away. "We'd best be going," he said, gruffly. "Before I make a fool of myself," she heard him whisper under his breath. "Put shoes on, grab a bag or whatever. I'll wait for you

57

outside. I need some air."

Tingling from toe to crown, Daisy hurried to find her best sneakers. She wet her lips, avoiding where his finger had been. Even the videos couldn't do justice to the kinds of electrical charges that'd coursed through her body when his finger had made its way slowly down her nose to settle on her lips.

She'd thought he was going to kiss her. She was more than a little disappointed that he hadn't. But there was no question that he now regarded her as a woman. He was probably still hung up on age, but age didn't matter for her purposes.

"Jones is the man," Nick declared. "He carries this team when he has to. And he's a team player when that's needed. He's the kind of person I like on my team."

Daisy nodded, biting down on a soft pretzel. The batter Nick pointed out didn't look any different than any other player, but he must be. At that moment, Nick's player swung. The bat made a cracking sound that surprised Daisy. She watched the ball sail over the leftfield bleachers onto Waveland Avenue. Now *that* was power. It was like watching a horse determined to get to the wire first over any and all challengers. And Nick Underwood clearly loved the game of baseball.

"Okay, that was the power game. Now watch this next batter. He needs to get a hit. One out. He may even try to bunt to get on."

"Ball one," cried the ump.

"Did you see that?" Nick asked, without taking his eyes off the batter. "He faked the bunt. Now the third baseman and first baseman are edging in toward home plate. The infield is getting smaller, making it easier for him to hit away."

Daisy wasn't certain she understood everything Nick was telling her, but she enjoyed watching the tension rise. They sat in the third row between home plate and first base. She could see the batter trying not to give away what he was going to do.

On the next pitch he swung and lined a ball over the third baseman's head. Nick stood and cheered wildly. For a man who was reasonably quiet at the race track, he sure made a lot of noise at a ballgame. As if sensing her question, he sat back down. "Hope I'm not embarrassing you. This is different. Money is involved with the horses. This is pure and simple recreation. Nothing is on the line for me."

"I didn't realize there was so much strategy involved in baseball. Games were on the TV at the group home, but I never bothered to watch. Looked too boring."

"Boring! There's as much strategy in baseball as in horse racing. Hell, there's strategy in anything worth pursuing."

Daisy grinned broadly, reached over and squeezed his thigh, then placed her other hand on his neck and her lips close to his ear. "Old man, you overwhelm me with wisdom far beyond my years. I'll bet there's a lot more you could share, if you wanted to."

Covering her hand with his, Nick lifted it and returned it to her lap. His fingers brushed her inner thigh; he jerked away as if he'd been singed by a blazing fire.

He awkwardly rose from his seat. "I've got to make a call. You want anything more to eat?"

"No, I'm fine. You're not going to leave me here alone for long are you?"

Nick sighed; his shoulders slouched. "Kid, I don't have the faintest idea what I'm going to do with you."

- o -

Stomping up the stairs toward the restrooms, Nick hoped his erection wasn't too damned obvious. What the hell had gotten into Willow today? There was no question what she was after. At least he didn't think there was. Though the only truth about women he'd learned was that not one of them was predictable.

She was too young. But dammit, he was a man. Why would she want to risk their partnership with romance? The only place romance ended up was broken hearts or strained goodbyes.

It wasn't that he didn't find her attractive. She was damn sexy. There was no difficulty imagining her body entangled with his. Earlier, at her apartment, he'd wanted to run his tongue over her lips and explore the interior of her mouth. That slight overbite intrigued him. It had possibilities that only made him grow harder.

So what was holding him back? Age. Pure and simple. But if it didn't matter to her, why should it matter to him? He had no answer. When he looked at her, he only saw Willow: vibrant, bright, captivating. What did she see when she looked at him?

Maybe it hadn't been a good idea to drop by her apartment. He'd wanted to see her laugh. He chewed a fingernail. Damn, the track was a safer place.

- o -

"You better stand aside unless you want to get soaked." Daisy, up to her armpits in soap suds, sprayed water over the bay gelding's back and down his flanks. He'd just run second in a claiming race for horses who had not won three races in their lifetime.

Nick moved away from the splattering water. "So should we try to claim a horse like him?"

Daisy straightened and assessed the horse as if for the first time. Without glancing at Nick, she returned to her task of bathing the animal. "Depends on how much you want to spend and at what level you want to compete. This guy is a twenty thousand dollar claimer who is earning his keep, barely."

"What if I wanted to buy four more horses to go along with Blaze? Using her as the foundation, let's think of two horses better than she is and two maybe not as good. Diversification is the key to the stock market; I don't know about the horse business."

Daisy walked over to the spigot and turned off the water. Returning, she began scraping excess water from Rocky's coat. "Probably as good as any strategy. You'd be competing at different levels, maybe trying to find your niche."

"How do I start?"

"You already have. You've been studying pedigrees and watching horses work on the track. I imagine you wouldn't want to go below thirty-five-thousand dollar claimers. A horse will go up or down the claiming ranks. He may become an allowance horse, or he may wind up running for a five thousand dollar tag and we'll hope someone claims him. But..."

"That's horseracing."

"Exactly. As far as the upper end goes, it really depends on how much you want to spend. I would recommend easing into the game. If Rainbow is worth a hundred thousand, maybe you could double that."

"Or triple it. Remember you always bet a little light from my perspective."

Daisy dropped the scraper in a bucket and glared at Underwood. "Don't count on that."

Nick pursed his lips and squinted at her.

Aware of his confusion, Daisy smiled inwardly and wondered if maybe she was learning a few things about seductive repartee. He'd certainly been quiet when they'd returned from the Cubs game. He hadn't even bothered to come into her apartment but begged off, saying he had to get back to his factory. No matter. She was beginning to enjoy this game. She'd heard people tell stories about landing a big fish. Maybe Underwood was her big fish.

"I need to get back over trackside," she said, drying her hands and arms on a towel. "Cassie has a contender running in the seventh. Do you have time to come along?"

"Sure. Is Travers a possible source for buying some horses?"

"Maybe. Her husband certainly is. That's pretty much what Clint does full time. He buys yearlings, trains them and then sells them as two-year-olds or three-year-olds."

"Sounds like a guy I need to meet."

- o -

"Hurry," Daisy shouted, grabbing Nick's hand, nearly dragging him through a throng of people. "We don't want to be late for the picture."

"Do you always go to the winner's circle when your friends have a horse that wins?"

"Of course," she said, over her shoulder. "And they'll come when Rainbow wins. That's the way it is. It's family."

They both were covering a lot of ground with long strides when Daisy pulled him through the winner's circle gate.

Cassie Travers, her auburn hair glistening in the sunshine and her smile as wide as possible, waved. "Hi there," she said, beaming at Daisy. The woman's eyes lowered to take in Daisy clutching the strange man's hand. Her smiled turned pasty.

Daisy dropped Nick's hand and stammered, "Cassie, I'd like you to meet a friend of mine. Nicholas Underwood. Nick, this is Cassie Travers."

Nick pumped Cassie's hand. "Heard a lot of great things about you. Congratulations on your win."

"Everybody, look this way," the photographer said.

On cue, everyone in the winner's circle smiled. Then the groom led the winner toward the test barn. Cassie joined Daisy and Nick as they walked back toward shedrow. "You've been a stranger, girl. Why don't you drop by when you're not busy?" She cast a meaningful look at Nicholas Underwood.

"I'm sorry. There's so much to tell you. I'll try to catch up with you later in the week."

"All right." Cassie scowled. "Nice meeting you, Mr. Underwood."

"Same here," Nick replied.

As Cassie returned to her barn, Nick stuffed his hands in his front pockets. "Why do I get the feeling that woman doesn't like me?"

Daisy put her arm through his and tugged him toward her barn. "Don't worry about Cassie. She can be overprotective, particularly of me or her kids."

"Guess I can understand that. Is that why you don't work for her anymore?"

"In part. We both knew it was important for me to try out my wings with another trainer. I've learned a lot from Cassie, and she was a big help in my landing the job with Sam."

"But."

"But she can be smothering. And she'll readily admit it. She can't quite believe I'm grown up and on my own now. Even though that's what she wants for me." Daisy stopped walking and turned to face Nick. "Cassie and Clint are terrific. Once they get to know you, they'll love you, and they have horse people contacts all over the country."

"Hope you're right." Nick ran the back of his hand across his mouth. "First impressions can be quite misleading."

- o -

"What do you mean you know what you're doing?" Cassie Travers pursed her lips, pacing rapidly back and forth in front of Daisy, who was lounging on a hay bale in Cassie's shedrow area. "The man's old enough to be..." She threw up her hands.

Daisy gave Cassie a lazy smile that she knew drove her up the wall. This brought back group home memories; she knew how to play that game well. Passive disinterest. That was the face she'd put on, and Cassie's Irish temper was in danger of raging out of control.

"I know what you're trying to pull. If you get me torqued off enough, you think I'll apologize and give you credit for having more brains than you actually have."

The small spitfire of a woman was about ready to wear down. At last she came to a halt in front of her. Cassie tried to glare and then a broad smile overtook her ire. "You say the man has made you part owner of RainbowBlaze."

Daisy nodded.

"He's not showering you with all kinds of other gifts

"Nope."

"I know how much Rainbow means to you; you must be walking on air."

"I am." Daisy crossed her legs at the ankles. "Being part owner puts a new perspective on the whole business."

Cassie nodded. "I just worry for you, girl. I know how much family means to you. Every time you think you're getting close to someone, they die or kick you in the groin."

Daisy shuttered her eyes.

"Don't try to hide from me, Daisy Ann Matthews. I know you better than anyone on this earth. You're up to something. And I'm not sure I like it. I saw how you looked at him and how he looked at you. If you're not in the sack with him yet, it won't be long."

Daisy blushed, but remained silent.

"I just don't want to see you hurt again. Okay. Enough social work and mom stuff. I can see I'm not making a dent. What is it that you like about him?"

Drawing her knees up under her chin, Daisy shrugged. "I'm not totally sure."

"He must have a lot of money."

"Yes, but that's not it. I don't see us having a future, if that's what you mean. I'm taking care of my emotions."

Cassie's eyebrows shot up. "If that's true, it will be the first time."

"He's fun. He treats me like I know something. I think he respects me for who I am."

"You sure he's not just trying to get into your pants?"

Daisy wrinkled her nose. "I wish he was. He's too bothered by our age difference."

"As he should be. Does he know how old you are?"

Daisy shook her head. "And don't you dare tell him. If you do, I'll never forgive you."

Cassie leaned against her tack room doorway. "I might like to interfere, but I won't. You know that. I guess there's some big lesson for you to learn in all of this; I just hope it's not the same old one."

"Which is?"

"You can't make family out of a mirage."

"I'm not looking at him as family." Daisy stood. Her fingers curled into fists and rested rigidly on her hips. "Nicholas Underwood is a nice man. He's experienced. He's too old, and that makes him safe."

Cassie studied Daisy for a long moment and then she glowed. "Well, I'll be damned. Do you mean you're looking at Nicholas Underwood as a sex object? Why, you calculating girl, you!" She paused. "You may be right. If he's as gentle and good as you think." Cassie pushed away from the doorway and resumed pacing.

Again, she stopped in front of Daisy. "Just be careful, Daisy. You're dealing with a lot of emotions that you haven't ever touched. And you're dealing with another human being. I don't want you hurt, but you don't want to hurt him, either."

"Are you telling me that you didn't have relationships with men without assuming they would lead to wedding bells?"

Cassie folded her arms across her chest. "Okay, you win. You're right. It's hard for me to let you go. But you will, whether I want you to or not. Just be careful. Practice safe sex. Give me a call if he turns out to be a louse. Clint will take care of him if it comes to that."

"Cassie!" Daisy scolded. "I'm hoping you and Clint will help Nick find some good horses to buy."

"Humph. Not until I know he's treating you like a lady."

"Then I might have to move up my time schedule a little." Daisy gave Cassie a little smile.

"Shit." Cassie turned and stomped into the tack room. Daisy laughed softly and walked back to her barn.

"Look what the cat drug in. Thought maybe you forgot the address of your office."

Nick shot an exaggerated grimace at his partner and plant manager, Thomas Harrison. Bald as a billiard ball, with skin as dark as walnut and teeth as white as fresh snow, Tom matched Nick's height but outweighed him by another fifty pounds. Not fat, just muscle. The man's smile was infectious.

"Had to come by and make sure everyone wasn't loafing. So how's it going?" Nick moved through the lobby to his office and sat down at his desk. Harrison slouched on the leather couch.

"We're on schedule. Should have two model X-Tens finished by the weekend and two T-Nines by the end of the following week."

"Good. Our buyers don't like to wait."

"Anyone who can afford these high priced canoes isn't used to waiting." Harrison leaned back and smiled. "But maybe waiting would be good for them."

"Right. How's the experimental model coming?"

"Another three weeks or so. You going to test it out, or do you want me to line up somebody else?"

"No. I'll do it." Nick fiddled with a pencil. He'd always taken pride in testing each of the prototypes before giving the go-ahead to craft more of them for sale.

Manufacturing handmade precision canoes required a lot of time and labor. His business would never be high volume, but it would be top quality. That was why he'd be the first to take the experimental canoe to the Boundary Waters of Minnesota and paddle it through its paces.

Nick frowned at the circles and squares he'd been drawing on the notepad. It would seem odd being away from her for that long. He brightened. Maybe he should take her along.

"So who's the woman?"

Nick slammed the pencil on the desk. "What?" He glared at his best friend.

Tom Harrison rolled his eyes toward the ceiling. "Come on, Nick, we've known each other since we were eighteen. You don't get this way unless there's a woman problem."

"What way?"

"Ignoring your business. Ignoring your friends. You were like this before you asked Ashley to marry you, and then again when you were mulling over the divorce. It's like you avoid everything else to focus on a woman that matters. For fifteen years you've been hot footing around with the ladies now and then, but you've been able to concentrate on business. Now look at you. You walk in here like a randy dog with his tail between his legs. So who is she? And when do I get to meet her?"

Nick raked fingers through his hair and stared blankly at his inquisitor. "How many times have I threatened to fire you?"

"Countless. Don't matter. You won't. We owe each other. Besides, I'm the best damn manager you'll ever find."

Nodding, Nick admitted, "That's the truth. Do you ever wonder what might have happened between us if we hadn't been thrown together in Special Forces?"

"This is old ground, Nick. You're trying to avoid my question. We would've never met, and you know it. So who's the damn woman?"

Nick balled a fist and examined his curled fingers. He loosened and flexed them. He blinked. "Her name is Daisy Matthews. She trains horses at Arlington Park."

"Horses. You mean race horses?" Tom cocked his head. "You mean you're getting into the ponies?"

"You remember Mike Barnes?"

Tom nodded. "Sure, he bought several of the last X-Tens and a half dozen T-Nines for some kind of resort he was buying in northern Wisconsin."

"When it came time to pay, he didn't have the cash. Instead, he talked me into accepting a race horse in payment."

Tom shoved back and laughed. "You are such a soft touch, man. It's amazing we make any profit. So the woman came with the horse?"

"Sort of. She's quite attached to the mare. If I sold the animal, she'd lose the horse, too. There was something in her eyes that I saw. Don't know. Anyway, I couldn't sell the damn horse, so now

I'm in the horse racing business."

"And in her pants?"

"No, she's too young. She can't even be thirty."

"Is she too young? Or are you too old?"

Nick glowered at him.

"Can't be too old if you can still get it up. She can't be too young if she's over eighteen."

"Harrison, sometimes you're beyond explanation." Nick folded his arms across his chest. "Willow is different. She's had a tough life. She grew up on the streets, the best I can figure out, and has pulled herself up with a little help from others. Courage, man, she's determined, and she's got guts."

"Sounds good. If what you say is true, she's probably a hell of a lot more experienced than her age would suggest."

Nick nodded. "No doubt about that. I wish she wouldn't dress so provocatively. She must draw guys like fresh honey attracts bears."

"Must be nice to look at."

"Oh, yeah. Tall, willowy, strawberry blond hair, legs that go on forever, and nipples that pout as much as she does."

"You sound hooked."

Nick flinched. "Nah, she's too young for an old guy like me."

"Can't get it up any more, huh? I've heard of a remedy or two."

"Cut the bullshit. You know that's not it."

"Well, you're not planning on marrying her, are you? So why should age matter this much?"

"Of course not. Why would I want to marry her?"

The phone rang and Nick grabbed it after one ring. He closed his eyes and breathed. It was a buyer checking on a delivery date. Who had he expected to call? During the past several weeks, she'd never once called him. He'd always called her. As he talked with the buyer, Nick watched Tom get up, wave and leave. Marriage? Not likely. Once was enough.

- o -

Holding the phone out away from her ear, Daisy cussed herself for not letting the answering machine take a message. But a call late at night often meant a problem at the stable.

"Every time you fuck up I lose money!"

Daisy shivered at Reggie's rage. He must be on something. But then he always was.

"Well, what do you have to say for yourself, bitch? Five losers in a row. And I really laid on them heavy. After three winners last week, I thought you were hot."

Screwing up her courage, Daisy replied, "You can't count on horses winning. Too many things can go wrong."

"Not if you get your facts right. I know how it is."

Daisy winced at Reggie's slurred words.

"Are you giving me bad information, bitch?"

"No, of course not."

73

"You better not. If I ever found out you were..."

Withdrawing into a shell she knew well from her younger days, Daisy whispered, "I didn't ask you to bet on those horses. Maybe you should stop betting."

"No! You just give me some better tips. We're depending on you. Maxine is depending on you. We're the only family you got, bitch. Don't forget it."

She heard his phone slam, and then there was blessed quiet. Daisy hung up and grimaced. She'd continue trying, for Maxine's sake, but there was no surefire way of guaranteeing winners.

Daisy rolled over and hugged Bear. Reggie would never be satisfied with sporadic winners. When would his patience snap? And then what?

- o -

"That's a no-brainer." Nick stretched his long legs out in front of him in Sam Gallagher's shedrow office. Sam sat in his desk chair chewing on his unlit pipe. Daisy sprawled atop an upside-down empty feed bucket.

Sam nodded. "So where do you want to race?"

Daisy watched Nick. She'd come to know his moods fairly well during the past six weeks. She knew what his decision would be. They had a choice of running RainbowBlaze in a mid-level allowance race at Arlington, a low end stakes race at Iowa's Prairie Meadows, or a similar race at Canterbury. The Canterbury purse was smallest, but money wouldn't be the key for Nicholas Underwood. He'd want to take Rainbow to Minnesota to share his newest passion with his family.

"We'll do Canterbury," Nick said. "Shakopee is just a short drive from Saint Paul where my folks live. It'll be good for them to see the Blaze. What do you think, kid?"

Daisy smiled in agreement. "Why not? It'll give me an excuse to see some new country. It won't be a long haul. Rainbow trailers well and should handle the trip fine."

"When do we leave?"

"I'll call ahead and take care of entry fees and stall arrangements," Gallagher said, making a note on a large desk calendar. "It would be good to give the horse a day or two to acclimate. The race is next Sunday. That gives you a couple days to prepare before you have to pull out."

"Ouch!" Daisy glared at herself in the full length closet door mirror. Why didn't anyone write clear instructions any more?

She read the folded instructions for the fourth time. The wax was certainly hot enough. Burning skin attested to that.

"Okay, again," she said, looking in the mirror. "Bend your knee and pull it towards your chest," she read aloud. She sat on a towel in the chair she'd placed before the mirrors. Maybe looking at her reflection was confusing things. But how else could she see what she was doing?

In that now-familiar cramped position, she applied the wax. The roller seemed to turn more smoothly this time. She relaxed, a trifle. Maybe this would work, after all.

"Now comes the difficult part," she mumbled, glancing over at the mirror. She'd never be a very good contortionist. "Okay, remember pull vertical, not parallel. Parallel hurts like hell."

With a quick jerk of the wrist, Daisy pulled on the wax remover strip.

"Shit, shit, shit!" she shouted, hopping about on one foot. "Whoever wrote that this might tingle a little bit never tried it." She glanced down at the removal strip and counted six hairs. "Damn! Nicholas Underwood, you'd better damn well appreciate what I'm doing."

Daisy sat back down and examined herself. She looked like she had a rash of pimples in a most unusual place. She slumped back and closed her eyes. Was this really worth it?

A bikini line was supposed to be a simple thing to accomplish. She didn't even own a bikini, but she loved the trim look of the women in the instructional videos. They looked sexy, and she wanted to look sexy. Hell, thousands if not millions of women had a bikini wax line. So what if it was painful? it was a small sacrifice to make.

She grabbed the box and went over the instructions again.

Half an hour later, perspiration poured off Daisy's brow. She raised her head and looked in the mirror. She stood.

"Done. That'll have to do. I can't take any more." The hairline looked quite fine, really. But where there had been hair before, now there were so many red bumps and ridges she looked like a war zone. She *felt* like a war zone. And women went through this every month or so? Whoever said women were the weaker sex?

Daisy groaned. She couldn't go to him looking like this; he'd puke. Would he put his tongue down there? She sure hoped so. She watched as her fingers tested the red dots. They didn't hurt as bad now. She admired the trim hair. It seemed to frame the target nicely, not that Nick wouldn't know where to find what he was looking for.

But how long would she have to wait for her skin to clear up? A couple days? Two weeks? Certainly it would clear before she had to go through this procedure again.

They'd be staying at a hotel in Shakopee. Those red pimples had better be history by the time they got to Canterbury, or she was going to be one unhappy girl. She'd put too much planning into her coming out party not to come out.

Chapter Four

Daisy sat on the edge of the bed in her hotel suite fighting back tears; her skin remained red and prickly to the touch. No way could she implement her plan to become a woman tonight. She shrugged and scowled at herself in the mirror. She'd waited nearly twenty-one years; another day or two shouldn't matter so much.

Glancing around the suite, she marveled at how some people lived. Nick had called it a small suite adjoining his identical suite. It was half the size of her apartment, and there was even a phone in the bathroom.

She was so inexperienced. She'd only been in motels when she was a child, and then only when her mother neglected to pay the rent. Those drab holes-in-the-wall weren't even in the same universe as this.

In her wildest fantasies, she could not have dreamed of a better setting for her sexual initiation. The suites were luxurious, and by putting her imagination in overdrive she could even conjure up a bit of romance—though she knew romance was not at the center of what she and Nick were about.

Shrugging, she rose from the bed and continued getting ready. Good thing she'd brought along one nice dress; it was actually the only nice dress she owned.

Nick would be rapping on her door soon. They were going to the Orpheum to see *A Funny Thing Happened On the Way to the Forum*. Nick's youngest sister, Angie, had a supporting role. His parents would also be there. Daisy shivered. She'd focused so much on her seduction of Nick, she'd forgotten that by coming to Canterbury she'd be involved with his family.

"Oh well," she muttered. "They're just people. And it's not like we're staying with them. Thank God."

Two hours later Daisy sat on the first floor of the Orpheum trying to concentrate on the antics taking place on the stage. The play was great, but sitting with Nick's family had turned out to be more unnerving than she'd anticipated. Angie Underwood was good. She was funny and had a body men must beg for. Nick had informed her that Angie was the nearly forgotten caboose of the family. She'd just celebrated her thirtieth birthday, and was the family's somewhat eccentric artist.

His parents were reserved and welcoming, although clearly puzzled by her presence. Nick had introduced her as part owner of RainbowBlaze and the person responsible for the horse's training. That seemed to suffice.

Nick's father had given her a shy smile, but otherwise ignored her. Nick's mother, Agnes, was more curious. Not too obvious, but obvious.

Thankfully, there was little time for small talk before the play. She and Nick would have to leave right after the show in order to be at the track by sunup.

The Underwoods planned to attend Saturday's race, and they had invited Nick and *his friend* to their home for Sunday dinner. Daisy drummed her fingers on the chair arm. She wasn't looking forward to Sunday dinner, but that was a ways off. A lot could happen before then.

Nick covered her hand with his, stilling her fingers. He leaned over and whispered, "You're doing great. Don't worry about it. Everything will be fine."

She pulled her hand out from under his, trying hard not to notice Agnes Underwood's tiny smile. Daisy frowned. Why was the woman smiling? What had she made of that little byplay?

Daisy flinched at the tap on her shoulder.

"Thought you were going to join us in the box seats for the post parade," Nick said.

"I can't. I'm too nervous about Rainbow." Daisy watched RainbowBlaze come on to the track for the seventh race post parade.

"She looks good out there, up on her toes and alert."

Daisy glanced at Nick. "I don't want to be rude, but I need to be alone right now. Make sure your family comes to the winner's circle. I should be ready to rejoin you by the tenth. Depends on how long it takes Rainbow in the test barn."

Nick grinned. By now he knew that winning horses were taken directly to the test barn to check them for illegal drugs. "You really think she'll win."

Glancing at the tote board in the infield, she said, "The bettors have her as the eight to five favorite. They respect her record and the fact that she shipped in from Arlington. She'll win, barring bad luck." Daisy grabbed her bare arms and bent over. "I can hardly wait."

"I know the feeling. As far as my folks are concerned, there'll be plenty of time with them tomorrow. They've got some kind of social function this evening so will probably leave right after this race. I better get back to them so they know about the photo."

"Okay." Daisy gave him a weak smile. "Don't be late. They don't wait around long for photos."

Her eyes followed Nick until he disappeared in the crowd. Daisy turned around, rested her forehead on the fence rail and closed her eyes. Her anxiety wasn't just about Rainbow. That morning her skin had finally appeared smooth and normal. This was going to be her day.

Some people preferred watching a race from high up in the stands and some by the rail. Daisy liked the rail because she had an up close and personal view of the horses straining to claim victory, she could hear the pounding of hooves, and at times dirt would even fly up and smack her in the face. At the rail, she wasn't a bystander; she was a participant.

"All in," she heard the announcer declare. And then the bell rang and the gates sprang open and the horses leaped out, each trying to get the jump on the others.

Daisy cheered silently when RainbowBlaze came from the seventh hole to settle in fourth position on the rail as the horses entered the clubhouse turn. The mare's running style was that of a presser, which Daisy thought was the best approach for winning routes. Up the backstretch, RainbowBlaze advanced into second. She held that position, running just off the leader's flank, until the eighth pole. Then with what appeared to be the easiest of moves, the mare lengthened her stride and raced on, leaving the rest of the field behind and crossing the finish line three lengths ahead of the closest pursuer.

Daisy clapped quietly. There had been little doubt about the end result. The bettors knew it, and she knew it. The Arlington shipper was the class of the field.

Smiling broadly, Daisy made her way to the track to collect her horse. She led Rainbow into the winner's circle. If only Sam and Cassie could have been there, it would have been perfect. Rainbow had won numerous races already, but this was a stakes race, and that made it even more special. Daisy looked up to see Nick rushing his parents and sister into the circle.

Nick kissed her on the forehead and patted Rainbow's shoulder. "That was a high. It's one thing to watch a horse that you've bet on win, but it's entirely different to see your own horse win. Wow! Well done, partner." He kissed her again — this time on the cheek.

Daisy blushed and directed everyone's attention toward the camera. After the click, Nick's father stepped forward and shook her hand. "Congratulations. I'm glad we could see that."

Next, his mother squeezed her hand. "Congratulations. You've really got Nick hooked. All he can talk about is you and the horses."

And then his sister. "Congratulations, Daisy. I'm really looking forward to spending time with you tomorrow. This is so exciting. It's hard to believe that you've accomplished so much with my brother."

Daisy frowned. RainbowBlaze bobbed her head up and down and began to prance, displaying her eagerness to leave the crowd.

"I'll catch up with you at the barn after I see my folks off." Nick looked like he couldn't stop smiling even if he tried. "This has got to be one of life's top experiences, kid. We definitely have to celebrate tonight."

Feeling slightly queasy, Daisy smiled. "You bet."

She led RainbowBlaze toward the test barn. Did Nick have any inkling of the kind of celebration she had planned for them?

Daisy gulped three deep breaths to clear her

head. Seduction must be like swimming in the cold water of Lake Michigan. You had to dive in quickly, or you'd lose your nerve. She rapped on the door between their suites and turned the knob without waiting for a response.

"Hey kid," Nick said, his eyes widening. He sat propped up on the king size bed with a folder on his lap. He wore pajama bottoms and nothing else. "I thought you went to bed an hour ago. I've been going over some dull reports."

His eyes scrolled up and down her body. She couldn't read the heavy emotion in them. She had on a thin nightgown and a robe which she hadn't bothered to close. As he'd said on an earlier occasion, if she wanted to hide her wares she should remember to tie the sash. She wasn't into hiding, not tonight.

"Damn," Nick said, "I've never seen horse slippers; they're sexy as hell."

Daisy looked in horror at her slippers; blood rushed to her head. How juvenile they must appear! Cassie had bought them for her sixteenth birthday and she'd loved them. Although they'd worn out on more than one occasion, she'd sewed them up. They often provided solace. Would they be her undoing tonight?

Nick put the folders on the nightstand. "So what's up? Still running on adrenalin? Can't sleep? It was a terrific day."

She saw his shoulder muscles tighten. Daisy tried to smile. She been bold, but now what? Those videos only showed people in bed, not how they got there. *Be practical, girl, be straightforward* had always been her grandmother's advice. She didn't know if her grandmother would approve of what she was doing, but that was probably the best advice she was going to get.

"I need your help," she blurted out. "I need you to make me a woman." She remained standing just inside the doorway; her escape route was handy if she failed.

It was his turn. She couldn't make him want her. Would he reject her?

- o -

Nick shook his head trying to clear the fog that was scrambling his brain. Had he heard right? He stared at Willow. He'd heard right. Her nipples were pouting big time through the flimsy material she no doubt thought was a nightgown. She stood tall, elegant and forlorn. Her long legs were spread slightly, making her appear more determined than ever, possibly even defiant. Her hair had been recently combed and he smelled perfume. Daisy never wore perfume. Until now.

And then there were those damn horse slippers. They were, in fact, sexy as hell. He couldn't explain that one; it was probably best not to try. He had enough trouble explaining his response to the young woman standing in those slippers.

Nick crossed his legs; he couldn't stand if he wanted to. She had him in a vulnerable position. He hoped she couldn't see his physical response to her need. Emotionally he was a wreck. This was Willow. He'd enjoyed sexual banter with her; he'd even fantasized about her. But she was too young. And if he had decided otherwise, he would have gone to her; he would not have waited for her to come to him.

He sighed in recognition of her vulnerability. Knocking on his door must have taken a lot of guts. Make a woman of her? Did that mean? His stomach lurched. Holy shit!

"What? I thought...You mean you're a..." Why the hell couldn't he complete a sentence? Her full lips turned up slightly. Goddamn, that overbite had to be one of the most erotic things he'd ever seen on a woman. It wasn't obvious until she smiled a little; it was obvious now and he felt himself drowning in her aura.

"I never said there were other men," Daisy said, softly. "You assumed because I was raised on the streets that I was wise in such matters. I had a grandmother who taught me how to take care of myself. You will be the first."

"But." Nick frowned. "You can't just walk into my room and make such a decision."

Chuckling, Daisy moved a step closer to the bed. "Trust me. This is no snap decision. I've been waiting for someone like you for some time now. I've been ready, but I wanted the right man. This should be done right, you know."

Nick arched an eyebrow. "Right? Doesn't that require some romance, some wining and dining, some dancing back and forth?" He stopped talking. They had done plenty of dancing back and forth. At least, *he* had. Did she have any doubts? "And how do you know what is right?"

"I've spent the last year watching educational videos. They've got good material on positions, oral sex, games, advanced positions. They answer just about every question that one can think of. And I've been doing a lot of reading."

"Videos! Books!" Nick gasped for breath. "You mean you've boned up, so to speak, on sex, and now you want to experience how it's actually done."

Daisy nodded. "Sort of. It's a matter of time. And I wanted to select who and when. Don't you want me?"

Nick steeled himself trying not to respond to the whimper in her voice. "Damn, kid, you've had me tied up in knots for weeks; it's not that I don't want you. Son of a bitch. But why me? What do you really want?"

Daisy's nostrils flared. "I'm not looking for marriage, if that's what's concerning you. I want an experienced man to make me a woman. I want a man I can trust. You're gentle, experienced, and I trust you. Isn't that enough?"

Nick got up and headed to the refrigerator. He didn't give a damn if she did see his erection. Maybe it would scare her back into her own bed. He sighed, reaching for the Chardonnay. *Be honest with yourself, Underwood. She'd crush your ego if she retreated now.*

"Okay," Nick said, uncorking the bottle and

reaching for two glasses. "Give me a little time. This is all coming pretty fast and hard, kid. I've desired you from the moment I saw you talking to Blaze. You were nearly as sexy then with straw in your hair as you are now in those adorable horse slippers.

"Come on. Join me for a drink. There's time. That's one of the things you learn with age and experience. There's time; we don't have to rush." Nick took her hand and pulled her close.

- o -

Daisy floated. The chilled wine bottle, cold against her back, sent shivers down her spine, but that wasn't the only reason she trembled. His lips had settled on hers and she responded eagerly. His hard arousal pressed against her crotch. He moaned her name. Her heart stopped. She'd worried that he wouldn't want her; she didn't have to worry about that anymore.

His tongue worked her lips apart, moving in to explore. It tickled the roof of her mouth; she used her own tongue to play with his. He withdrew; she was bereft. And then he drew her tongue deep into his mouth. He suckled her like a new born foal suckled its mother. Daisy's eyes sprang open. He was watching her. His eyes smiled.

Nick withdrew from the embrace. After placing the bottle and glasses on a small round table, Nick said gruffly, "The wine can wait. A different kind of thirst needs quenching." He gave her an amused look. "Maybe there is something yet to be said about the eagerness of youth."

His lips moved to the juncture of her neck and shoulder blade. Daisy marveled at the sensations spreading throughout her body. She didn't know what to do but stand there and receive. It was happening. Good God, it was happening!

She ran her fingers through his hair as he moved his lips to enclose a nipple. On her toes, Daisy stretched to her full height. Good grief, would she explode before he was ready?

"You don't know how often I've wanted to caress these exquisite nipples. They mirror your personality." He removed her robe and gingerly lifted the nightgown over her head. Briefly, he stood back, admiring her like she was a piece of art. She'd never forget the look on his face. Then he returned to her nipple—licking, nibbling, chewing. His hand squeezed her buttocks and worked its way around between their bodies. She leaned away, giving him room.

She moaned. She was already wet. His finger had no trouble with entry. "Is this okay?" he whispered.

She nodded, not trusting herself to utter a word.

"God, you're on fire down there."

"Where am I not on fire?" she murmured, wiggling her legs, wanting, demanding more.

Nick covered her mouth again. He withdrew his finger. She groaned. He shook his head. "I feel like some randy kid, but I don't think either one of us can wait much longer."

She nodded without meeting his eyes.

"Later, I'll show you a kind of loving that is so slow you'll think you're dying."

She already thought she was dying.

He guided her toward the bed and then stopped abruptly. "Damn, I hadn't planned on being seduced tonight. You didn't by any chance remember a condom in all your planning?"

Daisy smiled and picked up her robe. She retrieved a half dozen condoms and handed them to Nick.

He broke into a laugh. "You got one hell of a lot of confidence in me, kid." He opened a package and dropped his pajamas.

"Let me," Daisy whispered roughly. "I want to touch him."

"Okay."

Daisy knelt on the bed, running fingers over his full length. It quivered. So soft. Especially at the head. She reached lower and cupped him; she grinned when she heard Nick's growl. His vulnerability brought tears to her eyes.

"Enough," he said, his voice shaking. "Put the damn condom on, or there won't be any need for it."

After three tries and a little assistance, Daisy had the condom fitting snuggly. She reached for a pillow and tucked it under her buttocks. She spread her legs wide and waited. Her heart raced. She tried to breathe deeply, but failed. She fought to keep her eyes open; she didn't want to miss a thing.

He gave her a curious look. "I imagine the pillow is something you learned from the videos."

She nodded.

"This may hurt a little the first time," he said, kneeling before her.

She nodded. He parted her slick folds. It seemed like he played at her entrance for an eternity. He leaned forward and rolled a nipple between two fingers. That felt so good she reached for the other nipple and did the same.

His weight shifted over her body. He entered her gradually. Her eyes widened. At last, she held his full length in her most private chamber.

He hovered above her, holding himself up on both hands. "Are you okay?" he whispered, hoarsely.

Daisy nodded and smiled. He dipped his head and laved a breast. She splayed her fingers across his back, raised her knees, and squeezed his buttocks like she was asking a stallion to move.

Nick responded with a low growl and began moving.

If there was pain, she wasn't aware of it. She couldn't comprehend the fullness and emptiness she felt as he penetrated deep and then nearly withdrew. She wanted more; she needed more. She strained upward, meeting his thrust to keep him inside.

When had her eyes gone shut? Dammit, she wanted to experience all of this. She opened them. He was staring at her. His look was raw and savage. She'd never witnessed him on the verge of losing control. Was she having that affect on him? He was certainly having that affect on her. She struggled to stay present.

His eyes closed and then he churned in and out of her as if he were racing against life and death. She gripped him like a vise for fear that he might die, and then she disintegrated.

A few minutes later, Daisy tried to reconstruct what had happened. There had been little warning. Not at all what she'd expected. She was there, and then she wasn't. She was whole, and then she'd shattered into a million fragments of light. Somehow their bodies remained entwined as they lay side by side. His arms held her tight. He was still inside, but had softened. He must have climaxed, but she sure didn't know when.

God, she was warm and tingly all over. Couldn't they just stay like this forever? Maybe they should have died in ecstasy. How did you go back to the way things were?

His tongue traced her jaw line.

She smiled. She pried her eyes open. He looked nearly as satisfied as she felt. Maybe they never would move again.

"Are you okay?"

"I'm fantastic," Daisy whispered. "How are you?"

Nick smiled. "Feeling younger by the minute. It may be time for some wine. And then we'll see what else might happen. Just stay here, I'll pour the wine."

Daisy accepted the wine he offered and sipped it. She didn't like beer, but she did have a taste for wine. Cassie had given her some from time to time. Daisy blinked. What would Cassie say if she saw her now? Daisy blushed.

"It doesn't make any difference to me," Nick began, running his fingers lightly down her arm. "This was terrific, but why the charade?"

Daisy frowned. "What do you mean?"

"The virgin act. There was no hymen to break. You're not bleeding."

"Oh, I forgot," she said, idly pulling the sheet up to her throat. "I took care of that with a wine bottle when I was eleven." She flinched as she saw the horror sweeping across Nick's face. "My grandmother repeatedly warned me about being raped. Where we lived, young girls lost their virginity early, one way or another. I didn't want to give it to a rapist, so I took it myself. Figured if I got raped, it would hurt less if I wasn't still a virgin."

"Jesus H. Christ," Nick swore, cuddling her to him and kissing her forehead and eyelids warmly. "I'm so sorry."

She broke away. "It doesn't matter," she said, pulling her knees to her chest and clasping them tight, wishing the tears streaming down her face weren't telling a different story. "At least this — what we just shared — matters more. It's more than I had ever dreamed."

"Sounds like you dreamed about it a lot."

She smiled. "I suppose so. Not many girls who

live in group homes are asked to proms. I refused to be easy; my grandmother wouldn't have liked that at all. She drummed words of wisdom into my head. *What you've got between your legs is your most prized treasure. Cherish it and use it well. Don't give it away to just anybody who thinks he's a man."*

"But you just gave it away."

"Not to a boy."

"That's for sure." Nick wet his lips. "I want you to know that this was incredible for me, too. Thank you for sharing your treasure with me." He kissed Daisy on the tip of her nose.

"Sure." She blinked. "It's done now." She turned to eye Nick. "I am pleased. I'll always remember this night. Thanks."

He liked it when she blushed. He pulled the sheet back down and pressed a finger on her right nipple. Smiling, he watched it stretch when he removed his finger. Her eyes turned smoky. "You make it sound like this is a one night stand."

She stiffened under his gaze. "It is, isn't it?"

Nick frowned at her. She'd taken a huge risk coming to him, but she'd had no idea how desirable he really found her. She'd gotten him to deflower her. Was that all she wanted? Was that all she thought she deserved?

He gave her his most wicked grin. "You think you'll learn all there is about sex in one night?"

"Of course not."

He propped himself up on an elbow and looked at her, memorizing every curve and nuance of her lusciousness. He stroked the inside of her thigh.

She moaned. Brushing her trim curls, he said, "Maybe we could be lovers for a while."

Her muscles tightened and he sensed her withdraw.

"I don't know much about love, and I'm not sure I want to," she said, her voice thick with emotion.

"But you want to know more about sex."

She nodded.

He'd have to treat her as gingerly as she treated an injured horse. "Okay, well, if I'm a passable teacher..." He waited for a response.

She blinked. Her inner thigh quivered against his fingers. "More than passable, I think," she managed to say.

"Good. I've got the time, and it seems like the body is more than willing. Maybe I could further your education."

She arched an eyebrow. "For real? No strings?"

"I thought you trusted me. For real. Would you like that?"

"Yes."

He hadn't thought she could sound so meek. "Good, then it's settled. You'll continue teaching me about the horse business. And I'll continue teaching you about the sex business. Deal?" He offered her his hand.

"Deal," she whispered, placing her hand in his. "What if I'm a slow learner?"

Nick laughed deeply, pulling her closer. "I hope you are, Daisy. You shouldn't rush good sex anymore than you should rush a good wine."

Daisy closed her eyes and let the feel of his fingers grazing her belly soak into her pores. Did he realize he'd called her Daisy for the very first time? Odd, that *that* intimacy should scare her more than what his fingers were doing. Had she gotten herself into more than she'd bargained for? An image of Cassie Travers flashed before her mind. The woman was nodding *yes* and giving her an inexplicable smile.

Tension released from her upper body down to her toes. She'd just made a deal with a man old enough to be...well, old enough to know better. And she was relishing his touch as he dipped a finger into her moist crevice. His thumb found her button and she rose and faltered and then rose again. She soared as his tongue rimmed her belly button and his fingers continued working a special magic. She caught her breath and moaned. Jerking her knees toward her breasts, she ignored the man arousing her and rode the waves of ecstasy that she'd dreamed so much about. Only this was better, much better. And then oblivion overcame her senses and she slept.

- o -

An hour had passed. Wide awake, Nick lay beside the long-legged beauty, watching her sleep the sleep of a well satisfied woman. She'd wanted him to make her a woman; hopefully she realized it had taken both of them to do that, in the physical sense. But she'd always been all woman to him, and probably always would be.

Despite his glib words about teacher and student, what had he gotten himself into? There was no positive outcome to this arrangement. She was still too young. But damn, she was responsive. She exuded an innocent passion that was overpowering.

He'd been so close to embarrassing himself the first time she'd touched him. He hadn't had to worry about that for years.

Daisy Matthews was uncharted waters. He'd spent many days and weeks in a canoe on the Boundary Waters, where he often could not see where he was headed because one island followed another in endless chains. Sometimes islands seemed to emerge and change overnight. Even with a compass in hand, he had to trust his instincts and experience.

Daisy rolled over in her sleep. Nick patted her rear affectionately. "Guess that's what I've got to do with you, Daisy. Trust my instincts and experience and hope to hell I don't lose my way."

- o -

Daisy sat across from Nick's mother and father in their modest dining room unable to stop smiling. Angie Underwood sat at the end of the table closely scrutinizing her. They probably thought she was still thrilled because of Rainbow's victory.

Fortunately, most of the talk had nothing to do with her. Nick, sitting beside her, deflected any personal questions.

She chewed on a piece of ham, savoring it like she'd savored his loving earlier that morning. His tongue had found its way to her now not-so-private place. His words were seared on her brain: "Did you trim this for me? It's beautiful." The joy caused by his praise washed away any memory of pain. Though there must be an easier way to keep a bikini line. She'd have to do more researching on that.

His fingers squeezed her thigh, bringing her attention back to the conversation. "Yes," he said to his mother, "Daisy is an English major, aren't you, Daisy?"

She frowned, picking up threads of conversation. Vaguely, she recalled his mother asking her whether she was in college. She flushed. "That's right. I love the classics. But there's not a lot of time. I can only manage a course a semester."

Agnes Underwood smiled. "There's no rush. Sometimes education is best when you savor it step by step."

Daisy smiled while Nick choked on a mouthful of potatoes. "I hope you're right," Daisy replied, brushing her knee against Nick's thigh. "I don't want to miss a thing."

"So who's your favorite author?"

"That's easy. Shakespeare. Not a very original

choice. But he has such a deep appreciation for the tension between pain and joy."

"You could do much worse," Nick's mother said, sipping her coffee. "I still have a soft spot for Shakespeare even after all these years."

Daisy nodded at the woman, whose dark hair was sprinkled with gray. Nick's mother was thoughtful and likeable. What would she say if she knew how her son had spent his morning? *He's old enough to make up his own mind.* Daisy blinked at the older woman, who had not uttered a word. Did she know? How could she?

After dinner, the men took their coffee into the living room while the three women cleared the table and put away the food. The conversation was comfortable and light, mainly about horses, some about books and theater. She didn't know enough about the theater. While she'd read plenty of plays, few were contemporary. Maybe she'd pick up some by Sondheim. She shrugged as she put more dishes into the dishwasher. It was highly unlikely she'd ever see these people again anyway.

They did make her feel like she was part of things. Almost like she was part of the family. She shivered. But what if they really knew about her and Nick, or about who she was?

"Come on, Daisy," Angie said. "Let's go upstairs and freshen up. We can join Mom and the men in a few minutes."

Daisy watched Angie expertly apply lipstick and then blush to her cheeks and finally a little eye liner. Daisy only owned lipstick. She'd never learned about the other stuff.

"You're a beautiful young woman, Daisy, in case my brother hasn't told you."

Daisy felt herself blushing profusely. Angie was a head shorter, but more amply filled out. If either of them was beautiful, it was Nick's sister.

"If you don't mind a suggestion or two," Angie said, "you could make those high cheek bones and full lips stand out more."

Daisy arched an eyebrow. Angie's bubbling enthusiasm was contagious, like that of a bettor who'd just hit a trifecta.

"Nothing dramatic," Angie cautioned. "Just add a little subtlety and even more mystery. Can I try? It's part of what I do for a living."

Daisy shrugged. What did she have to lose, if it made Nick's sister happy? She could just wipe it off later. "Why not," she muttered.

"Good. You have such a natural beauty, we don't want to do much." Angie leaned over and pinched Daisy's cheeks. "You definitely have the look of a well loved woman. Nick must be good for you, and I expect you're good for him."

"What?" Daisy gasped.

Angie straightened and smiled. "Come now. You don't think everyone sitting at that table didn't know they were looking at a well loved woman?" Angie paused. "Well, maybe not my dad. I'm never sure what he sees.

"Let me look at you now. First, let's try a slightly darker shade of lipstick." Angie pulled out several boxes of assorted makeup kits, picked out the lipstick she'd been searching for and then applied it to Daisy's lips. "Great. Then a little rouge on the cheekbones. Excellent. Now a little eyeliner. Wow! Take a peek in the mirror."

Daisy looked and her eyebrows shot up. It was still her, but she looked more...more sophisticated.

"I love your hair," Angie said. "I wish mine had the natural wave yours does."

"But you're gorgeous," Daisy said, faltering. "You're voluptuous. Men must be crazy about you."

"Funny, I only seem to find crazy men. But you have the long legs men desire. You must be something in a bikini."

Daisy frowned.

"You do have a bikini?"

Daisy shook her head.

"Come on down to my old room. Most of my stuff is still here because I'm on the road with the theater group so much. Actually, we'll be in Chicago in a couple months."

"Great! I look forward to your next play."

As they entered Angie's room, Daisy's heart fluttered. The accoutrements of family were so evident. Pictures of Angie with her parents, with Nick, and with an older woman on picnics and standing in front of a lakeside cottage were on a pegboard.

There were pictures of Angie in various stage

roles and with friends. "Ah, here's one that should fit you."

Angie held in her hands the tiniest swimsuit Daisy had ever seen. It was light blue.

"Try this on. Let me see how you look. It should go good with your eyes, not that any man will notice that small detail."

Daisy's skin warmed. She wasn't unaccustomed to undressing in front of others. There was little modesty possible in a group home. Clearly, Angie was used to it from her stage life.

Taking a deep breath, Daisy shrugged out of her blouse. In minutes, she'd donned the brief pieces of material and tied the appropriate strings. She looked at herself in the full length mirror. Her eyes rounded. Was that really her? The bikini hid just enough to be mysterious and legal.

"You have a nice bikini line, but you'll have to move it in a little to accommodate this one."

"I can't accept this."

"Sure you can. It's brand new. The guy who bought it for me had no concept of size. It fits you like a glove. I'd just hang out over it. If you don't mind my saying so, you still look a little raw down there. What kind of kit did you use?"

Daisy told Angie about her harrowing experience with wax and hair removal patches.

Angie shook her head and giggled. "That procedure went out with cavewomen. Here," she said, pulling out a dresser drawer, "this is what you need to buy. Much simpler and, believe me, much less painful."

103

Daisy didn't hesitate. She reached for her purse and scribbled down the brand and the label, then reconfirmed the names of cosmetics Angie had used on her.

She examined the bikini line kit again and then smiled at Angie. "Thanks. Thanks for all your help. If this works like you say, I may not feel like such a human sacrifice."

Angie laughed. "I figure if I'm helping you, I'm helping my big brother. I've always adored Nick, but he's not been the best judge of women. It's nice to know that he's finally found one with enough gumption to match his own. Why don't you go ahead and change and stuff that bikini in your purse? I'll meet you downstairs."

Turning so she could see her backside in the mirror, Daisy flushed. Where had the back of the suit gone? Calling it a suit suggested it possessed more fabric than it actually did. She'd take it back to Chicago with her, but there wasn't any public place she'd ever wear it.

She grinned. Maybe she'd model it for Nick in the privacy of her bedroom. He might like that. And she might like his reaction. She ran a hand across her belly wishing it was his hand.

She'd planned on becoming a woman during this trip; she hadn't counted on returning with a lover. Having a man in her life was unnerving, yet her body tingled with anticipation.

"Looks like you girls have been playing makeup," Agnes Underwood commented when Daisy entered the living room. "I hope you don't mind, Daisy. Angie has been doing this since she was six or seven. It's really quite a stunning effect. Hope you like it. What do you think, Nick?"

Nick swallowed hard. Stunning. There must be a better word. *This* woman didn't look quite so innocent. This woman was as mysterious as the Daisy he'd known before, maybe even more so. More sultry. Goddamn, he wanted to throw her on the floor and make love to her.

He gritted his teeth. "She looks very nice, Mom. Daisy always does." He stood holding the comics over his fly. "We better get back now; we leave early tomorrow morning."

"It's not even three o'clock, son," his father complained. "I haven't had a chance to beat you at chess yet."

"That's okay, Dad," Angie chimed in, rising to escort her brother and Daisy to the door. "I'll give you a game. These two have to get a lot of sleep. I expect they've been celebrating too hard over their horse's win."

"Thanks again," Daisy said, returning Angie's hug. She waved at Mr. and Mrs. Underwood.

"You seemed all fired up to go. Was it something I said?" Daisy asked Nick climbing into the pickup. "I didn't mean to offend anyone."

"Just drive, Daisy. Don't go through red lights,

but get us back to the hotel as soon as possible." His breathing sounded ragged. "If we don't get there soon, you're going to have to pull over so I can take you right here in the truck. Whatever you and Angie did upstairs turned you into the most ravishing woman I've ever seen. And I'm determined to ravish you as soon and as often as humanly possible."

"Oh," she squeaked, grinding a gear as the truck lurched out into the street.

Chapter Five

"So what are you going to do with your earnings from Blaze's win?"

Daisy sat up straighter. She'd been in that foggy state between dozing and wakefulness. Nick had spelled her at the wheel; they were at the first tollbooth on I-90 outside of Chicago. She tried not to think too far ahead. She much preferred wallowing in the erotic memories of the past thirty-six hours. Her sexual education was proceeding quite nicely.

Would it ever end? Reality slapped her in the face like a raw wind off the lake. Money. He had a lot of it; she had practically none. He was from an upstanding family; she couldn't trace her roots beyond herself. And then there was her druggie sister and her sister's pimp of a husband. Reggie would sell his soul for drug money. He'd no doubt sold Maxine's body numerous times.

"I'm sorry. Were you asleep?" Nick asked after paying the toll and getting the truck and trailer back up to speed.

"No. That's okay. I guess I was just daydreaming."

"What about?"

Daisy blushed.

Nick smiled. "Yeah, it's pretty fantastic, even

reliving it." He blew her a kiss. "You can put that wherever you want it the most. So what about your share of the purse?"

Frowning, Daisy twisted in her seat to face him better. "I don't know. It doesn't seem right that I get that much money."

"You own twenty percent of the horse. You get twenty percent of the purse, less twenty percent of the costs. So what's not right about that?"

"I don't know. It just seems like I didn't earn it."

"The deal was you'd teach me about horses. Remember?"

Daisy giggled. "You sure are a wheeler dealer. I thought the latest revision of the deal was you'd teach me about sex if I'd teach you about horses. Seems like I'm getting more for my efforts than you are."

"No way!" He gave her a lopsided smile. "And I don't just mean what's going on in bed. Believe me, the teacher is getting as much pleasure out of that as the student is. Hell, I'd never be into horses if it weren't for you convincing me to hold on to Blaze. Haven't you ever heard of consulting fees? You've earned your share of the purse and more. So what are you going to do with it?"

"I haven't given it much thought." She clasped her hands in her lap and looked out the passenger window at the fence posts rapidly disappearing from view. Directing her attention back to Nick, she offered, "Maybe I'll put half of it in my college fund and half in a new account to save up for another horse purchase."

Nick nodded. "Sounds good, but don't you ever do anything just for fun? I didn't hear any recreational plans."

"I don't have time. Besides, it's largely a waste of money I don't have. Just because I have money today doesn't mean it'll be there tomorrow."

"Sounds like your grandmother talking."

A trace of a smile formed on Daisy's lips. "I suppose you're right. But it's true."

"Maybe. No celebrations? Back to the grindstone?"

Daisy reached over and ran a finger up Nick's thigh. "We've been celebrating ever since Rainbow crossed the finish line. Not that I'm complaining. I suppose we can always find time to celebrate something."

He grabbed her hand and held it against his inner thigh. "Now that's the truth, kid. Hell, we can always celebrate the fact that the sun came up, or that we're still breathing, or that you keep flunking your finals in sex education."

"You're right. I'll need a lot more tutoring before I even try that test again."

Daisy turned up the apartment window fan to high. She stood in front of the anemic breeze it produced and pulled the sticky tank top away from her skin. At ten o'clock at night, the temperature still hovered near eighty-five degrees and the humidity had to be even higher. If this didn't qualify as a steamy night in Chicago, she didn't know what would.

Her door buzzer rang loudly. Maybe she shouldn't have had the manager fix it. Nick wasn't supposed to come by tonight. They'd agreed on making some space for themselves. They'd been back only a week, and he'd been over nearly every night. Their lovemaking remained intense, but even that was curtailed for the moment. Her monthly cycle forced a recess in her education. Surely he knew that, so why was he here?

She dashed to the door and flung it open. Her heart tumbled; sex shouldn't make her brain dead or cost her street smarts. Why hadn't she peeked through the peep-hole?

"Bitch!" Reggie screamed, slamming her against the wall. "My tips. You didn't leave a message. There was a hundred to one shot winner this weekend. I should've had him."

Oh my God! She'd forgotten all about Reggie and his betting tips. Trying to show no fear, Daisy slipped out of Reggie's grasp and walked into the living room, buying time.

"I'm sorry." She sighed. "You know I had to take a horse to Minnesota to race. I've never been out of the state before; I guess I'm having difficulty adjusting. Maybe it's like jet lag."

Reggie frowned. "I've never heard of that. Don't know why anyone would want to leave the city. This place is big enough to have everything a body would want and then some."

His eyebrows shot up. "Bitch, it don't matter. You owe me. I lost money because you spaced out.

Sure you're not on dope? I could help you there, if you want."

"No! I'll get you twice as many tips this week."

"Make sure they're good ones."

"I can't guarantee winners."

"If you don't start doing better, you're gonna have to make those losses up to me in other ways."

Daisy recognized the too familiar leer. Her skin crawled. How long could she fend him off?

"You've always been a good looking piece, bitch. Ten times better than your sister. But I couldn't wait for you to grow up. Now you're all growed up real nice. And you owe me for not getting me bets last week. It's payment time."

Quickly, he narrowed the space between them and pulled her roughly against his body. His lips crushed against hers; stale alcohol nearly overpowered her senses. Instinctively, she bit down hard.

He recoiled and swung a fist. She ducked and Reggie fell to his knees. Fortunately, he was too drunk to do much damage.

"Don't ever touch me again," she said coldly, "or you won't ever be able to have children, not that that wouldn't make for a better world."

Reggie scrambled to his feet, wiping blood from his lips with the back of his hand. "Don't be so cocksure of yourself, bitch. When the chips are down, I've got something you want real bad."

"You don't have a thing I want."

"I have your sister."

Daisy's jaw dropped. She couldn't form a comeback.

"I could tell her how you seduced me," Reggie said, rubbing his crotch. "She's jealous of you already, you know. She knows you're prettier. All I'd have to do is call out your name when I'm banging her."

Reggie's eyes glazed over. Daisy's skin crawled.

"Or I could give her a little more drug candy. Bye, bye Maxine. It would be so easy. I can see I've given you plenty to think about, bitch." Reggie lifted Daisy's chin, ignoring her glare. "I've always wondered what your buck teeth would feel like scraping against my Roger down there."

"Given the chance, I'd bite it off," Daisy spat. "You've said more than enough. Get out of here. The tips for Saturday and Sunday will be on your machine by Friday night. And you'd better not hurt my sister."

"Right. Or what? I'm leaving. But remember, bitch, I always know where you live. Bye-bye!"

The door to her apartment slammed shut. Riveted in space, Daisy trembled and shook before pulling herself together enough to go into the kitchen and brew a cup of tea.

She had a complicated problem. Reggie wasn't about to go away. He'd never get enough money from her sister or from her. Why had Maxine ever married the guy, and why did she continue to stay with him? Drugs was the obvious answer. The man was a walking drugstore.

Nick! Good grief, she couldn't let him know

112

about Reggie and Maxine. It was bad enough that he knew she'd been raised in a group home. What would he think if he knew her sister was a druggie and part-time whore? And that her brother-in-law sold drugs as well as his wife to anyone with the right amount of cash?

Daisy gagged. If he ever found out about Maxine and Reggie, she'd be totally humiliated. He wouldn't want to be involved with her at all.

Memories of Nick's family gathered around the dining room table in Saint Paul flooded her. She cried. Was it envy, or loss?

"Hi Daisy, congratulations on RainbowBlaze's stakes win." Cassie Travers poked her head into Sam Gallagher's stable office. "I'd have been by sooner, but the baby's been sick."

Daisy's smile faded. "Nothing serious?"

"No, just a cold. It happens."

Daisy shoved her chair away from the old desk where she'd been scribbling down the weekly training schedules. Cassie settled down on a chair across from her. "It was great, Cass. Any victory is great, but a stakes race, no matter how small, that's something. It was worth the trip. Nick's family joined us in the winner's circle."

Daisy paused and cocked her head to the side. "I know I'm rattling on. I'm sure you know what it's like to own part of a horse that's won a stakes race."

"Uh, huh. I also know what it feels like to be a well loved woman."

Rolling her eyes, Daisy groaned. "Do I have a neon sign that's blinking? That's exactly what Angie said. That's Nick's sister." She sighed and closed her eyes. Looking back at Cassie, she said, "You're right, it is fantastic. I never knew it would be this great. He's so kind and gentle and understanding. I'm learning a lot."

"Bullshit. You're falling in love."

"No way." Daisy leaped to her feet, towering over her friend. "That won't happen. I won't let it. He doesn't want that. Neither of us does."

"I think you're babbling again."

Daisy plopped back down in the swivel chair. "You're often right, Cassie Travers, but this time you're wrong. Nick and I have a deal. And it's got nothing to do with love."

"It's okay, girl." Cassie crossed her feet at the ankles and leaned back. "You believe whatever you want. We'll see. So he's treating you right?"

"Of course."

Cassie nodded. "I guess when you're ready, you can bring him by and Clint and I can talk to him about buying some additional horses. If the man's serious about horseracing and he's good with you, we might as well take a percentage of his money."

Daisy laughed. "We should prepare for one of the fall sales: Keeneland, Barretts, Fasig-Tipton. If we get a yearling, would you be willing to keep him at the farm? For the usual fee, of course."

"Certainly. This *we* sounds quite definite. So you're part of the ongoing horse partnership?"

"Apparently. He won't have it any other way. And I'll be taking half of my winnings and putting it into a horse fund."

"What happens when all of this ends? When the prince sells his horses and Daisy Ann is left holding a pumpkin?"

Daisy glared and then softened. "I don't know. I can't see a good ending. I'll admit that. But Cassie, I've never dreamed these kinds of dreams. Let me enjoy the ride while it lasts. I know it won't. It can't. But it's happening now."

Cassie brushed a tear from the corner of an eye. "I know, and it's good to see you so happy. Remember, I'm here when you need me. Now what about this deal with Nick?"

Daisy flashed an eyebrow and grinned widely and opened her mouth to speak.

"Strike that question, girl." Cassie waved off Daisy's response. "I think I don't want to know the details of whatever the two of you have cooked up. You know where to find me."

Cassie stood. "I've got to get back to check with my assistant. Catch you later. Don't do anything I wouldn't do."

Daisy laughed. "That should give me plenty of leeway."

"Well, if you're going to have an affair with an older man, then you should at least benefit from having an experienced teacher." Stepping through the doorway, Cassie waved over her shoulder.

Daisy waved back absently. What was her sage instructor up to at that moment?

"You're acting like some damn kid with hormones on the loose." Tom Harrison leaned against the doorjamb at the entrance to Nick's office. "You sit in here and stare off into space like you're on some kind of excellent grass. You drag your worn out body in here an hour after starting time. Suppose a forty-two-year-old man might have a little trouble keeping up with a much younger woman. Maybe once a night should be enough, or heaven forbid you might think about skipping a night."

"We have skipped...a number of nights," Nick groused. "So I just lie in my bed with my eyes wide open wondering about her." Nick scowled. "You're absolutely right, Tom. I'm not the man I used to be."

"So what are you going to do about her?"

Nick sighed deeply. "Slow down before I get a heart attack. Seriously, I don't know. She's way too young. But she's an aphrodisiac—I don't mean just sex—I mean about life. Everything is so new for her; it's like seeing the world again as if for the first time. She's enthusiastic. Shy. Gutsy." Nick chewed on the fingers of a closed fist. "She's hopeful. Vulnerable. Passionate. Innocent. Worldly."

"Damn, you've got it worse than I thought." Tom sat down on a chair and rubbed a hand across his bald head.

"What do you mean?"

116

"What do I mean? Shit man, you're in love."

Nick jerked. "In love? No way!" He glanced out the window. No way could that be happening to him. He knew better than to let that happen. "I'm way too old for Daisy."

"Is she telling you you're too old?"

"No, but we've got a deal."

Tom laughed. "Why does that not surprise? You know you make deals with people half the time so you can avoid dealing with your own emotions. What's the deal?" Tom raised his eyebrows. "Of course. She helping you get into the horse business while you're sharing with her your wealth of sexual experience."

Nick winced and tried not to blush. The arrangement sounded so much more crass hearing it from Tom's lips than it had when he and Daisy were naked in bed.

Tom shook his head. "You should have been a scam artist. One of your deals, someday, is going to reach up and grab you where it hurts — in the heart. I want to meet this Daisy Matthews. I've got a hunch about her. And I haven't even seen her. You may be in over your head, my friend. You both may be."

Nick wished he could be certain Tom was wrong.

"Can you dance?"

"What?"

"Kid, you're not listening again." Nick cupped the bare knee poking out from her robe. They sat on the loveseat at her apartment reading the Sunday paper. He'd stayed the night. He liked waking up early in the morning so he could study Daisy sleeping next to him. Her place was so much more intimate than his. He'd never brought a woman to his house since his divorce. He squeezed her knee and smiled as her lips parted. "I said, can you dance?"

"Not really. We practiced some at the home, but we never went to a dance."

"Two weeks from last night is the End of the Summer Charity Ball for the continuing battle against AIDS. A lot of mucky mucks will be there. I've got to at least make an appearance. We'll have you dancing with the best of them by then. Should be fun." He watched pure fright sweep across her face.

"You've got to be kidding." She pulled away. "You can't take me to a ball. That's for society folks. I'm just a..."

"Just a young woman who trains horses and happens to be my business partner and my lover. Now who else would I be taking?"

"Anyone else. I won't go!"

Nick smiled. "I love it when you put on a defiant show like that. Of course you'll go. You placed me in responsibility for your sex education, didn't you?"

"Yes, but that takes place in bed."

"I beg to differ. We've actually found several other places that work just fine."

Daisy frowned. "You know that's not what I

meant."

"Okay. I was tweaking you on that one. But I think those videos you've studied may have left you believing that sex is only about positions and such. As your teacher, I'm here to tell you that your sex education must include romance. And that includes being comfortable with dancing, with holding a glass of wine in one hand and a plate of food in the other, with inane chatter that bores you to death to such an extent that you'll find hours of requisite lovemaking even more refreshing."

"You make it sound so easy." Daisy chuckled. "Is that what you think about when you balance a glass of wine in one hand and food in the other — lovemaking?"

"If you're beside me, or across the room, I'll have you undressed in my mind."

"Is this part of the romance you talked about?"

"Yes, it is. So you'll come along, right? Or do I have to drag you caveman style?"

She scowled. "I guess."

"Good. That's settled. Now, get your cute butt dressed; we're going shopping."

"Shopping?"

"Absolutely. Part of romance is when the guy takes the girl to Macy's and buys her a dress for the ball."

"Macy's! It used to be Marshall Fields — my most favorite place in the world. Each Christmas season, Mom would take us to the toy department. We might spend an hour or two just staring and dreaming. We'd watch the toy trains go round and round. And there were so many dolls." Daisy sobered. "One year she went back and bought something." The corner of her mouth turned up. "That's where I first met Bear, and I was so thrilled when he greeted me that Christmas morning.

"After Mom died, Maxine and I'd sneak into Field's to look. Grandma thought we shouldn't waste time dreaming." Daisy shook her head and hugged herself. "I still make at least one trip each Christmas season to stare at the dolls and all those stuffed animals."

Nick slid an arm around Daisy and nibbled on her ear. "I'm glad you dreamed. Maybe I can help you dream even more."

"You already have," Daisy murmured. "That's the problem."

- o -

Daisy tried not to gawk. The lobby at the downtown Macy's was a delight even when it wasn't Christmas. She'd so loved coming there as a child. But she always knew she didn't belong rubbing shoulders with people who could afford to buy things.

She was surprised Nick knew his way around the store so well. He'd taken her directly to the most classy part of the women's section.

Between Nick and the stylishly dressed clerk, they outfitted her from the skin out. They'd decided on a long black dress in matte jersey. It showed off her trim figure, according to the clerk. Side slits that came embarrassingly close to her rear not only allowed her to walk, they displayed her legs very nicely.

She had to agree with Nick's judgment, even if the dress did leave her feeling half naked. Its scooped back only enhanced that feeling. Would she ever get used to walking in the black stiletto heels? And then he wanted her to dance in them!

"This little black bag will be just the right accessory to carry." The clerk stepped back to look at Nick. "Doesn't she look elegant? A beautiful young woman. You must be proud of your daughter."

Daisy quickly covered her mouth with her hand. She did an about-face and watched Nick's reflection in the mirror. He turned pink and then red.

The clerk must have discerned her faux pas. "I am sorry." She paused for breath. "You must be a lucky man."

"That I am," Nick stammered. "Doesn't she need something around her neck, or maybe on her wrist? Nothing too showy. I'm sure she'd prefer something understated."

"You're absolutely right. Come with me," the clerk said to Nick. "The young lady can come along, or perhaps you'd like to surprise her."

"Surprise." Nick nodded. "We'll be right back, kid. You might try to get used to those shoes. I know they look like only a few straps, but they are sexy."

Daisy tried a few tentative steps. At first she wobbled and then she righted. Maybe it was the balance she'd learned from riding horses, but in a matter of minutes she was able to walk about without much difficulty. She remained uncertain about dancing.

"Let me put this on you and see how it looks," Nick said, returning with the clerk.

Daisy leaned forward and Nick clasped the chain at the back of her neck. When she stood she turned and looked in the mirror. It was a small jewel set in a silver setting. It sparkled like sun reflecting on new snow. The jewel was lovely; no one had ever given her jewelry. How could so much light come from such a small rhinestone?

"You have fine taste in diamonds, Mr. Underwood."

Daisy gasped and her hand flew to her throat.

"Not too much display. These matching earrings are just right. I'm not sure about the gold bracelet." The woman paused jutting her chin forward. "It may work." She shook her head. "Maybe not with this dress."

"No matter. The bracelet is separate. Okay, anything else we may have forgotten? How about you, Daisy? Did we forget anything?"

Daisy's eyes widened. Her nostrils flared.

"Ma'am," he said, ducking away from Daisy's censuring stare, "why don't you go ring this stuff up and I'll be right along? I think our young model may have a question or two for me."

"Of course. You look lovely, young lady. It must be nice to have a man love you so much. When you're finished, bring your purchases over to my register and I'll wrap them for you."

- o -

The woman was no sooner out of earshot than Daisy unloaded on Nick. "What do you think you're doing? This is a stupid waste of money."

"It's part of the romance, darling. We've got a ball to attend, and I expect my woman to be the best dressed woman at the ball."

"Romance? Bullshit." Her eyes snapped, matching the sparkling diamond resting at the crest of her rapidly rising and falling breasts. "I feel like a whore accepting this stuff from you. You don't have to buy me expensive things to get me in your bed."

"Whoa, now just a minute." Nick grabbed her by the shoulders. "I may be a lot of things. I may be too old. You may be mistaken for my daughter. But I'd never do anything on purpose to make you feel like a whore. You know that."

Daisy rested her forehead against his shoulder. She sobbed. "I'm sorry," she mumbled half coherently. "Where I come from, a guy only buys a girl things if he's trying to get into her panties."

Nick massaged the nape of her neck. "Humph," he whispered. "I'm already in them, so why would I bother?"

She poked him in the ribs.

He flinched.

"That's the point," she countered. "I don't know why you do most things. But this is off the charts. It's a waste."

"It's not." He raised her head and wiped her tears with his handkerchief. "Daisy, no man has ever bought you nice things. I know that. I'm different than most men. I just want to see you dazzle—and you do. Who knows, maybe there'll be some rich young man at the ball who will want to lay his claim on you."

"Right."

"Not that I'd let him. You're not ready to go off on your own yet. There are still significant gaps in your education."

A slow smile crept across Daisy's lips. "How come you want to buy me expensive clothes only to imagine me naked? Doesn't make much sense, when you can see me naked most any time."

Nick laughed a low guttural laugh. "You have to develop a keener sense for mystery and romance, my young lover. Yep, it's going be quite a while before you can go out on your own. Now, why don't you change out of these fancy clothes while I go make the salesclerk happy?"

"But I've never bought clothes that don't even have price tags on them. These have to be way too expensive."

"Don't worry about it. I'm way too rich. So make me happy and don't complain so much. You'd think you'd never accepted anything from anyone before."

Chapter Six

"It's like being in an art museum." Daisy stood in the center of the finishing room at Paddle Dreams Unlimited.

She'd had no idea what Nick had been talking about when he spoke of his shop. At least a dozen people worked in half a dozen rooms on canoes at various stages of construction. Visualizing the roughed-out frames in an earlier room as canoes had been difficult. But the beauty of these nearly finished products was beyond anything she could've imagined.

"No two are alike," she said. "People actually put these in the water? Aren't they afraid of banging them up?"

Nick and Tom Harrison both laughed at her. "A few people who buy these canoes are collectors, and those boats may never feel the water," Tom replied, "but most buyers want something that is one of a kind that performs like a duck in water."

"If they need repairing," Nick added, running a hand across the hull of one of the three completed canoes, "the owner can always bring it back here and we'll take care of it. The first year at no cost; after that they have to pay."

"So why are these canoes so expensive? How do you get the colors to gleam like that? I didn't see a painting room."

"No," Tom replied, smiling as if he was about to share a secret. "The color is there in the wood; we just have to be patient and skilled enough to let the natural qualities of the wood emerge. If you try to force it or shape it to fit your preconceived image, it won't pan out."

"Tom's right, Daisy. Look at this grain closely." Nick leaned over a canoe and pointed at a particular strip of wood. Daisy bent and narrowed her eyes.

"See how the grain undulates? The next strip is slightly different. It's more linear. The grain and the color change as the craftsman sands each wood strip. That's what makes cedar wood strip canoes so unique, and, depending on one's desires, so time demanding. You could work these pieces of wood for days. So you have dark strips — nearly black, variations of reds and browns, even some yellows. Most of what we use is western red cedar; sometimes we'll add Alaskan cedar to gain even more variation in color."

"Such attention to detail. I can't say I've ever thought about canoes before, but this is spectacular. And you supervise the entire process?" Daisy asked, turning to Tom.

"That's my job. But the men and women you see working here know what they're doing. Still, it's good to have another set of eyes looking things over.

"While each canoe is unique, there are no flaws. No rough edges, not the slightest flaw from the finishing process." Tom grinned. "Some of our workers want to run when they see me coming with my bucket of water and sponge. Dampening the wood causes the grain to rise. Scratches and poorly sanded areas turn darker than the surrounding wood, if you have good eyes to see. I have good eyes."

Walking back toward Nick's office, Daisy asked, "So how do you know the boat will float? I've seen some great looking horses that couldn't run a lick."

"That's where I come in," Nick said, waving to a young woman who had just looked up from her work, raised her goggles and smiled. She held a light power sander in her hand.

Daisy thought the woman smiled too boldly at her boss.

"While each of these canoes is unique, we are working with only so many models. Similar length, weight, strength and so on. We may make only a couple dozen of a given model. We don't want to become the local factory outlet for canoes. Anyway, I'm usually fiddling around with design and testing models. Once the prototype is constructed, I take it to the Boundary Waters in northern Minnesota to run it through its paces."

"Really. Sort of like the exercise rider."

"Would you like some more coffee?" Nick grabbed the pot and filled Daisy's cup, Tom's, and then his own.

"Have you ever had a boat sink under you?"

Nick smiled and shook his head. "If you're

halfway good at design, that shouldn't happen. I've certainly had to make changes, but I've never had one sink because of poor design."

"But they do sink?"

Nick frowned. "I forgot. You've never been in a canoe?"

Daisy shook her head.

"Like any small boat, canoes can swamp in heavy waves. If a storm is coming up, the wisest decision is to head for shore."

"Oh."

"Don't let him scare you," Tom admonished. "If he ever swamped a boat, it was to see what it was like. In water safety courses, the instructor will often ask you to tip over the canoe to teach you what to do in case it happens for real.

"What I like about Nick's designs is their simplicity. A canoe is the simplest of boats: it's a hull with whatever else is needed to hold it in place. Sometimes designers get carried away; Nick doesn't. The result is a simple, elegant, serviceable form of water transportation."

"I like your logo. The single paddle design with Paddle Dreams Unlimited in script is simple and elegant. Did you come up with that?" she asked, glancing at Nick.

Nick drank from his cup. "We both did. This is a joint venture. We both do just about everything there is to do in the building process. I just can't get Tom to try one out."

"Really?" Daisy cast an inquisitive look at Tom.

Tom glared at Nick before answering. "That's a

whole other story, Daisy. I'll just say I got too damn wet too many times saving your friend's ass while we served together in Special Forces. Now I only go near the water to take a shower."

"They look so pretty." Daisy looked at a picture hanging on the wall of Nick in one of his canoes with a forested island in the background. The place looked so remote and Nick looked so at home. That was a man she wasn't sure she knew. "I'm not sure I could get in one. But it must be serene to glide along in the water without hearing the sound of an engine."

"That it is. Maybe you'd like to come along when I test the next model. Is it about ready, Tom?"

"Soon. Another week or two at the most. Don't press it, Nick. You know we can't rush a good canoe, any more than a good wine, or a good...well, I'd best be getting back to work. Good meeting you, Daisy. We'll be seeing you at the ball, right?"

Daisy stood to shake Nick's partner's hand. "I'll be there. Nick has a hard time accepting *no.*"

Tom tipped back his head and howled. "Didn't take you long to learn that one. I'm not sure *no* is in his vocabulary. Bye."

She watched Tom Harrison enter the lobby and say something to the receptionist, who laughed and waved the man on. "I like Tom. He seems so at ease."

"He doesn't rile easily, but you wouldn't want to be around when he does. So how about taking a

129

canoe trip with me in a couple weeks or so?"

Daisy's brow furrowed. "No, I couldn't do that. I have to stay with the horses. I have a job that ties me down, remember?"

"Okay. I'm glad you liked the canoes. They are something else, aren't they?"

"So, that's it. You accepted my *no*. After what Tom said?"

Nick guffawed. "You two made me sound like some domineering kind of guy." His eyebrows arched. "I'm not into domination. Are you?"

"Certainly not."

"Good. Anyway, you've now seen what I do besides race racehorses and watch the stock market."

"At first when you talked about canoe building, I thought you were talking about a hobby, but I see now that this is your love. Do you know you talk about it using the same language you use to describe lovemaking?"

Nick's brow furrowed. "I hadn't thought about it quite like that." He paused. "I suppose you're right.

Chuckling, Daisy pointed at the various canoe designs covering the wall opposite Nick's desk. "A shrink might point out how you spend much of your time drawing the shape of a woman's most private part."

Nick stared at the designs. His mouth fell open. "Well, I'll be damned. The student is out-performing the master."

Daisy stood and kissed Nick on the cheek. "I'd

better get back to work myself. There are some questionable knees to check before evening."

- o -

After Nick's employees had gone home, he walked toward the large, airy sanding room where six canoes sat on sawhorses. It was there he'd find Tom. The man loved to rub sandpaper against wood. When others thought they were finished with the job or had given up on an unrelenting knot or scar, Tom would find a way to help the wood express its unique personality.

As Nick entered the room, Tom glanced up briefly and grunted. "Wondered when you'd get here."

"So what do you think?"

"About what?" Tom took a step back and eyed a swirl in the grain before returning to rubbing it.

"About Daisy, of course. I'm not here to find out what you think about the weather."

Tom stopped sanding and met Nick's eager gaze. "It's not important what I think. What do *you* think about her?"

"Come on, Tom. You know what I think. She's beautiful in an understated way. She has an innocent charm about her, and yet the strength of a tigress." Nick winced. "But she's too young. There are times when I totally forget our age difference. It's then that I soar like I've never soared before."

Tom nodded. "That's what I thought." Idly he

131

rubbed the sandpaper against the tips of his fingers. "So how young is too young? Do you even know her age?"

Nick shook his head.

"Why not? It would be easy to find on some record or another."

"I'm aware of that." Nick swung his legs over a sawhorse.

Tom grinned. "I don't think I've ever seen you this afraid of a little information. She's surely over eighteen, right?"

"Of course."

"Then her age is only a secondary matter. Hell, all you have to do is look into that woman's eyes to know that she's experienced more than most fifty-year-olds. I've seen that look. I grew up with it.

"What you see as innocence is often sharply honed wariness. I expect she's not nearly as innocent as you think. Certainly Daisy's naïve about a lot of things, simply because she hasn't been exposed to much outside of her small world. But she's shrewd. You better believe that."

Nick crossed his arms over his chest. Shrewd. Certainly. She'd clearly had a plan to seduce him. The videos, the bikini line, her coming to him. But not deceptive. His brow furrowed. "So what do you think she's after? My money?"

Tom shrugged. "That probably intimidates her more than anything. I expect you're a window onto an entire new world for her. She's from the streets, Nick. She doesn't expect to land you. That thought has likely never even occurred to her. Regardless of age, she won't see herself ultimately fitting into your world.

"If that's what you want, you'll have to convince her. And my guess is that won't be easy."

Letting out a deep breath, Nick stood up and stretched. "I don't know what I want. You sure she won't want me?"

Tom chuckled. "That would be a blow to your ego, wouldn't it? She may not know what she wants at this point—but I guarantee you she doesn't expect anything permanent, and if she thought you did, she'd run like hell. You're hung up on age, old man. If you become more than a window for her, then she'll probably get hung up on class differences, and maybe on not wanting you to see her past.

"In the long run, if you really want her, you're going to have to convince her not only that you love her but that she deserves it and that she belongs."

"Shit, I never knew you were a budding psychologist." Nick shoved his hands in his pockets. "Why do you think all of that?"

"Because I've been there. That woman may be young, but she's got a lot of pride. Probably hard earned against high odds. If you don't respect her, she'll walk away from you like you're the plague."

"She wasn't overly excited with the stuff I bought her for the charity ball. Hell, most women would have been thrilled and gushing their thanks." A wisp of a smile touched his lips. "Not my Daisy. She accused me of treating her like a high priced whore. Can you believe that?"

"Sure can. So you've already experienced the whiplash of her pride. A woman who has struggled hard to find something in herself to be proud of isn't going to be impressed with your wealth. I expect Daisy Matthews won't be bought with things. She's done without all her life. She won't want to get used to having more than she can afford to buy for herself, because you aren't permanent."

"So why does she accept owning horses with me?"

"Now that's a smart question. You've touched her soft spot with the horses. I'll bet she likely never dreams about a man like you, but she does dream about owning race horses. Besides, it's clear you don't know a damn thing about horses, so she's earning her own way there whether or not she chooses to share your bed."

"Chooses to share my bed? She's the one who came to me wanting to gain from my experience. I didn't..."

Tom walked over and tapped Nick on the shoulder. "Exactly. That's what I mean. You chose her for the horses. She chose you for the bed, and she can un-choose you whenever she wishes without jeopardizing the horse business."

Nick huffed. "She won't just un-choose me."

"The hell she won't. You're not used to being rejected, my man, but you better start wondering what it will feel like. Believe me. She does not see you as a permanent fixture in her life. She can't."

- o -

Daisy willed her heartbeat to steady. Was this what Cinderella had felt like before the clock struck midnight? The ballroom chandelier sparkled so intensely she couldn't stare at it for any length of time without hurting her eyes. She'd never seen so many people so dressed up. Most of the men wore tuxes. Nick was stunningly handsome in his black tux; the fit showed off his firm body.

Tom Harrison and his wife, Thelma, were equally decked out. She liked both of them. They didn't put on airs like some of the people she'd been introduced to that evening. Thelma was a substantial bouncy African American woman who made it clear she took no crap from anyone, including her husband. She seemed to know at least half of the people in attendance, and her booming voice could often be heard emitting laughter and occasionally venom.

"Come on, girl. You're starting to glaze over."

Daisy jerked her head up to see Thelma's toothy smile. The woman stood beckoning.

"These two men can protect each other for a few minutes. Let's visit the powder room; I think my face is slipping some."

Daisy rose and followed her guide. The powder room, as Thelma called it, had gold plated faucets.

Daisy stood and gaped at the blue and white tiled floor and walls. The entire décor provided a soft, lush atmosphere. In a bathroom, of all places. Daisy glanced at her reflection in the wash basin. What would the kids at the old group home think of her now?

"And who are you? Nick's niece, or what?" inquired a drop dead gorgeous raven-haired woman. The petite stranger had the kind of body Daisy knew made men go wild. Her ample bare cleavage left little to the imagination.

Before Daisy had a chance to respond, Thelma spoke up, her eyes gleaming. "Why, Claire, how nice of you to ask about Nick's friend. This is Daisy Matthews. She and Nick own some racehorses together. I understand from Nick that Daisy's an expert with horses and is busy teaching him a lot about the racing business.

"Daisy," Thelma said, turning to her, "this is Claire Donaldson. She once thought she and Nick had something going, but I guess she came up short. It's old history. And I do mean to emphasize old."

"Well, I never. She doesn't look old enough to be out of training bras. He's no doubt infatuated with her because he can manipulate her into doing anything he wants. Horses!" Claire Donaldson obviously found it difficult to look down her nose while glaring up at Daisy, but she gave it her best shot. "You might be able to put diamonds on a gutter snipe, but you'll never remove the stench of the gutter."

The dark-haired woman spun on her heel and stalked from the room. "Don't trip over your deodorant!" Thelma bellowed at the woman's back.

Daisy wanted to laugh and cry. She'd never even had the opportunity to say hi. "Don't mind her," Thelma said. "She's always been a jealous lush."

Daisy crossed her arms and leaned back against the vanity. She took a deep breath. "I've heard worse, much worse. But maybe she's not so far off. She sure had me pegged right away. Do I smell bad?"

Thelma laughed. "Tom's told me some of your story, girl. At least what Nick's shared with him. You had a rough time of it. So did Tom. So did I. I was raised in the projects. Tom comes from Woodlawn. We know the odors of rotting garbage, dried urine, winos—and of shattered dreams. Do we smell bad?"

"Of course not."

"And neither do you. It takes guts to make something of yourself. I expect that's part of what Nick finds attractive about you. You're not some simpering female who's looking for a sugar daddy.

"Now Claire? She's never had anyone threaten her with a needle or a blade. She's never had friends who were raped or killed. And she wouldn't know how to fuck a man if she had to save her life; she's the kind who only wants to lay there and fulfill her obligation while dreaming

137

about signing a dozen checks or credit cards.

"From my point of view, that stinks to high heaven, Daisy Matthews. So don't get bent out of shape over women like her. What you got is the real thing. Don't ever let anyone tell you any different. Okay?"

Daisy nodded. Thelma touched up her own lipstick. "Thanks, Thelma. You're the real thing, too."

"Damn right. Now let's get back to our men before some fancy hussies come along and try to lure them away."

- o -

"So how's my lovely date?" Nick asked, holding Daisy close to his body while he guided them through the steps of a waltz. He wasn't at all surprised that Daisy had taken to dancing with the grace of a swan. They'd practiced a few times at her apartment, and now no one would have guessed that the young woman in his arms was experiencing her first formal dance.

"I'm fine," Daisy whispered into his ear, "although my feet are getting a little tired. I've never had these heels on this long."

"Slip them off when you get back to the table."

Daisy leaned back and frowned at Nick. "I wouldn't do that. That would be uncouth."

"Ha. I bet if we peeked under all the delicate table cloths in this room, we'd find as many bare female feet as not."

"We're not going to do that!"

"No," Nick chuckled, "I'll try not to embarrass you. So, do you like Thelma?"

"She's a gem."

"Yep. And she thinks you're pretty great, too. She may be a little blustery, but Thelma is usually slow to develop friendships."

"So tell me about Claire Donaldson."

Nick scowled and missed two steps before regaining his stride. "So you met the shrew; I'll bet that was pleasant."

"Actually, Thelma chopped the woman up into tiny pieces before I could even say hello. So who is she?"

"A social climber who wanted to climb into my bed, but never got there."

"Really."

"You must know there've been plenty of women in my life, but not Claire Donaldson. So what did she have to say?"

"Not much, apart from comparing smells of gutter snipes and deodorants. She wondered if I was your niece."

"God, I hope no one is still wondering that," he mumbled into her ear. He moved his hand lower on her buttocks and pulled her tighter against his groin. His erection pressed just about where it should. He closed his eyes and breathed deeply her delicious scent. "You smell good enough to eat."

"Promises, promises." Her voice was husky. "Claire Donaldson, eat your heart out."

Two hours later, Nick lifted his head and grinned. "I like to keep my promises."

"Don't stop! Not now!" Daisy pummeled his back with her heels.

Nick smiled to himself and dipped his tongue, separating her engorged lips. She sighed in response. He liked it when she rested on the edge. Daisy was easily the most passionate woman he'd ever been with. Unexplored desire smoldered within her loins just below the surface. It pleased him immensely that he'd learned how to tap that unclaimed reservoir. It was his tongue and his lips that were able to draw her ardor to a near boiling point and then to back off, permitting it to subside of its own accord. The gradual build-up of erotic energy, the storing up of aroused synapses ultimately triggered an explosion as hot and volatile as anything he witnessed in nature.

"Now, Nick. Now."

Her murmured plea touched his brain and his heart; he could no longer withhold. He tasted her moisture. He tested her heat. He inserted a finger, probed her inner chamber and flicked his tongue along the bud at the apex of its opening.

"Oh my God!"

Her words encouraged his efforts. Her body tensed beneath and around him and then released and then tensed and released again. At last, she shuddered and pulled away.

For a moment, he was envious. Why was she able to ride an orgasm for so much longer than he could? And then with little rest, she'd be ready to search for another wave. Could he keep up with her? What about ten years from now?

Nick's eyes widened. Who cared about ten years from now?

"You were beautiful tonight."

Daisy gave Nick a lazy smile and reached for the sheet.

"Not just now. Earlier at the ball. I told you you'd be the belle of the ball and you were. Did you enjoy yourself?"

"Yes. But this was better. I prefer being here alone with you in my bed. I can be myself here."

"But not at the dance?"

"Sort of, but I have to be on guard and watch how everybody is doing things. Cassie made sure I learned the basics about eating out, but there were many more forks, spoons and knives tonight than were needed."

Nick chuckled and pulled her close to him. "I suppose you're right about that. Think of it this way. There was more work to go around setting the tables and washing the dishes."

"Right."

"Do you have a lock box?"

"A lock box? You mean at the bank?"

He nodded.

"No. Why? Do I need one?"

"How about household insurance?"

Daisy ran fingers through her hair, tugging at snarls. "Nope. I don't have anything worth

141

stealing."

Nick cleared his throat. "You do now. I'd suggest putting those diamonds in a lock box. I think you'd agree this isn't the safest neighborhood in Chicago."

She looked at him quizzically. "So how much household insurance do I need? I probably should have some for my office equipment anyway. I just haven't gotten around to it."

"Figure out what that stuff is worth, and then add another seventy-five to it."

Daisy sat up straight; the sheet fell to her waist. "You mean seventy-five hundred dollars, not seventy-five. Right?"

"You're learning."

Daisy exploded off the futon and began marching back and forth. "I can't accept that. That's a small fortune."

"A very small fortune."

"That depends on one's point of view," she said, bent over with hands on hips.

"Damn, you're a fetching woman when you get angry like that. Particularly naked. Could you hold that position?"

"You stay right where you are, mister. Are you trying to buy me?"

"Good God, woman, we talked about this before. Anything I buy you is yours with no strings attached. Can I help it that I'm rich and I want to give you something beautiful now and then?"

"Yes, you can." Daisy's lower lip trembled.

142

"You're enough without the diamonds and the fancy things." She turned away from him. "They only remind me how different I am. Like, I've never once thought of needing a lock box."

Nick let out a ragged breath. "Daisy, I want to ask you something."

"Am I stopping you?"

"No. I am." Nick sat up in the bed. "How old are you, Daisy?"

Daisy grabbed her nightshirt and laughed. She slipped it on; it only reached low enough to cover her belly button.

He smiled at this quest for modesty. She looked so damn fetching in that nightshirt.

"How old am I? You've been screwing me for two whole weeks and now you want to know how old I am? Don't worry, you're not subject to the Mann Act."

"I just want to know."

"We were talking about you giving me gifts I don't want or need, and now you've switched the subject. Okay, old man. If it'll make you feel worse, I have a birthday in three weeks."

Nick's throat constricted. She was stalling. He wasn't going to like what he was about to hear. "So how old?"

"I'll be a ripe old twenty-one."

Nick collapsed on the bed and closed his eyes. Not even twenty-one. He'd thought maybe twenty-three at the youngest; hopefully, more like thirty.

"I'll be able to drink wine, if you're still

143

interested in taking me out to restaurants. Haven't you noticed that I never drink alcohol when we're out?"

She was right. And he'd never thought much about it one way or the other. Wow. He'd been screwing around with a twenty-year-old. What was it Tom had said? If she's over eighteen, she's legal. He tried to take deep breaths. Well, she was at least that.

"Are you just going to lie there, old man? Speak to me." Daisy knelt on the floor beside her bed and placed a palm on his chest. "You've been very good, you know. But if you want to end this, I'll understand. Sort of. I'll be all right. You don't have to worry about me. And you can have all your things back. The diamonds. The clothes."

Her finger's tightened against his skin.

"But I won't give up my twenty percent of RainbowBlaze. I've earned that."

Without opening his eyes, Nick covered her hand with his. "I know you have. You don't have to give anything back. Ever. I've never tried to buy you, Daisy. Giving the stuff back would only make us both feel like that was why I gave you things."

He cracked an eye open. He hadn't ever seen her look so lonely and forlorn. "I don't know what I'm going to do with you, kid. Nope. I won't call you kid again, and I think it best if you drop the reference to old man." He paused. "You're not put off by the age difference? I'm forty-two."

"I've known that from almost the beginning. I

checked at the racing office. Age hasn't mattered to me. Why should it matter to you?"

"So you knew before you came to my suite?"

"Of course."

Nick voiced his next thought before he could stop it. "What if we were to have kids? I'd be leaning on a cane taking them to the Cubs game."

Daisy eyes rounded and then narrowed. "Who said anything about having kids?"

"I just did. Not that I'm planning on it."

"Good." Daisy sighed and traced a line from his chest to his belly button. "Let's not complicate things any more than they are."

"But we are lovers. You do admit that, don't you?"

"Certainly, in a matter of speaking."

"What the hell does that mean?"

"I don't know, but why are we arguing over semantics? I feel like I'm back in freshman English."

"I suppose you're right. But you won't try to give back the gifts."

"No." Her voice was meek. "But I don't have much to give you." She rimmed his belly button with a finger. "Except maybe me." She leaned over and replaced her finger with her tongue.

"As long as you give yourself freely. I wouldn't want you thinking you were paying me back for anything."

Daisy glanced up with a smile on her lips. "Oh, I'm going to pay you back all right, but not for the diamonds. This is for that delightful loving a

145

while ago."

Her fingers wrapped around his shaft. Nick tensed.

"Now, you'd better enjoy a twenty-year-old while you can. I won't be that young much longer. I skipped dessert at dinner with this in mind. I'll just hope Claire Donaldson is having a nightmare about us at this moment."

Nick chuckled and sank back into the pillows. He relished the warmth of Daisy's mouth surrounding him. Lovers or not. Twenty-one or not. Future or not. None of that counted at the moment. He was in the perfect place.

Chapter Seven

"Hi, Daisy, this is Angie. Angie Underwood."

"Hi, Angie." Daisy cradled the phone between shoulder and cheek while grabbing a pop from the fridge. "How are you? Where are you?"

"I'm in St. Paul with my folks for a couple days, then back to Austin, Texas for a run. But I wanted you to know that we're coming to Chicago toward the end of September. The twenty-eighth, to be exact. Our run will last through Thanksgiving and into the first week of December. I hope we can get together."

Daisy pulled out a kitchen table chair and sat down. "I expect to be here."

"So..."

Daisy listened to the silence.

"So I guess I have to ask. Is my brother still in the picture?"

"Oh. That he is. Don't you talk to him?"

"There's seldom time. And," Angie mocked, "he's never home anymore. I wonder why?"

"He does stay pretty busy."

"Right. How's that bikini line working out?"

"Fine. Your suggestion is much better. Not painless, but much better."

"Good. I won't ask if Nick appreciates it, but he'd better. So how's your class going?"

147

"What?" Daisy frowned and looked at the receiver.

"Aren't you taking a course on Chaucer?"

"Oh, that." Daisy sighed. "It's good. He must have been quite the character. He earns his reputation for being ribald. I have a final paper to write this coming week. And then I'll have about a month before fall term begins."

"Sounds like you stay pretty busy yourself."

"Angie, have you ever ridden in a canoe?"

"Of course, we spent our summers up north on lakes and rivers."

"Are they safe?"

Angie laughed. "You *are* a city girl. Of course they're safe, if you're with somebody who knows what he's doing. So Nick wants to take you to the Boundary Waters?"

"Yes, but I said *no*."

"But you're rethinking your position."

"Yes."

"This is bigger news than you might realize, Daisy."

"What do you mean?"

"Nick makes two or three trips a year up there to test out canoes or to just get away. When he goes, he travels alone. I've never heard of a woman tagging along."

"Not even his ex-wife?"

"Ashley? She'd never have gone. Too many bugs and too much wild. Doubt he asked her more than once."

"Really. Why me?"

148

"You're going to have to figure that one out for yourself, girl. I hope you go, and I hope the loons put on a show for you. Their calls at night are incredible. Got to run. Just wanted to stay in touch. See you in a month or so. Enjoy. Bye."

"Bye."

Daisy hung up the phone. Now why would he think she'd like the bugs and the wild more than his ex-wife had? Shrugging, Daisy forced herself to set Nick Underwood aside so she could focus on Chaucer.

"Thought we might find you here, baby," Maxine cooed, stepping through the Laundromat entryway. The early evening temperatures were still scorching, so the door stood wide open.

Daisy looked up from her book. She scowled at Reggie following behind her sister. "Hi, Maxine," Daisy said, rising from her chair and slipping her feet into flip flops. "How are you? What brings you to this part of town?"

"No *hi* for me?" Reggie sneered.

Both women ignored him. "I'm managing. Barely," Maxine said. "It's hard even getting food on the table. And the landlord can't understand that rent money is hard to come by with Reggie laid off."

"Cut the crap," Reggie interrupted. "So who's the suit?"

"What?" Daisy's heart leapt. Shit, somehow they'd found out about Nick.

"Oh, baby, I'm thrilled for you." Maxine placed

149

a cold, sticky hand on Daisy's bare shoulder. Daisy shrank from the touch. "I'm your sister, for God sakes—you're supposed to confide in me about the men in your life."

"What man?"

"This man!" Reggie pushed a newspaper in front of her face. "The guy who looks like he's fingering your ass."

Speechless, Daisy gawked at the society page. There were many pictures of couples and small groups attending the charity ball. There she was, cuddled against Nick. His hand hardly looked innocent. She read the caption under their photo. *Nicholas Underwood in a May to September romance? Who is the lucky princess?* Daisy felt color working up her throat. Princess? Not hardly.

"So who is he, baby? You can tell us," Maxine crooned. "We're family."

A dryer buzzed, propelling Daisy into action. "I've got to get the clothes out."

"That's okay. We've got plenty of time. Don't we, Reggie?"

"You've got more time than me."

Daisy tried not to react to her brother-in-law's snarl. She'd have to buy them off. She couldn't let either one of them get to Nick. They'd make him believe she was the gutter snipe Claire Donaldson thought she was.

"He owns a horse I train." Did her voice sound calmer than her swirling stomach?

"Well, isn't that handy."

"He looks like a handsome man, Daisy. Why

150

did he take you to such a society bash?"

Daisy frowned at her sister. Was it so hard to imagine that Nick just wanted to take her to the dance, to be with her for who she was?

"I don't know. He asked me. I said yes."

"Where the hell did you get the fancy clothes?" Reggie demanded. "And those rhinestones look almost real."

Thank God he didn't believe they were diamonds. "Nick bought the clothes. You know I can't afford them." Daisy focused on folding blouses.

"You mean you let a man buy you fancy things?" Maxine chortled bitterly. "And you always thought you were better than me. You're no different than me and our mother. You're no different. You're just a more expensive whore. You're trying to be one of those uptown call girls."

Daisy slapped Maxine's cheek before there was time to think. Reggie grabbed her wrist, squeezed hard and bent it backward.

"Bitch. I don't care who's banging you as long as we get a piece of the action. This guy's got to be rich. You're a bright girl."

Daisy gasped against the pain and Reggie's breath washing over her face. "You figure out how to separate some of that money from your boyfriend so we can all share in the wealth. You understand." He squeezed harder.

Sharp pain shot up her arm to her shoulder. She nodded. *God, don't break my wrist!*

Reggie dropped her arm. "Don't forget what I

151

told you before." He looked at Maxine. "I've got something you want."

"Ah, baby," Maxine said, rubbing the back of her hand against Daisy's cheek. "We don't mean to hurt you. You're the only family I've got. It's just that you've always been the lucky one. Look at me. I don't know when I'll ever get another dress, and you get a fancy dress. It's not fair."

Daisy's eyes turned smoky. Fair. What was fair? Maxine had chosen Reggie. She had to buy time. If it was just Maxine, she'd feel better about lending money.

Lending. What a joke. There would be no loan, only a gift. But Reggie really galled. He wanted to treat her like he was her pimp.

"So can you help us out? Even a little bit." Maxine's tone was saccharine.

"What do you need?" Daisy avoided eye contact with Reggie.

"A couple hundred would be great. A hundred would help." Maxine glanced furtively at her husband. "Even fifty is better than nothing."

"I'll see what I can do. It'll take a day or two."

"You better come through. You hear?"

Daisy nodded at Reggie and shrank from his threatening fist.

With hands trembling, Daisy folded her socks. Thank goodness Maxine and Reggie were leaving. The two of them sauntered down the sidewalk. As if more emphasis was needed, Reggie squeezed Maxine's neck and turned back to leer at Daisy through the Laundromat window.

Daisy rubbed her eyes. Was she in over her head? All her life she'd wanted to be part of a family. Now what family she had was threatening to mess up her life royally.

What would Nick do if she just came clean and told him about Maxine and Reggie? He knew some of her background. He could likely guess the rest. But that was different than having her relatives flaunting themselves before him. If they ever got their hands on Nick, they'd try to suck him dry of every cent he had. She couldn't allow that to happen.

Maybe she should just walk away from Nick. That would save everyone a lot of heartache. Daisy's blood chilled even in the sauna of the Laundromat. She couldn't let him go, not yet. She'd know when it was time to cut bait, and it wasn't now.

She slammed the dryer door shut. Why couldn't her so-called *family* stay out of this? For the first time in her life, a man was treating her like she was lovely and worthwhile. It might only be a dream, but it was too soon to wake up.

Daisy resolved to go to the bank in the morning and withdraw a hundred and drop it off with Maxine. She'd call to make sure Reggie was out. It wouldn't be enough. She knew that. There would never be enough money to satisfy them.

Daisy fought back the tears that had flowed for the past twenty minutes or so, ever since she'd watched RainbowBlaze take a bad step during a race over the turf course. She, Nick, Sam Gallagher, Cassie Travers, and a groom stared at the mare munching on grass near their barn. Rainbow refused to put weight on her left front leg. It wasn't broken, but they didn't need a vet to tell them that she had a severely bowed tendon.

Nor did they need a vet to tell them that RainbowBlaze would never race again.

Arms crossed, Sam Gallagher shook his head. "It's a damn shame. But it happens. A bad step. She could have broken her leg. Guess we're lucky, really."

Daisy nodded through blurred tears. They were lucky. If the leg had broken, they would have had to put RainbowBlaze down. Daisy shuddered at the thought. Nick again placed his arm around her shoulders giving comfort. What would she do if it weren't for him and her friends?

She never cried. Not like this. It was like there was a leak in some hidden pool inside her body and the entire pool was draining. She kicked at the dirt, angry both at what had happened to Rainbow and at her inability to control her emotions.

She'd never let people see her like this.

"When RainbowBlaze is ready and when you're ready," Cassie said, looking at Daisy, "we can trailer her back to our farm. She can recuperate there. She'll welcome the rest."

Again Daisy nodded. Had the tears drained her of her power of speech? "I know," she managed to blubber. "Oh, shit." She turned and buried her face against Nick's chest.

"It's going to be okay," he said, rubbing her neck and shoulders. "Sam says it's not life threatening; it just means her racing career is done."

"So now what are you going to do with her?" she whispered.

Nick glanced over Daisy's shoulder at Cassie and curled his lips into a hint of a smile. "Not me, partner. What will *we* do with her? She's a female. Can't she have babies?"

Daisy stilled, then pulled abruptly away from him. She whirled and looked at Cassie for confirmation.

"We'd have to test her to determine whether she can get pregnant," Cassie cautioned. "But she certainly has the pedigree and racing record that would suggest she'd be a fine broodmare, if that's what you want. There's always enough room at our place for a decent broodmare prospect."

"We wouldn't have to sell her?"

"I don't see why. As you know, Daisy, it takes time and patience to develop a broodmare and to bring a foal from a weanling to be a runner. But why not?"

Daisy looked inquisitively at Nick.

"Why not?" he agreed. "All that studying of bloodlines you've been foisting upon me may prove valuable after all. What do you say, partner? Should we be planning a meeting between our gal and some lucky stud?"

Smiling broadly, Daisy nodded and stabbed at

the tears with the back of her hand. "Why not? If Rainbow can be as successful at being a mom as she has been on the track, she should produce some very competitive foals."

Her equilibrium returned. Things would work out. Not the way she'd expected, but they would work out. "I'm going to brush her down," she said to Cassie. "Then we can load her for the trip to the farm. She'll enjoy being back there."

Two days later, Daisy and Nick visited their broodmare prospect at the Travis farm. RainbowBlaze hobbled about in a large paddock. Her leg was wrapped under the guidance of an excellent veterinarian who predicted that the mare would recover quite nicely—and that while the tendon would never be strong enough to support a racing career, it shouldn't prove a problem in the breeding shed or in the horse's role as broodmare.

RainbowBlaze came to the gate and whinnied softly. Daisy reached into her pocket for some carrots. "You're gonna be a bigger mooch than ever, Rainbow."

Leaning against the gate, Nick said, "I wonder who taught our girl that."

Daisy jabbed him with her elbow. "It's part of raising the foal. They need to know that they're cared for."

"I'd guess Blaze knows that all right. I'm really quite excited about her broodmare career."

"Hopefully, she'll be ready to breed by next spring. If she had to have a career-ending injury, this wasn't bad timing. It takes months to come down from the intensity and competition of the track to improve the odds of settling in a pregnancy."

"Sounds like we'll be running tests and setting stopwatches to find the right moment for her to get together with her man."

Chuckling, Daisy nodded. "I wonder which of us will be more nervous when the time comes."

Nick glanced sharply at her, but she maintained a steady gaze assessing the range of motion available to RainbowBlaze. Satisfied at last, she turned to Nick. "Cassie said she'd make some lemonade while we checked on Rainbow. Are you ready to quench your thirst?"

"Sure am, but I'm not positive lemonade will do it."

Daisy smiled at the dark passion evident in his pupils. "It's all you're going to get for the moment. So it better tide you over."

She swung their clasped hands back and forth as they made their way toward the house. It was good being back at the farm. She'd missed it. She'd spent nearly three years of her life here. It was so close to the city, yet at times, like right now, it seemed so far away. No smog. No Maxine. No Reggie.

"You two look quite content," Cassie shouted from the porch. "Quit lollygagging. I've got lemonade and cookies. Clint will come out and join us in a minute. The older kids are at a 4-H leadership camp. And the younger two are down for a nap. At least I hope they are."

Daisy and Nick sat on the old stuffed couch where Daisy had slept many a night listening to spring peepers and the mournful sounds of owls. The screened-in porch had been one of her favorite places on the farm. From there she could hear, see and smell the change of the land and the horses and yet still feel protected from the mosquitoes and the ghosts of the dark. It had taken her months to adjust to the relative quiet of rural McHenry County.

She glanced over at Cassie. She never was certain who she'd see. Cassie the social worker. Cassie the mom. Or Cassie the friend. This looked like Cassie the mom.

"RainbowBlaze is doing fine," Cassie said. "She's getting around pretty well. And how about you, girl? How are you doing?" Cassie glanced at Nick.

Daisy smiled shyly. "At least I've stopped crying."

"Good. Oh, here's Clint now."

- o -

Everyone stood. Cassie made the introductions.

Nick liked Clint immediately. The deeply tanned man had a crinkly smile, as if life was treating him well. Daisy had told him Clint was part Ute. Somehow he'd expected his host to be more reserved.

"So, Daisy, it's good to see you. Why don't we

all sit down?" Clint pulled up a chair to sit by his wife. "So this is the scandalous older man," Clint arched his eyebrows, "that Cassie's been telling me about."

"Complaining about, more likely," Daisy snorted.

"Maybe at first," Cassie admitted. "But I've come around. You have your life to live. Besides, I've seen enough of Nick to know that he's not going to go out of his way to hurt you."

"Thanks for your vote of confidence," Nick said, lifting his glass in mock salute. He leaned back and smiled. Whether Daisy saw it as such or not, this was part of her family. These two cared about Daisy and what happened to her.

"So I understand you're interested in purchasing some horses come fall." Clint redirected the conversation.

"Yes. Especially now, with RainbowBlaze unable to compete. You interested in working with us?"

Clint glanced at Cassie, who gave him a soft nod. "Of course. So Daisy will be involved in the purchases?"

Nick smiled. "She's my coach and trainer. I like the trainer to own part of the horses; I think it gives her a little more vested interest. She'll be in for twenty percent, like she is on RainbowBlaze."

Clint reached for his glass. "Fine by me. I know a number of owners who prefer that arrangement. Sometimes it's a little messier to dissolve partnerships that way, though."

"We'll cross that bridge when the time comes." Nick hadn't been able to keep an edge from creeping into his voice.

"I'll make sure you get copies of the major sales catalogs as they become available. In the meantime, you might also want to work with Daisy on claiming a horse."

"Actually, I'm trying to get Daisy to take a little time off. This past week has been quite hard on her."

Nick ignored Daisy's stern look. He figured Cassie might be an ally for once. She certainly knew how distraught Daisy had been over Blaze's injury. "I need to take a prototype of a new canoe up to Northern Minnesota and test it for my company. Thought it might be an opportunity for Daisy to get away and recharge a little."

"You're in between school terms, aren't you?" Cassie inquired.

"Yes, but I don't need a break. Horses are my life."

"Hmm, I find I need to get away from them in order to fully appreciate what they are. Sounds like a great change of pace. I assume the canoe is safe."

"Spoken like a mom," Clint teased. "I doubt Nick is going to market an unsafe canoe."

"The canoe is safe."

"So what are you afraid of, girl? You two are obviously sleeping together. Are you afraid of Nick?"

"Of course not." Daisy looked startled and

cornered.

"I didn't mean for us to gang up on you," Nick apologized. "If you don't want to go, you don't have to. I just thought it might be fun. To be away from all the routines and day-to-day pressures."

"I wish it were that easy," Daisy mumbled.

"If that's what's holding you back, Daisy, I can have some of my crew help back up Sam in your absence."

Nick watched Daisy color under three sets of eyes.

"Okay." Daisy breathed deeply. "I'll go, but I don't want to hear any bear stories. I've never been in the woods at night. I've never been in a canoe. I've never been alone with a man for any length of time."

She crossed her arms below her breasts and pursed her lips. Nick was reminded of a rebellious teenager. "I'll go. So can we talk about something else now?"

She looked stunned. Now why were there tears in her eyes—and what could he do to make them go away?

They stayed for supper, which gave Nick an opportunity to meet the two youngest Travers children. These two were a handful, and he knew there were two older children away at camp who were from Clint's first marriage. What was it about kids that snookered him and scared the hell out of him at the same time? They seemed malleable one moment and then intractable the

161

next. Like Cassie's youngest child, they could beam you the brightest smile and then when you stooped to pick them up give you the most hair raising scream. Kids made him feel dumb. Clint moved back and forth with ease from one child's roller coaster emotion to the next. So what kind of father would *he* be? Paranoid.

He drained the last of his coffee and peeked over at Daisy. Only twenty. A lot of women were mothers by that age. But it seemed too young. She needed more time for herself. At that moment, she let out a gleeful scream and hoisted the three-year-old to her lap. Between giggles Daisy and the child played patty-cake. Daisy was at ease with children. Would she be a good mother? Apparently she'd had less than an adequate mother, but then she'd had her grandmother. Nick looked at Cassie, who was giving him a warm smile. Yes, Daisy certainly had sufficient role models for motherhood.

Nick shook his head and inhaled sharply. Why the hell was he thinking about kids? Or about fatherhood and motherhood? He stared at Daisy. *She* was. Why? Son of a bitch.

He was a goner. Tom was right. There was no way he wanted to spend the rest of his years without Daisy. He hadn't fully understood it until watching her with the kids, but he needed her to be more than lover. He needed her to be wife, mother and soul-mate.

In his peripheral vision, he saw Cassie stand and stretch. Her words sounded like they came from across a great expanse. "Daisy, why don't you and Clint take care of the dishes and the kids? I need a break. And I'd kind of like to show Nick something before you all go."

"Sure. No problem." Daisy's lips turned up. "Right, little one," she said to Angela, Cassie's youngest daughter. "We can do dishes and play games while your mommy is up to no good."

Nick followed Cassie toward the barn, exchanging idle chatter about the weather. They entered the tack room that also served as an office. Cassie rummaged through a beat up trunk full of ribbons, clothes and assorted odds and ends. She was searching for something specific. Nick leaned against the doorjamb, watching, waiting.

"Here they are," Cassie said with a glint of triumph in her eyes. She held in her hand a pair of pants that were sorely in need of repair.

"Do you know what these are?" she asked.

Nick shrugged. "They look like a pair of pants."

"They're riding pants. Scarred. Worn. More holes than I'd care to mend. These were Daisy's when she first moved in with us. They started out new, but Daisy didn't have an easy time with the horses at first. Her height made her feel awkward, so she acted awkward. Horses would throw her to the ground because they couldn't figure out what she wanted them to do. After a cuss word or two, she'd get back up, determined to learn how to be with them."

Cassie laid the pants across the messy desk. "I

gave her lessons, but as often as not she didn't *get* it. She had to learn her own way—by feel. She didn't trust what I said; she had to feel what I said. Too often that meant landing on her butt. There was never a question of her quitting. The only questions were how long it would take her to learn to ride and how many pants we'd have to go through before that happened." She smiled with pride. "Fortunately, it only took one pair.

"All the riding ribbons and trophies in that trunk are Daisy's. She became an excellent rider, and as you know, there's no one who cares more about horses than that young lady."

Nick nodded, keeping his own counsel. The redhead had more than a pair of pants on her mind.

Cassie continued, "So how well do you know Daisy?"

"I know she has a lot of guts, if that's what you mean. I know she's had a rough time. That she was raised by her grandmother until the woman died. That she then went to a group home, where you met her and that you took her in. She's great with animals, and apparently with kids, from what I saw today. She's bright and witty. And frankly, I wish she were older."

"Good. Do you realize how young she is?"

"I do now."

Cassie chuckled. "You have my sympathies, sort of. She's always looked much older than her age. And for the most part, she behaves that way."

Nick stepped over to the desk and ran a hand

along the tattered pants. "Again, spoken like a mom." He compressed his lips and eyed Cassie. She wasn't the enemy; she only wanted the best for Daisy. Nick sighed. "I wish I had a magic wand so I could make her older, but I can't do that."

"No, nor can she."

"When I'm seventy she'll be almost fifty." He scowled. "When I'm eighty she'll nearly be sixty. How about ninety and seventy?"

"That does sound better," Cassie agreed, with sparkles in her eyes.

Nick looked at the wall calendar showing two horses running free on the open range somewhere in the West. "At least if I die young she'll be a wealthy widow," he snorted.

"You really are serious, aren't you?"

"Dead serious."

"Is she?"

"She doesn't know that she is yet."

Cassie laughed. "That sounds so much like Clint. He was ready long before me."

"Yeah, well, Daisy can't bring herself to believe that such things are possible. She doesn't allow herself to dream big enough."

"But she's capable of dreaming big."

"Oh yeah."

"This doesn't surprise me, really. Daisy is a passionate, attractive, competent young woman. I was hoping she'd find someone closer in age, but you are a very upstanding, resourceful man." Cassie bent over the desk and pulled out a file. She gave him an offhanded smirk. "You checked out very well. Daisy may not have informed you that my husband is also a silent partner in a local private detective agency."

Nick's laughter came from deep in his diaphragm. "I've heard of protective mothers, but this is pretty extreme."

"Maybe. I just wanted to be sure you were a good guy and not one of those creeps who make a practice of preying on young girls. Knowing what I do about you, I expect you would have done the same thing if you had been in my shoes."

"No doubt about that. Does that mean you're on my side?"

"No, I'm on Daisy's side. Whatever she chooses to do in the long run, I will support her. I expect you are very good for her, at least right now." Cassie paused and closed the file. "You two come from very different worlds. You may be able to accept each other, but will you be able to function in each other's world? I don't know. Do you?"

"Nope. But if she wore out those pants learning to ride, I expect if she decides she wants to live in my world, nothing and no one will be able to stop her."

Cassie stood. "I bet you're right about that. Why don't we head back? I don't want her thinking we're plotting a conspiracy out here. But be very clear Nicholas Underwood—she will have to choose you. You won't be able to buy her or cajole her. If you try to guide her with a tight rein, she'll toss her head and bolt."

Nick frowned. "I've learned that already."

As they left the barn to walk toward the house, Cassie asked, "So have you met Daisy's half-sister yet?"

Nick stopped and looked down at Cassie. "No, I haven't. I'd completely forgotten about her. Daisy only mentioned her once or twice."

"That's not surprising." She squinted at him and the setting sun. "If you and Daisy do get serious, there'll be trouble from that corner."

"How's that?"

"Maxine's married to a lowlife bastard. Reggie is a smalltime pimp, drug dealer and who knows what else. He's been in and out of prison a few times, but nothing big. I've threatened to turn Clint and his partner on him, but Daisy would never forgive me. It's the only blood family she has."

"So how does that affect me?"

"Reggie and Maxine have bloodhound noses when it comes to money. When they find out about you, they'll be trying to figure out some way to tap into the *rich man*. It could get uncomfortable for Daisy. Knowing Reggie, it could get downright nasty. I only had to meet him once after Daisy moved in with us to tell the bastard that he wasn't welcome on my property or around my family."

"Sounds like a great family," Nick responded sarcastically. "But I'm not holding Daisy responsible for her family, and I'm fairly good at protecting my own."

"I suppose you are, but Daisy may not turn to you for help. There is still a lot of street in her. She'll try to take care of any problems herself and will be just as inclined to protect you as you are to protect her."

"Now that's ridiculous. I sure as hell don't need protection. I'll whittle the punk down to size if he gives me the excuse."

Cassie shook her head. "You don't understand. Reggie is lowlife. He won't stand up and fight you. He'll threaten Maxine. He'll threaten Daisy. He might come after you, but if he does, it will be in the dark and you won't see him."

For a moment, Nick's stomach knotted as it had so often when he and Tom Harrison staked out a target when they were nineteen and twenty. "I'm pretty good in the dark," he muttered, "if I have to be."

Cassie placed a hand on his arm. "Don't do anything stupid. Maybe I shouldn't have said anything. Maybe I'm just an overly protective mom, but I felt you needed to know. Daisy wore out those riding pants in part because she wouldn't ask for help when she needed it."

Chapter Eight

Daisy inhaled the crisp, clear air. She perched on an outcropping of granite and stared across the bluest water she'd ever seen to yet another island. There would be another island beyond that one. That was the way it had been for the past three days paddling in the Boundary Waters Canoe Area.

Two spruce trees towering above her sang a playful tune on the soft breeze. She held several small pieces of red-veined jasper. The area abounded with jasper, along with wildlife, and birds, and trees, and fish. Things she knew so very little about.

She set the jasper aside, pulled her knees to her chest and fixed her gaze on Nick, who continued paddling back and forth in figure eights, in tight circles, then in larger ones. He was running the prototype canoe through its paces again. Every now and then he'd stop and place small strips on the bow of the canoe. While the canoe had functioned perfectly from her perspective, Nick had discerned that with a single canoeist, it planed a bit too much. And there was the slightest of pulls to the right. He was a perfectionist.

Daisy rubbed her arms vigorously. She'd found muscles in her arms, legs and back that she never knew existed. Paddling required effort. Although Nick did seventy percent of the work along with the steering from his position in back of the canoe, she'd come along fairly well and at least contributed a decent share. And then there was portaging. Nick handled the canoe and she carried much of the gear.

She looked across at the horizon. They'd driven through flat marsh, bogs, and rather scruffy looking trees to get to the boundary waters. Yet when it came to portaging a canoe, there was no flat land to be found, and whether coming or going, it was uphill or downhill.

Scratching at bites on her bare legs, Daisy tried to ignore the gnawing pain. She smelled like the inside of a Deets bottle. There were many unnamed biting insects, but the mosquito stood out as the most fierce and pesky. She'd become accustomed to the clinging repellant odor. Maybe because Nick smelled just as bad as she did.

Daisy stood and stretched in the warm mid-afternoon sunshine. The days warmed up nicely, yet the nights were surprisingly chilly. Splashes of red, orange, and yellow were everywhere among the many shades of green spruce and pine. Early autumn had already arrived, and it was only mid-September. She'd expected more broadleaf trees. Nick had informed her that they were too far north for most maples and oaks. Still, there was an enchanting amount of color to warm the spirit.

While she'd never considered herself much of a religious person, standing on the granite rock looking out over the water onto the next island made her think of an e. e. cummings poem she'd had to memorize in English class: *I thank You God for most this amazing day: for the leaping greenly spirits of trees and a blue true dream of sky; and for everything which is natural which is infinite which is yes.*

Daisy breathed a *yes* embracing the sanctuary in which she stood. She'd never known such a place. So wild. So serene. So other worldly. So fundamental. It was all of those things and more. In the middle of the night, she'd huddled closer to Nick listening to the screams of a prey falling to a more powerful or more cunning hunter.

She was privy to that balance of survival: who would win and who would lose? Out here, there were seldom additional opportunities for second or third place finishers. Out here, the victor didn't receive a blanket of roses, but rather life and the chance to hunt again. The loser — she didn't want to dwell on the fate of the loser.

"Totally engrossed? I could have been a bear," Nick teased, encircling Daisy from behind, rubbing his groin against her buttocks.

Daisy didn't startle. She'd heard his approach and knew what he would do. His strong arms comforted. Being here with him had shown her aspects of Nick Underwood that she hadn't seen in the city. He seemed less demanding, less hurried — if anything, even more gentle and patient.

She liked having Nicholas Underwood for a

lover. Not just as a teacher, but for a lover. Daisy compressed her lips. That acknowledgement was a huge, dangerous step. But she'd taken it with her eyes open. She hoped her heart would survive.

"So how's your first love doing? I saw you playing with those lead strips again."

"Playing. I'll have you know that's serious business." Grinning, Nick rubbed his cheek against her ear. "By the time we're done, I'll know precisely what we'll have to change to get it just right."

"And a Paddle Dreams Unlimited canoe has to be just right." Daisy leaned back into Nick resting her hands on his rear. "You certainly have high standards."

"Yes, I do. And that goes for my women, too." He ran his tongue over her earlobe.

Daisy shuddered. Was it caused by the wind that had suddenly quickened, by his tongue working its erotic magic on her ear, or by his words? High standards. If he only knew.

"So do we paddle on, or do we stay camped here?" she asked, wanting to be practical.

"Why don't we spend another night here? There's no hurry. That'll give us time to catch supper. I'd just as soon not do freeze-dried again. We should supplement our supplies."

"Sounds good to me." Daisy broke their embrace and started to walk back toward camp. "You have to catch the fish. So far I can't even get the line out over ten feet."

"You only tried it for the first time yesterday. It

takes a while to develop a knack for casting," Nick said, matching her stride.

"Good thing you have quick reflexes and ducked yesterday, or I could be minus a guide."

"I've been hooked before. It's painful, but I survived."

Daisy glanced warily at him. He maintained a straight face. There were still times when she wasn't sure if he was kidding or serious. Well, she had no plans to hook him, with a gigantic fishing lure or with any other kind of hook. Yesterday was a near accident, a mistake that could have been a lot worse. Today she'd be more careful.

Daisy leaned forward over the front of the canoe stretching her back muscles. They'd only been fishing half an hour, but it felt like four times that. There was no explanation why the fish liked his lure better than hers. She'd at least mastered — well, sort of mastered — getting the damn thing out in the water. It still splashed loudly enough to chase away anything with fins within a hundred yards. Nick said she might get a big Northern angry enough to attack her lure. Not likely.

Reeling in her line slowly, Daisy glanced up over at a nearby tree. It was a huge spruce that probably had been struck by lightening more than once, because half its branches were dead. But it wasn't the branches that had raised her heart into her throat.

"Is that what I think it is?" she whispered, pointing toward the tree.

Nick followed her line of sight. "Ah, good girl. We've been joined by one of nature's best fishers, the bald eagle. Now, if we catch a fish we have to be careful and stow it before Mr. Eagle wants to come and claim it."

"You're kidding. Right?"

"It's never happened to me, but I've heard such stories."

"Yeah, well, people will say most anything. Damn, he is big. Look, here he comes. He's huge!" The bird swooped low over the water, dropped suddenly, and then with a powerful lurch rose from the water with a large fish clasped firmly between its claws.

"Shouldn't have to worry about protecting our catch for a while," Nick said dryly. He paused. "Spotting that eagle means you've been blessed."

Daisy recast her silver spinner. "So now what kind of story are you telling me?"

"I'm serious," Nick said, using a paddle to reset the canoe into the dying wind. "According to many Native Americans, the eagle is the most sacred spirit found in nature. When eagle appears, it's a reminder to move beyond the shadows of former lives and be open to new illumination. Eagle teaches to love the shadow and the light. If you can do that, then you will fly freely like the eagle."

"That sounds like a lot of bunk..." Daisy's rod bent; line raced out of the reel, making a shrill hum. "Holy shit!"

"Set the hook!" Nick quickly reeled in his line

and grabbed the net. "Pull back on the rod sharply. Okay, now you can let him run a bit."

"Let him. You got to be kidding," Daisy said, through clenched teeth. "He's doing whatever the hell he wants to do. Damn, my arms are tired already."

"Relax. He'll tire. Go with him. But be prepared to take up any slack line in case he decides to make a run toward the boat. Here he comes. Reel!"

"Shit," Daisy muttered, cranking the reel handle as fast as she could. Nick turned the canoe, or her fish would have gotten clean away. That fish had to be tiring; when he hit the end of her line, she was able to hold him and turn him. Maybe by instinct, maybe remembering something Nick had said, she began to guide the fish back and forth from right to left.

He surfaced some twenty feet from the boat. Daisy gasped. He was big. Bigger than anything she'd seen Nick catch. She wanted to land this fish more than anything else at the moment. The fish jumped and then dove. Daisy let him take more line. She sensed the fish weakening; the battle was won. By the time she reeled the Northern up to the canoe, she was as exhausted as the fish.

"You've got a monster, girl. Nice fish." Nick's voice was laced with pride. Leaning over carefully, he placed a gaff hook through the fish's gill and lifted him into the canoe. He reached for a paddle. "We're heading for shore before this guy gets new life. We have supper and breakfast, at least."

"Now that I have some understanding of what I'm supposed to do, we're quitting?" Daisy protested.

"There'll be other opportunities. We don't have a choice—if I put this guy over the side, he's going to drag us across the lake. If you're too worn out to paddle, that's okay."

"Oh." Daisy put her rod aside and reached for the paddle. "That was thrilling. I never had a clue what it would be like to catch a fish. Even watching you didn't prepare me."

"Sometimes you just have to have the experience." Nick steered the canoe toward shore. "And the next time it will be easier. But be prepared. We don't always land them. This guy could have gotten away several times, but you did what was needed to keep him on without breaking the line."

Daisy stepped onto the shore. She plopped down on the bank before her legs gave out. Landing that fish had left her depleted. She let Nick pull the canoe out of the water.

"Well done, partner," he said, grinning. He hefted the Northern and grabbed the waterproof camera he always had handy when canoeing. "Here, you hold the fish and I'll record this moment for posterity. Cassie won't believe it otherwise."

Daisy smiled broadly with her hand held high to keep the fish's tail from hitting the ground. "His teeth sure look sharp."

"Razor sharp." Nick snapped a picture. "A

couple more. Like I said before, don't go putting your fingers anywhere near a Northern's mouth. That's why we have the long-nosed hook remover."

Tucking the camera back in a waterproof gear bag, Nick turned and asked. "So are you ready to clean your catch?"

"No way!" Daisy held the fish out arms length.

Nick laughed. "All right. I'll clean it. Why don't you gather some wood for a cooking fire? I'm so hungry I can almost smell the fish frying."

"Okay." Daisy's stomach rumbled, but she wasn't sure it was from hunger. She'd never eaten a fish she'd actually caught. That seemed so personal. They'd developed a relationship in the fight. She'd felt the full flush of victory when Nick hauled the fish over the side of the canoe. Where had that triumphant feeling gone?

- o -

"So are you glad you came along?" Nick asked. It was their last night on the water.

Nick warmed at the sight of Daisy's soft smile. "Yeah," she admitted, "you were right. This was great. Just to know that a place like this exists is a treasure."

As she stared into the fire, Nick saw a wistfulness etch her frame as if she were trying to hold onto something, but knew she couldn't. Without looking at him, she asked, "So how was it for you? You found out everything you needed to know about the prototype?"

"That I did. But that was secondary. Having you with me is what made this trip exceptional. Watching you embrace the unknown. The eagle. The loon. The flicker. Fishing. Sleeping in a tent. Paddling. The stars.

"You're a very expressive person, Daisy. You breathe new life into old things for me. How many eagles have I seen? Watching you totally amazed with your first fish. How many fish have I caught? Yet, your first will be one of my most memorable fish stories. You bring freshness to the wilderness. Maybe it's those first encounters that are the most pristine and the most lasting." Nick hunched over before the fire. "Maybe I'm just showing my age."

Continuing to concentrate on the flames of the fire, Daisy said softly, "By the way, you should know that you're now making love to a twenty-one year old."

Nick turned his head sharply. "What?"

Daisy chuckled. "Today's my birthday. I told you it was soon."

"Why didn't you tell me earlier?" He couldn't believe she hadn't let him know about such an important day. "We would have done something to mark it."

Daisy reached over and squeezed his thigh. "Nothing you could have done would be better than this past week. Being out here. Just having this time alone with you. No cell phones. No responsibilities. It's been beyond my wildest dreams. I thought you'd be happy that I turned twenty-one."

He heard the sexy pout in her tone. "I am pleased. It's just...I should have done more."

"Nonsense." Giggling, Daisy said, "So now I'm half your age."

"That makes me feel a hell of a lot better!" Nick shook his head, picked up a stick and leaned over to rearrange the burning logs.

"Funny how it works." Daisy leaned back on her hands. "I've been thinking. A person twenty-one is half the age of a person forty-two. But when the forty-two year old is sixty-two, the twenty-one year old will be forty-one, approximately two-thirds the age of the older person. So you see, I'm catching up with you."

Nick scowled and then laughed from his belly. "Only a college student could come up with that one. But I'm glad you're thinking ahead."

It was Daisy's turn to frown and withdraw. "It was purely hypothetical. I know how sensitive you are about our age difference."

"Now, now, I didn't want to send you into a tailspin. It's your birthday. So tell me, what's your favorite birthday memory?"

Daisy stiffened.

"Shit," Nick cursed. "That must have been a bad question. I'm sorry. Can we start over? So it's your birthday. That's great."

"Don't," Daisy whispered. "It's okay. Cassie always did something. My grandmother made sure we had a cake." Daisy paused. Her shoulders sagged. "When I was real young—four, I think—I remember my mother making a cake. We had party hats. The three of us and a man; I don't recall who he was. He was just there, I think. Anyway, that's the year I got a doll with a frilly dress. The year my mom died she forgot my birthday. She was already pretty far gone, I guess."

"I'm sorry."

"It's okay. I survived. But to answer your question, my favorite birthday memories are two: getting the doll, and being here with you watching this fire."

Nick's heart suddenly expanded. Could a man choke to death on love? He kissed Daisy on the cheek. She turned and pressed her lips against his. It was a soft yet powerful kiss. There was no urgency in the embrace; it was fresh, assured, and filled with promise.

She wasn't going to like what he had to say, yet he had to say it. She was too extraordinary to let slip through his fingers. He cleared his throat. "I know you don't want to think about a real future between us."

Her body shuddered against him, but she didn't raise her head from his shoulder. "I can't," she muttered.

"I know. And I'm not pressing you. I just want to be clear on one thing right now. We've kidded each other about you being the student and me the sex education teacher." He chuckled softly. "Thankfully, there have been numerous occasions when those roles were reversed."

She smothered a laugh. At least he had her attention. "You seem to have come around to the idea that we're lovers."

Her head moved hesitantly on his shoulder. She was so still he feared she might break. "All I want is for us to be clear that we're in a committed relationship."

Again he felt her muscles go rigid. "I'm not talking about living together or anything else. Just that there are no other partners." She softened; he was on target.

"And that if either one of us desires to move on, we have the good graces to inform the other and break it off with as much dignity as we can muster." He paused.

There was silence.

"Well, what do you say about that?"

"Fine with me." Daisy shrugged. "It's not like I have a bunch of guys knocking down my door. You're the only man I've ever slept with." She grew silent.

Nick could hear gears turning in Daisy's brain while she sorted out the implications of what he'd said. "Have there been other women...since that night in Shakopee?" she whispered.

Nick's response was quick and firm. "Absolutely not. You are actually the first woman I took to bed in three years. There never seemed to be much of a point. Oh, I was fairly active for a while after the divorce. Proving myself, I guess. But then I sort of lost interest. Until you came along."

181

"If I remember correctly, I had to almost beg you to make love to me that first time. It was quite embarrassing at first." Daisy leaned back and looked at Nick.

He was afraid he'd lose himself in those smoky orbs.

"So would you have hit on me, if I hadn't come to you first?"

Glancing at the fire, Nick shook his head. "I don't really know. God, I wanted to. I wanted you from the moment I saw you bent over working on Blaze. Have I ever told you you have the cutest, tightest ass I've ever seen or held?"

Daisy placed a finger across her lower lip and gave him a pensive look. "Yes, I believe you have, several times. How about if you'd known my age?"

Nick recoiled. "No way."

"Yet here we are."

A hint of triumph colored her words. She was beginning to drive him nuts. If he even hinted at a long term future, she'd withdraw. Yet, their relationship was much more than frantic coupling, even for her.

"Can you tell me what kind of wood we're burning?" Nick asked.

"I think it's a combination of willow, ash, and birch. It's what I could find that was down."

"You know I've never told you my nickname for you is Willow."

"No you haven't," she said, turning to stare softly at him.

"It's not just your delightful willowy frame. It's also your gray eyes. They remind me of willow smoke, particularly when you pout or when you're all sultry and ready to climax."

A small smile separated her lips. Her overbite became a little more distinctive. And her eyes were definitely shimmering like willow smoke. "I like that," she murmured. "It makes me feel even more a part of this wilderness. That was a nice gift, Nick."

"Willow is used in making sweat lodges in part because a willow branch will bend and yet maintain its strength. It's very difficult to break a willow branch."

"Interesting."

"And a lot of carvers will seek out the diamond willow to fashion walking sticks, not only because of its strength, but also because as they carve the outer layers of bark away, natural colorful diamond shapes emerge in the grain of the wood."

"I'd like to see that."

"We'll pick up some before we get out of northern Minnesota. The marshes up here are overrun with diamond willow."

"Diamond shape." Daisy tilted her head away from him and then gave him one of her more provocative looks. "Isn't that like the shape of a canoe and..."

"You do have an erotic mind, Willow. And I like that a lot. Why don't we put this fire out and turn in for the night?"

"So you can explore another diamond shape?"

Daisy teased.

"Exactly. Would you like that?"

"Immensely."

They both remained silent and turned their heads, listening. The low, rolling melodic sounds came from a distance across the water and then a response from nearby. The eerie conversation intensified, and then quieted.

"The loons are even more mournful tonight," Daisy said in a hushed tone. "They must know it's our last night here."

"Maybe. Soon they'll be leaving to head south for the winter. Maybe they're making sure their mate isn't left behind." Nick stood and began to put out the fire and then changed his mind. "Would you like to sleep out here tonight? With the frost we had a couple nights ago, the mosquitoes are gone. If it gets too cold, we can always go into the tent."

"Great!" Daisy rose and headed toward the tent. "I'll get the sleeping bags. It'll be fantastic having the stars as our blanket."

- o -

Had she ever been more satisfied? Daisy snuggled next to Nick. His arm draped across her breasts and their hips pressed together while he snored softly. Their tender lovemaking still warmed her. Drowsy and sated, she could not sleep. The stars seemed so close she should be able to reach out and touch them.

Why did they have to go back? Daisy closed her eyes briefly. Of course they had to go back.

A smile crept across her face. Wasn't there a children's story about wishing upon a star? She opened her eyes. There were countless stars. What if she wished Reggie was sent away to prison for a very long time? He deserved it. Wouldn't Maxine be better off without him? But wasn't that a mean wish? *Why can't they just leave me alone?* She closed her eyes, willing sleep to take away her dread.

You'll be okay, girl. You're the only one who can help you. Keep your wits about you and trust no one. The words of her grandmother came to her like the call of the loon out of the darkness of the night. *Yes, Grandma,* she screamed silently. *I know.* Aloneness spread through her muscle fibers like a cancer. "Never turn your back on blood." Daisy began to tremble and then she was shaking.

Nick pulled her closer. "Are you cold?" he asked, half awake.

"No," Daisy mumbled. "It was a bad dream."

"Oh."

His regular inhaling and exhaling let her know that he was asleep again. She compressed her lips and then let out a big breath preparing to do battle with wakefulness.

She opened her eyes. She squinted. Her eyes widened. "Oh my God," she exclaimed, poking Nick.

"What the..." He rose to a sitting position.

"Look. Look at the sky!" Daisy was standing now—even naked, she wasn't chilled. "It's

185

spectacular. I've only ever read about it. The dance of the lights. There aren't enough words to describe what's going on inside me."

"I know." Nick stepped up behind her, encircling her in his arms.

The warmth of his body covered her backside like a blanket. It felt right. She felt whole. No matter what happened tomorrow or the next day, in this moment standing under the Northern Lights, she was whole.

"They seem to have a life of their own, pulsating first one direction and then another." She arched her neck. "Some of them are directly overhead. God, it's like they are enfolding us. I wonder if anyone else is noticing."

"Probably. Although not too many people are likely out at one o'clock in the morning."

They stood and watched for minutes. "Look at that red panel of light. It's coming out of the lake. There's another. Green. White. Red. What's happening, Nick?"

Nick chuckled softly in her ear. "It's an illusion. All the sheets of light are still coming from the sky—from the sun, actually. But it sure does look like they're bouncing off the water."

"There's something very primal about this."

"We could come back hundreds of times and not see a light show like this. I think you're looking at nature's birthday candles just for you." He nibbled on her ear.

His arousal pressed against her bare bottom. She wiggled, encouraging him. His lips brushed her shoulder; his hands cupped her breasts. Already, she felt her breathing shorten. His teeth nipped at her shoulder. She gasped.

With him at her back, she felt helpless to participate. She reached around to squeeze his butt. He bit her shoulder harder. She moaned. He rolled a nipple between thumb and finger. She gave in to self-pleasure and stroked the unattended nipple.

"I like it when you help," he whispered, hoarsely. "There's something primal about that, too."

His words acted like a whip. Through half-closed eyes she watched sheets of red and green dance across the lake while her fingers roamed across her belly to her mound of curls. She was soaking. His hand joined hers. Two fingers entered her heat — one hers, one his.

It was too much. It was just right. "Now!" she screamed, jerking against him. "Now." She stilled. He held her as she crumpled to her knees.

Then she positioned herself on hands and knees and rotated her rear in invitation. "I'm ready, are you?"

An inarticulate grunt was his response. He entered her with a single swift push. He paused, catching his breath. She squeezed down. He yelped and began to move. She smiled, keeping her eyes open. She wasn't going to miss the lights playing upon the water.

He leaned over, pushed her hair aside and ran his tongue across the base of her neck. Daisy threw her head back, encouraging him. A coiling sensation began tightening within her loins. "Deeper," she groaned.

"You want deeper," he muttered, rising to his feet.

"Ah." Her entire body smiled. It was the coupling of wild horses. He slammed into her with a fierceness she'd not experienced. She greeted each thrust by arching her back, taking as much as she could and demanding more. She wanted to swallow him up. She wanted to possess him. She never wanted to let him go.

It couldn't go on forever. He let out ragged breaths; his thighs quivered against her rear. He pulled back and forged ahead again and her world exploded into reds, greens, and whites. No longer were they watching the lights. They *were* the lights.

In some small corner of her mind, she was aware that Nick was cradling her as they both collapsed to the sleeping bags. She forced her eyes open. The lights were gone. They had disappeared as quickly as they had come. She couldn't be sad about their leaving, for she had been royally blessed by their presence.

She listened quietly to Nick struggling for breath. At last he spoke, "Now *that* was primal. Are you okay? I didn't hurt you, did I?"

"I couldn't be better. Yes, that was memorable. There will never be another birthday like this one. You can stay right where you are if you want, but I think I'm going to sleep now."

Chapter Nine

"It's a pretty little town," Daisy remarked, peering out at the main street and stores with old-time storefront facades.

Nick nodded. "Virginia's done a lot to maintain its small town charm. It's a mining town, actually. Lumber and taconite have been its lifeblood. Taconite still is. This whole area is deservedly known as the Iron Range. According to old timers, the Range supplied most of the iron ore needed to support the World War II effort. Lot of Finns and Swedes live up here: hardworking, nose-to-the-grindstone kind of folk."

"And why are we stopping here?"

"I want to say hi to an old friend. Missed him on my last trip through."

Daisy grinned. It seemed Nick had an old friend just about everywhere they'd been. They'd stopped at an Ely outfitter before entering the Boundary Waters so Nick could do some backslapping and find out what kinds of bait and lures the fish were hitting.

Coming back from Ely on their way to Virginia, not far before the divide that Nick informed her was the point where waters ran north instead of south, he'd pulled off the main road onto a narrow dusty lane and stopped at a small farmhouse seemingly in the middle of nowhere. An older woman had come out and greeted Nick like he was a long lost relative. Turned out he was. She was an older cousin, and was not only happy to see Nick and his friend but was more than willing to have Nick collect diamond willow branches from her marsh.

After sharing a glass of lemonade, they were on their way again until he turned into the small town of Virginia. At this rate, they might not make it back to Chicago until Christmas. Idly, Daisy pressed her nose against the SUV window, trying to imagine what Christmas was like up here in the north country. It must be pretty, with lots of white snow. She'd always enjoyed the first snow of the season, but far too quickly the white flakes turned into blackened mounds that she had to climb over or avoid one way or another.

Nick angled into a parking spot. "We're here. Come on."

She followed close behind until Nick stopped in front of Witala's Jewelry Store. "You have a friend who works here?"

"Frank owns the place. We go back a long way." Nick grabbed Daisy's hand. She allowed herself to be pulled through the entryway.

"Well, look what the wind blew up from the south," said a tall, thin, balding man standing behind a counter of jewelry displays. He was beaming, obviously pleased to welcome Nick.

The two men shook hands and slapped shoulders. This was a man ritual with which Daisy

190

was becoming quite familiar.

"Frank, want you to meet my companion, Daisy."

Daisy shook the extended hand and made the appropriate grunts, wondering what companion was supposed to convey. Sounded like more than a friend. But not too much more. She could live with that. After last night, Nick could call her most anything and she'd follow.

She tried to plug herself back into the conversation. The men had gone through the weather and sports. She figured it was about time to leave.

"So what do you have in necklaces, Frank?"

Daisy scowled.

"I can't match your taste or your billfold, Nick."

"I'm not looking to impress. I just want to see if you have something that can be a memento of our trip."

"I don't need another memento," Daisy protested. "I have all kinds of memories. And you took loads of pictures."

"How about something with an opal?"

Frank smiled at Daisy. "The man can be stubborn."

"I've noticed."

Frank turned and walked with a noticeable limp ten feet away and pulled out a thin oblong box which had not been on display. He brought it back to where they stood and carefully lifted the lid. Five pendants were richly displayed against a black background with fine gold chains tucked underneath.

"Now you're talking," Nick declared. "Looks like three opals."

Daisy glared. She wouldn't know an opal if it reached up and bit her. They all looked stunning.

Nick plucked one from the box and held it up so the light played off the jewel. Daisy gasped. The pendant had come to life. Little specks of red, blue, and green danced across a white background, vividly reminding her of the way the lights had danced the night before and then of their lovemaking. She knew color was racing from her ankles to her hair roots, but it didn't matter. Nick was right. The opal was a perfect memento of so very much.

She didn't flinch when he smiled and placed the chain around her neck and fastened the clasp. She tried not to tear up, but she did smile broadly and hugged Nick tightly. Was she behaving like a little girl? If so, so be it. This was a gift she would treasure forever.

After Frank ran Nick's credit card and took care of the business transaction, Nick and Daisy prepared to leave.

Frank winked at Daisy. "You've got quite a man there, young lady. Take good care of him. In my book, he deserves it. I wouldn't be alive if it weren't for him and Tom Harrison."

"Can it, Frank," Nick growled. "We've got to get going. Catch you next time, through."

"Will do, but I would have bled to death that night if you guys hadn't stayed back to help."

Frank turned a warm smile on Daisy. "Hope to see you again, young lady."

"So what was that about?" Daisy asked, struggling to keep pace with Nick heading for the car.

"It's a long story."

"I've got the time."

"I don't. It happened long ago. In a faraway place. I don't care to go back there. Okay?"

Daisy registered the pain in his eyes and nodded. "Sure. That's okay." It was okay, but her curiosity was running on overdrive. Maybe Thelma would fill her in, or even Tom. She didn't have to be too bright to assume that it had something to do with their time together in the army. And that her man had been courageous in the face of danger.

- o -

They drove until dark and stayed overnight at a motel in central Wisconsin. The next morning they had breakfast in the adjacent café. Nick peeked over the rim of his coffee cup at Daisy nibbling on scrambled eggs. She was typically so buoyant and robust in the morning, making him feel like he'd already lost a step or two. But this morning she behaved differently.

There was a melancholy quality about her that he'd seldom witnessed before. Her eyelids drooped; her posture slumped, as if she had the weight of the world on her shoulders. He smiled to himself. The clincher was that Daisy usually ate her breakfast like she'd been starved for a week, but this morning she played with it.

"So what's up?" he asked. "You out of sorts?"

Daisy raised her eyes from her plate to meet his. The sadness in them tore at his heart. She shook her head in response.

"Worried about your horses?"

"It's not that." Daisy swallowed and looked back down at her eggs and bacon. "I guess I've never had a mountain top experience before."

Nick frowned.

"I've heard others talk about going away on retreats or vacations and having such spectacular times that they had a hard time going back. I'd always thought that was so much bunk. But now I know they weren't lying."

"But life goes on."

"Yes, but not like that night under the Northern Lights."

"No. That was a peak moment. But there will be other peak times. Maybe at the track. Maybe at your place or mine. Maybe back in northern Minnesota. Try as hard as we might, we can't hold on to the moment. We can only remember it and look forward to the next one."

He watched her smoky eyes liquefy. "Damn, I sound like some old wise sage."

Daisy chuckled. "You've probably had many peak experiences. Sometimes I feel like such a novice at life."

"You're doing great." Nick reached across the

small round table and stroked the back of her hand. "You have a lot of wisdom, too. That's part of what makes us work—we're both open to hearing the other's wisdom."

"Sometimes you get pretty hard of hearing," Daisy quipped, a small smile forming on her lips.

Nick withdrew his hand, feigning pain. "Usually when you're not willing to dream big enough."

"I'm not used to dreaming big." Daisy lifted a coffee cup. "I normally dream about making it through the month with my bills paid, maybe about getting into the winner's circle more often, or of having enough money set aside for taxes, and," her voice faltered, "being part of a real family."

Daisy stopped talking. Nick watched her scatter pieces of egg across her plate. She'd just revealed more of herself than she had probably wanted to. Why couldn't she trust him more? After all they'd shared, she was still reticent to talk about herself, as if she were afraid of his censure.

He remembered the tattered riding pants Cassie had shown him. Daisy had conquered a lot in her short life. That should be a source of pride, not shame.

"Do you see much of your sister?" he asked. "I'm sorry, I've forgotten her name. You've only mentioned her once or twice."

Daisy flushed. "Her name is Maxine. She's my half sister; we had the same mother." She put her fork down and dabbed her mouth with a napkin.

195

"It depends. Sometimes I see her once a week, and then it might be a month until I see her again."

"So what does she do for a living?"

"She's a waitress."

"And her husband?"

Daisy frowned.

"I vaguely remember you saying she got married while you were still at the group home."

"He does odd jobs," she lowered her eyes, "and is currently laid off."

"Oh."

"Can't we talk about something else?" Daisy said, balling up her napkin. "I don't think my sister and her husband can be of much interest to you."

"No problem." Nick kept his voice even. She was withholding. What and why made him curious. But he wasn't about to press her. Cassie Travers had been less than pleased with Daisy's family, but that didn't mean Daisy didn't love them or that they weren't important to her. He'd tread lightly, but at some point he'd have to find out more about them.

He watched Daisy drift back into her own thoughts. What had his sister called her? Waif-like. Well, at the moment that was an apt description. Daisy must believe she was an unlikely Cinderella waiting for the clock to strike twelve.

But didn't she know the whole story? It was only Cinderella's foot that fit the glass slipper. And it was only Daisy who could win his heart as she already had.

It would take time. But in the end, he would win her over to his way of thinking. He expected her heart was already there or very close, but her head was an entirely different matter. He'd tread gingerly, but he'd not let up. Not now; not ever.

- o -

Daisy scowled at the offensive cold bacon. It wouldn't be cold if she'd eaten it when she should have. But Nick's probing had been so disconcerting.

Why did he have to go and spoil things? Oh, he saw a longer future for them than she did. But even what he saw remained unclear. Certainly, he couldn't be thinking marriage. And she wasn't convinced she wanted to be anybody's mistress.

They were fine just the way they were. Lovers. He had his place and she had hers. Funny, she'd never even seen his place. She'd met his family, but didn't know where he lived.

That was okay. That was his secret. Her family and her family's history was her secret. He didn't need to know, and if he ever did find out, then she wouldn't have a lover or a horse partnership. No, things were okay the way they were. In fact, what they had was far more than she'd ever expected, and probably far more than she even deserved.

Her upper lip curved slightly. Nick Underwood was her Prince Charming. He'd brought adventure to her life in ways she'd never allowed herself to dream about. They would be buying some more horses shortly. Her career as a trainer was about to take off. And she had a man in her life. Daisy felt herself warm. She had a lover and wasn't ready to let him go.

She'd have to work doubly hard to keep her two worlds separate: the exhilarating dance with Nick and the seamy side with Reggie and Maxine. She could do that, if no one pressured her more.

She peeked quickly over at Nick and then away from his inquiring eyes. Would he be satisfied with what they currently shared? She wasn't certain. Reggie and Maxine were another matter. They'd never be satisfied.

Why did she feel like a street urchin waiting for her fantasy life to go poof like so much smoke? Willow Smoke, he'd called her.

Maybe she *was* like willow smoke, waiting for the wind to change and blow her away. Tears formed in her eyes. She shook her head, refusing to let them be seen. Why couldn't she even permit herself to hope and dream?

She dreaded going back to her apartment.

"Maxine! What happened to you?" Daisy's heart palpitated wildly. She threw an arm around her sister and assisted her to the loveseat.

The shorter woman walked with a limp. After flopping down on the couch, she looked at Daisy through one squinted eye. The other eyelid was closed shut, laced with yellow, purple and black hues.

Daisy sat beside her on the edge of the loveseat. "Tell me what happened. Did he hit you?" Her fingers balled into fists.

"No," Maxine snorted. "I fell into a door."

"Bullshit, I'm not some little snot-nosed kid anymore. I know what I see. Boy, if I could get my hands on him right now, I'd throttle him."

"No. You don't understand. Reggie loves me. He doesn't want to hurt me." She lifted a hand to her face. "This isn't as bad as it looks. He was high."

"When the hell isn't he?"

"He's been having a hard time of it lately. He can't get steady work, and the cops are sniffing around again. They never leave him alone."

Daisy frowned. At least there was some hope. "Why do you stay with him?" Maxine recoiled. It was a dumb question.

"I love him." Maxine tried to smile, but even that effort appeared painful. "Maybe someday you'll understand. But you got to find somebody to love first."

"And then I'll be happy being a punching bag?" Daisy rose to her feet, distressed with her impatience. "So what happens now?"

"I'll be all right. He'll make it up to me."

Daisy didn't want to ask how he might accomplish that.

"Every couple fights now and then, Daisy. You need more experience with men to know what I'm talking about. But if there were no fights, there wouldn't be any making up."

Her sister's crooked smile turned Daisy's stomach. Was there any hope for the woman? Not as long as she was strung out on drugs; not as long as she remained under Reggie's thumb. "You could kick the habit, Maxine. I'd pay for it."

Maxine gave Daisy a horrified look, as if she were listening to an alien.

"I'd stand by you to support you."

"Right," Maxine responded bitterly. "Goody-two-shoes would hold my hand and kiss my ass while I heave up my guts and shake to death."

Her sister's features softened. "It's okay, baby. I know you care. And I love you, too." Maxine brushed a curl from her brow. "But I can't do what you want. I don't think you really know what you're asking. It's not so bad. If we could just get ahead so we wouldn't have to move again, and if the cops would leave us alone. We're not bothering anybody. Not really."

"Good grief, Maxine, Reggie sells drugs. He beats on you whenever he's in the mood. That's not bothering anybody?"

Maxine clasped her hands at her waist. "He doesn't sell to nobody who doesn't want to buy. He doesn't make anybody buy."

Daisy closed her eyes. There was no use telling her sister that some of her husband's buyers were likely kids who were just trying to be cool.

"And he beats me because he loves me. He can't help himself. You don't understand," Maxine wailed. "You don't even try."

"All right. All right, we're not getting anywhere

going down this road. We never do. So what else is happening?"

"Work is slow. With the layoff at the factory, we're getting fewer customers in the diner and smaller tips."

Daisy blew air from compressed lips. "Okay, so how much do you need?"

"What?"

"How much money, Maxine?" Daisy crossed her legs at the ankles. "How much do you want this time?"

"Could you spare three hundred?" Her voice was hoarse.

Daisy listened to her sister cough, possibly covering embarrassment. "You might save a lot of money by cutting out the cigarettes."

"I know. I try from time to time. It's hard, but you wouldn't understand that either."

"I'll have to write you a check. I can't get that much out of an ATM." Daisy rubbed her temples. When would that splitting headache let up? "When is this going to end, Maxine? How is it going to end?"

Maxine's eyes rounded. "I don't know, baby. I don't know. I wish I did." She started to sob. At first, her sobs were soft and then they began to wrack her entire body.

Daisy slipped an arm around her sister and held her tight. They both sobbed. This might be the first time in years that she and her sister had genuinely communicated.

After what seemed like minutes, Maxine

whispered, "So tell me about your man. He looked so handsome in the newspaper. But he looked pretty old."

Daisy laughed softly. "He's older, but he's a gentle man. He's..." Daisy caught herself. She wasn't about to share much information about Nick with her sister.

She might have shared a few tears with her on the couch, but that didn't mean she could trust Maxine not to blab everything to Reggie. "He's a nice man for the time being, but I don't expect it to last much longer."

"I'm not surprised," Maxine replied, placing a comforting hand on Daisy's. "He doesn't look like he'd have much in common with us."

Stiffening, Daisy tried to calm her irritation. "We have horses in common, that's enough."

"Yes, I suppose. I still don't know how you're able to work with those beasts, but that's not news." Maxine hesitated. "Well, if you'll write that check, I'd best be going. Reggie gets antsy if I'm gone too long."

"What would it ever take for you to call the cops on him?"

Maxine moved gingerly to stand and laughed. "You got to be kidding, baby. You don't turn on the man you love. Not for nothin'."

Daisy wrote the check at her makeshift dining room desk. She clinched her upper body to slow the shivering. How would Nick ever understand this world? She'd been raised in it and still couldn't fathom how her mother had accepted her lot in life, or how her sister was managing hers.

She stared at the check. Their grandmother had been so emphatic about blood being thicker than water, but did that mean Daisy had to allow her sister and brother-in-law to suck her dry?

- o -

Tom Harrison clapped his hands. "So you got her working with wood? That's good." He admired the diamond willow stick Daisy was carving.

She sat on a straight-back chair in the mold room with the willow stick in her hands. She'd already peeled half its bark and was digging at the grooves of a troublesome knot. Several shades of reddish brown were already evident.

Daisy smiled at the tall black man. "I think your job is safe. This is a lot of painstaking work."

"It takes getting used to. But I can tell you have a good ear for wood."

She looked up, inquiring.

"You don't hack at the wood. You're letting the wood guide you. How far or how deep to peel or dig. Which grain to highlight and which to let be. It's all in the manner of listening. Some people have a good ear for music. Some have a good ear for animals. Some have a good ear for wood."

"Daisy's got a good ear for horses, that's for sure," Nick interjected, stepping over from where he'd been examining work on the frame for a new canoe. "And you may be right. It looks like she

203

can listen to wood pretty good, too."

"So how do you like mosquitoes, Daisy? Do you understand why they're Minnesota's state bird?"

"I could do without another mosquito for a few weeks," Daisy said, idly rubbing old bites on her arm. "Though sometimes I think the worst part about them is the bug spray."

"What you gonna do with the stick when you're done with it?" Tom asked, rubbing a finger over a carved section. "This will sand out real nice. Some folks don't want to sand—they think it looks better rough. I'm partial to sanding. How about you?"

A smile tugged at Daisy's lips. "I'll try sanding this one and then I'll have something to compare a rough-carved one to. I sure do like how your sanded canoe strips turn out. The one we took to the Boundary Waters was even more beautiful in the water than sitting here. The first time I sat in it I felt the kind of awe I feel when I sit in a church pew. Not that I've sat in one of those often."

"Maybe that's why it's still awe inspiring. You didn't say what you plan on doing with it?" Tom pointed. "The stick."

Daisy shrugged. "Probably put it in the corner of my living room for decoration. Don't think I need a walking stick yet."

Tom sneaked a peek at Nick.

"Don't even think about going there," Nick growled.

Chapter Ten

"How's MrShowman coming along? Haven't had time to get out to the track this week to see him."

"I know." Daisy curled her toes in the Lake Michigan beach sand where she and Nick had shared their picnic lunch. Their recent claiming horse had looked quite good in his early morning workouts.

She didn't plan to tell Nick she'd appreciated the breather his business trip had provided. While she liked Nick a lot, she valued her space and her privacy.

Sometimes he could be too overpowering and, well, just too present. "MrShowman is training quite nicely. We'll try him in a Starter's Allowance or an Optional Claimer in the next week or two. Preferably on the grass."

"At a route, right?"

"That's the plan." Daisy sucked in a deep breath of cool air. "I like it here by the lake," she said, staring off across the expansive body of water. The sand dune point on which they sat was protected from the westerly breeze. Remnants of their lunch still lay scattered on the blanket. A few late hanging-on ants were having a feast.

"Clint called last night. About Keeneland."

Daisy leaned back on her hands and looked up at Nick sitting cross-legged beside her; his attention seemed concentrated on a speck out on the horizon, but she wasn't fooled. His sensors were monitoring her reactions very closely. "So are you going to the sale?" she asked.

"We all are. Cassie, Clint, you, me."

Sitting up straight, Daisy busied herself scraping sand from between her toes. "What do you mean? Sam needs me here. I can't keep taking time off and traipsing across the country after you."

"You'll be earning your pay. Sam wants you to help represent his interests. He'll pick up ten percent of whatever I buy, and you'll get twenty."

Daisy jerked to her knees and yelled, "Why do you keep doing this to me?" She dropped her voice. "Making decisions on my behalf. Giving me parts of horses that are far too expensive for me. How do you know I want all that responsibility? That I'd even want to go to Keeneland? That can be a snooty crowd, from what I hear."

"Actually, the fall sale is more like a fair atmosphere, not nearly like the dress up ball of the spring and summer sales. At least that's what Cassie said. She seems to think it would do you good to see firsthand the next level of the business."

"Am I being ganged up on? Why does everyone think they know what is good for me?"

"No one wants you to do anything you don't want to do." Nick sighed and picked up a handful of sand and sifted it through his fingers. "If you don't want to go, you don't have to. I thought you'd enjoy being away and spending time with me and Clint and Cassie."

Daisy flopped back down on the blanket and squeezed her eyes shut. "It's not that I don't want to go. I just wish someone had asked me before deciding I would of course tag along."

"I'm sorry." Nick ran his fingers along her bare leg. "Sometimes I presume too much and act too quickly. You're right, I should have asked first."

She groaned at his downcast look of contrition. Would he ever learn to treat her as an equal? She couldn't escape, however, the pure adoration on his face, nor the vibrations caused by his fingers moving lazily along her thigh.

"So, will you consent to come with me to Keeneland, young lady? I'm afraid it would be quite boring without you. And I might wind up buying a three-legged horse."

Was she becoming addicted to his mesmerizing ways? She laced her fingers through his and drew them upward, resetting them where she desired them most. Could he feel her heat through the fabric of her shorts? "I think Cassie and Clint would make sure the horse had four good legs." She wiggled her fingers and in doing so also his; a soft moan emitted from her pursed lips. "But I would miss you. And I wouldn't want you casting about for my replacement. How long will we be gone?"

"No need to worry about replacements. I'll

wear out before you do." He cocked his head.

She knew he was trying to read her response, but she was keeping it closely guarded.

"Probably three days," he added." He squeezed her fingers. "I'm glad you decided to come."

"Oh, I expect to do that frequently. You may be limp by the time we get back."

"I hope that'll be only a temporary condition."

"It better be." Daisy lifted his hand and placed it on the blanket. "Maybe we should tidy up here before we do something in public that will embarrass both of us."

After disposing of their garbage and stuffing the thin blanket and leftovers in backpacks, Nick and Daisy mounted the bike, with Nick in front and Daisy behind. Riding along the lake front, Daisy appreciated the opportunity to stretch her legs. She'd been shocked when he'd arrived at her place with a two person bicycle.

Sometimes she thought the man was merely eccentric, and other times simply nuts. This was one of the latter times.

She matched her pace to his and they moved quite smoothly along the bike path, as if they had done this many times before. Nick glanced over his shoulder and gave her a wicked smile. "How's it going back there?"

"Quite peaceful," she responded, ignoring his innuendo. "Do we have a destination?"

"Only when we get there."

Daisy nodded. Why did that not surprise?

Nick wiggled the front wheel back and forth as

he announced, "It's the process that counts. If the process is good, we'll get to where we're going."

Daisy shook her head. And there were moments when she thought she was hanging out with a burned out druggie. That wasn't the case. Nick Underwood didn't require any artificial substance to give him a high. He seemed to have them quite naturally and quite often.

"Daisy, Daisy, give me your answer, Do!" He sang off key at the top of his lungs, "I'm half crazy, all for the love of you."

She poked his ribs hard. He continued bellowing like a lovesick bull. Giving up, she closed her eyes and hoped no curious onlookers would recognize her.

His words washed over her with more meaning than perhaps intended. No man had ever sung to her, even in jest. Only her mother sang to her when she was very young.

There was comfort in his words, in his presence. Daisy took a deep breath and tried to relax. That his singing to her was comforting was good; maybe it would balance all that was scary about having him around too much. A girl — even she — could get used to this pampering.

Nick was a very serious businessman, but it was his capacity for play that amused Daisy and endeared him to her. He had wormed his way into her life in a big way. It was becoming more difficult to imagine her life without him.

While he could make her laugh, he could also touch a part of her that she thought she'd walled off from exploration by any outsider. Nick Underwood was dangerous for Daisy Matthews. Daisy gripped the handle bars tight. She had to commit that mantra to memory and repeat it like a rosary.

It would be painful enough when they had to say good-bye. She could not allow herself to care about him too much.

"How about an ice cream cone?" Nick hollered, leaving off his singing and interrupting her thoughts.

"Sure," she replied, grateful for the suggestion and the fact that he did not renew his interest in serenading her.

Within minutes, they were both devouring vanilla cones. Nick tried desperately to catch a glob of ice cream before it slid off his cone onto his hand. She giggled and handed him a napkin.

"Saved again," he said. "You have a habit of doing that, you know."

Daisy shrugged and ran her tongue along the lip of her cone, trying to stay ahead of her own meltdown.

"You're becoming quite habit forming," he added.

Her eyes bugged wide at his strained nonchalance. Again, she held her tongue by busying herself with the cone.

"I've had worse habits," Nick quipped.

"Oh?" Daisy raised her chin briefly hoping that his line of thinking might redirect the conversation from them to prior bad habits.

"We don't want to go there." Nick scowled. "Don't you ever eat ice cream?"

"Huh?"

"My cone is nearly history, and there you are still running your tongue over that cone like it's the last one you'll ever have."

"Maybe I like savoring things more than you do," she said, exaggerating her pout. "Besides, I'd think you'd appreciate that I'm using this opportunity to practice."

She lopped off the top of the cone and gulped it down while Nick's eyes darkened with banked passion. She loved rattling him. How had her mantra so quickly vanished? Oh well, she couldn't recite a mantra with her mouth full anyway.

Nick pulled his eyes away from her and looked toward the lake. He turned back to her. "I didn't realize eating an ice cream cone could be so erotic." His voice was strained. "If you could hurry a little, it might help. Or do you enjoy torturing me?"

"A little," she admitted, "but torture is not my thing."

"Good. Although at the moment, taking you over my knee seems like an appropriate option."

Daisy popped the last bit of cone into her mouth and munched as slowly as she could before saying, "We've got a lot of work to do to prepare for Keeneland. I know Clint will be well prepared, but we need to do our own homework."

"You have the catalog at your place?"

"Sure."

"Maybe we can begin this afternoon."

"Why not?"

"Oops, I almost forgot Angie is coming into town. Told her I'd meet her at the airport. You want to come along?"

"Nope. I'll catch up on schoolwork. If I don't make more progress soon I'll have to drop the class. You do take up a lot of my time, you know."

"Is that a complaint?"

Daisy shook her head, her blond hair billowing about her neck. "Not really. Tell Angie I'm looking forward to seeing her for lunch tomorrow."

Nick lifted the bike half up and paused. "You knew she was coming? You already have made time for her? Without me?"

"Yes. Yes. Yes." Daisy straightened the bike and swung a leg over it. "We don't need a chaperone. I like your sister a lot. We've talked on the phone several times since our first visit. Besides, if you were there, we couldn't talk about you."

Nick frowned and mounted the bike. He began to pedal rapidly. He seemed so intent on being a part of her life, yet there were occasions when he seemed hesitant about her being part of his.

Daisy sat across from Angie Underwood at the South Side Bistro near the university campus. Angie's eyes still bugged as large as Daisy had remembered. The woman appeared to be in a constant state of amazement.

"I think," Angie said, pointing her fork with a tomato slice, "my big brother is infatuated with

212

you. It's hard to get him to talk about anything but you. If not you, then horses, which is a poor substitute for you. You seem to have quite a way with men. I'm envious."

"Don't be." Daisy glanced away from the other woman's intensity. "I haven't been around many to compare."

"Ah, the shy Daisy," Angie cooed. "I remember now. It's just that you look so good and Nick is so consumed with you that I forget you're not a femme fatale."

Daisy's mouth fell open. "Me? Hardly. Isn't that a little dramatic?" She reached for a french fry. Or was she a temptress? Was she just playing with Nick like a kid played dress up games? They had no long range future. Infatuated. Consumed.

Those were different sentiments than love. He cared for her like she did for him. But they were safe. There was the age thing. The horse partnership. When would it end? *How* would it end?

"Yoo hoo! I'm still here."

Daisy blinked. Angie came back into focus. "Oh, I'm sorry, Angie. I guess my mind wandered a bit."

"Uh, huh. I like you a lot, Daisy." Angie paused and wiped her full lips with a napkin. "You're good for Nick, but I worry."

"Don't worry about me. I'm a big girl."

Angie shook her head. "Oh, when we first met, I worried about you, but now I worry more about my brother."

Daisy's brow furrowed and her eyes narrowed.

"Anything else that I can get you ladies?"

Daisy acknowledged the waiter. "No," she stammered. "I'm fine. You, Angie?"

"I'm okay."

Angie waited until the man stopped at the next table and reached for his order pad before continuing. "I don't think you'd deliberately harm Nick. But he's much more serious about this relationship that you seem to be."

"Serious?"

"Come on. A girl knows when a guy is serious. I should talk. Well, at least a girl knows when a guy isn't serious."

Daisy blinked. Her brain might fry before it caught up with Angie. "I still don't know what you mean."

"Okay. I'll spell it out." Angie took a deep breath and let it out slowly. "I believe my brother is within an eyelash of asking you to marry him, and he has no clue that you will turn him down."

Gasping, Daisy clamped a hand over her mouth. She couldn't stop her heart from racing or her ears from hearing. She closed her eyes. It couldn't be. Not yet. He wouldn't force the issue yet. They hadn't had enough time together. She wasn't ready to lose him—not yet. There was no escaping Angie. She sat three feet away waiting for some kind of response. She'd have to tough it out.

"I think you're wrong." She hoped she was right. "Nick knows we're from two different worlds. He's infatuated with being the prince to a Cinderella. But in his heart, he knows the slipper doesn't fit."

"You're full of shit, if you believe that." Angie's voice turned accusing. "And another thing. My brother won't be easily dumped."

"But it wouldn't work. Not marriage. He doesn't know who I am." Daisy squeezed back tears. "I don't want him to ever know."

Angie leaned back in her chair and brushed unruly curls from her forehead. "So you've got a skeleton or two in your closet. Who doesn't?"

"Some of my skeletons are very much alive, and if they knew about Nick being at all serious about me, they'd do everything in their power to drain him of his money. These aren't society types, Angie. They're scumbags. But they're family. The only family I've got."

"So you're trying to protect Nick while you explore this relationship?"

"Sort of." Daisy nodded. "I guess so."

"I'd bet he'd feel more protected if you leveled with him."

"I can't. He'd never understand my sister and her husband. And they'd have him for breakfast."

"Somehow I think you're underestimating Nick—and yourself, for that matter."

"I'm not. I'm quite sure Reggie, my brother-in-law, has mob connections."

"Oh." Angie's shoulders slumped. "I think I'll go back to worrying about both of you."

215

"This is a pretty heady game," Nick announced, hoisting his Margarita in salute. Clint, Cassie and Daisy responded in kind. The dim lighting of the bar at the top of the Manfried Hotel did nothing to conceal Nick's glee.

"You mean it's not every day you plunk down three hundred thousand for a hope and a dream?" Cassie's eyes were sparkling.

"Damn right. And I didn't know if that fat guy in the rumpled suit was going to give up or press the bid. Don't know if I could have stopped at our three hundred fifty thousand dollar limit."

Clint nodded knowingly. "Sometimes we get caught up in the bidding war and wind up paying more than a yearling or a two-year-old is worth. You see that happen in the sales pavilion every day. I'd say you have a pretty good stomach for this sort of thing."

"Yeah, I think this is more my niche than the claiming game. Here, everything happens in front of you. Daisy has more patience for claiming horses than I do. What do you think, Daisy? Is this my niche?"

"As long as you have enough money to throw around and lose, there's no problem." Her fingers tightened around her drink. "I'd prefer to take a horse somebody else has given up on and give him a jumpstart on his career. Or better yet, raise a contender from a foal. Maybe RainbowBlaze will produce a stakes winner."

"Won't you enjoy training Hip sixty-four—the yearling we just bought?" Nick failed to hide the censure in his tone.

"Of course I will," Daisy protested. "He's a beautiful chestnut colt, exudes class and has an impeccable pedigree. Why wouldn't I?"

"Thought maybe he was tainted because of his price tag."

Daisy frowned, paused and pushed her chair away from the table. "I didn't mean it that way. I've got to go to the ladies room," she whispered, before grabbing her purse and rushing down the hallway.

Nick watched her leave and then directed his scowl at his drink. "Guess that didn't come out quite right." He balled a napkin in his hand trying to ignore the telltale looks cast between Cassie and Clint.

Shortly, Clint excused himself in order to talk to a fellow sitting at the bar about a horse that would be in the sales ring in the morning.

Nick pursed his lips and said nothing, wishing he was somewhere else. He'd expected Cassie to follow Daisy, but he wasn't that lucky. Instead the redhead cleared her throat to speak. She had the look of an inquisitor.

"So you both are sensitive about money."

Nick gave Cassie a fake smile and then let it fade before responding. "Suppose you're right about that. Money spooks the woman."

"Maybe it's your comfort with money that spooks her most. She's never really been around

217

much money. Even when she stayed with us at the farm. Clint and I are doing all right, but," she smiled sweetly—too sweetly to Nick's liking—"you're in a different league from us. We're better at spending other people's money than our own."

Seeing no need to respond, Nick remained silent.

"Another round?" the scantily clad waitress asked.

"No, I'm done," Nick said. "How about you?" he asked Cassie.

"No. I expect we're all done."

"Just bring me the bill," Nick told the waitress. Once she left, he said, "Since I'm the big spender I'll take care of the drinks."

Cassie grimaced. "You're angry, Nick, and you appear to be hurt. I didn't mean to judge you. It's just a fact that you're wealthy and Daisy is relatively poor. She's not bothered by the differences in your ages—that probably bothers me and you more—but she has yet to adjust to being around your kind of wealth. That doesn't make either one of you good or bad. It just is."

Nick slumped back in his chair. He ran fingers through his thinning hair. "Suppose you're right. I just thought it'd thrill her to be part of buying Hip sixty-four. Instead, she threw him in my face."

"I'm not certain she meant to do that," Cassie soothed, "at least not as harshly as it came out." Cassie folded her arms and eyed Nick intently. "My father may have influenced Daisy. He was your basic hands-on horse trainer. He never

218

wanted to buy the big horse. He wanted to raise him from a foal. That was the real dream."

"Did he?"

"Depends on what you mean by a big horse. He never made it to a Triple Crown race—never expected to. But he felt he raised a good stakes contender in Cassie's Hope. That was good enough for him. After her, and after I returned to training full-time, he agreed to buy better quality horses because he knew his time was running out, and he felt I deserved to work with more horses who could compete at higher levels."

"Maybe that's Daisy's hang up," Nick offered. "She may think we're just buying a winner. But we all know that even top sales horses often fail to win back their purchase price. It's a gamble. A big one."

"That you're able to take. That she can't. Daisy has to question her role in all of this. You buy a horse, and no matter what the cost, she picks up a nice percentage. How does she earn that? Maybe she feels a little like a kept woman."

"Daisy? Kept?" Nick leaned forward. "I don't think so. She's the brains of this outfit, and its backbone. She provides the labor and the savvy. She's got to know I'm not trying to buy her."

"Aren't you? Are you afraid she won't want to hang around with a slightly balding, forty something fellow, if you can't buy her expensive horses to play with?"

"No! That's not the way it is." Nick's windpipe constricted. He massaged his diaphragm. "She can't think that."

"Why not?" Cassie's pupils flashed warning signals. "In her world, everything is bought and paid for one way or another, including women. They might be whores that pimps manage. Or they might be more glamorous arm candy for guys who can afford to pay much more. But they're still bought."

Nick's mind exploded. Was he actually using Willow? Was she a willing partner? Had he bought her like a piece of meat? Surely, she could walk away from him if she wanted to. But could she? Really? Had he cut off her escape by feeding into her love of horses? He closed his eyes, trying to avoid some of the accusing answers.

"I know you don't want to hurt Daisy." Cassie's voice was soft. "But how will you avoid it?"

"Marry her," he blurted out.

"It takes two people to do that. Last I noticed, Daisy doesn't exactly see herself as the future Mrs. Underwood playing hostess to the business world. I expect that scares the hell out of her, if she even allows herself to fantasize about it. You don't live in a cocoon, Nick. Even if you can't see that, you can count on Daisy being aware of it. You bring a lot of trappings with you. I expect most women you've known were bedazzled by all the glitter you bring with—but not Daisy. Have you met her family yet?"

"No."

"I'm not surprised. That's likely intentional." Cassie paused. "You scare her, you know. Maybe you should be a little more afraid of her." Cassie rose, picked up her purse and headed toward the ladies room.

Nick remained alone at the table. He shut out Daisy's friend's words by turning his attention to the strains of *Mack the Knife*. He didn't want a relationship with any woman to be based on fear. On that point, Cassie Travers was absolutely wrong. Daisy might be hesitant about his money and his age, but she wasn't afraid of him. And her family didn't matter to him one iota. And if it took some money to make her relatives happy, so be it. His first wife hadn't come and gone without costing him a sizeable sum of money. He lifted his glass and drained it. Setting it back down on the table, he grinned thinly. Women were costly. Period.

- o -

Daisy looked up from her reading, not that she'd turned a page in the last half hour, to notice Nick watching her reflection in the floor-to-ceiling window of the top floor suite they shared overlooking the Lexington skyline. Why did the man have to be so stupidly rich?

She regretted her strong words in the bar. Cassie had helped her realize that underneath a lot of bravado, Nick was just as anxious about the two of them as she was. Maybe in different ways. She hadn't wanted to hurt him. And now they had to clear the air. He would choose to ignore the

221

friction and go on as if nothing had happened. She couldn't let that happen. The pain ahead of them was inevitable without permitting wounds to fester.

She cleared her throat. He turned to look directly at her. His passion simmered behind an uncharacteristic guardedness. She could go to bed and make up with him, but she wouldn't allow herself to fall into that trap.

"We've got to talk, you know," Daisy said quietly.

Nick raised his chin. "Somehow I thought you would say that." He folded his arms at his chest and leaned back against the window. "So what's on your mind?"

Only twelve feet separated them, but it might as well have been twelve miles. "I shouldn't have said what I did in front of Clint and Cassie. I didn't mean to embarrass you or hurt you."

"I'll get over it."

"Why do you have to continue buying me things?"

Nick took a step closer. "Why can't you just accept things?" he demanded. He retreated to the window. "I'm sorry. I know you've gone through a lot of changes in a short time."

"Gone through?" Daisy huffed. "Stuck in. Maybe going through. But hardly gone through." She stood, tugged the sash of her robe tighter, and swept hair back from her face. She placed her book on the end table and moved to the window. With four feet separating them, she stared out at the city lights. At last she said, "Why do you have to keep buying me pieces of horses?"

His eyes appraised her while he took his time to respond. At least he wasn't going to give a pat answer.

"I'm coming to understand how much that bothers you. As crazy as it may sound, I wanted you to own part of Hip sixty-four because it's the way I do business. Clearly, you've done more thinking about it than me. Even Clint says many owners want their trainers to own a percentage."

"But twenty percent!"

"If that's too much, we can talk about it. I'm not trying to buy you, Daisy. You've got to know that."

Daisy shivered against the cool of the window. "In my heart, I know that, but it still doesn't feel right. And what must others think?"

"Others be damned."

Glaring hard at Nick, Daisy said, "See? You don't understand. The track is my world. What do other trainers think? What does Sam really think? You come marching in like some fairy godfather and turn my world upside down. It matters to me what others think."

Nick pushed his glasses back onto the bridge of his nose and exhaled. "Okay. It matters. But to me, what you think matters most. So if twenty percent is too much, we can cut it back. How's fifteen? Ten? Damn, what you contribute to this partnership is at least worth that."

Daisy's mouth curled upward. "Sometimes I

think you're just too naïve about what I can and cannot do." She hesitated before reaching out enclosing his hand in hers. "But I do appreciate your confidence and your willingness to listen to what I have to say. If you insist on keeping me in the horse partnership, then maybe we can do something like this..."

"We're not changing what's already done."

She squeezed his fingers. "Hear me out. We won't change what already is. But in the future, on claimers I'll accept ten percent. On any purchases over a hundred thousand, the most I'll take is five percent. Even that seems like far too much."

"Nonsense. I couldn't get those horses to the track without you."

"You and I both know you could get any trainer on shedrow to work with your horses, Mr. Underwood."

"Maybe, but it wouldn't be nearly as much fun."

She arched her eyebrows.

"And I don't mean the bed," he added quickly. "How many trainers are going to spend the time with me to teach me the ins and outs of the horse business? Half of them would probably like to keep me ignorant so I won't interfere."

"You're probably right about that. A lot of trainers won't tolerate owner interference."

"Yeah. I won't be part of something I can't *interfere* with if I'm putting up the dollars. So you see, you're worth every percentage point you have in a horse."

She opened her mouth to speak. He pressed a finger against her lips. "You're my ticket to knowledge about this business. You protect me from getting duped." He sighed deeply. "Oh hell. I concede to your desire to lower your percentage of ownership in future purchases, but are you aware that I'm not buying your favors by including you in this horse partnership?"

"My favors," she said. Was it her heartbeat or his that sounded like dynamite exploding? She'd pled her case and he'd listened. How many men would do that? A part of her warmed, recognizing the truth of his words. He wasn't trying to trap her. Hopefully, she'd feel less trapped. But she still wanted him to spell it out, so she gave him a quizzical frown.

"Favors. You know. Shit. Maybe there is something to generational differences. Dammit, I'm not buying you horses so you'll have sex with me."

Daisy giggled. "I never thought you were. I thought you were after more than sex. That's what scared me."

Nick turned several shades of purple. He opened his mouth to speak and then snapped it shut. Whatever he wanted to say went unsaid. She expected that was best. She knew they needed to talk, but not about everything. Not all at once. She wanted more time with him, much more time.

"Speaking of favors," she whispered, huskily, "I'm kind of in the mood for distributing favors, if you're receptive."

"Oh, I think I can be talked into that." He lifted her chin with a finger. "You know you can be quite the salesperson when you want to be. I thought that's what *I* brought to this partnership."

Daisy leaned forward and brushed her lips lightly across his. "As part of the younger generation, I'm still learning and developing." She took a step back from him, untied the knot at her waist and shrugged her shoulders. Her robe pooled at her feet. "So what do you think, partner? If I'm getting less money, I'll need more loving to keep everything equal."

- o -

"Now why didn't I think of that," Nick said gruffly, pulling Daisy into his arms.

His spirits soared. He hadn't lost her. They'd weathered the storm. Daisy slid a hand inside his robe and ran her fingers down his spine to his buttocks. He crushed his mouth against hers. The pent up sparks that had separated them now joined them.

She broke their kiss and led him toward the king sized bed. His robe joined hers on the floor.

Quickly, she became the aggressor. He did nothing to dissuade her. She wanted him; that was all that mattered. He watched her corn silk hair bobbing between his legs. Her warmth threatened to undo him.

She stopped. "Damn girl, are you trying to kill me?" He lifted his pelvis, pleading for more.

226

She ignored his pleas and dropped him from her mouth. Bereft, Nick shut his eyes and tried not to swear. She was in charge, and that was the way it should be. She moved to straddle him. He opened his eyes to meet her smoky stare. With her eyes locked on his, she slid forward and lowered herself onto the tip of his shaft. There she remained suspended — attached but aloof. She tossed her head from side to side and her blond hair flew about like a child's kite on the end of string. Never taking her eyes off his, she toyed with a nipple of one breast and then the other. When had she become such an accomplished tease?

Nick used every ounce of self-control available not to grab her hips and seat himself firmly in her liquid chamber. She was ready; her moisture dripped his entire length. Yet she waited, boldly challenging him to take over. He refused to do so.

She fluffed the curls at the top of her mound. She flicked her tongue at him. He could feel her fingers touching her, touching him. He loved to watch her discover her own responses as well as his. Her breathing became shallow; she gnawed on her lower lip. Nick waited, trying not to twitch a muscle. The pantomime unfolding before him was too precious to disturb. Daisy's eyes drifted shut; he was sure she couldn't wait much longer.

And then as if at last gravity prevailed, she slammed to his groin and swiftly rose and fell until her mouth contorted. Clearly she was in that place where pain and joy joined into a kind of holy ecstasy. She whimpered and leaned forward, clasping the hair on his chest, running her tongue along the crease of his neck.

Needing to delay no longer, Nick levered his thighs upward, rapidly finding his own release. His brain spun like a top. He waited for it to settle while hugging Daisy's body tight against his own. She might not be ready to talk about a long run future, but there was no way he could ever give this woman up to her demons or to his own. They would make it work.

She breathed evenly against his shoulder. It had been a difficult day for Daisy and a tense evening. She deserved to sleep. Nick closed his eyes and slid a palm down her back. There was no need to shift his weight, because she snuggled better than a down comforter on a cold wintry night.

- o -

"Oh my God!" Daisy flipped her cell phone off and with shaking fingers placed it back on the breakfast table. Her wide misty eyes caught Cassie's gaze. Daisy's hands covered her mouth.

"What is it, Daisy? What's happened?"

Daisy shook her head.

"Is it Maxine?"

Daisy nodded and whimpered, "Yes."

Cassie pushed back her chair to kneel by Daisy and rub her arm. From his chair next to Daisy's, Nick leaned over and massaged her rigid neck muscles.

"How bad is it?" Cassie asked softly.

"Bad." Daisy looked at her friend and stand-in mom through watery eyes. "She may not make it." Gulping for air, Daisy added, "That was Reggie. The story is Maxine was mugged last night. She's at Cook County Hospital. She has a ruptured spleen, a broken arm, a severe concussion."

"Sounds like Reggie did a number on her this time."

Daisy nodded, trying not to feel. She had to get back to Chicago. Reality crushed any more storybook fantasies. Nick had heard everything and could easily fill in the blanks.

"I've got to go." Daisy focused on Cassie, not wanting to see what expression might be on Nick's face. "Can you help me get a plane?"

"Of course I will. I'm so sorry, Daisy, but there was no way you could protect her forever."

Daisy nodded. Nick withdrew his hand. The end would come as quickly as the beginning. She closed her eyes and tried not to pay attention to him. He was punching numbers into his cell phone.

"Cindy? This is an emergency. I need a private jet at the Lexington Airport as soon as possible. If one is here, fine. If not, get one from the nearest airport. Make the arrangements. There will be two passengers."

"Make that four," Cassie interrupted after catching Clint's eye.

"Cindy, make that four passengers to Chicago Midway. That's the closest airport to Cook

County. Do whatever it takes to clear our landing. Call me on the cell when you have things confirmed. We'll be heading to the airport shortly. Thanks."

Daisy stared at Nick. Her lower lip trembled. Her body shook. She allowed him to gather her in his arms. Her ears did not lie, but she still had difficulty believing.

He rubbed her back. "I'm sorry, Daisy. We'll get there as soon as humanly possible. I wish I could say everything will be okay. But no matter what, we'll be there with you."

"I'm scared," Daisy managed to mumble against his shoulder.

"I know. You have every right to be."

She pushed back from him and ran her fingers across his cheek. Struggling for words, she managed, "I thought you wouldn't want anything to do with me after learning about Maxine and Reggie. He's a real lowlife. And," she whimpered, "Maxine isn't much better. But they're all I've got."

Nick chuckled in her hair. "That's where you're wrong. You've got a lot of people who love you. Cassie, Clint, Sam, Thelma and Tom, and me."

"But they'll come after your money," she wailed.

"They might try, but it won't do them any good. Remember, we've got Thelma in our corner, and she can handle just about anybody."

Daisy snickered at the image of Thelma taking on Reggie. She'd put her money on Thelma in a fair contest between the two, but then Reggie would never fight fair.

"We'd best be on our way. By the time we pack and get to the airport, Cindy will have a jet waiting for us."

"But what about Hip one-thirty-two? You wanted to bid on him."

Nick scowled at Daisy and stood to pull her chair back from the table. "Who's always telling me there will be another horse and another race? Horses are important, but not as important as family."

Chapter Eleven

Sterile. Daisy had never been in an intensive care room before. Scrubbing and putting on a hospital gown over her clothes before entering Maxine's room had only heightened her anxiety.

"These are precautions," the nurse said, trying her best to answer Daisy's questions. "The doctor will be by later this afternoon. Your sister is holding her own. She's a fighter."

Daisy nodded. She held Maxine's fingers in her hand while doing her best to ignore the tubes and monitoring cables that formed a massive complex of lines to and from her body. Lights blinked on four machines. The intermittent beeps mesmerized only to be broken by occasional ragged breaths her sister made around the tube stuck down her throat. Cleaning detergent odors mingled with those of the human body to assault the senses. Daisy nearly gagged on the metallic taste encrusting her tongue.

"Five more minutes," the nurse instructed. "You can talk to her. She may be able to hear you; we're never certain. The doctor doesn't want to rush her because her body needs this time to heal. I know she'll be pleased that you're here, so I'll leave you be for a few minutes."

Daisy listened to the nurse's retreating

footsteps. She tried to sort out what had happened to Maxine. "Ah, Maxine," she whispered. "Why can't you let him go? I'm so sorry. Life shouldn't be this hard for anyone. I'm here now. You're going to be okay."

Daisy's shoulders sagged. Who was she kidding? If her sister did pull through, she'd never challenge Reggie's so-called *witnesses* to the mugging. How much more could she take? How much more could any of them take?

Cassie and Clint had gone home. Nick remained in the waiting room. He'd been on the phone checking on the police report. She shuddered. She'd finally buckled under pressure from Clint and Cassie to allow Clint's detective agency to do some digging into Reggie's affairs. Maybe the only way to protect her sister was to get her husband behind bars—for a good long time.

So far he was nowhere to be seen. She was actually somewhat surprised he'd bothered to call her. Apparently the doctor had wanted contact with another family member, if at all possible. The doctor probably had identified Reggie as an abuser right away.

Daisy flinched at the light touch on her shoulder. "Times up," the nurse said. "Why don't you get some rest? It'll be another couple hours before Doctor Anderson is by. I'll let you know when he's here."

"Thanks." Daisy stood and smiled wanly. "I'll be in the waiting area."

"So what did you find out?" Nick asked, holding Daisy in his arms. "Are you okay?"

Daisy stepped back, slumped down on a vinyl armchair and accepted the Styrofoam cup of coffee Nick handed her. "Nothing new to report. She's still not awake. I guess that's normal. The doctor won't be by for another couple hours or so. I'll wait for him." She sipped the coffee. "There's no need for you to stay, Nick. I'm here now."

"You can't get rid of me that easily," Nick said. "I've got nothing more pressing to do than be here with you. Tom and Thelma send their love. Sam says to take as much time as you need. Angie wants to know if it's okay to come by."

A corner of Daisy's mouth turned up. "My, you have been busy. I don't really want to see anyone else today."

"Even me?"

"No, I didn't mean you. You've been a rock throughout this. I just don't want to share this world with Angie or anyone if I can help it."

Nick squeezed her neck gently between thumb and index finger. Daisy closed her eyes and leaned into him. If she wasn't careful, she'd begin to purr.

"You don't seem to realize that your friends see you as a strong young woman who cares, maybe too much. No one is going to be put off by your family."

"That's easy for you to say." Her voice was muffled with exhaustion.

235

"We can't be responsible for our relatives or who our parents were."

"At least you know who your parents were." Daisy ground her fingernails into her palms. What had made her say that? Was she that vulnerable? Now he knew she was a bastard. She looked at him with horror on her face.

"Don't," he said, leaning over to kiss her forehead. "Don't be ashamed. Given what you've said around the edges, I'm not surprised. And it doesn't matter to me. Not one bit. I have a lovely woman sitting next to me that I care about deeply. I don't care if you are descended from the likes of Huck Finn or the Queen of England."

Daisy managed a tiny smile. "I doubt that either of those are likely, since one is fictional and the other out of the question."

"Maybe. Just don't think that you're the only one with questionable roots."

Daisy frowned. "What do you mean?"

"Well, it just so happens that on my mother's side there is a grandfather whose father remains unknown. A bastard, they might have called him in his day, but I'm darned proud of him. He became a successful railroad engineer. And if it hadn't been for him, there would be no me."

"Angie said there were skeletons in your family too." She raised one eyebrow. "Are there more?"

"Oh yeah." Nick sighed and then stood. "But another time. Now we have to see about getting you some food. I don't want you fainting."

"Somehow, I think you just avoided answering

a question. But you're right. I'm famished. But I don't want to leave. If the doctor comes by early, I don't want to miss him."

"That's okay. I'll just snoop around a bit." He gave her his wicked smile. "I'm pretty good at snooping."

"I've noticed."

"You hang here and I'll see what I can find to eat."

- o -

"Wake up, bitch!"

Daisy's eyes jerked wide. Dazed, it took her a moment to identify her surroundings. She must have dozed. But there was no question who was shaking her by the shoulder.

"Take your hands off me, Reggie." She scrambled to her feet. He never had liked the fact that she stood a good four inches taller than him. "If you came to see Maxine, she's still limited to ten minute visits."

Reggie backed up a couple steps and sneered. "I'm not stupid. I know that. So are you satisfied?

"What do you mean?"

"If you'd come through with more dough, your sister wouldn't have to walk the streets at one in the morning looking for johns."

Daisy blanched. Was he telling the truth? He just wanted her to believe Maxine was mugged.

"I can see that you got the picture, bitch. Not a pretty one either. But bread is bread. And we'll get

237

it any way we can. Which reminds me, you better stop by billing before you go anywhere."

"What do you mean?"

"Somebody's got to pay for all of this. We ain't got any insurance, you know. Unless you want us to be at the mercy of the county."

Daisy groaned. "I'll check into it. There must be a way to pay."

"Oh, there's a way all right." Reggie moved forward and Daisy backpedaled until she felt the wall against her buttocks.

"Your rich boyfriend can spring for it. About time he started paying his own way in this family. He should know it's going to cost him to get a virgin piece like you."

Instinctively, Daisy slapped her brother-in-law. He staggered, momentarily retreating. Regaining his balance, he came in low with his shoulder, slamming Daisy against the wall. Slanting a forearm against her throat and pressing a knee against her crotch, Reggie shouted, "Don't ever try anything like that again, or you'll be in bed next to your sister."

Daisy fought for breath. She wanted to close her eyes but wouldn't give Reggie the satisfaction.

"I'm only gonna say this one more time, bitch. You better figure out a way to separate super stud and some of his cash. You're not gonna leave us lying in the gutter while you ride the gravy train. Accidents happen every day. Look at your sister. Could be you. Could be him. You understand?"

Daisy nodded. Her eyes rounded. She saw Nick

running in from the hallway with a man in a white coat right behind him.

The weight was yanked from her throat; she slumped to the floor gasping for breath, but she couldn't take her eyes off of Nick. She'd never seen this side of him. He was ready to kill.

Nick spun the shorter, beefier man around and slammed him against the wall. He blocked a blow to his body and struck a solid blow to Reggie's midsection and a second to his nose. Reggie crumpled to the floor. Blood from his nose spurted over his shirt.

"You broke my fuckin' nose, you bastard." Reggie reached for his boot.

Nick stomped his foot on the man's wrist, pinning it to the floor. "If you try for that pig sticker again, you'd better be able to handle it a lot better than your fists."

Reggie yelped.

Without taking pressure off the man's wrist, Nick bent over and pulled a thin five inch blade from its hiding place in Reggie's boot.

Nick glanced at Daisy. "I suppose introductions aren't necessary," Nick said, stepping aside to cradle Daisy in his arms. "This must be Reggie— the outstanding citizen of Cicero. I'm Nicholas Underwood. You're lucky you're still alive," he growled at Reggie.

"You'll wish you weren't before I'm through with you," Reggie gasped, bracing himself against the wall, trying to stand. "This isn't over. Not at all."

"Not if you don't want it to be," Nick agreed. "You just be careful, little man. Any accidents happen to Daisy, and I'm coming after you. You won't have enough hiding holes to keep me away."

"Nick, please don't antagonize him more," Daisy pled, tugging on his elbow.

"Sandy," the man in the white coat said. "Call security. I want this man removed from the premises. And he is not to be allowed back in."

"Who the hell are you? I'm Maxine's husband."

"I'm Maxine's doctor, and I've had to repair your handiwork. Don't tell me otherwise. The cops don't believe your story either. But their hands are tied. Mine aren't." Doctor Anderson looked at the nurse. "Like I said. Make sure security doesn't let him back."

"But what about my nose?" Reggie wailed, clutching his handkerchief over his nose.

The doctor grunted. "Doubt one more broken nose will harm your looks or disposition. You'll heal a lot faster than your wife."

"I'll press charges," Reggie squealed.

The doctor looked around the room at the nurse, Nick and Daisy and then shook his head. "I don't think you have any witnesses to back up your story this time." Two security officers entered the room.

"Get this vermin out of here, gentlemen," Dr. Anderson ordered. "Make sure you put your gloves on before touching him. I wouldn't want you catching anything."

"I'll get you, too, Doc," Reggie shouted over the shoulder of a guard hustling him from the room.

"Don't waste your breath on me." Dr. Anderson shook his head and turned toward Nick and Daisy. "If I'm not threatened twice a day, I don't feel like I'm doing my job." He invited them to be seated.

"Are you okay?"

Daisy smiled at Nick. "I'm fine. I was pretty shook, but now I'm okay. How about you?"

"Never felt better. It's good to get the adrenaline going now and then."

"I'm worried. Reggie's threats aren't idle."

"Neither are mine."

"I've got a busy schedule, you two," Dr. Anderson interrupted. "I'm afraid you'll have to sort out your family troubles on someone else's time."

"Sorry," Daisy replied.

"That's all right. As to your sister, we're keeping her under heavy sedation at the moment, but we'll begin to back that off in the morning. I think she's doing okay, given the circumstances." Dr. Anderson looked toward the doorway where Reggie had left and shook his head. "Some women never learn to give up on a guy."

Daisy nodded. "Will she make it?"

"Oh, I think so. Unless there's complications. With any luck, she'll be out of intensive care in two or three days. Then it's just a matter of getting her back where she can manage for herself. People don't stay in hospitals any longer than necessary these days. Sometimes not even long enough."

Daisy held her chin in her palm. "Before he attacked me, Reggie was saying something about not having insurance, and that I needed to pay her bill."

"I don't handle the financial end of things, but this is a county hospital. There are a lot of patients here who have no insurance and can't afford the services. Don't worry about your sister's bills. There are programs that can help with that."

"If it's a matter of money..."

"Don't even suggest it," Daisy ordered, glaring at Nick. "That's exactly what Reggie wants, for you to start paying their bills. If you ever begin, there will be no end. I can guarantee it."

Dr. Anderson laid a hand on Nick's shoulder. "I expect that's excellent advice. I see these kinds of situations far too often. The county will help out. You both pay your taxes; let the county do its thing. It will do the minimal, but it will be adequate medical care."

- o -

The next morning, Daisy opened her eyes in a strange bed. Quickly, she closed them, sank back into the down pillows, and pulled the sheet up tighter. She stretched a hand out to her right. She was alone.

Prying her eyes open again, she checked the red numerals on the clock. Ten o'clock. Good grief. She never slept that late. Still, she hesitated to climb out into this new space.

Nick had brought her back to his Kenwood home. No way could she convince him she would be safe at her apartment with Reggie on the loose. She was touched by his concern for her safety, but she wasn't sure bouncing around in a fourteen room house with a multimillionaire was good for her health, either.

They'd arrived after dark. Even then, Daisy recognized the old Tudor house standing at the head of a wrap-around driveway for what it was: a mansion. No doubt the place had a manicured lawn and beautiful gardens. Nick had told her about Mary Brown, an ageless woman in her eighties who was his live-in housekeeper.

Daisy moaned. The house had to be large enough for at least a half dozen live-in housekeepers. She hadn't seen many of the rooms. Just the kitchen, dining room, Nick's bedroom and the adjoining bathroom. All were decorated with taste.

Nothing gaudy or flashy. She guessed it was solid and fairly masculine. There was no showy display of money.

From what she'd seen thus far, the interior of Nick's home was understated, much like Nick himself. Daisy hugged herself; she couldn't believe she'd flown on a private jet. Maxine!

Daisy's eyes sprang open. She had to get back to the hospital—Maxine could awaken at any moment. Daisy threw back the covers preparing to climb out of the massive oak bed when she heard a light rap at the door. Pulling the covers back up, she croaked, "Come in."

"Ah, you're awake. About time. Though I heard you've had a bad time of it lately. I'm Mary Brown. Let's get you out of bed before you can't move."

Daisy gripped the sheets between white-knuckled fingers. She tilted her head, trying to comprehend the slightly bent black woman with a broad smile showing several gaps of missing teeth. Nick was right, the woman was ageless. She had the bounce of a sixty-year-old. But the gun-metal gray of her hair and the deep creases in her skin spoke of decades of hard work and pain. The woman's smile line indicated there had also been plenty of joy. That pleased Daisy.

Stepping closer to peer at Daisy, Mary Brown said, "So you're the young lady who has Mr. Underwood turned inside out. I wouldn't have expected less. Come on now, let's get you dressed."

Finding her voice, Daisy replied, "I'm pleased to meet you, Mrs. Brown, but I don't need help getting dressed."

"Call me Mrs. B., Miss Daisy. Everyone else does. And I've been helping folks get in and out of clothes, making meals, and cleaning up messes in this house for over sixty years. It's what I do. Now put that sheet down and get out here. Time's a-wasting."

Frowning, Daisy climbed out of bed. Naked, she felt extremely vulnerable before the older women even though she towered over the housekeeper.

"My, my. You are a beauty. So tall. But you've got the right stuff in the right places. I'll make the bed while you get some things on. You can freshen up in Mr. Nick's bathroom, if you like."

Daisy grabbed a bra, panties and slacks and tried not to dash too rapidly to the bathroom. She wasn't surprised to find Mrs. Brown still there tidying up when she stepped back into the bedroom. Partially clothed, she didn't feel at such a disadvantage. What did the old woman make of her relationship with her employer?

"So you've lived and worked here a long time. Before Nick bought the house, I imagine."

"Oh heavens, yes. Nick wasn't even a dream in his mommy's heart when I moved here. The Prestons bought this house in the late thirties. I came to work for them shortly after; I was the nanny to their five children. Lived in the carriage house back then." Mary fluffed a pillow. "Missus passed on and Mister had to be put in a home. That's when Mr. Nick moved in. I never moved out. It's been good.

"Though I've got to say it's been better since his Missus moved out. She could be pretty snooty at times. Didn't like me hovering about when they had parties. Wanted me to serve, but not be seen. Now I don't know about you, but I haven't figured out how to be present but not visible."

Daisy laughed. "No, I haven't figured that out, but I've wished I could more than once."

"Ain't that the truth. Girl, you're good. I can see you and I are going to get along just fine."

"I don't expect to be around much. This was kind of an emergency, my being here."

"Hah. Emergency. Emergency. I know my Mr. Nick. You're here because he wants you here."

Giving up on finding a better top, Daisy tugged on a silk tan blouse she'd planned to wear at a special dinner in Lexington.

"I'll have your things cleaned by the time you get back."

"You don't have to do that, Mrs. Brown. I'll be going back to my apartment soon. By the way, where is Nick?"

"Ah, yes, I almost forgot." The elderly woman pressed a palm against her forehead. "He wanted you to know that he had to go to the shop for an important meeting this morning. Expected you would want to go to the hospital. He left the jeep for you. He didn't think you'd want to drive his Triumph."

"He has a Triumph?"

"Uh, huh. One of his many toys. He used to be into cars, but I heard tell that you got him into the ponies. Now, that's a lot better, from my way of thinking."

Daisy didn't even attempt to conceal her grin. "And, why is that, Mrs. Brown?"

"It's Mrs. B., girl. My husband, Andrew, bless his soul, had one obsession—in addition to me, of course—and that was the ponies. He used to watch them at Washington Park. One of his greatest thrills as a young man was watching Seabiscuit run. He talked about that horse until the day he died. Enough of this prattle, you must be starving. I've got breakfast warming."

Scrambled eggs with body, thick bacon, home made juice, strong coffee and buttery toast. Had she found culinary heaven? "This is great!" She beamed at Mrs. Brown who was obviously pleased with her houseguest's compliments.

Feeling refreshed, Daisy couldn't resist trying to find out a little more about the habits of Nicholas Underwood. "So Mrs. B., does Nick often leave you to entertain his women guests?"

Mary laughed heartily and pulled out a chair to sit down. "You're not very subtle, Miss Daisy, but that's okay. I like people who are direct. No. To tell you the truth, you're the first woman Mr. Nick has brought home since his divorce. I was shocked to learn this morning that a female was in the house."

"Well," Daisy said, avoiding eye contact. "I wouldn't be here if it weren't for the emergency."

"Right. Sure." Mrs. Brown shrugged. "Believe what you want. It was just a matter of time. Mr. Nick has sense enough to hold on to something special when he sees it."

"How do you know he thinks I'm special?"

"He bounces."

"He what?"

"He bounces when he walks. The man hasn't done that in years."

Daisy shook her head, trying to understand. "Maybe it's the horses. Or a new canoe idea. Or maybe he just decided to bounce."

"He scares the bejeebers out of you, doesn't he?"

Gulping the remainder of her orange juice, Daisy nodded.

"For whatever it's worth, Mr. Nick is the kindest white man I've ever known. He could have let me go at any time. And where would this old woman go? I've outlived most of my friends. We had a son, but he was killed in Vietnam."

"I'm sorry." Daisy placed a hand on the older woman's arm.

"Yeah, well. It happened. Long time ago. But...anyway, Mr. Nick kept me on."

"You seem to like him a lot."

Mary gave Daisy her broadest smile. "Oh yeah. He makes sure I get to church on Sunday. He does much of the grocery shopping anymore. But he can be cantankerous at times, but then I just pay him back."

"Now, I am curious. How do you pay him back?"

"I dress up in the white nanny outfit I used to wear in the old days. I've done it a few times when he's had guests over. It embarrasses him to no end. Threatens to burn the damn clothes. Says it makes me look like his slave and him some kind of master. It's always worth a chuckle or two, and then he's over nice for a while."

Daisy convulsed with laughter. She could easily

imagine Nick straightening his glasses, running his hands through his hair, pacing about and ordering his housekeeper not to look like a slave. And she likely just stood in one place and listened politely with no intent to heed his orders. Nick had difficulty with women who didn't follow orders easily.

"So you will go to the hospital?"

"Yes, my sister may be waking from the drugs."

"You'll be back?"

"Yes, I have to work things out with Nick. I'm perfectly safe in my own place."

"Maybe not."

"What has Nick told you?"

"Don't be cross with him. He only told me enough so I would call the police if a Mr. Reggie Lassiter shows up on our doorstep."

Daisy's shoulders sagged. "I hope my coming here hasn't put you in danger, too. Nick wasn't supposed to find out about my family."

Shrugging her shoulders, Mrs. Brown replied, "It don't matter. I've probably seen worse than your brother-in-law. And Nick would've found out sooner or later. It won't matter to him."

"It does to me."

"Shouldn't. You're strong. You've got street sense, girl. You can handle whatever comes your way. Even Nicholas Underwood."

"How can you tell?" Daisy wanted to believe.

"Your eyes. You have honest eyes that see much. And the way you carry yourself. Like a cat ready to pounce or flee, depending on what she sees."

Laughing, Daisy said, "I hope you're right. You sure pay a lot of attention to how people walk."

"Yes, I do. I've spent many more years than you watching and scheming to protect myself and what's mine."

"So your sister didn't come around today?"

Daisy shook her head at Nick, who sat beside her on the leather couch before a small fire in the marble fireplace. It was unseasonably cool, and the fire warmed her chilled bones. She'd just returned to the Kenwood house after spending the day being sentry at her sister's bedside.

"No. Doctor Anderson thinks maybe tomorrow, but it's hard to predict." Daisy tucked a leg under a thigh and rocked forward. "He says she's resting comfortably and healing and that's what's important."

"Any sign of Reggie?"

"Hardly," she replied, placing a hand on his arm. "I don't think we'll see his face until his nose recovers."

Nick grunted. "Just don't count on it. He's going to be a problem."

"He always has been."

"Did you meet Mrs. B.?"

Daisy brightened. "Oh yes, early this morning. Well, not so early, I'm afraid. She's quite the woman. Sounds like she came with the house."

"She did. The seller almost made it a condition of the contract. Keeping her on was one of the best

250

choices I ever made. This place functions because she knows what to do. I dread thinking of the day when she won't be around any longer."

Gazing at the fire, Daisy nodded. "We seemed to hit it off right away. So you don't bring women here."

"Ms. B. also likes to gab." Nick patted Daisy's thigh. "Yes, you're the first woman to sleep in my bed since I split with my ex."

"So why me?"

"Can't explain that entirely. You delight me in ways I never dreamed off. Maybe it's your youthful enthusiasm."

"Did you take advantage of my vulnerability yesterday to bring me here?" Daisy eyed Nick without accusing.

Taking a deep breath before responding, Nick replied, "Yeah, I imagine I did a little. I've wanted to bring you here for a while now. But you seemed so put off by my money, I waited. With your safety in question, it was a no-brainer. Oh, you could have gone to the Travers farm, but that's a long commute. I could have put you in a hotel, but bringing you to my home seemed right at the moment. I hope it doesn't bother you too much."

"Oh, I'm adjusting; maybe too well. It's a beautiful house. I love the hardwood floors and the French doors and the built in cupboards. It's so spacious a person could get lost here. And Mrs. Brown is a real card. And it's good to know more about who you are."

"Good. I'm glad you like it. Then you'll stay."

Daisy crossed her arms. "Only until my sister can get on her feet. I'll need to be with her as she recovers. Then I'll go back to my place. I admit that Reggie unsettled me yesterday, and I do like your support, but eventually I have to stand on my own." A harshness had crept into her voice that she couldn't explain.

Nick slid his glasses up his nose and glanced over at the fire. "That's good enough for now. Let's take it a day at a time and see what develops."

Daisy snuggled into his outstretched arm. It was going to be difficult to keep her guard up — her emotional guard. She could get used to his lifestyle and his constant presence if she wasn't careful. And then what would she do when he was ready to move on to some other woman, or to some other toy? Wasn't that how Mrs. Brown described the horses? His latest toys?

At nine-thirty the next morning, Maxine opened her eyes for the first time since arriving at the hospital. Slowly she focused on Daisy and whispered, "Hi, baby."

Daisy nodded, forcing back tears. "Hi there yourself, big sister. It's been a while."

"How long?"

"Three and a half days. The nurse told me to press the button when you came around."

"Where?"

Daisy cringed at Maxine's dry whisper. "You're at Cook County in the ICU. Doctor Anderson says you're coming along nicely."

Maxine winced. "So much for him."

"Well, well our patient has decided to join us. That's good. My name is Rebecca. I'm your nurse." Rebecca checked various monitors. "How do you feel?"

"Like shit!"

Rebecca chuckled. "I bet." She looked toward Daisy. "Everything checks out okay. I'll let the doctor know that she's come around. It's okay to stay for a while, but don't tax her by getting her to talk much."

"No problem. It's just such a relief to see her eyelids open and shut."

"Maxine can have small sips of water when she wants. She'll need your help. Her throat is terribly dry from the tubes." The nurse looked at the chart again and scribbled a note. "I'll be in and out, and the doctor will be by later."

Daisy nodded and directed her attention back to her sister. She looked a mess. Her face was laced with bruises and her left arm was in a cast. And she looked tired, so tired. "Don't try to talk," Daisy said. "You need to sleep so you can heal."

Maxine's eyes widened. "Sorry," she groaned. "You should be working."

"Work is taking care of itself. For now, you're the top priority. Would you like a sip of water?"

Maxine nodded.

"Let's see if we can do this." Daisy held the cup with the bent straw. With effort, Maxine opened her lips. She took three small swallows and pushed the cup away. Daisy placed it back on the stand.

"Know what you're thinking." Maxine whispered, closing her eyes. "What?"

"He didn't do it."

"Who?"

"Reggie."

Daisy tightened her grip on the bed rail. She wasn't about to tell Maxine Reggie had attacked her in the waiting room while his wife was just holding on. "You can tell me about it later."

"Won't be different then." Maxine coughed and gagged. Daisy wiped her mouth with a tissue. "Was hit by a car. Never stopped."

With mouth agape, Daisy was at least pleased that her sister's eyes remained shut. Obviously, Reggie had never had an opportunity to tell Maxine their cover story.

Shaking her head at the half broken woman, Daisy feared there was nothing Reggie Lassiter could do to her or anyone else that would force Maxine to turn him in to the cops. Unlike the common wisdom regarding alcoholics, Maxine apparently had no bottom. Or if she did, it was nowhere in sight.

Chapter Twelve

Cornered. For two weeks Daisy shuffled her feelings regarding Nick as if they were a deck of cards. There were moments, like when he held her in the middle of the night after an upsetting dream, when her heart burst with an emotion she feared naming. And at other times, she wanted to scream bloody hell when he assumed he knew what she wanted.

If only he would listen. If only she could be clear. If only she could be clear with herself.

She was sending him confusing signals, but she couldn't help it. He was driving her nuts. She didn't want to break off their relationship, yet she desperately needed some breathing space. Getting back to her own apartment had to be a priority or she would go crazy.

The rope she held between her fingers went slack. Startled, Daisy let out a groan. "I'm sorry, young man. You're right. I wasn't paying attention." Hip sixty-four didn't answer; he calmly stood and stared at the woman standing in the middle of the round pen hanging on to the end of his lead rope.

She had been lunging the yearling outside the barn at the Travers farm, investigating how much the colt knew about voice commands and how well he paid attention to what his handler desired. Daisy snorted. He was paying more attention than she was. Damn, they had to agree on giving the horse a name fairly soon. She was tired of calling him Hip sixty-four.

Tired. That about summed up her life. Too much Maxine. Too much Nick. Too little Daisy.

She walked toward the yearling, who stretched out his neck for a treat. "Not now," she said. "I know it was my fault, but I can't reward you for stopping on your own and wheeling to face me.

"You have the glossiest coat I've ever seen." Daisy ran a hand along the yearling's spine and then lifted his tail. At first the animal stiffened, but then he relaxed, accepting her touch. After she'd run her hands along his belly and up and down each leg, she stood and reached into her pocket. "Good," she praised, letting the chestnut take a treat from the palm of her hand. "You're going to be easy to handle. Easier than some other males in my life."

She hadn't seen Reggie since the debacle at the hospital. Maxine had been home for a week and was managing, but according to her, she hadn't seen Reggie either. Daisy didn't know whether to believe her sister or not, but she could at least hope Reggie had finally fallen down a manhole.

It would likely be another month before Maxine could return to work. Daisy shook her head. She'd had no choice but to give her sister money this time. What was the alternative? Maybe that was why Reggie wasn't showing up. Maybe he

256

realized she'd be an easier touch to pay her sister's way if he wasn't around. It might be worth taking Maxine on as a dependent, if that meant Reggie would stay out of their lives.

She knew that wasn't possible. She sighed. Reggie's nose for money was too good for that to happen. He knew about Nick, and he knew Nick had money. That was enough to keep him on her scent. She just hoped the hatred he harbored for Nick wouldn't outweigh Reggie's greed. If he hurt Nick, he'd run the risk of cutting off the money train.

Daisy shivered. There was no doubt in her mind that Reggie was holed up somewhere devising a plan to separate Nick Underwood from as many dollars as possible. And Reggie would see her as the key to his plan.

Hip sixty-four butted Daisy with his head, knocking her off balance. She straightened and pulled on the lead rope. "Okay, you're right. I better put you back in the paddock if I can't pay better attention than this."

"So how's it feel working with a three hundred thousand dollar Keeneland purchase?" Cassie asked, walking down the steps from her porch toward Daisy, who was stowing gear in her pick-up.

"Humbling," Daisy acknowledged. "Whoever prepared him for the sale did a nice job. That young fellow has the smoothest trot. The way he holds his head, you know he knows he's

257

something special."

"We'll have to wait and see about how special. A lot of things can happen between here and the track. Do you want some coffee?"

Daisy removed her working gloves and shook her head. "No, I better be getting back. I've got a lot of sorting yet to do."

Cassie sighed and leaned against the fender of the truck. "Don't expect we're talking about odds and ends."

Giving her friend a faint grin, Daisy replied, "Not hardly. I've got to get out of that place, Cassie. I'm sorry, I didn't mean to shout, and I know you like Nick a lot. But..."

"Listen to me, Daisy. I've made it clear to you and to Nick that I will support you no matter what you choose to do. What I think about Nick doesn't matter. It's what *you* think that does."

"I know, but that doesn't make it any easier. I just feel like I'm suffocating. There's too much clutter in my life. I can't even find my damn clothes."

Chuckling, Cassie quipped, "That's probably a bigger problem for you than for Nick."

"Right." She paused and squinted at Cassie. "Do you think he loves me? He says he does."

"Do you think he does?"

Daisy banged a hand against the pickup door. "You're answering questions by asking questions. Are you going to be my social worker, my mother or my friend?"

Moving closer to Daisy, Cassie squeezed her

shoulder. "I'm sorry, I know how you hate that. But I can't really say. I know Nick thinks he loves you. But does it feel like it to you—not in your head, but in your heart?"

Daisy took a deep breath before answering. "I don't know. I don't know what I'm feeling anymore. One minute I think I must be in love and the next I think I'm a fool."

"So we're really questioning *you* being in love with *him*." Cassie's lips turned up. "It's okay to question such an emotion. My goodness, there probably isn't anything more powerful or far reaching than love."

"But that's just it. I don't even know what love is supposed to feel like." Daisy sagged until she sat on the running board. "I'm such a mess."

"No more so than much of the population that struggles with intimacy. Listen, Daisy, I think you were wise to prepare yourself about sexual matters by reading and watching videos, but they probably didn't do much to teach you about love."

Daisy scowled. "I've only been around one couple who I think is really in love, and that's you and Clint. Maxine hardly counts. And you guys seemed different. I'm not you, Cass."

"And you shouldn't be. You have to be yourself in matters of love, as in working with horses or with anything else. I hope we've helped you feel loved, but I expect there remains a large hole for you. Maybe you expect too much of Nick and too little of yourself."

"Now what's that supposed to mean?"

"Maybe you expect him to fill that hole by himself. I'm not saying you do, but if that's what's happening, then you may need to rethink your own role in a love relationship. It takes two people to truly experience a loving relationship."

"I think I know what you're getting at." Daisy closed her eyes and paused. "I'm not sure I'm ready to give as much as he needs, or even as much as I need."

"And maybe that's the answer. Maybe you're not ready. That doesn't make you the bad guy, nor Nick either for that matter."

Daisy pushed herself up from the running board and brushed off her jeans. "You may be right, Cass. You've given me even more to sort through. Thanks. But I do have to go. Make sure Hip sixty-four doesn't get into trouble."

"I'll do that. Now, you give me a hug before you go. I won't tell you to stay out of trouble. It seems to be finding you these days without you looking for it."

"That's for sure," Daisy whispered, hugging the smaller woman who'd thrown her a lifeline on more than one occasion. Yes, she'd think on her words. Carefully.

Maybe she just wasn't ready to decide.

"So you'll be leaving us soon."

Daisy peered at Mary Brown. How had that woman read her mind again? Having showered and dressed, Daisy had been trying to decide whether to pack before talking to Nick or after. It might be safer to do so before, but if he found out she was all packed he might be wounded more than she wanted. This wasn't going to be a painless departure, but she didn't want to torpedo their entire future either.

Mrs. Brown stood in Nick's bedroom doorway with her feet spread wide apart.

Closing the closet door before answering, Daisy turned and said, "Yes, I need to get back to my place. I'll be closer to help Maxine. And...well, I just need to be there."

To her surprise, Mary Brown chuckled and entered the room. "I'm not gonna bite your head off. Mr. Nick's the one you gotta worry about. Not me. Just be careful, girl. There's too much evil lurking around you."

Daisy scowled. "Maybe. But I can't hide out here any longer."

"Do you love him?"

"Who?"

"Now I *am* gonna get mad. I'm not stupid. Do you love Mr. Nick?"

Daisy sank onto the bed. "I wish I knew." She glanced up at Mrs. Brown. "I don't even know what love is."

"Now that's a crock of spoiled milk, if you ask me. Your momma loved you. I know she didn't do great by you, but maybe she did her best. Your grandma loved you. You know that now, don't you?"

Daisy nodded.

"And them people at the group home you told

me about. And them who took you home to live with—they loved you, right?"

Again Daisy nodded.

"Then don't tell me you don't know what love is. You've felt it. It's touched your heart and your soul. Do you feel it from Mr. Nick? And do you feel it for him?" Mrs. Brown shrugged her shoulders. "I suspect you know the answers to them questions, but you're too afraid to see them. But, that's okay. No matter. When you're ready, then you'll see. In the meantime, I wish you well, girl. You've been good for Mr. Nick. Though his bounce has been sagging a little of late."

Without waiting for an answer, Mrs. Brown headed for the doorway. Before stepping out into the hall, she turned and announced, "I'll cook up a good meal for you when you're ready to come back. You can count on that."

Daisy threw herself on the bed. She hadn't even thanked the woman. They both knew she'd be gone before breakfast.

- o -

"You don't look so good," Tom Harrison said, glancing up from polishing a section of cedar on the bow of a canoe. It was early evening and the rest of the employees had gone home. Tom was doing his typical touchups. "If those circles around your eyes get any darker, the authorities will accuse Daisy of abuse."

"Wouldn't be too far off," Nick responded

262

flatly. "I'm losing too much sleep." Nick scowled at Tom's raised eyebrow. "From worry."

"Oh. Is that asshole brother-in-law still bothering her?"

"He hasn't shown his face since the incident at the hospital. And that bothers me. I'd like him to be out in the open where I can keep track of him."

"I can understand that. You think he's dangerous."

"Anyone who carries a blade in his boot is potentially dangerous." Nick ran his fingers through his hair. "Clint Travers has his people at the agency checking Lassiter out. So far he shows up with loose connections to the mob. He seems to have fallen out of grace. I wouldn't be surprised if he didn't try to scam them, or maybe he's just too much into drugs. He's a dealer and a user.

"The cops want to nail the guy for selling around the area schools, but every time they think they've got him, a witness decides they didn't see anything after all. He's had a small string of women working for him, but their number is decreasing. I'd say the guy's sources of income are drying up and that makes him even more dangerous. And makes Daisy more of a target."

"And you," Tom pointed out, putting down his sandpaper, moving to straddle a sawhorse.

"Yeah, probably. I'm going to talk with the people who installed our security system in the morning. Want to make sure we're as well equipped as reasonable. Maybe I'll check into a private night watchman, too. It certainly wouldn't surprise me if our macho man might try to attack me through the business." Nick squared his shoulders and crossed his arms. "If he tries anything here, his ass will be flayed."

"That's more like it." Tom grinned. "Maybe we should stand guard, for old time sakes. It'd sure surprise the bastard to be looking down the barrels of two Uzis if he shows up with a torch in his hand."

Nick shook his head. "I'm not ready to go there yet. Maybe he won't even try anything." Nick rubbed the bridge of his nose and straightened his glasses. He took two steps back toward his office, hesitated and turned back to his friend. "You know she's going to leave me."

"Ah, damn." Tom brushed fine sawdust from his jeans. "I'm sorry, man. When?"

Shrugging his shoulders, Nick said, "Don't know. She hasn't said anything yet. I just know. Soon, I expect. Something is wrong between us and I can't figure out what it is. If I could, I'd fix it."

"Maybe it's something you can't fix," Tom offered.

"Maybe."

"Is it the age thing?"

"I don't think so."

"She won't tell you?"

"I'm afraid to ask."

"Oh. You can't make her stay." Tom stood and walked around the canoe, squinting, looking for any sign of imperfection.

264

"I know that. Can't make the woman do a damn thing."

"So is she unhappy with the horse partnership?"

"No, not that. Oh, she thinks I give her too much of the horses for her contribution, but I don't think so. Besides, I've agreed to reduce the percentages in the future." Nick ran his hands along the smooth contours of the canoe. "No, I think she's upset that I'm now involved with her family. And she's still put off by my wealth. I don't know what else is bothering her, but something sure is."

"That might be enough," Tom said, dryly.

"There's more. And she's stubborn as hell. Won't listen to reason."

"You mean she won't cowtow to Underwood logic, don't you?" Tom grinned broadly. "She's got spunk, Nick, and she values her independence. She probably needs some space and time to figure out what's going on around her and what *she* wants to do."

Nick looked at his palms and flexed his fingers. "So what am I supposed to do?"

"Depends on what you want." Tom ducked his head and examined a tiny knot in a wood strip. "If you're done with her and ready for another woman, you help her pack her bags and wave goodbye."

Nick's stomach knotted and his fingers balled into fists. "That's not what I want. And you know it."

"Good. Then you might want to figure out how you can help her do what she needs to do. If she needs time, give her time. If she needs space, give her space."

"But how can I protect her if she leaves?"

"How can you protect her if she stays? If she's in danger, and from what I know I assume she is, you can't provide twenty-four hour lock-down security. Sounds to me like at some point this brother-in-law will have to be dealt with. He's more likely to be flushed out of his hole if Daisy's at her apartment than at your place."

"I don't want to use her as bait."

Tom looked directly at Nick. "She is, whether you like it or not. The question is who's prepared to move in if the bastard steps over the line?"

"Ah. Surveillance." Nick closed his eyes and pinched his nose. "God, she'd call it an invasion of privacy. Or Nick taking control again."

"Maybe. But she doesn't have to know, does she? The point is to nail Lassiter. If you find out along the way she's bedding three young studs, you'll have to deal with that. But once Lassiter is off the streets, the two of you will be in a much better position to sort out what you may have between you. Until then, Lassiter is the wild card. And a wild card can trump the best of hands."

Nick shoved his fists in his trouser pockets, nodded at his friend and without replying made his way back to his office.

Sitting at his desk, he pondered his choices. She was going to leave. No way could he make her stay; he wouldn't want her unless she could match his love. Otherwise, what was the use?

He'd do what he could to provide for her safety, whether she liked it or not. Clint Travers was high on his list for a phone call. But that could wait another day. He had to make sure they didn't let up on the horses during this period of redefining their relationship. While he wouldn't try to buy her with horses, he wasn't above using their mutual interest in them to remain in contact. What else? He'd think of something.

Nick rose, picked up his jacket, and with his jaw firmly set, headed out of the canoe factory to his Jeep. He tried not to worry too much about what was waiting for him at home.

Nick gazed at Daisy sitting across from him in a captain's chair at the kitchen counter. It was Mrs. Brown's night off, so the two of them had shared a meal of cold cuts, fruits, veggies and wine. Daisy looked as bad as he felt. Her eyes were red and her cheeks swollen. They'd both been uncharacteristically silent while eating. Now with the dishes cleared and coffee before them, he waited for Daisy to speak.

"We have to name Hip sixty-four," she said. "I hate calling him a number."

Nick cocked his head. That wasn't what he expected to hear. He nodded. "Do you have any ideas?"

"I do. How about Paddle Dreams?"

"That's great." Nick found it hard to breathe.

Did this mean that he'd been misreading her moods these last two weeks? Maybe she was just upset with Maxine and Reggie. He watched her gather herself by taking a deep breath before eyeing him with that look of determined vulnerability he'd grown to love and dread. No, he hadn't misread her.

"I've got to move back to my apartment," she whispered. He wished he could erase her pain and his own.

"It's not that I don't like it here and appreciate what you've done for me, but I have to be on my own. At least for a while."

"So are you saying we're finished?"

Her eyes clouded over. "No, not unless you want us to be finished."

"You know I don't," he admitted. "Far from it. I want you to..."

"Please don't say it," she interrupted. She gagged. "It would only make this harder."

"Okay. So how do you want to play it? We're not finished, but you're moving out. It's your game. So what are the rules?"

Daisy brushed a lock from her forehead. He noticed that her hand lingered a moment longer at the corner of an eye.

"I don't know. I'd still like to do things together. The horses and the track. But not sex."

"No, not sex." He sounded mocking. And maybe he intended to be just that.

"I don't want you out of my life, but I don't know what to do with you. You want more than I can give. Or at least am ready to give." Her eyes implored a response.

Nick sighed and shook his head. "I don't want you out of my life either. I love you. I want you even more in my life." He watched her scowl. "But I won't go there, not now." She relaxed a little. He gave her a tight smile. "Maybe we should go back to square one."

"What do you mean?"

Nick leaned back in his chair. "We kind of got started without much romance. Oh, there was some banter. But I never had the chance to really romance you."

- o -

Daisy reached for her coffee cup. She swallowed slowly and reddened, remembering rapping on the door of his suite in Shakopee. "That wasn't your fault."

"It wasn't anyone's fault. And I'm eternally pleased that you took the first step. I doubt that I would've. Not that I hadn't fantasized about you a lot. I just figured the age difference made you off limits."

"Hah. So much for your figuring." Daisy clamped her mouth shut. It was so easy to fall into a pleasurable bantering with Nick. If she wasn't careful, she'd succumb to the comfort of their relationship and never leave. But wasn't love about more than comfort?

"I know you're determined to leave," Nick said.

"I won't try to make you stay. Might as well try to make water run up a ten percent grade. I want to make a deal with you, though."

Daisy lowered her head. *Be careful, here he goes again. This is where things will get sticky. He's not going to just let me fly away on my own.* She shivered. She wasn't sure she wanted to fly away entirely on her own. "What do you have in mind?" she whispered.

Placing his hands around his coffee mug, Nick said, "First, as to your security."

Daisy flinched, but remained silent. It didn't surprise her that this would be his first point.

"I know we can't provide for your complete security." His voice shook. "But as long as Reggie is out there you are at risk."

"No more than usual." Why couldn't she sound convincing?

"The ante has been upped, Daisy, and you know it. I want to put a security system in your apartment."

"What good will that do?"

"It may help you sleep better. I know you won't be able to avoid the creep entirely, but at least he won't have the element of surprise on his side. Do you agree?"

"It's your money."

Nick withdrew as if she'd slapped him.

"I'm sorry, I didn't mean to be snide. And I do appreciate your concern for my safety. But you also have to realize that I was raised on the streets, Nick. I have a graduate degree in street smarts."

"Good. Second, I want to continue growing our horse partnership. I don't want to switch trainers. Are you still interested in managing our horses?"

"Of course."

"Good. Third, I want to see you on a regular basis. Some at the track, but I also want to escort you to plays, to the art museum, to the Bulls, to places you want to go."

"The romance you talked about?" Daisy eyes rounded.

"Yes. Do you agree?"

She should scream no, but the word would not form on her lips. It would have been the easy way out. Instead she answered, "Yes, if I can say no."

"Allowed."

"Good."

Nick smiled broadly.

She loved to watch him when he thought he was on a roll.

"No sex." He scrunched his mouth. "I understand, but that's going to be hard."

"Hard on both of us," Daisy admitted. She'd miss his arms clutching her to him or his hand lazily patting her buttocks in the middle of the night. Familiarity. She'd grown accustomed to that. Too accustomed.

"Good. But part of romance may include touching and even kissing."

It was her turn to smile. "Yes, if I agree."

"So what do you think? Do you have anything else to offer at the moment?"

She met his gaze steadily. "I do have an

additional thought. We once agreed that while seeing each other, we would remain committed, that is we wouldn't see other guys or women. Do you still want that?"

"I know what committed means." His brow furrowed. "Do you still want that?"

"Yes," she squeaked.

"Good," he gasped. "I wouldn't want it any other way. I'm sure you don't know how much time you'll need."

Eternity, maybe. Daisy shook her head. "No."

"I don't want to put any more pressure on you, but you do need to know I won't wait forever either. How long? I don't know."

"That's fair," Daisy heard her voice say. Why couldn't she stop her hands from trembling? "I better go pack my things."

"You'll stay the night." He chuckled. "I won't break the rules. I promise. There are at least a half a dozen beds that you can choose from. First thing in the morning, I'll have a security team over at your apartment installing a monitoring system."

Daisy flashed her eyebrows and nodded. "Thanks for understanding. I need some breathing room."

Nick stood and placed their coffee cups in the sink. "Don't give me too much credit." His voice cracked. "I didn't say I understood. I'm just not ready to give up on us yet."

Wanting to avoid displaying more tears, Daisy ran toward the stairs.

Chapter Thirteen

Daisy studied her reflection in the mirrors on her bedroom wall. It had been a nerve-wracking day. She looked as frazzled as she felt. She hugged herself. It was good to be back in her own space.

She slipped into a nightshirt and knelt on the futon. Clutching Bear to her chest, Daisy cried a new round of tears. Would she ever stop crying? She'd always prided herself on not being like those other women who cried when any little thing went wrong. "Oh Bear," she whispered. "It's not just a little thing. My entire life is falling apart."

She'd left Nick's house before dawn. There was no need for further goodbyes, with him or with Mrs. B. The security people had already installed a motion and sound system. Little red lights blinked at her wherever she went. She'd be in more trouble if she forgot it was on. Grudgingly, she admitted she did feel safer in her protected cocoon, but she couldn't stay inside her apartment forever. And at some point, sooner than later, Reggie would learn that she was back.

Daisy turned off the light and crawled under the covers. With Bear tucked in the crook of her arm, she closed her eyes, but sleep refused to come. "Oh, Bear," she moaned, "I love you so much. So why do I feel so bereft, so alone?"

"Ah Baby, thanks for bringing by the groceries," Maxine said. "I'm getting better day by day, but it really helps."

"I'm glad I can help," Daisy responded, putting frozen foods away.

Maxine sat at the kitchen table with a cup of cold coffee in front of her and a cigarette in her hand. The ashtray on the table was overrun with butts. "I'll get the rest later," she said. "Why don't you come and sit down for a bit? You look like you're running yourself ragged taking care of me and doing your job, too."

Daisy poured herself a cup of coffee and joined her sister. Maxine was right; she was fraying at the edges. It had been a week since she left Nick's house. Other than the security system installed in her apartment, there was no evidence that he any longer cared she existed. He hadn't been at the track, and he hadn't called.

Maybe he was waiting for her to make the first contact; after all, it had been her idea to move out.

She stayed busy. That was the one positive thing about Maxine's situation: her sister filled up time. But that wouldn't last. She'd have to take care of herself pretty soon. "So how are you doing, Maxine?"

"I'm coming along. Tired as hell of staring at these walls. I've always known this was a small place, but it's beginning to feel like a cell. It will be good to get back to work just to see some people."

"I suppose. Guess I'm more of a natural recluse than you."

Maxine stubbed a cigarette in the ashtray. "I don't know about you," she huffed, "but I need people around me. I need to hear stories and laughter. Even bad jokes are better than none." She smiled at Daisy. "You'd be surprised the jokes people tell waitresses. Particularly men."

Daisy shook her head. She didn't really want to hear about jokes or men who bantered with women. "So when do you expect to get back to the café?"

"I've talked with the boss. I'll give it a try week after next. It might be only a half a shift at first." Maxine lit another cigarette. "I'm surprised Scooter is willing to be that flexible. Usually, it's his way or the highway."

Maxine lowered her long fake eyelashes. Her sister was hiding something. While Maxine was a heavy smoker, Daisy seldom saw her smoke one cigarette after another.

"Oh, I meant to tell you," Maxine began, catching Daisy's eye and then looking away, "Reggie was by last night."

All of Daisy's senses went on alert. "Oh?"

"Yes, it was so good to see him. He's been very busy, you know. That's why he wasn't by at the hospital or here sooner. Some important contacts had a job for him—out of town." Maxine drew a last puff from a cigarette before grinding it to bits in the ashtray. "He had to leave again." She smiled wistfully. "But he did manage to stay most of the night."

Daisy closed her eyes. Maxine was trying to hide more than the fact that Reggie had been by. Her sister was back on drugs. The hospital stay had been hard for Maxine. The hospital might have just replaced one drug with another. And the last week or so, Maxine was ready to jump out of her skin on some days and then mellowed out on others. She'd found a supplier to tide her over, but now her main man was back.

Daisy wanted to kick herself. Why hadn't she seen it all along? If it had been anyone else, she would have noticed more signs. But it was her sister and Daisy so wanted her to do the right thing...to dump drugs and Reggie.

"Reggie wanted me to give you a message," Maxine cooed.

"What's that?"

"He just wants you to know that bygones are bygones and he holds no grudges against you or your boyfriend. Can you believe that, baby? He wants us to be a regular family. Once he gets this job done, he'll come back home where he belongs."

And pigs can fly! How could her sister be so gullible? She had no common sense or any other kind of sense. Daisy's stomach lurched. She had to get out of there before she barfed. Pushing her chair back, she stood and went to the sink to rinse out her cup. "I've got be going," she said. "I've got a horse who needs some medication within the hour."

"Horses!" Maxine scowled. "That's all you care about. You could spend more time with me. And aren't you going to say anything about Reggie? He's being mag...magnanimous. And you don't even say squat."

Daisy's shoulders sagged and her chin dropped to her chest. "Maxine, I want you to be happy. I guess if Reggie makes you happy, so be it. But I can't trust him."

"You don't want to trust him." Maxine reached for the nearly empty pack of cigarettes. "He's going to make more money than your Nicholas Underwood. Because...because he's more of a man."

Suppressing a grin and the memory of Nick's foot squashing Reggie's wrist to the floor in the hospital waiting room, Daisy nodded. "You believe what you want, Maxine. I can't live your life for you."

"Thank God for that. I wasn't born to be a goody-two-shoes like you. It's amazing to me that any man would want to share a bed with you. That Underwood must be hard up."

"Thanks for your love and concern, but I haven't seen Nick for a week."

"Oh?" Maxine's eyes narrowed. "You mean's he's no longer in the picture?"

"Doesn't seem to be."

"Damn, Reggie won't like that. He wanted us to be a family."

"Right. And if you believe that you must think Reggie is Santa's elf." Daisy couldn't stop her legs from shaking.

"That's enough," Maxine screamed. "Out of my house. Now! I don't need your help or your money. Go! Beat it!"

Daisy grabbed her purse. "I'm out of here. You know how to get hold of me if you need anything."

"I won't."

"Right."

"This time take the pill like a good boy," Daisy muttered, trying to push the dosage over MrShowman's tongue with her fingers. At last, he swallowed, and Daisy withdrew her arm and massaged the gelding's throat. "Well done, big guy. Makes me think that all males should be gelded. Might make them more tractable."

"Ouch," rasped a deep voice from outside the stall. "Do you have any particular male in mind?"

Daisy peeked swiftly over her shoulder and tried to control the pace of her heart. She patted MrShowman on the shoulder before stepping toward the stall door. "Thought you learned not to sneak up on someone working with a horse."

Nick pulled on the brim of his hat. "And it's good to see you, too. I did learn that lesson. But your reference to gelding all the males you've ever known sort of got me off kilter a bit."

"That's not what I said," she protested, unlatching the door and stepping out into the alleyway.

"No, but it's what you meant. And I still might

like to have kids someday, if I can ever convince the right woman to have me."

"Good luck. So what are you doing here, Mr. Underwood?"

"Two things," he said, with a smug grin. "I'm checking up on my investments. And I'm here to make a date with that *right woman* I just mentioned."

"Oh." Daisy crossed her arms. "I thought you weren't going to pressure me."

"I'm not. But I'm not going to lie either. I am a man of honor, after all."

"I hadn't noticed."

"And you didn't miss me at all this past week?"

Daisy's skin tingled. "Oh, has it been a week already?"

"You don't do coy very well, kid. Lying doesn't become you. So how is our fellow doing?"

Welcoming the change of subject, Daisy peered back into the stall. "He's fine. We'll try to enter him in a one mile race on the grass next Saturday."

"Good. It's about time. I was beginning to think that owning racehorses only meant paying bills. He's got to run in order to have a chance of making any money. Any more thoughts on another claim?"

Daisy shook her head. "I haven't had time to think about that. Sam's made a rumbling or two about a couple horses that should run during the next couple weeks. You'll probably want to talk to him about it."

"I'll make sure the three of us sit down and go

over the possibilities. Thelma's called me four times insisting on getting into this horse business."

Smiling, Daisy replied, "I can understand why you're asking. When Thelma sets her sights on something, I expect she's quite tenacious."

"You're right about that—like a badger. But she's not the only one. So would you prefer going to a Bulls game, or to a symphony Saturday night?"

Daisy took a step back. She'd agreed to go out with Nick, so why was she so intimidated? She bent over and slapped dirt from her jeans. When she looked back at him, she saw that wicked smile of his. Had he looked down her shirt, or was he just admiring her butt? She winced, trying to appear nonchalant. "Okay. I've never been to a symphony. I couldn't tell one musical instrument from another."

Nick nodded. "I'm glad you haven't lost your sense of humor, kid. I'll go try and track Sam down. If I don't see you before, I'll see you Saturday. Oh," he reached over and plucked straw from her hair, "has Reggie come around yet?"

"Not yet."

"He will."

"I know."

"You be careful."

Daisy nodded and walked toward the tack room. She wasn't about to get into a prolonged conversation about Reggie, if she could avoid it. As she rechecked the medicine and feed schedule, she could hear Nick whistling, strolling down shedrow. Daisy brushed her messed up hair back from her face. Why did she tingle so? Maybe because she'd never been on a formal date.

"So what does a girl wear to the symphony, Angie?" Daisy leaned against the door of Angie Underwood's cramped dressing room. Angie sat before a mirror tilting her head to one side and then the other. She tied her hair up and then untied it, letting it fall loosely around her shoulders.

Nick's sister turned on her stool and grinned broadly at Daisy. "Didn't you go with Nick to a charity ball?"

"Yes."

"That would be fine, if you want to dress up. If you don't want to be that fancy, then drop down a notch." Angie turned back to the mirror and plucked at her eyebrows. "It's pretty hard to go wrong anymore. Almost anything goes at the symphony or the theater these days, unless its opening night. Now, that's a gala affair."

"Nick didn't say it was opening night."

"Then it probably isn't. We can check that out easily enough. So my brother is back on your scent?" Angie pursed her lips and blew Daisy a kiss in the mirror.

Daisy frowned. She wasn't entirely comfortable talking with Angie about her brother. But Angie seemed more than comfortable. "He asked me out."

"And you said yes."

"I told him I would before I left his house."

"But you could've said no."

"Sure."

"Then why did you say yes?" Angie turned around to face Daisy. "You've told me why you wanted to be back in your own apartment, and I think I understand why Nick intimidates you. But I wonder if you're playing with my brother or with yourself?"

"I don't know what you mean." Daisy glanced over at Angie's dressing screen.

"I'm a woman, Daisy. You're not talking to Nick now." Angie rose and slipped out of her wrapper and stepped over to a rack of gowns.

Daisy watched Angie unabashed, clad only in panties, stand back and try to decide among her choices. Again, Daisy wished she'd been blessed with such a figure. She'd always been too tall for her age. Girls chided her and boys hated the fact that she was a foot taller than them. But that was then. Now she'd found a man who matched her height and seemed quite pleased with her body. Daisy shook her head. What was Angie saying?

"Hey you, leaning against the wall. Did you come to talk to me or stare at me or ignore me?"

"I'm sorry," Daisy mumbled. "I'm not playing with Nick or myself. At least I'm not trying to."

Angie shrugged into a long pink gown. It was a period piece from the 1880s. "So there's a chance that Nick will be able to successfully woo you?"

"What?" Daisy pushed away from the door and stepped over to button the column of tiny buttons

282

going down the back of Angie's dress.

Angie turned her head. "Thanks. That you'll agree to be my sister-in-law, silly. Isn't that what all of this is about?"

A tiny button slipped through Daisy's fingers. She scowled. She tried again. Having secured it in its loop, she moved on to the next and finally commented, "Can't we just go out and enjoy each other's company? Why does it always have to come down to marriage, kids and forever?"

Angie shrugged. "Maybe because Nick is aware of a time clock ticking that you're not. It's okay to have fun, Daisy. I'm not condemning you for that—not hardly. Not me. But you've got to know Nick wants more than that."

Daisy glanced at Angie's image in the mirror and nodded.

"So you're not ready to really commit, nor are you ready to let him go yet."

"Something like that."

"Thanks for doing my buttons," Angie said, sitting back down before the mirror. She picked up a brush and began running it through her hair. The woman's eyes smoldered; it was the only sign that the outgoing, congenial Angie Underwood was angry.

"I've never seen my brother so in love. He's besotted. Any other woman who pulled a stunt like you did by walking out on him would have been left in his dust. He'd never give her a second thought."

"I didn't exactly walk out on him," Daisy

283

protested. "I only stayed with him for a short time because of an emergency. I never agreed to live with him. And how do you know he loves me so much? He's been married and with many women before me."

Angie smiled into the mirror. Her flashpoint of anger had apparently subsided. "But not since you. You want to know about his first wife and the other women? His wife was much more interested in Nick than he was in her, but she came around at the right time. Nick was feeling the need to be a family man. Only Ashley wasn't too excited about motherhood once they were married.

"She wasn't a bad woman, I don't mean that, but she saw Nick as a way up the business and social ladder. Much more than a husband and a father, and I expect as a lover. As to *other women,* Nick hasn't had a relationship that I know of that lasted more than two months. And I doubt there was anyone for two or three years before you arrived on the scene. No, my brother doesn't dispense love like it's a freebie in a grocery store."

"I didn't think he did," Daisy retorted. But Angie's words left her more confused than ever. If there had been so few women that Nick had cared for, how did that explain her?

"So do you love him?"

Daisy wanted to ignore the bug-eyed, curious woman in the mirror, but she couldn't. "You don't give up, do you?"

"No. It's a family trait. So do you?"

"What?"

"Do you love him?"

Daisy sat down on a stool beside Angie. She wanted to collapse. She shook her head. "I don't honestly know. I don't know how I would know."

Angie applied rouge to her cheeks. "Well, do you think a lot about him when he's not with you?"

Daisy nodded.

"Do you miss him when you're alone in your bed at night?"

Daisy nodded.

"Does he make you laugh?"

Daisy nodded.

"Do you get goose bumps when I ask you if you love him?"

Daisy lifted her arm and Angie stared at the rows of small pimpled bumps. Laughing softly, Angie said, "Daisy Matthews, like it or not, I'd say you're in love."

"But it can't go where he wants it to go."

"Where you want it to go?"

Daisy let out a repressed sigh. "Maybe."

"Because of your brother-in-law?"

"Yes."

"Maybe he'll take Nick more seriously now, after the escapade at the hospital."

Daisy shuddered. "That's what I'm afraid of."

- o -

Nick sat in a box overlooking the finish line.

285

Thelma chattered her nervousness while Tom rested his eyes. They had a chance to claim a filly in the fifth race. Nick worried about what Thelma might do if they lost the claim.

Leaning forward, Nick rested his chin on his hands and stared at the tall blonde in tight jeans, maroon shirt, and ball cap stepping out on to the track and snapping a lead rope to the number three horse in the first race of the day. Daisy exchanged a few words with the jockey and then led the gelding back toward the barn. It had run a decent third.

He watched Daisy pat the animal on the shoulder and whisper something, no doubt endearing, into its ear. Nick wished he could trade places with the horse. He shook his head. *You've got it bad, Underwood. Real bad.*

His eyes did not stray from the woman leading the horse away from the track. Her bottom swayed that alluring motion that he expected had attracted men since man and woman became aware of each other. Daisy led the horse around a corner and out of view.

Nick leaned back and ran his fingers through his hair. He couldn't remember ever having a woman tie him and twist him about in so many directions. Usually, he was in the driver's seat. But not with Daisy Matthews. That didn't particularly bother him. What bothered him was that he cared too damn much. Too much about her, and too much about what she thought of him.

He'd been a fool to let her walk out of his

house. He'd been more of a fool not to just let her keep walking. He'd be a bigger fool yet if he let her slip through his fingers.

Nick pushed his glasses down and squeezed the bridge of his nose. Daisy might have some legitimate qualms about her feelings for him and about sharing her life with him, but Reggie Lassiter remained at the crux of his problems with Daisy. He could not figure out the claim the man had on Daisy. Was it simply her sister and Daisy's fierce sense of family loyalty? Did Lassiter have designs on Daisy? Had he abused her? Clearly, Maxine stayed with her husband even though the man had nearly killed her. Could Daisy be from the same mold as her sister? Daisy was proud. She had more courage than most anyone he'd known. So how did Lassiter manage to terrorize her so?

Clint Travers had called the day before to tell Nick that they'd finally traced Lassiter. He had resurfaced. He'd been seen visiting Maxine. There was now a tail on Lassiter as well as on Daisy. The slime ball was cautious, but he'd screw up sooner or later. And Clint expected that his man would be there to nail him when he did.

As for Daisy, it had surprised Nick to learn that she'd visited his sister at the theater. The two of them were thicker than he liked at the moment. He didn't want Daisy picking up any more family ammunition than she already had. She knew a hell of a lot more about him and his family than he did about hers. Though he had to agree he wasn't certain he really wanted to know more about her family. He just wanted Daisy, and he didn't give a damn about her sister or her brother-in-law.

Nick stood and stretched. Why was he so melancholy? Damn, he had a date with Daisy that night. MrShowman would be running in the seventh and they still had a shot at a claim in the fifth. He should be feeling like he was at the top of his game. Instead, he was down. Maybe it was the lack of sleep, and Mrs. B. was constantly harping on his poor eating habits. The damn woman couldn't stop pestering him with hints of wondering when that gentle, tall, beautiful Miss Daisy would be back.

Tall and beautiful, no doubt. Gentle? No way. That damn Miss Daisy fought hard. She'd freely given him her virginity, but he wanted more, much more. And now she was fighting and clawing like a cat from hell. Nick blew on his fingernails. Well, this old Tom was more wily than most.

- o -

Repressing an urge to sing and dance, Daisy tiptoed toward the shower. What a day it had been already, and Nick would be picking her up within the hour.

Stepping into the shower, she turned on the pulsating stream of water as hot as she could stand it and reached for the soap. She soaped her breasts and belly and then each long leg, recounting the day's events.

There was another horse in their barn. Blue Horizon, a three-year-old filly, had shown promise in two races as a two-year-old and then six more during her three-year-old campaign. Sam felt that he and Daisy could possibly improve the horse to be a decent runner in allowance races.

Daisy let the water cascade over her hair. She held her breath and then stepped out from under the water and shook her head. She grabbed a towel and began vigorously rubbing herself dry.

She grinned, thinking that Thelma had to be the happiest person at the track that day. The woman had screamed and danced when she found out that their claim had been successful. And Tom had nearly had to pry his wife away from the stable when it was time to go home. Thelma would likely become a pest, needing to know every little burp Blue Horizon made, but it would be fun having the expressive woman around more often.

Daisy reached for the blow dryer and frowned. Why couldn't she be the free spirit Thelma appeared to be? But she was too much of a worrier. As she dried her wavy hair, she watched her breasts rise and fall with each move. Too bad Nick wasn't there. He always enjoyed watching her shower and get ready. It gave him an opportunity to pamper her with his eyes and his fingertips, he'd say.

Her skin flushed. Well, he wasn't here. And she had to erase those kinds of thoughts from her mind or she really would be in trouble. This was their first date, not the continuation of jumping in and out of bed like two randy rabbits. She tried to suppress a smile; she'd always been fond of bunnies.

She glanced at the clock. *Damn, he'll be here soon and I'm not even close to being ready. Quit lollygagging, girl.*

Slipping on the gold dress she'd purchased at Macy's after conferring with Angie, Daisy admired the new look. She'd decided to treat herself; she could afford it now. There should be a limit to frugality.

The dress was certainly beyond that limit. It was classy and sexy at the same time, hugging the contours of her body like a jockey riding low over a horse's neck and withers. While the vee neck made a hint of suggestion, the mid-thigh hemline showed off her thighs and legs very nicely. A gold chain gathered the satiny material at the waist. She slipped her feet into gold pumps and pronounced herself ready for the symphony.

Daisy's brow furrowed. Jewelry? She hadn't bothered about going to the bank to retrieve the diamonds. The gold bracelet seemed like too much gold. She plucked the opal from the jewelry box. She latched its chain behind her neck and tucked it into the vee of her dress.

Pirouetting before the bedroom mirror, she smiled mischievously. She wasn't ready to walk away from whatever she had with Nick, and she didn't want him all of a sudden deciding to break things off between them. She certainly didn't want him to forget what he was missing. Appraising herself yet another time in the mirror, she concluded he wouldn't.

- o -

Scrunching down in his seat and sticking a leg out into the aisle, Nick released a satisfied sigh. His fingers enfolded Daisy's hand atop the arm rest between their two seats. He looked at Daisy and grinned. With eyes rounded and posture straight, Daisy's attention was completely fixed on the orchestra. She was so expressive. He loved to watch the music move her almost to tears, and then a smile parted her lips, and then a foot would tap lightly. Daisy couldn't just sit there and listen — she became an instrument. She became the music. It was that spirit that enabled her to communicate with horses on a level he couldn't totally comprehend. Her capacity for exploring sensations was what allowed her to become such a creative lover.

Had he ever been that innocently enthusiastic? She was so mature and honed by the streets that he was surprised each time he witnessed her childlike quality as she embraced new experiences without question or hesitation.

Nick squeezed her hand. When she'd met him at the door of her apartment, childhood qualities were not what had crossed his mind. She was absolutely stunning in that gold dress. He grinned, remembering. She'd been so proud that she'd selected and bought the dress on her own.

He wagered that that was one of the few times she'd gone out and splurged on herself. She'd demonstrated superlative taste; he could not have done better himself. That the dress rode nearly up to her butt when she sat down was simply an added benefit for him.

Damn, he already missed what she could do to him with those fit, long legs.

Don't go there, old buddy. This is hard enough without torturing yourself. Was she trying to torture him with her choice of apparel? He groaned, shifting his position to provide his arousal more room. Hell, it would be excruciating sitting next to her in that dress or if she'd worn a sweat suit.

Nick was startled to see Daisy rise to her feet and clap her hands loudly. Belatedly, Nick noticed that everyone around them was standing and applauding.

The conductor was bowing to the audience and inviting the musicians to stand.

"That was fantastic," Daisy said, turning to Nick. Her eyes were shining. "Thank you for bringing me. I never thought I'd enjoy the symphony. It's such a complete experience. You get caught up in the music whether you want to or not."

"I'm glad you liked it." With one hand, Nick took Daisy by the elbow and guided her up the aisle. His other hand rested low on her back. If she was bothered by this intimacy, she didn't show it. "We'll stop at one of the pubs nearby for a drink, and you can tell me all about it."

They sat in a darkened corner of Henri's sipping White Zinfindel. He was in danger of being mesmerized by Daisy's mood swings. First, she'd chatter endlessly about the mood of the music, or the instruments she'd learned to name, or how the conductor performed like a skilled horse trainer, or the glitter of the audience. And then she'd withdraw as if she were seeking the protection of a private cave. He doubted he'd ever grow bored with this young woman so filled with mystery.

"So do you think we should do another symphony sometime?" he asked.

"Oh yes, that would be great." She leaned back away from him. "If that's something you'd like to do." Daisy ran an index finger along the rim of her glass. "You know so much more about culture than I do."

"Don't overrate that. My mom saw to it that we kids got to the performing arts. Sometimes she had to drag me kicking and screaming. Literally."

Daisy giggled and quickly covered her mouth.

"It's true. I guess all of that encouragement did have some effect, though it impacted Angie more than me. But at least my mother tried."

Daisy sobered. "I don't imagine my mother ever stepped into a symphony or a theater."

Reaching across the small round table, Nick covered Daisy's hand with his. "You're a well-read young woman, Daisy. You've picked up more culture, as you put it, than many folks who attend the symphony or the opera or the theater or the ballet on a regular basis."

Scowling, Daisy asked, "What do you mean by that?"

Nick cocked his head toward her. "I suppose there are many patrons of the arts who search for the kind of meaning you so evidently find. But there also those who go because they want to be seen by a certain crowd. Culture for them is something to be worn, rather than tasted and savored." He squeezed her fingers. "You are a taster and a savorer. And I love that about you. Along with a lot of other qualities."

Nick watched the color rise in Daisy's cheeks. She closed her eyes as if she could block out his praise—though he expected she privately cherished his words before preparing to flee from them. That was okay. He didn't expect to woo her in a single night. But he was planting seeds. He hoped that if he planted enough seeds, some would come to fruition.

At some point during the past week of soul searching, he'd come to the realization that one of many reasons Daisy might be unable to accept his love was that she couldn't fathom herself loveable. He'd have to show her that what they had wasn't all about sex. Though it might be hard to convince the woman dressed in gold of that fact if she could see the current size of his erection.

- o -

"Oh, Bear," said Daisy, squeezing Bear to her breasts. Even with Bear, the bed didn't feel complete. "Sometimes I don't remember why it's so important to have my own space.

"It was a magical night. You would have loved it. The musical instruments came to life; I thought they were making sounds just for me. And the crowd—such beautiful people." She frowned. "Nick says a lot of them are just there to be seen. I don't know about that. But if so, what a waste.

"Bear, I can't believe it. Daisy Ann Matthews goes to the symphony with a handsome escort. It might as well be Daisy Ann Matthews wins the lottery.

"You know, maybe he really does love me. Could it really be?" Daisy shook her head. "Sometimes I think you're on his side, Bear. I know there aren't sides, but it feels that way.

"He loves me because I'm a taster," she whispered. She closed her eyes, remembering the taste of his skin.

She clutched Bear in one hand; her other hand covered the curls at the juncture of her thighs. She brushed them lightly. Applying more pressure, she teased herself. Her breath quickened and her heart rate picked up. Abruptly, she withdrew her fingers and rolled over.

She would wait. She would wait to be with her lover. She would wait until she could taste him and he could taste her. If nothing else, she could savor the dream.

Chapter Fourteen

At four o'clock in the afternoon, Daisy made her rounds checking her charges, making sure hay-nets held enough hay, and refilling water buckets with fresh water. A groom raked the gravel alleyway in front of the Gallagher barn.

Daisy clamped the hose tight in one hand to cut off its flow while dragging it to the next stall. There she let the water rush forth, filling the next bucket. She loved this routine. While the early morning hours were precious in nearly inexplicable ways, the late afternoon feeding marked the end of a busy day. Either she or Sam would be back later to make sure the horses were safely tucked away, but this was the last prolonged interaction with them.

Of course, race days were a little different for those horses that might be running late in the afternoon. But they didn't have any horses running on this day. She could hear the echo of the crowd as horses neared the finish line, but it seemed to come from a world far, far away. If she didn't know better, that world and this world would appear to have little or no connection. That world was competition; this one was nurturing. That world was fast-paced; this one was slower. Yet this world of liniments, leather, hay, majestic

297

beasts, and soft nickering wouldn't exist without that world of excited and disappointed bettors, of proud jockeys and cantankerous owners. Both worlds shared a fondness for chasing dreams across a canvas of many defeats and fewer triumphs.

"Well, I finally found you, bitch."

Daisy whirled at the all too familiar voice. Water splashed the dirt in front of Reggie's feet, splattering his shining black shoes with blotches of mud.

"Shit, woman!" he bellowed. "Get that hose away from me. These are two hundred and fifty dollar shoes."

Trying to remain casual, Daisy walked slowly to the side of the barn and turned off the faucet. She rolled up the hose, ignoring her brother-in-law's efforts at cleaning his precious shoes. Where had he gotten the money to buy such expensive shoes? And why hadn't he given some of that money to his wife?

Tucking his handkerchief back in his pocket, Reggie seemed to remember why he was there. He peeked in a couple of stalls before addressing Daisy. "Nice looking horseflesh. Understand you're moving up in the world. Sort of like me." He grinned a crooked smile.

Daisy fought back rising bile. "How did you get back here? This is a restricted area."

Reggie laughed derisively. "You mean like your apartment. That fancy security system don't mean shit if someone really wanted to get in. I've got contacts. Lookie here." He pointed at his visitor's badge. "See, I belong."

The two of them would never belong in the same place, but holding her tongue, Daisy waited for Reggie to tell her why he was there.

"Yep. Nice horseflesh. I understand you own a part of some these money machines." He sneered up at her. "You've been holding out on me. But," he raised his hand as if to stop her protest, "I know you've been busy with Maxine and the boyfriend. I can understand you not keeping me informed of your business ventures."

He took a menacing step forward. "But now I'm here, bitch. And I know. And I've figured out a nice way for you to share some of that wealth with your family."

"Oh?" Daisy stood tall, refusing to back down.

"Yep. Your boyfriend gave me the idea. That security system he had installed." Reggie tapped his temple. "You might say a lightbulb went on. I should've thought of it myself. Protection. Protection is the name of the game."

"I don't understand." Daisy crossed her arms. She tried not to look around for help. Unless he actually tried to harm her physically, no one would be able to discern from a distance that she wasn't simply having a discussion with a potential owner or an old acquaintance. If he wanted to push her around, Reggie Lassiter wouldn't pick such a public place. He appeared much more in control of himself than usual—that was even more frightening.

"Oh, you will understand, bitch." Reggie's lips curled and he emitted a harsh laugh. "You might say I'm offering you insurance." He shook his head. "No, that's not true. I'm telling you to buy some insurance, from me, Reggie Lassiter."

Daisy's brow furrowed.

"Let's make it black and white, bitch. You pay me five hundred a month, and I'll see that nothing bad happens to these damn animals you own. If you don't pay me," Reggie shook his head in mocking concern, "I can't guarantee their safety. You get the picture."

Wishing she could rub her throbbing temples, Daisy nodded. He was blackmailing her.

"And if you think you don't need the protection, think again, bitch. If I can get back here this easily, any scumbag can."

Daisy closed her eyes and almost laughed. The man was ludicrous, but he was dangerous. What choice did she have? At least he wouldn't be beating on her sister. And it wasn't as if she couldn't afford it, at least for the time being. As long as her partnership with Nick lasted. Of course, if she didn't have the partnership, she wouldn't have the horses, and Reggie wouldn't have the leverage. But he'd still have her sister.

Opening her eyes, Daisy saw a burly security man marching toward them. "Excuse me, ma'am, is this man bothering you?"

Daisy hesitated. She saw Reggie's eyes narrow in warning and she shook her head. "No, it's all right. He's not bothering me."

"I'm glad to hear that, he's in enough trouble." The track security officer turned to Reggie. "You're no longer welcome here, Mr. Lassiter. I was just informed to escort you off the premises."

"On whose orders? I've got clearance." Reggie backed away and the security officer placed a hand on Reggie's shoulder.

"Let's not make a scene, Mr. Lassiter. I'm just following orders. Your clearance has been revoked."

"Who says?" Reggie clinched his fists.

"I say. And my two colleagues coming up from behind you agree with me." Reggie turned his head sharply and groaned.

"Now, let's go along quietly. We don't want to scare the young lady or the horses. Both can be temperamental, you know."

Daisy decided not to take umbrage at the man's poor sense of humor. She liked the idea of Reggie being escorted off the grounds, though she knew that wouldn't reduce the risk to her horses.

"Okay, you win," Reggie said to the officer and then spun toward Daisy. "You remember what I said, I'll expect to hear from you the first of the month. Don't be late."

Daisy watched her brother-in-law being led away between two security officers. It was uncanny that they had come along when they did. And who had tipped off the track office about Reggie? Had they really banned him from the premises?

Apparently they had.

She breathed a sigh of relief. Still, she knew she'd have to pay the protection money. Given all the things the bastard might come up with, that was the least intrusive. And she knew she was protecting more than the horses. She was protecting Maxine and Nick, and maybe even herself.

Leaning against the stable, Daisy gazed at the spot where Reggie had stood when he made his threats. How long would five hundred dollars satisfy Reggie's greed? Probably not for long. She huddled against a stiff, cool breeze. How long would money satisfy Reggie Lassiter's lust for blood?

Daisy pulled into a parking spot across from her walkup apartment and scowled. Directly in front of her sat a familiar red Jeep; its driver opened the door to get out. After the unsettling encounter with Reggie, the last thing she needed was the doting attention of Nicholas Underwood. Her lips thinned in response to Nick's set jaw.

"Hi," he said. "How are you?"

"I'm fine," she replied, stepping out of the pickup and grabbing her purse.

"Are you going to invite me in?"

She folded her arms across her chest and leaned against the pickup fender. "Only if you're going to be civil. You look like someone bit your tail real hard."

"Let's get off the street, if you don't mind." Nick took Daisy by the elbow and escorted her toward her front door.

Daisy shook her head and pulled out her keys. Was she getting paranoid, or was Nick looking around like he was expecting company?

"You want something to drink?" she offered, once they entered her dining room.

"Sure. If you have wine open, that'll be fine. Or a pop will do."

She heard his footsteps following her into the kitchen. This Underwood mood was unusual. He was tense, almost combative. As she opened a bottle of Prairie Fume, she took the initiative. "So, how was your day? I didn't expect to see you this evening. Is something wrong?"

"I don't know. I was hoping you could tell me."

"I've got to sit on something soft." By way of explanation, she added, "It's been a day of being on my feet most of the time."

They carried the glasses into the living room. Daisy sat on the loveseat. Nick remained standing.

Daisy sipped from her glass. "So why are you really here? You don't have your romantic face on."

Nick sat down in the wing chair and exhaled. "Damn, why is it so important for you to keep me in the dark?"

"What?"

Nick tilted forward. His eyes flashed sparks. "I understand you were involved in a bit of commotion out at the track today."

Daisy refused to look away. Her mind raced. How had he found out? How much did he know?

303

Did he know about the blackmail? Did he know she'd agreed to Reggie's demands? "Oh, you mean Reggie?"

"Was there more? What did he want? Did he hurt you? Did he threaten you?"

Daisy feared that Nick would break the wine glass clenched in his hand. "No, he didn't hurt me," she said, maybe too quickly. "He wanted me to know that he was back."

"And?"

Lurching to her feet, Daisy glared at Nick and then turned her back on him. She stared at the small gas fireplace. "Why do you have to know everything that happens in my life?" she demanded. "You have no right."

"I love you." Nick rose and wrapped his arms around her, drawing her back into his chest. "I don't want you to get hurt," he whispered. "I don't think I could stand that."

Daisy closed her eyes and all her senses turned to mush. Why did love have to be so complicated? She shuddered against his strength. "I know," she managed to say, "but I'm okay. No one is going to hurt me."

"What about Reggie?"

Turning in his arms to face him, Daisy said, "I don't think Reggie is interested in physically hurting me." She smiled thinly. "If I were hurt, his wife wouldn't be able to bum off me."

"He wanted more money?"

Daisy shrugged and walked toward the kitchen. "He always wants more money."

304

"What drives me up the wall as much as anything," said Nick, his voice rising, "is your damn evasiveness. Are we in this together, or not?"

Leaning against the sink, Daisy responded sharply, "Not entirely. No. You don't run my life like you do some corporation. You see danger where I don't. If I want to give money to my sister, that's my business, not yours."

Nick stood in the corner of the kitchen, apparently searching for words. She had never seen him look so helpless. Wanting to say something, to do something that would comfort him, she took what she believed was the wiser course: she said and did nothing.

Throwing up his hands, Nick said quietly, "So I'm not supposed to concern myself with Reggie Lassiter. I'm not supposed to concern myself with your safety."

She nodded, hoping she looked more defiant than she felt.

"So, I'm supposed to sit on my hands and wait to see if you can ever come up with enough money to satisfy your sister and brother-in-law or until Reggie crosses the wrong guy and either winds up in jail or in a casket."

Daisy's eyes rounded. She remained silent.

"That may be what you want, but I can promise if the bastard goes after anything that's mine, I'll strike back harder than he's ever known."

"I'd expect you to protect your own," Daisy protested.

"Just as I'd do."

She pursed her lips at his smug smile. "Oh no, you don't. I'm not yours. Our relationship doesn't give you any right to protect me."

"Right." He stepped forward and lifted her chin with an index finger.

Electricity snapped through her body. He was going to trap her somehow. He had that look of victory on his face.

"So, my young lady friend, what in the hell are you attempting to do on my behalf by keeping secrets if not protecting me? Protecting me from knowing more about your family. Protecting my financial assets from Reggie. Maybe even my property. I wouldn't be shocked if the bastard didn't threaten our horses or the canoe factory."

Daisy clamped her eyes shut. "No, not the canoe factory. Not yet," she whispered.

"The horses?" She nodded.

"Damn. And you were going to pay him off and fight him alone."

"He's my brother-in-law." She opened her eyes. "Not yours."

"Well, that's a situation I'd like to rectify."

Daisy lost her breath and stepped sidewise, eluding Nick's grasp. "Please, don't make things more messy than they already are."

Nick backed away and removed his glasses. He reached for his handkerchief and began cleaning them. He was stymied. The woman was twisting him in more directions than what showed on any compass he'd ever held. Was he a fool? If he was a wise man, he'd just walk away and leave this beauty and her sultry overbite to the wolves. He winced. He'd always enjoyed being regarded as the fool. There was more than one corporate executive who was left wondering how he had been outmaneuvered by such a laid back innocent as himself.

But Daisy Matthews was more wily than any business executive he'd ever dealt with. Clint Travers had tipped him off as soon as Reggie was spotted entering the stable area. But he had to pry the information out of Daisy. She was still hiding from him, but he'd stumbled across another motivating factor for her. She was trying to protect him. Should he laugh or cry? How did she think she was going to protect him from the likes of Reggie Lassiter?

And she knew he wanted to marry her. But each time he made even an oblique reference to such a possibility, she fled emotionally, and if she could really fly she'd be long gone from his presence. The woman was becoming hazardous to his ego.

"So, what do you want me to do, Daisy, crawl into a hole and wait for you to sort out your life?" He wet his lips. "If so, you haven't yet learned that there will always be things to sort out in your life. Probably even when you're ninety."

Nick watched that trapped look reappear in her eyes. It wasn't there often—but it was that look that tore his insides up more than anything else. She looked so alone, so helpless. So in need of what he wanted to give her.

"So, what do you want from me, Daisy? Don't leave me hanging."

- o -

Trembling, Daisy struggled to speak. Why was it so much easier to talk to Bear than to Nick? She closed her eyes and imagined Bear. She chewed her lower lip and then whispered, "I don't want to lose you. I want you with me, Nick. But I can't marry you. So don't ask." She whimpered. "Not now. I want you to hold me, if you would."

His arms enfolded her and she laid her head on his shoulder. He stroked her back, calming her trembling. "I want you," she said, "but you've got to let me be me."

"I know," he moaned into her hair. "I try, but I don't want to see you hurt."

"Nor do I want to see *you* hurt." She leaned back against his arms. She smiled through tears. "Do you think we can be together and not hurt each other?"

"Not likely," Nick admitted.

"I suppose you're right." She ran her fingers along his smooth chin. Her heart clutched. There was only one way to free it. She needed to give love. She needed to receive love. She bent forward and traced his lips with her tongue. Nick froze in place like a statue. "To hell with the pain," she said, her voice husky. "Show me how much you love me, Nicholas Underwood. Right here. Right

308

now."

She covered his lips with hers. She separated his lips and her tongue probed his mouth. His tongue greeted hers and then entered her mouth. She sucked his tongue until she feared tearing it out by its roots. Already her reservoir was filling. She soared. She'd missed him so. She'd kiss him for hours if other parts of her body weren't so insistent on demanding equal treatment.

Without breaking their kiss, she reached for the button on his shirt. He continued probing her mouth, searching as if for something long lost.

Frustrated, wanting to feel his skin against hers, she broke the kiss. She tore at her blouse; buttons skittered across the floor. Her bra followed. At last, she rubbed her hardening nipples against his. She breathed deeply, reveling in his scent. Nick groaned loudly. His hardness pressed against her loins.

"Are you sure?" he asked, hoarsely.

"Most definitely." She licked his corded neck muscles in case he didn't believe her words.

"You're not going to run from me when we're done."

"Not hardly.

"Good." He reached for her belt buckle and she worked to undo his. In tandem, they divested each other of remaining clothes.

Nick laved her breasts, first one and then the other.

"God, I've missed you so," Daisy whimpered, leaning back against the counter.

He began to work his way lower. Daisy grabbed his hair. "No need for that. I'm so ready. I have to have you inside me now, before I crumble."

Nick smiled broadly. "I aim to please. Right here?"

"Right here." Daisy wheeled to face the counter and bent over. "See if you can find the mark.

"Oh my God," she groaned, feeling his fullness probe her entry. "Why did I ever think it was a good idea to do without this?"

"It was a crazy idea," he said, biting her shoulder. "I can attest to that."

She turned her head and grinned. "A little less talk and a little more action, please."

She'd offered herself, and now it was her time to receive. He filled her until there was no empty space remaining. Her entire awareness focused on that one over heated pleasure spot and then fanned out to take in his hands deliciously squeezing her buttocks and the countertop cool against her nipples.

Nick set a languid pace. She squeezed, wanting more, urging him to quicken. "Hell," he groaned, "you win. Slow can wait."

He pulled nearly out and slammed his hips against her buttocks. Daisy gripped the counter top tight. "Way to go, old man," she teased. "I need you now. All of you."

His hips churned against her rear until she lost track of him entirely. She remained conscious only of that tiny place in her own body that loomed so huge. And then it grew, it spread like fire out of control threatening everything in its path. It leapt about, first here and then there beckoning, urging her forward. And then when she was certain she'd be totally consumed she was cast out into the darkness until she found herself resting on soft grass near a cool spring. Had she found heaven?

From a great distance, as if through an echo chamber, she heard his voice. "Are you still with me?"

With considerable effort, she pulled herself back. Her eyes popped open. Reality rapidly returned. She was confronted by floral wallpaper and two dirty pans.

"I'm here," she managed to whisper. "Wow." She sighed deeply. "Maybe there is something to be said about abstaining."

"Not enough," Nick growled, stroking her back.

The next morning was Daisy's day off and she took pleasure in serving Nick coffee in bed. She crawled back in beside him and took a swallow from her cup.

"A guy could get used to this," Nick said, winking at Daisy. "You're a full service woman."

"Like you," she smirked, "I aim to please."

He nodded. "And you're very good at that. So. Now what? This is fantastic, Daisy. But where do we go from here? Or am I just an old fuddy-duddy for wondering."

"No, you're not that." She ducked from his

gaze and blushed. "I'd say sex is back in our relationship."

"That's a safe assumption," Nick replied, reaching over to brush a nipple through her thin nightgown. "And?"

"So, do we have to have everything laid out in concrete?"

"No, not at all. I just want to have realistic expectations." He shrugged. "I assume this doesn't mean you're ready to move in with me?"

Daisy's features clouded. "No, I'm not ready for that."

"Not yet," he pried.

"Not yet."

"But it remains a possibility someday."

"A possibility."

"But we could spend the night in Kenwood some of the time?"

She nodded.

"Good, I can live with that. And what about Reggie? Am I supposed to turn my back and ignore that he's a danger to you, to me, to us?"

"I can handle Reggie," Daisy snorted. "You would just make things worse. He already hates you. I want to contain him in my own way."

"And you won't accept advice."

Daisy shook her head.

"Okay, I don't like that, but what choice do I have? I love you. Hopefully, in time you'll grow to trust me more and understand that your problems are my problems."

Daisy sipped her coffee. They'd never agree on

how to handle Reggie. If she could get Nick to turn his back, as he put it, maybe that would be the best and most she'd get from him. He'd never fully appreciate the danger he brought down on himself by simply staying involved with her. But she couldn't sort all of that out. Not now. She needed him too much, and apparently he needed her too much for either of them to simply walk away from what they had.

Accommodation. That was one of those big words she'd learned in her introductory sociology class. Migrating populations often had to learn to accommodate to existing cultures. And to a certain extent, existing cultures had to accommodate to the new ideas, tools, and norms of the migrating population.

Well, Nick had migrated to her culture, so he'd have to accommodate the best he could.

"So," she said, with a trace of incredulity, "when you next have a problem at Paddle Dreams Unlimited, you'll come running to me for advice. Maybe I can even tell you what to do."

Nick scowled darkly. "That's different, and you know it."

"Maybe. But I doubt we're going to get further by fighting about it." She grinned. "Do you want to fight or make love?"

"What a question," Nick responded. He set his coffee cup down and then relieved Daisy of hers. "Let me show you which I'd prefer."

Daisy allowed herself to be comfortably pulled into his arms. They'd only worked out a truce of

313

sorts, but life was far better this morning than it had been the previous morning. Her grandmother had always told her to be thankful for small blessings. Daisy smiled. Oh yes, she was thankful this day for blessings, small and big.

- o -

"So how do we contain Lassiter?" Nick stared hard at Clint and Cassie Travers, who sat across from him in their farmhouse kitchen.

"I wish I could be more positive." Clint traced a design on the kitchen table cloth. "But the guy is cagey. Hell, the cops have been trying to collar him for years."

"I don't know how such a dumb ass can outsmart so many people."

"It's a matter of time. He'll overstep; he'll cross the line. He probably has in the past, but no one was watching at that moment. Now we're watching."

Nick squeezed his arms tight. Daisy would have a fit if she knew he was there talking to Clint and Cassie about Reggie, but there was no way he could just sit idly by and watch the bastard drain her, either.

As if reading his mind, Cassie pushed her chair away from the table and rose. "I don't suppose Daisy has any idea you're having Reggie tailed."

"Nope. She'd think I was interfering."

"And what will she think if she finds out you have a tail on her, too?"

314

Nick grimaced. "She'd go ballistic."

"I don't like being part of this subterfuge." Cassie removed their coffee cups from the table.

"You wouldn't be part of it, if you had kept your nose to yourself," Clint declared, scowling at his wife.

Cassie stuck her tongue out at him. "I learned long ago that I'd better keep my nose in everything that goes on around here, or I could be in deep trouble.

"Don't worry about me," she said, smiling sweetly at Nick, "I won't go share your secrets with Daisy. Any more than I share hers with you." She picked up a towel and began wiping the table.

At least she was taking out her anger on the table rather than on him.

She looked back up at him. "One of these days the two of you are going to have to learn to trust each other more than you do, or your secrets are going to destroy a damn good relationship." Cassie glared at her husband. "I have chores to do in the barn," she said tartly. "See that you control yourself while my nose is absent."

Clint chuckled. "Or you'll pry it out of me later."

"Of course. I always do."

The redhead sauntered through the kitchen to the porch swaying her hips with purpose. Nick laughed. There was little question how she'd wheedle information from her husband.

Wincing at the slamming of the porch door, Clint arched his eyebrows. "Women can be

315

infuriating no matter how long you've known them."

Nick nodded in agreement.

"We'll keep the surveillance on Reggie. Do you want to keep it on Daisy?"

Glancing at the doorway, Nick knew Cassie was right. If Daisy ever found out he was having her followed, she'd flay him over a slow burning fire. But it was the only way he knew he could keep her safe. And even then there were no guarantees.

He shrugged his shoulders and pushed his glasses firmly against the bridge of his nose. He nodded at Clint. "Yeah, Daisy, too."

Chapter Fifteen

Daisy scrutinized Blue Horizon, who was entering the practice starting gate under the guidance of her female exercise rider. For once, Thelma Harrison was quiet, resting her arms on the rail fence beside Daisy. The part owner had made it a habit to come out to the track whenever Blue was scheduled for a workout.

This day was no exception. Blue would be working four furlongs from the gate. This would be a huge preparatory work. If she showed something and came out of the breeze fit, then they would try to find a race for her within the next two weeks.

"Blue looks terrific, doesn't she?" Thelma murmured.

"She's full of herself this morning. We'll see how she comes out of the gate. Soon we'll know."

Daisy punched the button on her stop watch as soon as the gate popped open and Blue Horizon lunged forward under the encouragement of her rider. Blue's strides lengthened and she tucked her head down to her broad chest like she enjoyed what she was doing. Daisy smiled when the filly blew by where they stood. She glanced down at her watch and let out a low whistle. "Forty-eight flat. Very nice." She turned to Thelma. "I believe

317

we do have a racehorse here."

"I sure hope so. Tom's having second thoughts. But I love that beast. I just hope she can do well."

"We'll see soon enough. Some horses work fine in the morning, but run poorly in the afternoon." Shading her eyes from the early morning sun, Daisy studied the filly approaching her. Nothing looked amiss. The horse looked like she'd prefer to run another mile or so. "I don't think Blue will disappoint," she said to Thelma. "She's got a nice set of wheels. And smooth action."

Both women followed the exercise rider and filly back toward their barn. "It amazes me that this track is right in the middle of the city," Thelma said. "Arlington is beautiful, but this is much more handy for the city fan."

"Sure is," Daisy agreed, never taking her eyes from the legs of the filly walking in front of them. "Many days I just walk to work when we're running here at Hawthorne. Funny, I love Arlington, but this is home. Guess I've always been a south side girl."

"Know what you mean. Tom and I moved to the near north for a while, but we missed what was familiar. We're in Kenwood now—close to forty-seventh. Not in the kind of mansion Nick has, but we're doing fine." Thelma chuckled. "We're back where it's safe to be a White Sox fan. Don't know how Nick can be a Cubbie, though, and live on the south side. But then he seldom does what's expected."

Daisy glanced sharply at Thelma, who was

giving her a slow smile. Pursing her lips, Daisy said, "That's for sure."

They reached the barn and Daisy placed a halter loosely around Blue's neck and then helped the exercise rider slip off the saddle and bridle. "She wanted to run. I had to work at getting her back down to a gallop," the rider explained.

Daisy nodded. "She looked good out there. Thanks. We'll have two more ready to go tomorrow morning."

"Great. I'll be here. Got to run. Cassie has a couple for me to work yet this morning."

Daisy paid little attention to the young woman jogging off toward Cassie's barn; she was focused on Blue's knees. Daisy bent and rubbed her fingers gently and knowingly up and down each front leg. She worked her fingers in and about the knees feeling for heat, feeling for something wrong. Blue never flinched and her knees felt tight and cool.

Satisfied at last, Daisy stood and blew out a lung full of air. She turned toward Thelma and gave her a brilliant smile. "Thelma, we'll race within the next two weeks."

"Hurrah," Thelma squealed, dancing a little jig.

Blue raised her head and backed up. Her eyes flared. "Oh, sorry," Thelma apologized. "I forgot."

"It's okay," Daisy replied, handing Blue over to a groom. "Just don't do it again. A lot of horses aren't as laid back as Blue Horizon. So would you like some coffee? I've got some brewing in the tack room."

"I seldom pass up coffee. You ought to know

319

that by now, girl."

"These cups may not be the cleanest," Daisy said, filling two cups with coffee. "I've been meaning to take them home and run them through the dishwasher. Sam will never do it. He wouldn't care if the cup is black as long as it holds coffee."

"If you'll help me remember, I'll take 'em home with me. The least I can do for the partnership." Thelma cast her eyes about the cramped space. "It's hard to believe that this is headquarters for a multi-million dollar franchise."

Daisy pushed both hands through her hair. "I don't think of it that way. The owners are the ones with the millions."

"Yes, but this is offices for the management team."

"Sure. I guess that's right."

"Not many businesses would have their core management team work in these kinds of surroundings."

"Maybe management loves their work more here. Besides, my office is outdoors at the track, in the stable, and at my desk at home where I spend a lot of time looking at potential races."

"Speaking of potential." Thelma raised her eyebrows. "How goes it with our Nicholas Underwood? I understand the two of you are a hot item again."

A hot item! She glanced at the calendar on the wall over the desk. The days were flying by. Her life had become almost comfortable. She'd sent Reggie a check through Maxine, and hadn't seen either one since. Her nights were split fairly evenly between her apartment and Nick's house.

A hot item. You could say that, all right. Their sex life had never been hotter, and she couldn't imagine it getting hotter still. But maybe. She gave a Thelma a shy grin and was too aware that she was blushing. "We're doing fine, Thelma. We're doing just fine."

"Harumph. Sounds like more than that to me."

Daisy scowled. "What has Nick been saying?"

"Now don't get your back up, girl. Nick hasn't said much at all. It's just how he behaves."

Chuckling, Daisy said, "You and Mrs. B."

"What? I know Mrs. B. Everybody does. What's she got to do with this?"

"She claims to know what a person is feeling by the way they walk."

Thelma placed her coffee cup back on the desk and jutted out her chin. "And you, of all people, question that. What the hell were you doing when we came back from the track to the barn if not watching how Blue walked? The way she walked communicated something to you. Now it didn't do much for me, because I don't know horses, but I know people. And Mrs. B. is right. If Nick gets any happier, we'll have to tie a rope around him like they do to hot air balloons."

Daisy shook her head and leaned back in the swivel chair. "That sounds like a lot of hot air to me. Though you do have a point about the horse."

"So are you going to marry the man?"

Daisy sat up straight. There was no easy way to

avoid the question. She wished she had an answer that would satisfy Thelma; hell, she wished she had an answer that'd satisfy her own curiosity. "Why is the marriage thing so important?"

Thelma steepled her fingers. "It might be unusual for the younger generation, but traditionally when two people love each other they get married and," Thelma's voice cracked, "if they're lucky, they have some kids."

"I'm sorry, Thelma. You and Tom would make such great parents."

"It's okay. We've adjusted," she smiled weakly, "the best we can. But we were talking about you, girl. What about you? Don't you want children?"

Tilting her head to one side, she paused and then responded, "I haven't really thought much about kids. I wouldn't want my children to grow up like I did."

"No, of course not. No mother would want that. But you have Nick Underwood. Your children wouldn't know the poverty and stench that you knew. They would be raised in an entirely different world."

"And that bothers me, too," Daisy confessed. "I've planned and worked hard all these years to improve myself and to have a better life, but I don't want to forget where I came from. You know, there was a lot of good back there, too. People did the best they could with what little they had. No one will love me more than my grandmother. And," Daisy pressed her forehead between thumb and index finger, "my mother

322

loved me. Maybe the booze, and drugs, and guys were her way of self-medicating a broken heart. But I know she loved me."

"I'm sure she did, honey. I'm sure she did. And you'll never totally leave that world behind when you marry Nick. And you can raise your children in ways that they can appreciate the gifts that they have and maybe even understand their roots."

Thelma scrunched her mouth as if debating with herself. "But you need to be careful, girl. The further we get from those days of real hardship, the more likely we glamorize them. It's kind of perverse, I guess. We struggle so hard to make a better life. We succeed. And then we look back with fond memories." Thelma shook her head.

"Maybe it's family that we're remembering more than the circumstances," Daisy offered.

"Maybe you're right. So when will you say yes?"

Daisy smiled broadly. "Thelma, you sure are persistent. I really don't know what I'm going to do. Nick and I seem so different. And we seem so right. And I can't really leave my world behind, even if I wanted to. I still have a sister and a brother-in-law."

"Ah yes, I've heard what that lowlife tried to do to you in the hospital, of all places, while your sister was just hanging on."

Daisy shrugged. "We can't pick our relatives."

"No, but we can pick husbands." Thelma puffed out her cheeks. "One thing for certain, you and Nick will have some tall children. You might have your own basketball franchise."

"How can you say that?" Daisy turned away from Thelma and picked up a pencil and started crossing off things from her to do list. "Like I said, I don't even know that I want to have children."

Thelma stood. "Well, maybe you ought to think a little more about Nick. You've got a lot of time to think about being a mother, but he doesn't have nearly as much time to think about being a father.

"Cripes, if you had a baby next year, Nick would be sixty-two when the kid graduated from high school." Thelma rose. "Thanks for the coffee, Daisy. Keep me posted on Blue. And think about what I've said. You've got the world opening up before you like a beautiful iris, but a flower wilts if it isn't properly nurtured."

Daisy didn't trust herself to look at Thelma. She nodded, keeping her glassy eyes fixed on her work schedule.

"Kids," she snorted. Why was everyone insisting on making things more difficult for her? She knew she was in love. She didn't need anyone to explain that to her anymore. But she needed time to figure out what to do about it. She needed time to handle Reggie.

She doodled on a piece of paper: circles, squares and hearts. She toyed with making box-like letters. Daisy. Nick. Underwood. Daisy Underwood. She gawked at the words. Her breath stuck somewhere in her throat.

Daisy leaned over the desk and rubbed a finger over the letters. The name looked good. It looked

324

right. Could she become Mrs. Nick Underwood?

God, how old that sounded. No, she'd be Daisy Underwood. Maybe Mrs. Daisy Underwood in some settings. But Mrs. Nick Underwood would be far too formal and stultifying. What had he called her while they were in the Boundary Waters? Willow. From the beginning, he'd thought of her as Willow. She chuckled. Had Mr. Underwood been searching for his own Diamond Willow when he stumbled across her in the barn?

Daisy blinked and Thelma's words came back to her. Children. She hadn't really fantasized about having children with Nick. Maybe that was a fantasy beyond fantasy. But was Thelma right?

Nick's time clock was ticking much faster than her own. Did he even want children? They'd never discussed children. Of course, she wasn't even willing to talk about marriage, so how could they talk about children?

What a mess. This brand new world everyone seemed to think was open to her didn't come without its costs. And she wasn't even sure that all the price tags were clearly posted. Time. She needed time to decide what to do about Nick, about Reggie, about herself. Daisy shivered, aware that she wasn't totally in control of that time clock either.

Later that afternoon, Daisy stepped out of Nick's shower and heard the downstairs doorbell ring. She threw on a robe and hurried down the curved stairway so Mrs. B's nap wouldn't be disturbed. She opened the door a crack and it was shoved in her face. She stifled a scream. Reggie stood before her with a cocky grin on his lips.

"Didn't think I'd find you here, bitch? When are you gonna learn? I'm not stupid, like that sister of yours."

"What do you want?" Daisy folded her arms tight across her abdomen suddenly wishing that the doorbell had awakened Mrs. B. The old woman was so hard of hearing she'd probably never flinched.

Reggie's eyes scrolled up and down her body. She glanced down and saw her bare feet poking out beneath the robe. At least the robe was thick, but she was still presenting him with much more of a show than she wanted. And he was taking every advantage of it he could. He stepped through the doorway and closed the door behind him. Daisy stepped back into the foyer glancing furtively over her shoulder. No Mrs. B. When would the woman get up to begin preparing supper?

Reggie laughed at her. "No need to be afraid of me, Daisy girl. You've always been the one I've wanted, you know that. I've just been biding my time with your sister until you grew up." He paused and ran a leering eye over her body again. "I'd say you've grown up real fine," he drawled. "To bad that bastard, Underwood, got to you first, but that's life. You can't always be first. At least you should be well broken in now."

"Don't you touch me!"

326

"Or what?" Reggie sneered. "You gonna sic that crotchety housekeeper on me? Or maybe your shining knight will show up. Nope, he went to Winnetka on an errand. Maybe he's got another pussy stashed up there." Reggie laughed. "Wouldn't surprise. But I didn't risk coming here to talk about Underwood. I came to talk about us. About our little arrangement."

Daisy scowled and tried to breathe normally.

"You must have misheard the deal, bitch. I only got one check from you. I said five hundred a week."

Daisy gasped. "A week," she squeaked. "You said a month. I can't come up with five hundred a week."

Rocking back and forth on the balls of his feet, Reggie glanced about the foyer and ran a finger along its rich oak trim. "Oh, I think you can come up with that, and much more. I'm not blind. You've got yourself a real gravy train. All you have to do is keep Underwood satisfied." Reggie lurched forward and grabbed Daisy by the arm.

"Ouch. That hurts."

"Not as much as you'll hurt if you don't come through with the bread. I think you've been holding out on me. You've got more than enough cash. If not, I'm sure Underwood will do most anything to keep you in his bed. And he probably wouldn't miss a piece of silver disappearing. He'll give you any jewelry you ask for." Reggie snickered and squeezed harder. "Maybe I ought to go to a jewelry store with you and pick out what I want."

"No," Daisy moaned, trying to back away. "I'll come up with the money, somehow."

"You better, bitch. Remember, you're simply buying insurance protection. It's a cost of doing business. It's a cost of being part of my family. Nothing too bad will happen to your precious sister, or damn horses, or that prissy Underwood, or even you, dear one," he said, moving his hand to cover a breast, "as long as you take care of my needs."

Daisy grabbed his arm with her free hand. She yelped and fell forward as he twisted her breast in his fist. Momentarily blinded by the pain, Daisy bit her lip not wanting to scream. Thankfully, Reggie released her and stepped back.

"Remember what I said, bitch. You be responsible to your family and no one will get hurt." He snickered at her massaging her breast. "And you if think that was pain, you haven't experienced pain yet. I'll expect five hundred dollars each week." He moved to leave and stopped. "And no more checks. Cash only. You give it to me or Maxine. Take care now, Daisy darling. We don't want Mr. Underwood to discover our little arrangement."

When she heard the door latch closed, Daisy whirled and raced up the stairs. Back under the shower, she thoroughly scrubbed every spot on her skin that Reggie Lassiter had touched. He was defilement personified.

Daisy's tears mingled with the streams of water

from the showerhead. Five hundred a week. Regardless of what Reggie thought, she didn't have that kind of money. Unless she touched her college fund. Her lungs heaved with her sobs.

Everything had been going so right. Five hundred a month wasn't right, but it wasn't a great burden, either. Two thousand was an entirely different matter.

Could she talk to Maxine? Would she be able to make Reggie be reasonable? Hardly.

She could save some money if she dropped out of school. She did have some jewelry she could hock. Reggie was right. Nick would buy her most anything she asked for, but she wouldn't do that.

And she wasn't a thief. Damn if Reggie Lassiter would turn her into a thief. She'd figure out a way. She had to. Maybe they'd get lucky and win a few more races. The extra purse money helped.

One thing Reggie didn't have to worry about was her telling Nick about their arrangement. This was her family that was causing all the trouble, and she'd deal with them one way or another. Why had Reggie and Maxine been easier to handle when she was dirt poor? Reggie was right about one thing—he and Maxine were her family.

Daisy gingerly touched the rising bruise circling her left breast. She squeezed her eyes shut. Family didn't do this. Reggie was no more a blood relative than the man in the moon. Or the cow that jumped over the moon. Daisy shook her head. Was she going crazy? If this pressure cooker didn't drive her crazy, nothing would.

"Damn," she muttered, "Nick will be home soon." Stepping out of the shower, Daisy dried off. She put powder on her bruise, but she knew Nick would notice it before it went away. She'd have to concoct a good story to explain the discoloration. She shuddered — that was so like Maxine. She was becoming too good at lying, at not telling the whole truth. No wonder Nick couldn't trust her. Hell, she wasn't sure she could trust herself any more.

Nick had raced home as soon as he'd heard that Reggie Lassiter had shown up there. He failed to understand why Clint's man couldn't intervene. Clint had explained that the detective's hands were tied unless Reggie had tried to break in. Someone from the inside had opened the door.

That someone had to be Daisy. Mrs. B. wouldn't let the man in, and she would have told him about Lassiter ringing their doorbell. Daisy, however, remained silent and distant throughout supper. She'd said she had a lot of work to do and, after helping clear the dishes, she'd disappeared into the upstairs room that she'd set up as a makeshift study/office.

Getting up from the desk in his study, Nick scanned his bookshelves. Too bad there wasn't a book that could provide a clue to what really made Daisy Matthews tick. She loved him; he was assured of that now. She needed him about as much as he needed her, but there was still a heavy chain that held her back. And he wasn't entirely certain that Reggie Lassiter was the complete problem.

Lassiter. The bastard. Nick's fingers balled. What he'd give to be alone in an alley with the creep. If they didn't get him soon, he might have to take matters into his own hands.

Nick ran a finger down the spine of a book. Lassiter wasn't the only factor holding Daisy back. She simply seemed unsure about making a lifelong commitment. Nick squinted at the small lettering on a book. Maybe that wasn't too surprising. Other than Cassie Travers, everyone who had mattered to Daisy had died or left her when she needed them most.

Slamming his fist against the wall, Nick muttered, "I'm not leaving. Why can't she trust that? What more do I have to do to earn her trust?"

"You're very quiet tonight. Was it something I did?" Nick asked, crawling under the covers and cradling Daisy.

"No." She sighed against him. "I'm just a little preoccupied."

"Care to tell me about it?"

He sensed her hesitate. Her breath seared his bare skin.

"There's a lot of work for my class. We have a horse off his feed badly. The vet hasn't been able to figure out his problem yet. I want to stay at the apartment the next few nights. It's so much further to commute to the library and the track from here."

Nick stiffened.

She circled his nipple with a finger. "It'll only be a few days. I'll get my paper written; then I'll be back."

"That's what you want."

"Yes, it's what I need. I do love you, Nick," she whispered. "Don't question that."

He sighed. "I know. And I love you more than I can ever say. It's just that I'm not sure what's happening anymore."

"Welcome aboard."

Nick leaned over and brushed his lips across her forehead. She inched away. Now, what the hell. She wasn't telling him about Reggie paying her a visit. She wanted to be away from him for a few days. And she was withdrawing from his embrace.

"Do you have something else on your mind?"

"No," she yawned. "I guess I'm just exhausted. It's been a hard week."

"I understand. Why don't you just roll over and we can cuddle? You'll be asleep in no time."

He'd never tire of the pressure of her rear against his groin. He grazed his lips across the back of her neck. And cradled her breast... She jerked away as if he'd hit her with a hot poker. "What the hell?" he demanded. "What's wrong, Daisy? Let me look at you."

Nick pulled down her nightgown, trying his best to ignore the shame and the tears filling Daisy's eyes. The black, blue and purple blotches on her breast made his stomach curdle. "Son of a bitch," he screamed. "That bastard did this to you. I'll have him killed before dawn."

"Don't talk foolish," Daisy yelped, sitting up in bed, tugging the gown up around her. Her eyes narrowed. "How did you know Reggie was here?"

Nick was out of the bed and pacing. How could he have left her so unprotected? His house had a security system, but she'd opened the door.

"Why did you let him in?"

"I didn't think. He barged in."

"But you opened the door."

"I didn't want to disturb Mrs. B."

"Disturb..." Nick threw back his head. "That's super. You risked your own neck so you wouldn't awaken Mrs. B."

"Yes."

Nick refused to be put off by Daisy's meek tone. She was still sorting out pieces to the puzzle and he had only a limited amount of time to find out what had transpired that afternoon in his own house. He came to a halt by the bed and crossed his arms. "So what did he want?"

Daisy looked away. "What do you think?"

"Money."

He watched her nod her head a fraction.

"Did you pay him?"

"I will."

"How much?"

"That's none of your business."

"The hell it isn't." Nick clenched his fists. "That asshole comes to my house and manhandles my

333

woman and it's not my business?"

Daisy breathed deeply. "I'm pleased to be your woman, Nick. I really am." Her voice rose. "But that does not make me your property. I won't have you treat me the same way Reggie does."

Crestfallen, Nick slumped down on the bed. "You know I'm not doing that."

Daisy shook her head. "Both of you seem to think you can get me to do anything you want like I'm some kind of puppet."

"Not true. And you know it. I wouldn't do a thing to harm you." His eyes rounded, staring at her partially bare breast.

Glancing down at herself, Daisy rearranged her gown again. "Oh, you wouldn't leave bruises on my body. You'd leave them on my heart, on my soul."

What could he say to that? How could she think that of him? What had he ever done to her that might make her think that?

She folded her hands on her lap. Carefully, she interlaced her fingers and then looked at him boldly. "So how did you know Reggie was here, Nick? And how did you know he was at the track the day the security officers escorted him off the premises?"

Nick pinched the bridge of his nose and reached for his glasses. He'd need every bit of armor he could muster before this spat was concluded. His head already throbbed.

"Well?"

She looked detached. He knew it was one of her

favorite defenses for self-protection. "You had him followed, didn't you?

"I'll bet Clint Travers is behind this. And Cassie hasn't breathed a word. Everybody's looking out for poor Daisy Matthews, aren't they. Nobody thinks I can take care of myself."

"You shouldn't have to take care of yourself by yourself," Nick mumbled.

"I have for most of my life. So how is this so different?" She raised her palm, stopping him with his mouth open. "I know, you're going to tell me that love is different. I don't know about that. Others loved me, and I still had to wind up going it alone. Why should I become dependent on someone else taking care of me?"

Nick reached to pat her thigh but withdrew his hand. "I'm not trying to make you dependent," he explained. "God, Willow, I've looked for you all my life. Now having found you, I can't stand the possibility of losing you. I can help. I want to help. If you'll let me."

"Seems like you're doing a pretty good job of that behind my back."

Nick could not discern from the glint in her gray eyes whether she was still angry or was teasing. He wasn't about to take a chance and guess wrong. "It seemed like a good idea to have Reggie followed. He's got to screw up someday, and then we'll have him behind bars for a good long time."

Smiling thinly, Daisy replied, "I can't say I'd have anything against that." A sob rippled through her body. She closed her eyes and opened them. "And I don't want to lose you either, Nick. I'm not sure I spent my life looking for you, but now that we've come this far, I don't want to lose you either."

"I'm glad for that." Nick tried to breathe while resisting smothering her in his arms.

Daisy's mouth drooped. He wasn't sure he didn't like her defiance more than this wrenching sadness. "So how long have you had a tail on me?" Her voice was a hoarse whisper.

His shoulders slumped. "Aw shit," he muttered. "I knew I should have told you. Cassie said we had to tell you. I just didn't want you to worry or feel like a bug under a microscope."

"So what do you think I feel like now?" she whimpered.

Her chin fell to her chest and her eyes closed. She sat like that for minutes.

Had he ever been so scared? She'd walk out on him for sure now. Why didn't she say something? Anything would be better than this damn silence.

- o -

What to do? Daisy tried to gather her wits behind her shuttered eyelashes. She'd smoked Nick out, that was for sure. At first, she'd been furious. Then she'd begun to see what was happening through his eyes. Yes, he had been searching for a willow when he found her.

She should get out of bed and leave. She had

336

every reason to. She had every right to. But she loved him, and he loved her. Didn't she have a right to cherish that, too?

It probably really didn't make much difference for Nick to know about Reggie blackmailing her. He already knew her sister and brother-in-law had their hooks in her for money. That he and Clint had a man following Reggie seemed only prudent. What would it take for that guy to intervene? But then, Reggie had closed the door before he'd accosted her.

Did Reggie know about the tail? She refused to let her brother-in-law win by robbing her of what she had been searching for: family. She could make that with Nick. She knew that now.

Given that Reggie had crossed a threshold to physically abuse her without being provoked, she shuddered to think what would happen next.

She peeked through her eyelashes at Nick. The man looked about ready to come apart. Could he feel worse than she did? One thing was certain now: she loved him with her whole being. She'd die before giving him up.

Slowly, Daisy raised her head and opened her eyes. She wet her lips and grinned a little. "You look like hell, Mr. Underwood." He searched her face as if for clues.

There was no question he was searching for hope. And she was done withholding. "I believe my favorite line from Ibsen is in his play *Ghosts: Things are not so desperate as you think.*"

With that said, Daisy reached for his hand and

pulled him to her. "We'll muddle through, Mr. Underwood. I'm not sure to where, but we'll muddle through."

Nick's smile split his face. "God, I'm relieved to hear that. So what's this Mr. Underwood business?"

"Don't know." A warm glow crept from her neck to her cheeks. "I guess I've become fascinated with the name of late." She yawned. "Maybe we can talk about it later. I really am tired now. Have to be back at the track in about six hours."

"Okay," Nick said, fluffing up a pillow. "We still have more to talk about. Reggie's not just going to disappear, even if you are paying him off."

"I know. And I do love you," she murmured, backing her buttocks against his crotch.

"And I love you. Sweet dreams, Willow Smoke."

As she drifted off to sleep, Daisy revisited the campfire in the Boundary Waters where Nick had shared his secret name for her. She recalled how the northern lights danced across the lake. She relived their primal mating under those lights.

That was part of her life now. No one was going to steal it from her.

Chapter Sixteen

Daisy left the doctor's office clutching her stomach. She felt worse than before entering.

Angling across the parking lot toward her pick-up, Daisy crumpled the Xanax prescription in her hand and threw it on the pavement. She'd take the medicine the doctor prescribed for diminishing the itching, but damned if she would take a drug to reduce the increasing anxiety attacks. Drug dependency was not a risk she was willing to take.

It had been over two weeks since Reggie confronted her at the Kenwood house. She'd made two payments already. They hadn't been too difficult, but she knew it was just a matter of time. She was in over her head and sinking fast.

Resting her forehead on the truck door, Daisy gulped in air. What else could she do? She'd dropped her class at the university. There was no way she could concentrate on her assignments, and it would save some money. If she moved in with Nick, which he wanted her to do, that would save a bundle of cash.

But that was a hell of a reason to make the move. She thought she wanted to move in with him anyway, but the money issue was a cloud making reasoning difficult. And if she did move in, Reggie would simply hike the amount of protection payment he wanted. There was no end in sight.

Sam had told her to take some time off from work. It was the slowest season of the year for their stable, but he'd also been clear that her lack of focus made it dangerous for her and for their high priced horses. He was sure if she took some time away from the pressure of the track, she'd be fine. Daisy laughed a dry laugh. Sam had no inkling about pressure.

Daisy wiped the back of her hand against her brow. She was sweating profusely on a chilly November day. Climbing into the cab, she realized she needed to talk to someone she trusted. With shaking fingers, she started the engine, drove out of the parking lot and headed for the Travers farm.

"First things first," Cassie said, after hugging Daisy and ushering her into the kitchen. "I'm fixing you a bowl of chicken noodle soup. And then we'll talk. Your old bed is still available upstairs if you need to rest."

"I don't know what I need," Daisy wailed, frustrated with her lack of control.

"That's okay. We'll sort things out," Cassie soothed. "We always do."

Daisy nodded.

Taking small sips of soup and munching on saltines, Daisy began to perk up a little. Cassie had kept the conversation light. Daisy waited for her cue.

"So are you going to tell me about it?" Cassie asked, softly.

Daisy shrugged. "You've probably guessed most of it. Nick hasn't formally asked, but he's made it clear he wants us to get married. Reggie is threatening to hurt everyone and everything I love if I don't pay him protection money." Daisy paused. Was it her voice that sounded so distant, so detached?

"I've been a mess lately. I dropped out of school. Sam has told me not to come to work for a while because I'm too much of a risk to the horses. I've got to come up with the money. But Reggie keeps increasing what he wants. I can't do it much longer." She stared at Cassie, afraid she was going to bawl like a two-year-old. "I'm not going to steal from Nick to pay Reggie off."

Cassie leaned back and pursed her lips. "So that's what he really wants—to bleed Nick dry."

Daisy choked back tears and nodded. "What can I do? The more involved I am with Nick, the more in danger I put him. Without Nick, I can't pay off Reggie for very long." Daisy pushed the empty soup bowl aside and laid her head on the table and sobbed. Cassie's fingers rubbed her neck, and sobs came from her toes.

"It's okay," Cassie whispered. "Let it out. Let it all out. You've bottled up so much over the years. You've got a lot of tears saved."

Between sobs, Daisy mumbled, "I don't want to lose him. He's become more like family than anyone but you and Clint."

"I know. It hurts sometimes to be in love."

"But I can't keep Reggie from gouging Nick. I want to fly to the moon."

Cassie chuckled softly. "I've had a few moments when I've wanted to do that. My guess is you're not giving Nick enough credit, and maybe you're empowering Reggie more than you should."

Rubbing her eyes, Daisy sat up. "What do you mean?"

"Have you told Nick everything that's going on—how much Reggie is demanding, your dropping out of school, your trip to the doctor, Sam asking you to take some time off?"

Daisy shook her head.

"I suspect the two of you together could come up with better solutions than either one of you can by yourselves. Sounds like he's not pressing you as hard as I think he should because he doesn't want to risk losing you. Yet what do you have in the long run if you can't problem solve together? If you can't trust one another enough to share your darkest fears?"

Daisy heard. But it was as if she was there and yet not there. She couldn't integrate what Cassie was saying—the message seemed garbled in code.

Cassie squeezed Daisy's shoulders. "Why don't we take you upstairs? You look like you could use a nap. Let me give you something that will help you relax a little."

Daisy didn't know how long she'd slept, but

she wasn't ready to open her eyes and join the world. In her mind she played again what Cassie had said. Was her stand-in mother right? It sounded so simple when Cassie said the words. But what would Nick do if she told him everything? She didn't want him to chase after Reggie and get in trouble with the law. Would he find a way to pay off Reggie and get her brother-in-law off their backs? Maybe he could afford to do that, but she doubted that he would.

Cassie was right. If she and Nick were to have a future, they had to find a way to talk about all those things that mattered — the bad as well as the good. He already knew she was a bastard. But was she really ready to tell him her mother had been a whore? Was that the kind of mother and heritage he wanted for his children? Was it pride that kept her from sharing her darkest secrets and her deepest fears — that somewhere in the recesses of her mind she was so afraid that Reggie would win, would get his hooks in her so deep that he would turn her into a whore like he had her sister? Were the daughters destined to re-live their mother's fate?

"Grandmother," Daisy wailed across time, "what do you do when blood goes bad? You were right about so many things, but not about everything. I can't do this alone. Not anymore. I have to go beyond blood for help, or I'm going to die. And I'm not ready to die. There is so much hope. I see it in his eyes when he looks at me. Why can't I feel it now?"

Nick knocked on the Travers' porch door and opened it at the same time. He rushed into the kitchen. "Where is she?" he asked Cassie, who was wiping her hands on a towel at the kitchen sink.

"Upstairs at the end of the hall on the right. Why don't you slow down and take a deep breath." Cassie reached for the coffee pot. "You sure didn't let any grass grow under your feet getting out here from the city."

"No. Is she okay? What's this about her seeing a doctor?" Nick accepted the coffee cup Cassie shoved at him but refused to sit down.

"She broke out in hives. That's why she went to the doctor." Cassie leaned back against the kitchen counter and brushed back a lock of hair from her forehead. "The girl's a nervous wreck, but she's got to explain that to you. It's not my place to say." Cassie frowned. "She's vulnerable, Nick. She needs you, and I'm not certain she knows it. Daisy's always been so fiercely independent. Go slowly with her," she said, pointing toward the stairway leading to the second floor.

Nick nodded, put his coffee cup on the counter, and took two stairs at a time. His heart raced and his nose twitched. At the top of the stairs, he steadied himself. Go slowly. How the hell could he go slowly if he stormed into her room like he was putting out a house fire?

He leaned against the hallway wall and

344

pinched his nose. Damn, he was scared. What if she was ready to walk out on him? She'd run to Cassie's comforting arms, not to his. Was there more going on with the doctor than Cassie reported? He had to get to the bottom of what was happening or he'd self-destruct. But Cassie was right, he had to go slowly. *Take a deep breath. You're a patient man; so be patient, damn it.*

He stepped into the bedroom at the end of the hallway and saw Daisy tucked in a fetal position facing the window. Her eyes were closed and her breathing shallow. Her blond hair formed a halo against the white pillow case. One hand gripped the quilt tightly. The other lay, more relaxed, atop the covering.

Vulnerable, Nick thought. Yes, vulnerable, but breathtakingly vulnerable.

He moved noiselessly and knelt between the bed and the window. She must have sensed his presence, for her eyes fluttered open and closed. A tiny smile slipped across her lips. Nick rubbed the back of her hand and she flexed her fingers, welcoming his.

"You don't have to wake," he whispered. "Just know that I'm here. And I'm not leaving."

He was rewarded with a slight nod. It pleased him that Daisy's grip on the quilt lessened and her breathing became deeper and more rhythmic. He braced himself against the bed and waited.

He watched the woman who had captured his heart sleep. And he made a decision. He had given Daisy a lot of room and time to deal with Reggie

Lassiter. Her time was up. Nick wouldn't bully her, but neither would he be shut out. Even if it meant losing her, Reggie had to be dealt with. The parasite would bother Daisy whether Nick remained on the scene or not. There would be no more pussyfooting around with the creep—family be damned.

Nick maintained his vigil by Daisy's bedside, mulling over their relationship and planning for their future. He smiled and squeezed her fingers. As long as he might live, he'd never forget the willowy woman with straw sticking out of her hair challenging his right to be near her barn. Or the waif-like blonde who stepped into his suite with an offer he never could have resisted. Or the woman who spoke to horses as if they understood. Or the woman who led him to the pinnacle of ecstasy beneath the northern lights. Or the woman who helped him see life through fresh eyes and an earthy wisdom. The woman he could not live without.

"I brought the two of you some tea," Cassie whispered, entering the room. "I'll put them here on the dresser. She should be waking soon."

"Thanks," Nick replied, watching Cassie tiptoe to the hallway.

- o -

Groggily, Daisy clutched the object in her hand to her breast. Its warmth against her body jogged her memory. She flushed, but did not open her

346

eyes. It wasn't Bear she held in her hand, it was Nick.

Vaguely, she remembered him being by her bedside. She recalled his words: "I'm not leaving." A comforting warmth spread throughout her body. Was she visibly glowing?

He had come to her. And he was staying to comfort her, to help her. Could she let him? Would he stay if he knew everything? Could she tell him?

Daisy squeezed her eyes tighter. She was so tired of running. From Nick, from her past, from their future.

Slowly, she cracked an eyelid open. A smile flickered across her face when she saw that he had nodded off on his knees, slouched over the bed, firmly clasping her hand.

"Hey, you," she whispered.

He jerked immediately alert.

She basked in the warmth of his welcoming smile.

"You're awake," he said. "How are you? You've been asleep for several hours."

"Really?" Daisy drew herself up from her quilted cocoon and stretched. "I had no idea. I must have been more exhausted than I realized."

"That doesn't surprise. Cassie brought up some tea about five minutes ago. It should still be warm. Would you like some?"

"Sure. I'll get up. Don't treat me like an invalid." she warned.

"Sorry. You still look pretty beat."

Daisy swung her legs off the bed and ran her hands through her hair snarls. "Guess I'm not ready to run a race. I'm sorry if I snapped at you. I'm glad you're here, Nick. You didn't have to come. I'm going to be okay."

"I know you are," he said, handing her a cup. "And I did have to come. This is where I was needed."

Daisy nodded. "Maybe more than I ever knew."

"Right. So what's happening, Daisy?" He winced. "No," he groaned. "That's not how I wanted to say that." He shook his head and grazed her arm with his fingers. "I know I can be fairly demanding at times."

Daisy grinned. Who would've thought that Nicholas Underwood would admit that little fault of his?

"What I meant to say is that I'd be willing to listen, if you would like to share some of the things that are bothering you. Aw shit," he muttered. "That sounded like Cassie." He narrowed his eyes. "We're in this together, Willow. When you're up, I'm up, and when you're down, I'm down. You get the hives and I itch all over. Our bodies are a team even if we haven't quite acknowledged that. Can't we work together to deal with whatever we have to?"

Daisy's eyes glistened. "I want to, but it's not easy. I've been getting by on my own for so long." She rubbed her nose. "But you're right. I figured that out this afternoon. I either have to push you out of my life, or we have to work this thing out together."

She watched Nick stop breathing and his pupils dilate. "I don't want to push you out of my life, Nicholas Underwood. Sometimes life is nearly unbearable with you, but it would be totally unbearable without you."

"I think that was a vote of confidence," Nick said. "But there's more?"

"Oh yeah, much more. We've got to talk about who I am. You may want to change your mind about me; I'd fully understand."

"Nonsense. So what is Reggie really after? And how much protection money is he asking for?"

Daisy felt her resolve waver. But maybe this was the easiest place to start. "Five hundred a week."

"Five hundred." Nick's eyebrows arched. "You don't have that kind of money, do you?"

"Not for long."

"Okay, we can handle that. Maybe he'd like a lump settlement." Nick scowled. "We'll do whatever it takes to get him off our backs."

"It won't be that easy. He'll blow it and want more. Or he'll decide he wants to be a business partner. Maxine says Reggie wants you to be part of the family."

"Not because he likes my looks."

"No, I'm sure he hates your guts. But you have wealth, and he wants it."

"Good," Nick said, rubbing his hands together. "We know what Reggie wants, and we'll just have to make sure he doesn't get it. According to Clint, the word on the street is that Reggie's chest-deep in quicksand. He's not seen as trustworthy. He's bragging about having a new banker and that he's preparing to move in to a higher level of drug pushing in Cicero. That will put him in direct competition with the mob."

"Not good," Daisy muttered.

"No, not good for one's health or longevity. If the cops don't get him, the mob will. But that squeeze may also make him more unpredictable and even more dangerous."

"Reggie's always been grandiose and paranoid."

"So where does all of this leave you with your sister? I know she's the only family you have."

Daisy shrugged. "It's hard to love someone who is only using you or allowing herself to be used. Maxine doesn't have enough self-respect to help herself." Daisy paused and rubbed her eyes. "I've been protecting her for years. Or maybe I've just been fooling myself all that time, hoping that we'd be a real family that cares for one another. I guess the last experience with Maxine in the hospital and recovery showed me how far gone she is. She can't be there for me unless she dumps Reggie. Do I believe the world is flat?"

"It's a matter of perspective." Nick finished his tea and placed both their cups on the end table. "So is there anything else you want to tell me? You're not holding back something about your health?" He paused. "The doctor visit?"

Daisy let her eyes drift shut. "No, not that. I'm

not dying. I'm not pregnant." Her eyelids flew open. "You didn't think that, did you?"

Nick glanced down at his hands. "It crossed my mind. Would that be so terrible?"

Wilting before his questioning eyes, Daisy hugged herself and plunged ahead. "Only if you don't mind that your children's mother is a bastard and their grandmother was a whore." Her fingers balled into fists. She couldn't stop the tears. Damn it, not now—how could she tell his reaction if she couldn't see?

And then she felt his arms close around her and pull her tight to his body. She wailed. Her body shook. Was she coming unglued? His hands stroked her back. His words were muffled in her hair. She sobbed until there were no more tears. Her body quivered little aftershocks. At last, she leaned back against his hands.

"You look incredibly gorgeous even when you cry." Nick bit his lip. "Have you been torturing yourself because of those things you couldn't control? Did you think that what your father or mother did would mean that much to me?"

Daisy shrugged, not trusting herself to speak.

"People make choices. They play the cards they're dealt. I don't always believe individuals make the best choices, but I really can't judge because I haven't lived my life in their shoes. As for you," he lifted her chin, "you've maximized the cards you were dealt. I hope our children will be as resourceful and able as their mother."

Daisy felt her cheeks burn and her body

threaten to implode. She shook her head trying to find equilibrium. There must be something she should say, but her thoughts were a jumble. He wasn't walking away. And he'd just said that their children should be like their mother. Good grief. She knew with every fiber in her body what was coming next, and she wasn't going to run anywhere but into this loving man's arms.

"So," Nick said, wiping tears from her cheeks. "This is not the ambiance I had in mind for this, but this is the right moment."

Holding her breath, Daisy watched Nick reach into his pocket and bring out a small jewelry box.

"I've been carrying this around for a few weeks now, trusting there would be a right moment and that I'd be bright enough to recognize it for what it was."

He lifted the case top and plucked out the largest diamond ring Daisy had ever seen. He dropped to his knees beside the bed. He bent and kissed her fingers. "Daisy Ann Matthews," he said, staring brightly into her eyes. "I very much want you to be the mother of my children." He smiled even more broadly. "But I'm old fashioned, I guess. Would you marry me first? I love you."

Daisy nodded. "Yes," she managed to whisper, and then grinned so wide it hurt. She giggled. "I guess I'm old fashioned, too, and I love you so much."

Nick slipped the ring on her finger and kissed her fingers one by one. She reached for him and slanted her lips across his. He responded hungrily.

She deepened the kiss. Love oozed between them and through them. She'd never felt this loved before.

The next morning she woke in Nick's bed. In *their* bed, she corrected herself. She lifted her left hand and gawked. How many times had she stared at diamond rings through the plate glass windows of jewelry stores, never quite allowing herself to dream of having one of her own? It was true. He'd asked. And she'd said yes.

She stretched and yawned and brought her knees up to her chest. Staring at the clock, Daisy laughed. It was mid-morning, but she had no place she absolutely had to be. There was no class to go to, and Sam wouldn't want to take her back so soon. That didn't matter. She'd agreed with Cassie and Nick that she needed to take some time for herself and kick back. No way would she allow herself to get spoiled, but this was okay.

Checking her skin for blotches, she was relieved to see that the fiery redness had subsided and she no longer itched. She grinned. By tonight she'd be ready to love Nick like a fiancé should.

Fiancé. Daisy gulped—she had to plan a wedding. She didn't know the first thing about weddings. But Angie might. Maybe Cassie, but her wedding had been a tiny ceremony in Salt Lake City.

She heard muffled footsteps in the hallway. She waited, holding in a giggle. The door cracked open and Mrs. B. stuck her head in the room. Once she saw Daisy awake, Mrs. B. opened the door wide and gave Daisy her broad gap-toothed grin.

"Good to have you back, Miss Daisy. And for good." She tilted her head. "Mr. Nick does have it right, don't he? You did say yes?"

Laughing, Daisy leaped out of bed and hugged the older woman. "Oh, that's right. Can you believe it?"

"Well, it's about time. Mr. Nick couldn't stop grinning and humming this morning. Told me he had a surprise. He just about gave me a stroke when I heard the news. I'm so happy for you, girl. This old house is gonna have some life again. Won't be no time and we'll have younguns tearing around here and you for sure won't know which end is up."

"Mrs. B., let's take this a little bit at a time," Daisy mocked, narrowing her eyes. "I don't know about kids. And I already don't know which end is up."

"That may be true, but I ain't getting' any younger. And I've not diapered a baby in so long I may have plumb forgot."

"If I need to know, I'm sure you'll be able to show me. Now what do you know about weddings?"

"Nothing that'll help you much. I don't know about rich folks' weddings." Mrs. Brown paused and then grinned. "Though I can help you with the caterer for the reception."

"Oh goodness," Daisy's hand flew to her mouth, "I may be in way over my head. I wouldn't have the foggiest idea of how to deal with a caterer."

"You'll learn." Mrs. B. placed her hands on her hips. "I don't expect Mr. Nick is marrying you because you're good with caterers. He don't need a social secretary. He need's a wife and mother with fire in her gut."

Daisy laughed heartily. "Well, if that's what he wants, I guess he found her."

An hour later Daisy walked down the sidewalk in front of the Kenwood house besieged by one of her favorite whirlwinds: Angie Underwood.

"So do you have a date set for the wedding?" Angie asked, swinging her arms rhythmically in power walk mode. "I'm so thrilled for both of you. And Mom and Dad are, too."

Daisy matched the shorter woman easily stride for stride. Angie had come by to congratulate her and "catch up on the news," but had to keep up with her morning workout before racing back to the theater. What a life! It made the backside at the track appear sedate.

"We don't have a date set. Sooner than later, I expect. Do you know anything about planning weddings?"

Angie stopped her forward motion and grabbed Daisy by the arm. "I'd love to help. I've been a bridesmaid a few times. It can't be too difficult." She pursed her lips and waited for a bus to drive by. "How many people? Two to three hundred, I imagine."

"Two to three hundred! I don't know that many people."

"Come on, girl. Remember who you're marrying. This will be a society bash. You have your friends at the track. Nick has business colleagues and friends. Plus people from various social circles. Plus the family. You've only met some of them."

Daisy placed her arms across her stomach and squeezed hard. "Can't we just elope? I had no idea this would be a social event."

Shrugging her shoulders, Angie turned and renewed their walk. "I doubt it. Nick is going to want to show you off. Besides, you're going to want to let all the females of Chicago know that Nick is now your man and they have to maintain their distance. We'll have to work on an announcement for the society page for the Tribune."

"What?"

"Of course. You were news at the Charity Ball. Don't think snaring Nicholas Underwood, one of the most sought after eligible bachelors in Chicago, won't be news!" Angie grinned broadly. "You're going to be the envy and the scorn of more than one distraught female in the city."

Daisy flashed on the image of Claire Donaldson. That woman would go ballistic when she learned Nick would marry his gutter snipe. Daisy wished she could be there when Claire received the news. Should she be more forgiving? Daisy narrowed her eyes remembering the scene

356

in the elegant bathroom when Claire had made it clear she didn't belong with Nick. Forgive? Hell no!

"So it's going to be quite a bash," she said, squaring her shoulders. "It'll come and go like most things. I can handle it, if I have to. If you'll help, that is."

Angie checked her watch and slowed their pace to a mere walk. "You won't be able to keep me away. First, you two have to decide on a date. Then we can reserve a church and hotel for the reception." Angie's lips formed a bow. "I expect my brother will want to be in charge of the honeymoon."

"Mrs. B. wants to help with the reception."

"Great!"

Daisy came to a halt. "Oh my God, a dress."

"We can begin shopping day after tomorrow. That's my day off. You'll look stunning in a long white gown. Or maybe it should be long in the back and mid-thigh in the front, showing off your long legs. I've been to a couple weddings where the bride wore something like that. Very eye-catching."

"I'm not sure I want to be eye-catching. And do you think I should be wearing white? Good grief, Nick and I are living together."

"So?" Angie burst out laughing. "You mean that virgin thing?"

Daisy nodded.

"There wouldn't be much of a market for white wedding gowns if women conformed to that

357

tradition. Anyway, you've only been with one man. And this is your first wedding. Right?"

"Yes."

"That's virginal in my book. White it is. Eye-catching you'll be, whether you want to be or not. We better head back, I've got to be at the theater in an hour. I'll hop in the shower at your place, if you don't mind."

"Of course not. And thanks for being willing to help."

"It's great to have you in the family, Daisy." Angie gave Daisy a bear hug. "Just don't worry about fitting in. You already do."

"What do you think about eloping?" It was a futile question, but she wanted to give it a try. They had just made love and were nearly asleep. She had her arms around Nick, her breasts crushed against his back.

He pushed his buttocks tighter against her groin and chuckled. "I've been wondering when you would think of that. Sounds like your chat with Angie about weddings got you up on your toes. Elope? No way. I wouldn't want anyone to misunderstand. I want to show off my bride to the entire world."

He rolled over and looked in her eyes. "I'm so pleased and honored that you chose me. I'm not going to run away and hide. We'll be married here in Chicago. You can choose the date. I'll be there. You can choose the church, if you'd like. I'll work on the hotel and the honeymoon."

Daisy shook her head.

"Now what's wrong?"

"We'll both work on the honeymoon. Whoever said that's the groom's prerogative?"

"Hmm. You may be right. We'll work on the honeymoon together. Where would you like to go?"

Daisy frowned. "I hadn't actually thought about it. Don't people go to Niagara Falls or something like that?"

Nick's laugh erupted from his belly. "Daisy, as Mrs. Underwood, you'll have to dream a little bigger than that."

"Oh."

"We could do Paris, or London. The Caribbean would be nice this time of year. Or maybe Australia or Tahiti."

"Australia," Daisy squeaked. "I've dreamed of going there someday. Australia and New Zealand. Is that really possible?"

"Of course it is." He ran a finger down her nose. "You can count on it, darling. I'll get my secretary to begin working on it tomorrow. So how soon can we do this wedding?"

"Don't know. But not soon enough; life has got to be simpler after we're married. I'll have a better idea once Angie and I see about a dress. Won't you need a lot of lead time for a reception facility?"

"That's not going to hold us up. If we can't get a hotel, then we'll clear out a couple rooms at the factory and hold it there."

"That would be fantastic!" Daisy squealed. "Paddle Dreams Unlimited would be on all the invitations. I like that a lot."

"Would you prefer that to the Pump Room or the Drake?"

"Absolutely!"

"Then that's what we'll do. It'll be the talk of the town. It will be outstanding."

"You already are the most outstanding thing in my life," Daisy murmured. She leaned over and kissed the tip of his nose. He reciprocated. She kissed his eyelids. And he did the same. She ran her lips up and down his neck and knew for the second time that evening they'd make the kind of gentle love that turned her insides to warm butter.

Would there ever be enough time or enough energy to get her fill of him? Probably not, but she'd try. She was determined to do her very best at trying.

Chapter Seventeen

Daisy scurried from her pickup to the entrance to her old apartment. She glanced quickly up and down the street before unlocking the door. As she entered the dining room, a wave of emotions swept over her.

Was it simply nostalgia? This had been her place for nearly two years. The living room love-seat showed signs of wear. The bookcases were boards and brick. The computer should be gathering dust in a secondhand store. But these were her things.

Daisy walked down the hallway to the kitchen. There was nothing there she needed to take. This was stuff for the homeless shelter or the home for abused women. She stepped into the bedroom and smiled. She'd miss the simplicity of the futon and the intimacy of the mirrors. Damn, those mirrors had witnessed a lot. A lot of tears. A lot of joy. And some great lovemaking.

Space would be found in the big house for the futon. Maybe they should have it bronzed and set up as a shrine to sexual exploration. Daisy knelt on the bed and chuckled. She'd better not suggest that or Nick would see that it was done, and then she'd have to explain to every visitor why they had a bronzed bed.

Daisy moved to the closet and pulled out an old brown suitcase that had so many scuff marks it could have been used by skateboarders for practice. She might as well get to work; she'd come for her clothes and necessities. The furniture could wait.

She wanted to be quick. Nick would have a fit if he knew she'd come to the apartment without him. Daisy scowled. But she probably wasn't alone. Clint's man was likely out there somewhere watching. The man must be good; she'd never spied him, and she'd tried on many occasions. She shuddered. Maybe Nick had called him off in deference to her feelings. She wasn't certain she felt safer knowing she was being followed or not.

It didn't take long to pack the clothes she wanted. She glanced at the bed and smiled. Her favorite pillow would come along. "And yes, you too, Bear," she whispered. "You didn't think I'd leave you behind, did you?

"You're going to be shocked by your new surroundings. You're moving up in the world, Bear. Clean sheets, weekly. Mrs. B. freshens the air daily. You'll like her. She'll be someone else you can talk with. Now, Nick. You already know him. He'll be kind, but for the most part he'll sort of ignore that you exist. Don't expect him to talk to you. He doesn't even talk to the horses." Daisy shrugged. "Maybe some day he'll come around. We can hope."

Daisy stood and clutched Bear in one hand and reached for the suitcase. "Guess we better be going before I get too mushy about leaving. We've had some good times here, Bear. But we'll have even better times where we're going."

Taking a last look around, Daisy fought back tears again. But she had to get back. She stepped into the entryway and opened the door. Her jaw dropped and her heart beat rapidly.

"Hi baby," Maxine cooed. "You *are* here. We were just going to ring the buzzer. Were you going somewhere?"

Daisy set down her suitcase and Bear. She nodded. She couldn't help but gawk at Reggie standing by her sister dressed in a dark suit, gray shirt, and gray tie.

Moving up in the world? He dressed like he'd already arrived.

Both Maxine and Reggie crossed the threshold and Daisy led them into the living room. Her mind raced. Where the hell were the guys who were supposed to be following Reggie and her? Of course, Reggie hadn't done anything wrong. And she'd refused to get a restraining order on him. Now what? She'd bluff her way.

"You just caught me in, actually. I'm going to be away for a few days—at a horse auction, in New York."

Maxine took a seat on the couch. Reggie remained standing. Daisy stood her ground and wet her lips.

"Come on, baby," Maxine said. "You never could lie to your sister. What's up? There's more to the suitcase than that. Are you moving in with

363

him?"

Maxine's hand flew to her mouth. "Look at that rock on your hand. Good God, Daisy! He asked you to marry him?"

Daisy didn't know if she should be more angry at her sister's disbelief or frightened that she'd been found out.

"Come here and show it to me, baby."

Daisy stepped toward her sister and held out her hand, but her concentration was focused on Reggie, whose eyes glassed over. He was high on something.

"God, that must be worth a small fortune!" Maxine shrieked. "You sure are the lucky one; you always have been. But I am happy for you, Daisy. You've really made something of yourself."

"Bullshit. She just must've screwed the guy blind," Reggie declared, taking a step closer. His eyes narrowed, his chin jutted out and his hand shook.

Daisy shrank from his outstretched hand until the gas fireplace prevented her from moving further back.

"I should never have let him get to you," he mumbled. "He took what was mine all along."

Daisy had a hard time understanding his slurred speech. It wasn't the first time he'd referred to her as his. Her skin crawled at the thought. She took a step to the side; her right hand grazed the diamond willow stick she'd carved and she grasped it firmly.

A crooked smile swept across Reggie's face. It

was as if he'd received an electric jolt. He moved with new energy.

"You did real fine, darling. You've got a helluva lot more brains than your sister. Sometimes I forget." Reggie reached for Daisy's hand. "Let me look at that rock."

Caught between wanting to flee and not wanting to cause a fight, she let him lift her hand. His eyes shone with unvarnished greed.

"A small fortune, all right. I could take it now," he sneered. "But there's a lot more where that came from. You got the right idea, darling. You marry the rich son of a bitch. As soon as his insurance is changed to name you as the one to collect, I'll see that he meets with an accident."

"No!" Daisy screamed. "I won't marry him."

"Oh, yes you will, bitch." Reggie shoved her hard against the fireplace. "In the meantime, I'll take care of your druggie sister. With both of them out of the way, we can get married. It will be great. Just you and me. Me with a gorgeous broad and tons of money."

Daisy glanced quickly at Maxine, who had turned chalk white. Her mouth was ajar and her eyes had widened into raw terror.

"Until death us do part, bitch. Give me a little something to seal our vow." Reggie leaned into Daisy, crushing her legs against the fireplace. His lips came down hard on hers. She jerked her head to the side. He swung it back with one hand and crushed her breasts with the other. Her eyes squeezed tight. She had to do something; she had to get out of there.

Reggie dropped a hand to her crotch. When he pulled on her jeans zipper, Daisy's brain surged into overdrive. She focused her energy on that willow stick. Reggie had the zipper down and was totally absorbed with clawing at her panties.

With all the might she could muster, Daisy crashed the willow stick onto Reggie's head and brought her knee up sharply between his legs. He stumbled backward and fell to the floor with one hand reaching for his bleeding temple and the other for his crotch.

Daisy saw him writhing on the floor and spun toward the entryway where she grabbed Bear to her chest and ran. She hit the sidewalk in a full run and swerved left heading for the El station a block and a half away.

She neared the corner and heard what sounded like firecrackers coming from behind her. Glancing over her shoulder, she saw Reggie firing a gun toward something across the street from her apartment.

It must be Clint's people. She didn't slow her stride. She couldn't count on them stopping Reggie. The man was a crazed animal. She wasn't even sure a bullet would stop him. He wanted her, and if he couldn't have her, he'd kill her. Life had become that simple.

The entrance to the train station loomed ahead. Should she risk it? If there wasn't a train soon, she might be trapped on the platform. Mercifully, she heard the screeching of the train and ducked under the turn-style hoping no one would notice her.

Gasping for air, she stepped into the open door of the train just before it closed. The warmth of the car hit her full force. She stumbled into a seat and trembled, clutching Bear to her throat.

The lights in the car went off momentarily. Why wasn't it moving? Was something wrong? *Not now!* She stared out the window. Who had fired the gunshots? Was it Reggie? Or Clint's detectives? Where was Maxine? What must she be thinking? If she was even alive.

Daisy shook the tears away. She had to think. She had to maintain some cool. She had to think through her escape.

Where would she go? Paddle Dreams Unlimited? No. Reggie would expect that. She had to warn Nick. Why hadn't she put the cell phone on her belt rather than leaving it loose in the pickup?

She wanted to crawl into a hole. No, she'd be safer in a crowd. No way would she let Reggie find her alone in an alley. She'd go downtown. Where hundreds of people would witness his rage. And maybe if she were lucky, she'd find a cop.

She pressed her nose against the dirty window and her eyes rounded in horror. There was the stumbling figure of Reggie Lassiter making his way up the sidewalk toward the platform stairs. Clearly, he was in pain. He appeared to be dragging his right leg. She couldn't have caused that much damage with the willow stick. He must have been shot by Clint's men. But where were they now?

The train lurched suddenly, throwing Daisy forward in her seat. She laughed hysterically and rubbed her forehead. Better to get a bump from the train that was finally moving than from whatever Reggie had in mind to do to her.

She leaned back and breathed. She was free, at least for a while. She had a plan. "Bear," she whispered, "I'll protect you, and you can protect me. It's Christmastime. There will be lots of people downtown. And Reggie has no idea where we're headed."

- o -

"She did what?" Nick stared at the phone in disbelief. "Why the hell didn't they stop him first?"

Nick pinched his nose. "Yeah, I know they're not superheroes.

"How's your man doing? Good. Then what happened?" Nick listened closely to Clint Travers. "Son of a bitch. Well, that's that.

"How about Maxine? Good, I think. So no one knows where Daisy fled to.

"You've got your people combing the streets. That's great. Just great. It's Christmastime. She'll be hard to find in the crowds.

"No, she won't come here. She'd think she'd be putting me in danger. No, she'll run the other direction. Downtown."

Nick leaned back in his chair and tried to breathe normally. "I've got a hunch where I'll find her. Yeah, I'll let you know if I do. And my cell is on if you come across her first. Yeah, let's check back in two hours no matter what."

Nick grabbed a jacket and raced out into the reception area. Tom turned away from the receptionist to stare at Nick. "You going to a fire or something?"

"It's Daisy. She's had a fight with Lassiter and ran. I've got an idea where she might be heading."

"I'll come along. Let me get my coat."

"No!" Nick grabbed Tom by the arm. "Stay here just in case she comes here. I doubt she will. But if she does, I need someone I can trust who can handle trauma."

Tom pressed his lips together and nodded in agreement. "Suppose you're right. You call if you find her. I'll let you know if she shows up here. But I don't figure she'd want to lead Lassiter here."

"Exactly. I'll be in touch."

Nick turned the key in the ignition of his Triumph. A light drizzle continued to fall. The windshield wipers whisked away the water. Was he right? It was Christmastime; that was the key. Would the child inside Daisy flee to that place of her Christmas childhood dreams? He sure hoped so. Macy's would be crowded.

And that was where he wanted her — in a

crowd, where she'd be less apt to do something crazy or catch pneumonia than if she'd gone underground in the back streets of Chicago. The weatherman had said the drizzle could turn to sleet or snow.

Nick turned on the heater and pulled out of the parking lot. He expected either option was a likely choice for Daisy. He prayed that her fond childhood memories would win out and lead his woman to safety.

- o -

It was hard moving rapidly through the Christmas crowds, but Daisy weaved in and out of the package-laden shoppers. She ignored their shouts of protests and craned her neck around often to see if she could recognize Reggie coming up behind her.

The way he'd been struggling to move on the sidewalk by the El platform, he shouldn't be too close. Her mind couldn't convince her heart. Reggie always bounced back.

Her heart would pound right out of her chest if she didn't stop soon. Once on State Street, Daisy slowed a little. All the stores were decorated, turning the street into a fairyland. She hugged Bear tighter and opened the door leading into Macy's.

Inside the entryway, she stepped out of the traffic and simply stared at the huge Christmas tree stretching above the first floor. She shook her hair and realized how she must look to passers-by. Like someone who had crawled out of the gutter. She brushed her clothes, and shook Bear gently. "Sorry," she said, "but we'll be dry in here. Do you remember? Bear. Let me show you around. It's Christmastime; it's time to dream."

Daisy chuckled at the little girl's voice coming from her mouth. Was it really her?

She peered around at the crowd. No one seemed to notice her talking to a stuffed animal. They were safe. She'd have to find a phone and call Nick. Certainly, there would be a phone in such a large store.

"Come on, Bear. I want to show you something."

Daisy walked to the escalator and got off on the fifth floor. She walked down the aisle and smiled. Just as they had when she was young, toy animals lined both sides of the walkway. She'd always believed there were more toys in this one store than anywhere else in the world.

And she had always known that Santa had a spare toyshop right behind that wall. There were just too many toys to ship them all from the North Pole. Daisy frowned. How she'd loved to come to this place to look and to dream. But never had any of those toys found their way to her house.

Except Bear. This was where she'd first seen Bear. It was love at first sight. And she'd been so amazed when he'd shown up that next Christmas morning.

"Here we are, Bear. This is what I wanted you

to see. Look at all your friends. There must be over a hundred bears. And look. Look at the elephants and the giraffes." She giggled. "And just imagine, there's a turtle! I think we need to get you a friend, Bear. I'll have to spend more of my time with Nick, and we wouldn't want you getting lonely." She looked down at herself and scowled. "But I ran off without any money. We'll just have to dream about it, I guess."

Daisy knelt on the floor before the stuffed animals. She couldn't explain why she felt so fuzzy. Her world was spinning. She gripped Bear tighter still.

Exhausted, she let her eyes close. Who was that man coming toward her? Was he friend or foe? She couldn't move a muscle. She tried, but neither her legs nor her arms would move.

His arms enclosed her. Pulling back, Daisy tried to raise a hand to protect herself. Her hand didn't respond. She tried to scream, but no sound came out. But she could hear.

"It's okay. It's me, Nick. You're in shock. I saw it in the army. It'll subside, Daisy. We'll get you to a hospital; they'll start an IV and soon you'll be as good as new."

Nick. Nick! Daisy closed her eyes and opened them. He was coming into focus. She was warming in his arms. "No. No hospital," she whispered. "I'll be fine, now that you're here."

"We'll wait a few minutes and see." He took off his jacket and wrapped it around her. "Are you warm enough?"

"Can I be of assistance?" a clerk asked. "Is she okay?"

Nick nodded. "She just fainted. The excitement of the season. I think she'll be okay soon."

"We have medical staff in the building if you need them," the clerk said, giving them a skeptical look.

"Thanks," Nick replied.

"I don't want to talk to anyone else," Daisy said, rubbing the numbness from her arms. Nick rubbed her legs. Soon they began to feel normal.

"Nick, be careful. Reggie may be right behind you. He was chasing me and I ran. I didn't want to endanger you. How did you know I'd be here?"

"It was a hunch. Isn't this where you always come at Christmastime?"

"Yes, but—what about Reggie? He'll kill you, if he can."

Nick took Daisy's hands in both of his. "Reggie Lassiter isn't going to kill anyone, Daisy. He's not going threaten anyone anymore."

Daisy shook her head, trying to comprehend. "But..."

"Listen to me, Daisy. I don't want to shock you more, but you need to know you're safe. Reggie is dead."

"But I saw him coming up the sidewalk by the El."

"Yes, I'm sure you did. Apparently, he had to wait for another train. One of Clint's people climbed to the top of the stairs and saw it happen. Reggie fell in front of the oncoming express.

373

Witnesses couldn't tell if he was trying to flag down the train and slipped, or if he was shoved. There were a lot of people milling about."

"Oh my God." The enormity of what had happened penetrated Daisy's haze slowly. She looked down at Bear and back up at Nick. Her eyes were dry. "You didn't have him killed?"

"Of course not."

"And not Clint."

"Certainly not."

Daisy frowned. "Maybe it was the mob."

"Maybe. We'll never know for sure. You know how wet things were this morning. And the story Maxine told the police would suggest that Reggie was out of touch with reality, whether he was on drugs or just flipped out naturally."

"Maxine." Daisy laced her fingers together. "What happened to Maxine?"

"She's quite distraught and worried about you. The police checked her into a women's shelter for now."

"She must think I got her man killed," Daisy wailed. "She'll never forgive me. Now I have no blood family at all."

Nick lifted Daisy's chin and smiled at her. "Not true. Not at all true. It was Maxine who made the first nine-one-one call. She was doing what she could to stop Reggie from hurting you."

Daisy's eyes grew even wider. "Maxine called the police on him? That's huge! Did she tell them that Reggie planned on killing her as well as you?"

"She did."

"What about the gunshots?"

"The guy following Reggie and the woman following you tried to stop Reggie when he ran out of your apartment. He must have been expecting them. He winged the man who'd been following him. The woman shot Reggie in the leg and then tended to her partner. Once she had him settled and nine-one-one called, she hightailed it toward the El station arriving only in time to confirm that Reggie was indeed killed."

"So no one was chasing me all this time."

"Nope. Clint's had a team of folks looking for you, but you gave everyone the slip."

"Except you."

"Except me." Nick leaned over and kissed Daisy on the forehead. "And I kind of like it that way."

"Me too," she murmured, draping her arms around his neck. "I think I'm ready to go home now. There's so much to think through and work through, but I believe what I need is Mrs. B.'s chicken noodle soup. Somehow I think she and Cassie have the same recipe."

"Can you walk, or should I carry you?"

Daisy stood and tilted her head. "I may have to lean on you some, but if you try to carry me out of here, we'll be arrested for sure. Now, give me an arm." She glanced down at the floor. "Oh my, I nearly went off without Bear."

Nick bent to pick up Bear and hand him to Daisy. He hesitated, then frowned at the stuffed animal. "You don't suppose Bear would like a friend, do you?"

"That's the first time you've call him by name." Daisy's lips turned up. "I think he'd like a friend to talk with now and then when I'm not around to listen in."

Folding his arms, Nick said, "I didn't mean to take it that far. But what the hell." She watched him scan the multitude of stuffed animals.

"So which one? I didn't know they made so many."

Daisy stuck her arm through his. "Why don't you select one? I'm sure it'll be just right."

"Okay. Let me see." Nick plucked one up and eyed it carefully. He looked at it so long Daisy wondered if he wasn't communicating with it.

"Yes, how about this turtle?"

"Bear and I like Turtle a lot. We've already met." She cocked her head at Nick. "So why Turtle?"

Nick tipped back his head and laughed. "I thought he might slow you down a bit. Bear doesn't seem to do that at all."

Daisy blushed. "So is that what you want to do? Slow me down?"

"Damn right." His eyes gleamed brightly. "How else are we going to make a batch of little Underwoods?"

Chuckling, Daisy allowed herself to be pulled into his arms. "It's a batch of Underwoods now, huh. You may be right. If the process of making them doesn't slow me down, tending them certainly will."

"You won't be alone. I'll be there in the making process and the tending as well."

"Oh, I'm counting on that, Mr. Underwood. If we're going to create a family, then we're going to *be* a family."

"Okay kid, I've got a deal for you. Maybe we should get you home to that chicken noodle soup, a hot bath, and some rest. And then we can think about beginning that making process."

"Sounds like my kind of deal, old man," Daisy replied, grinning broadly and carrying Bear and Turtle toward the clerk. "As soon as I get my strength back, which may be any minute now, we'll see what kind of stamina you really have."

"Let's at least wait till we get home," Nick cautioned.

Daisy put her arm around Nick's waist and pulled his hip to hers. "Maybe, maybe not."

Epilogue

Daisy Matthews Underwood stretched carefully to reach the overhead light, not wanting to disturb her sleeping husband. She settled back into the comfort of her first class seat. They were flying to Melbourne. The next three weeks would be spent playing in Australia and New Zealand. While there, they'd check out Australian racing, which was emerging as a force in the thoroughbred world.

Otherwise, little attention would be devoted to Underwood business interests. Nick had been quite insistent that a honeymoon should be devoid of business matters, other than horses.

Crossing her legs at the ankles and rotating her neck, Daisy tried to work out the excess tension that had been building for weeks. She chuckled to herself.

Tension. Good tension. Not the kind that built because of fear for safety, or fear of secrets revealed.

Good tension, resulting from planning such frivolous things as a wedding, reception and honeymoon. Each had been perfect. At least the wedding and reception had been, and she had no doubts about the honeymoon. At last she and Nick were alone together.

She closed her eyes and a smile spread across her lips. Everyone that mattered had been at the wedding: Cassie and Clint, Mrs. B., Tom and Thelma, Sam, all the Underwoods, and there were lots of them. Even Claire Donaldson had come, not that she mattered. But her presence had given Daisy a perverse kind of pleasure she'd seldom experienced. Rarely had she possessed something anyone else wanted.

She placed a hand on Nick's thigh. Now she did.

And it still didn't seem quite real. She glanced down at the simple but stunning wedding band resting next to the diamond. It was real, all right. She was Mrs. Daisy Underwood. The prince had found his princess, and neither was disappointed.

The wedding had been much more thrilling than she'd imagined. Angie had convinced her to go with the wedding dress that had a miniskirt cut in front with a long sweep-away trail. Enough cleavage showed to be sexy without being gaudy. A hair stylist worked on her hair for three hours. She hardly recognized herself when she looked in the mirror.

For one brief moment, she could have been a Victoria's Secret model. Daisy's eyes popped open. "In your dreams, girl," she murmured.

Apart from the exchange of vows and watching Nick's eyes swell with pride when she came down the aisle, the highpoint of the day had been having Maxine stand up as her maid of honor. Daisy had never been more proud of anyone than of her sister. She'd made the choice to dry out and change the direction of her life. Daisy hoped that with Reggie gone, Maxine would be able to conquer her fears and remain sober and drug free. It would be the hardest challenge Maxine would likely ever face. And Daisy planned on providing whatever support she could.

Her sister was back at the residential program now. Thankfully, she'd been able to come to the wedding. She still looked pale and shaky, but was able to flash a genuine smile and at her own request left the reception early. "No need for me to stand by all of this temptation, baby," she'd said. "You go off and have a fantastic honeymoon. And when you're back I'll be three weeks further into this program. It may be two steps forward and one back. I may want to cry on your shoulder, but I'm gonna beat this thing. It started when I reached for the phone in your apartment to call nine-one-one." Daisy remembered her sister's shaky, but broad smile. "We're family, Daisy. We're gonna make it."

Daisy rested her chin on her chest. They'd make it, all right. So much had happened in such a short time. So many doubts, so many fears. It seemed odd now those fears had wielded so much power for so long. Nick had helped her see through some of them. Others had too: Cassie, Mrs. B., Angie, Thelma. Still, she'd been the one who had to stand up and battle her own demons. But not alone.

Never again would she have to feel totally alone.

Daisy rested her head on Nick's shoulder and grinned. He had such big plans for them on this trip to continue working on making a little Underwood. Although not certain, she expected they might have already achieved that goal. But then—she kissed Nick's shoulder—one shouldn't take such matters for granted.

A batch of Underwoods, he'd said. Maybe, maybe not. But she'd sure enjoy the process. Those videos had been helpful, but they'd never come close to capturing the magic of lovemaking.

Romance. Nick had wanted to expose her to romance. Well, he'd certainly succeeded at that. And she wanted more. Much more.

She'd learned at last to dream big.

- o -

The End